The Quaker
AND THE Rebel

Books by Mary Ellis

THE NEW BEGINNINGS SERIES
Living in Harmony
▶ http://bit.ly/LivinginHarmony

Love Comes to Paradise
▶ http://bit.ly/LoveComestoParadise

A Little Bit of Charm
▶ http://bit.ly/LittleBitofCharm

THE WAYNE COUNTY SERIES
Abigail's New Hope
A Marriage for Meghan

THE MILLER FAMILY SERIES
A Widow's Hope
Never Far from Home
The Way to a Man's Heart

STANDALONES
Sarah's Christmas Miracle
An Amish Family Reunion

▶ We have video clips showcasing our books.
Check them out at the web addresses above.

MARY ELLIS

HARVEST HOUSE PUBLISHERS
EUGENE, OREGON

Scripture quotations are taken from the King James Version of the Bible.

Cover by Garborg Design Works, Savage, Minnesota

Cover photos © Chris Garborg; Bigstock / jpegisclair

This is a work of fiction. Names, characters, places, and incidents are products of the author's imagination or are used fictitiously. Any resemblance to actual persons, living or dead, is entirely coincidental.

THE QUAKER AND THE REBEL
Copyright © 2014 by Mary Ellis
Published by Harvest House Publishers
Eugene, Oregon 97402
www.harvesthousepublishers.com

Library of Congress Cataloging-in-Publication Data
    Ellis, Mary,
    The quaker and the rebel / Mary Ellis.
        pages cm — (Civil War heroines series ; Book one)
    ISBN 978-0-7369-5050-3 (pbk.)
    ISBN 978-0-7369-5051-0 (eBook)
    1. Governesses—Fiction. 2. Underground Railroad—Fiction. 3. Quakers—Fiction. 4. Virginia—
    Fiction. 5. United States—History—Civil War, 1861-1865—Fiction. I. Title.
    PS3626.E36Q35 2014
    813'.6—dc23
                                                                                        2013026762

Printed in the United States of America

            13 14 15 16 17 18 19 20 21 / LB-JH / 10 9 8 7 6 5 4 3 2 1

ACKNOWLEDGMENTS

Thanks to

- James A. Ramage, Regents Professor of History at Northern Kentucky University. His biographies *Rebel Raider: The Life of General John Hunt Morgan* and *Gray Ghost: The Life of Colonel John Singleton Mosby* were the inspirations for Alexander Hunt in this story.

- Henry Robert Burke and Charles Hart Fogle and their book, *Washington County Underground Railroad*. Their book, along with other valuable Underground Railroad sources for the Ohio River Valley, were invaluable for this book. Henry R. Burke is a direct descendent of John C. Curtis, who was born in the Shenandoah Valley and escaped slavery to become a conductor on the Underground Railroad in Stafford, Ohio.

- The countless authors of history I have pored over for years, including Shelby Foote, Bruce Catton, Ed Bearss, James M. McPherson, and Mary Elizabeth Massey.

- Philip LeRoy, who loaned me his copy of *Killer Angels* by Michael Shaara. The Pulitzer Prize-winning novel opened the eyes of this history lover to the wonders of historical fiction.

- Donna Taylor and Peggy Svoboda, who read the rough draft of this novel years ago and encouraged me to keep at it.

- The Western Reserve Historical Society, Cuyahoga Valley Civil War Roundtable, and the Peninsula Valley Foundation of Ohio and GAR Hall, whose appreciation for Civil War history has kept my passion alive locally.

- My agent, Mary Sue Seymour; my lovely proofreader, Joycelyn Sullivan; my publicist, Jeane Wynn; my editor, Kim Moore; and the wonderful staff at Harvest House Publishers. Where would I be without your hard work?

- My husband, who stomped around an inordinate number of battlefields, museums, monuments, cemeteries, and historical inns and bed-and-breakfasts for years in the name of research.

ONE

*M*iss Harrison?" a soft voice queried. "Please come in and take a seat."

Emily, startled from her open-mouth perusal of the painted ceiling, stared in the direction of the voice. She thought she'd been shown to an empty room to wait, but a wren-sized woman sat near the windows in a wicker chair with wheels. She hurried to the woman's side, bobbed her head, and then bent her knee in a small curtsey. "Mrs. Bennington," she said. Never in her life had Emily done such a thing. She'd only seen a curtsey in theater presentations, but the astounding elegance of the house seemed to warrant one.

"Oh, my. What lovely manners you have," the woman said, patting a chair beside her.

"Thank you, ma'am," Emily said, perching on the edge. She judged Mrs. Bennington to be around thirty-five, younger than her mother had been, with an unlined forehead, green eyes, and dusky blond hair. Delicate, that's what Mama would have called her.

"Your letters of reference from Mrs. Ames and Miss Turner glowed with praise for your accomplishments. My husband and I are glad you've come to our backwater island to polish the rough edges off our girls. They both attended grammar school in Parkersburg for six months of the year, and we've had tutors here, but now they require refinement. They still run wild through the garden like savages. Annie, especially, needs to learn deportment." Mrs. Bennington inhaled a deep breath and sighed. "I am aware of your loss, Miss Harrison. And in time I hope you will come to regard us as your family."

Surprised by the statement, Emily drew back from the lavender-scented aristocrat. "I'm afraid the situation will be temporary, Mrs. Bennington, as I'm engaged to be married. When my fiancé returns from Washington, I shall go back home to Marietta."

She knew her voice sounded haughty, but she couldn't help herself. From the moment the flatboat rounded the turn and she viewed Bennington Plantation, she'd been on unfamiliar ground. A carriage had been waiting at the dock to drive her to the mansion. Then an elderly black gentleman in finer clothes than any owned by her father opened the door, bowed, and ushered her into a foyer larger than her entire house. Pink and cream marble lay beneath her feet, and a crystal chandelier overhead cast harlequin patterns on the polished steps to the second floor. The butler had to wrestle her portmanteau away as she stood gaping at her surroundings. The butler spoke perfect Queen's English without a trace of the slang she'd expected from a slave. *He was a slave, wasn't he?* She'd followed him to this salon, and here she was—behaving rudely to her new employer without other options for her future.

"Of course, Miss Harrison. We'll be happy to have you for as long as possible. I only meant I hope you'll relax and find comfort with us." Mrs. Bennington's smile filled her face and didn't fade when she addressed a servant carrying in tea. "Thank you, Lila. This is Miss Harrison. She will be our new governess."

The reed-slim black woman bobbed her head and murmured, "Pleased to meet you, miss." Lila retreated before Emily could reply, so she addressed Mrs. Bennington instead.

"That is another matter, Mrs. Bennington. My family does not condone slavery. Although I respect your authority here, I won't be waited on by anyone. I shall do my own laundry and prepare my own meals." Her defiant tone clashed with the rarefied atmosphere in the room. "My family is Quaker." Emily lifted her chin.

If her well-bred employer was shocked by the outburst, her face revealed nothing. "Of course, as you wish. We're willing to accommodate you in any way." Her voice sounded like a trilling flute, musical and soothing. "Let's discuss your curriculum. I thought perhaps literature, poetry, penmanship, and French in the morning. My favorites are Lord Byron and Tennyson. Mathematics and whatever science lessons you think necessary for young ladies after luncheon. The girls rest in the late afternoon, and their dinner is served in the kitchen at six. You may eat with them or you're welcome to join my husband and me at seven in the dining room." With that, Mrs. Bennington settled back against the chair with a dismissive air.

"The curriculum sounds fine, ma'am. I believe it is well within my knowledge and abilities." Feeling foolish, Emily searched her mind for something reconciliatory to say. Drawing a blank, she began a sheep-like retreat from the room.

"Oh, Miss Harrison, we have something in common."

Emily halted in the doorway and turned.

"I also come from Quaker stock. From Massachusetts, originally. Since my marriage, I worship in my husband's Presbyterian church when in town, but my sister in Front Royal is still Quaker. That is how she raised her son, Alexander, although she hasn't had much luck converting my brother-in-law. Alexander takes the Quaker precepts very seriously, and for that reason he hasn't joined the Confederate Army." She studied Emily as though waiting for a reaction.

Emily shuffled her feet, unsure of the expected response. "Yes, ma'am."

"You would like Alexander, I think. He's about your age, quiet and studious. He always has his nose in a book and loves classical literature that leaves me weary. You'll meet him tonight if you choose to dine with us. He's visiting for a few days." Mrs. Bennington smiled warmly.

He sounds like a crushing bore. "It would be my pleasure, ma'am," she replied, hot and uncomfortable in her traveling dress. She was eager for the interview to conclude.

"I'm sure you're tired. Joshua will show you to your room. You'll meet the girls tomorrow after breakfast. Good afternoon."

Emily cleared her throat and stopped fussing with the ribbons on her dress. "I will do my best with your daughters, Mrs. Bennington. I apologize if I offended you earlier. I'm very glad to have this job." She bobbed her head and left, almost knocking the butler over as she rounded a corner in the hall.

He looked down his aquiline nose as though gauging potential madness. Apparently satisfied she posed no immediate threat, he said,

"If you will follow me, miss, I'll take you to your room as *quickly* as possible."

Emily's face burned with embarrassment until she closed her bedroom door. Her battered trunk and reticule had been left at the foot of the bed. She was blissfully alone. Pulling off her scratchy bonnet and unbuttoning the top of her high-necked dress, she opened the French doors to her balcony and stepped out. She breathed deeply, both from the luxury of privacy and from the clean, tangy scent of the river. With a clear view of the water and of the far bank, Ohio and freedom were only yards away.

Doesn't it make the slaves yearn to swim across? To be so close, yet still so far?

"No matter how nice you are, Mrs. Bennington, you are still a slaver," muttered Emily under her breath.

In the fading light of the sunroom, Augusta Bennington pondered the young woman she had just hired. She felt compassion and a touch of pity for the strong-minded, tenderhearted idealist. Emily reminded her of another outspoken woman who had wanted to change everything wrong with society—herself. But now Augusta was complacent and weak due to infirmities and simple ennui. A fiery abolitionist living on a slaveholding plantation? This was exactly the influence she sought for her sheltered, insulated daughters. But convincing her husband of the wisdom of her decision would be another matter altogether.

"What in the world are you doing in my kitchen?"

A loud voice caught Emily by surprise. She dropped the towel she had been using to fan smoke from the room. The towel landed near the stove burner and burst into flames. Emily jumped back in fright.

"I was trying to fry eggs and potatoes, but the grease got too hot." She peered at her blackened meal stuck to the skillet.

"Land sakes." The woman elbowed Emily out of her way. She picked up the flaming towel with the tip of a poker, flung it down on the brick floor, and doused it with a shovel of sand from a nearby bucket. Next, she wrapped another towel around the handle of the pan, pulled it from the burner and covered it with a heavy lid. Then, with her hands on her hips, she turned toward Emily. "Who are you?"

Emily cleared her throat and straightened her back. "I am Miss Emily Harrison, the new governess, ma'am. I'm very pleased to meet you, Mrs.…"

The woman's forehead furrowed with confusion. "All right, you're Miss Harrison, but what are you doing in my kitchen? You could have burned the place to the ground."

Another person I've gotten off on the wrong foot with. "I was preparing myself dinner."

The woman arched an eyebrow. "Dinner is served in the dining room at seven if you're eating with Dr. and Mrs. Bennington, and at six in the kitchen if you're eating with the girls. I don't know why no one told you that." Shaking her head, she began to clean up the mess on the stove as though Emily were no longer there.

"No, ma'am. I won't eat food prepared by slave hands. I will do for myself while I'm here. I believe that—" Her voice faltered. The cook had stopped wiping and turned to her. The expression on the woman's face caused Emily to back up a step.

"My name is Matilde Amite. You met my husband, Joshua, this afternoon. We're not slaves. We are free people of color. I'm paid a salary to cook here, and this is *my* kitchen. Make no mistake about that. Should you wish to peel your own potatoes or shuck your own peas, that don't make no-never-mind to me. But you'll do it outside, not making this kind of mess in here."

"Oh, I thought…I mean…I am sorry, Mrs. Amite."

"Never mind. There's no harm done." Matilde returned to cleaning her stove as Emily slunk from the room. She headed toward the house but did not get far.

"Good afternoon, miss. You look as if you're running from the scene of a crime." A tall man appeared out of nowhere, directly in her path.

Emily gazed into pewter-gray eyes set in an angular face. He had the longest hair she'd ever seen on a man. He wore tall boots, tight breeches, and nothing else. His tautly muscled chest was bare—no shirt, no jacket. She gasped at his near nakedness, yet she couldn't seem to avert her eyes.

"Excuse my appearance. I'm on my way back from bathing in the river. I enjoy it on a hot afternoon, don't you?" As though that explained his effrontery, he continued. "What happened? Did I over-hear correctly that you tried to burn down Matilde's kitchen? I've never heard her sound so vexed." His smile etched deep wrinkles around his eyes as though he was enjoying the situation.

"Not at all, sir. It was merely a misunderstanding." Emily's focus flitted between his face and the pectoral muscles of his chest. "If thou would be so kind as to cover thyself, I would be grateful." She motioned to the lump of clothes tucked beneath his arm. "I am a betrothed woman. It's highly improper for me to see thee in such state of undress," she stated primly, allowing her gaze to wander again.

He was taller and thinner than her fiancé, but his sinewy limbs made him appear strong and powerful. Emily felt a pang of shame for having compared this stranger to Matthew and finding him even slightly lacking.

"Great Scot! Do you mean I'm too late? We have only met, but you're already betrothed to another? I'm having the worst string of luck. What kind of misunderstanding with Matilde?" He obliged her by putting on his frock coat, but he neglected to button it. Tiny drops of water clung to his chest and sparkled in the reflected light.

Momentarily speechless from his sarcasm, Emily soon recovered. "I was preparing myself something to eat for supper."

"Are you saying Matilde refused to cook for you? What could you have done to offend her this quickly?" His tone sounded aghast, but his gray eyes twinkled with amusement as though enjoying her discomfort.

"I simply said I wanted to cook for myself and not partake of food prepared by slave labor. I am a Quaker." Her statement resonated with pride and dignity. "We abhor the practice of keeping our fellow man in bondage."

"I assumed you were Quaker from your thee and thy, but Matilde is not a slave. Where did you get that idea? I'm certain she set you straight on that fact." He crossed his muscular arms over his chest as Emily watched.

"Yes, Mrs. Amite corrected my incorrect assumption. I'm pledged to speak like the Benningtons, but occasionally I lapse when nervous." She flushed, uncertain where to cast her gaze.

"I apologize for making you nervous. I had mistaken you for the governess my aunt hired to tame my two wild cousins." He slicked a hand through his damp hair. "You must be a newly hired cook. Perhaps trained in Paris? I'm sure the Benningtons look forward to your cuisine." He ran his eyes over her from head to toe. "Judging by your initial performance and thin frame, they should have no fear about growing plump in middle age."

It took Emily a moment to recognize his ridicule. But when she did, she responded with her usual lack of poise. With flaming cheeks she clenched her fists and spoke through gritted teeth. "My culinary abilities are none of thy concern, I assure thee. Good day!" Picking up her skirt, she flounced past him...or at least she tried to. Precisely at the same moment, he stepped into her path. She bumped soundly into his bare chest. Emily hissed like a feral cat and maneuvered to the left.

But the horrid man moved in her way again. "I do beg your pardon."

When she lifted her gaze, they were mere inches apart. Her skirt blew against the leg of his trousers. She staggered and lost her balance on the flagstones.

He reached out to steady her, his fingers spanning her waist. With an exaggerated inhalation, he breathed in her soap's lingering scent. "My, you smell good. Not like any cook we've ever had. They always stink like onions and garlic." He sniffed her hair in a noisy fashion. "You smell like honey and lemon balm," he declared with obvious satisfaction.

This was too much. Emily jumped back from him. "Sir, I must insist you stop sniffing me like a dog. It is most inappropriate!" She smoothed the wrinkles from her skirt with both hands. "I'm not a cook. I *am* the governess your…aunt…sent for. I'm Miss Emily Harrison from Marietta." She wiped her palm on her skirt before extending her hand.

He stared for a moment. Then he grasped her hand tightly, drew it to his mouth, and placed a kiss on the freckled skin of her knuckles. "What a pleasant surprise. I am charmed to meet you, Miss Harrison."

Aghast, Emily yanked her hand back. "That is most inappropriate, sir, without my gloves on!"

"I was just wondering where your afternoon gloves were."

"I doubt that's what you were wondering. If you would please excuse me." Emily stepped to his left even as he mirrored her action.

"I beg your pardon. We seem to be at cross purposes." He retreated an inch.

Folding her arms over her chest, Emily stared him squarely in the eye. At Miss Turner's School for Ladies, she had practiced this look in the mirror to use on unruly pupils. "I must insist that you stand still so I may pass." She enunciated each word, leaving no question as to her displeasure.

He remained ramrod straight with his arms tightly at his sides. "Certainly, but I wish to properly introduce myself so that our first, memorable encounter won't leave you with the sole impression of impropriety." He bowed deeply, his long hair falling across his brow. "I am Alexander Wesley Hunt, of Hunt Farms."

"Nice to meet you." Bobbing her head, Emily sprinted by him while she had the chance.

"Of Warren County. It's outside of Front Royal." His voice rose with intensity. "We live east of the Shenandoah Mountains. Perhaps you've heard of our farm?"

Emily hurried up the path, not pausing until she reached the safety of the portico. Then she glanced over her shoulder.

He stood where she'd left him, rocking on his heels in a fit of uncontrolled laughter. He cupped his hands around his mouth and called, "Please don't rush into an impetuous marriage until I've had an opportunity to redeem myself."

Seething with fury, Emily marched into the house and climbed the servants' staircase. This cocky man was the bookworm nephew Mrs. Bennington had spoken about? He certainly didn't look serious and studious. He was the most obnoxious person in the world! Now she could add him to the growing list of people she had offended since arriving on the island. Why the impertinent, half-dressed man had managed to rile her, she couldn't say. But she paced her room long into the evening, recalling his taunts and thinking of the retorts she wished she'd uttered. Why would a nephew bathe in the river, yet act as though he owned the place? And why was she unable to get him out of her head?

That night she stood on her balcony and watched the calm flat water of the Ohio River. Occasionally a laden flatboat riding low in the current broke the smooth surface on its way south. Nightjars and whippoorwills called to her from swamp willows on the riverbank. Their sorrowful cries deepened her near-consuming melancholia. Exhausted, she crawled into bed and snuggled under the covers without any supper, either with the Benningtons or their daughters. After the day's events, she found she had little appetite. "I'll make you proud, Mama," she whispered in the darkness. She fell asleep as soon as her head hit the goose down pillow.

I'll make you proud.

Emily awoke to sunlight streaming into the bedroom, a fragrant breeze stirring the lace curtains, and a thump at the door. Throwing her wrapper over her nightgown, Emily padded across the thick carpet. A growl in her stomach reminded her that she'd skipped dinner. Smelling food through the closed door, she answered the knock with gratitude.

Alexander Hunt held a steaming breakfast tray in outstretched hands. "Good morning, Miss Harrison. I trust you slept well." He moved the tray closer for her inspection. "Here is your breakfast. You must be famished this morning. Matilde said she cooked this food herself, and that you should eat every bite of it."

"Good morning." Emily didn't move. She looked from the tray to him and then back to the tray.

"May I come in?" He nudged the door open with his foot. "Perhaps I can set this on your balcony and share a cup of coffee with you? We have another gorgeous morning."

"You may certainly not, sir," Emily belatedly recovered her wits. "I am not dressed." She folded her wrapper about herself more securely and knotted the belt. Foolishly, she had answered the door as though she still lived on the farm with her parents. His furtive glances from her neck to her toes reminded her otherwise.

"Please express my appreciation to Miss Matilde. And thank you, Mr. Hunt, for delivering my breakfast." She took the tray and tried shutting the door with her knee, but his boot was too quick.

"I remembered your Quaker convictions. Because I knew you wouldn't eat food unless carried by free hands, I volunteered for the task." Folding his arms across his waistcoat, he rested against the doorjamb. "And I can assure you, I am no man's slave…or any woman's, either. At least not yet."

Emily stared at him in disbelief. "Were you sent by the devil specifically to needle me, Mr. Hunt?" She glanced down the hallway, not wishing the Benningtons to overhear the question.

Straightening, he leaned toward her without a shred of decorum. A lock of hair fell across his temple. "No. The devil sent me initially…to buy horses." He winked and ambled down the passage with his thumbs hooked in his pockets.

She glared at his back until the smell of the food roused her senses. Inhaling the aroma of coffee and fried ham, she almost inhaled everything on the plate: hotcakes, thinly sliced ham, a poached egg, strawberries in cream, and a pot of strong coffee. She devoured every morsel at her balcony table. Thank goodness the cook turned out to be a paid employee because Emily didn't know when she had eaten a meal so delicious. The way her garments hung from her shoulders, she was slowly starving to death from her own cuisine.

Once revitalized and dressed for the day, Emily slipped down the staircase and out the front door, thankfully unobserved by anyone. Tulip poplars and giant black walnut trees shaded the expansive lawn. Standing on the flagstone terrace, she surveyed the mansion that would be her home for at least the next several months. The main building was a three-storied Georgian with painted wood shingles and brick chimneys at both ends. A large Palladian window crowned the front door, and an open belvedere topped the third floor like a huge cupola. A covered portico connected two separate wings to the house—the right housed the kitchen and pantries, but the left was locked and shuttered. Everything was balanced, symmetrical, and tidy, from the matching pillars to the identical chimneys in each wing. She stepped back to crane her neck skyward.

"Miss Harrison?" A voice startled Emily almost out of her shoes.

She turned to see a copper-skinned woman of about sixteen, fashionably and expensively dressed, approaching from the flower garden. "Yes?"

"I am Lila, Miss Margaret and Miss Anne's maid. You met my parents yesterday, Matilde and Joshua." Her expression betrayed nothing. "If you'll follow me, the girls are eager to make your acquaintance." Her speech was clear, articulate, and cultured. Her accent contained a Southern inflection, perhaps New Orleans, and not at all what Emily expected in Virginia.

"Pleased to meet you." Hurrying to keep up, Emily followed the young maid to the location of her initial interview. Two tow-headed young ladies stood as she entered the sunny room. The taller of the two extended her hand.

"Miss Harrison? I am Margaret. This is Anne. And I see you've met

Lila," she said politely. She dipped the tiniest of curtseys. "We're so glad you've come to be our teacher." Her smile seemed genuine, and Emily warmed to her immediately.

"Yes, we hated that sour old Mr. Tate," said the younger sister.

"I believe what my sister is trying to say is that we had outgrown his curriculum—"

"Yes, that and he smelled badly," Anne interjected as she clasped her hands behind her back.

"Smelled bad," Emily corrected.

"Oh, did you know him too?"

"No, I've never met him, but smelled badly indicates something was amiss with his nose," said Emily as Margaret attempted to stifle a smile.

"Something *was* amiss with his nose, Miss Harrison," Anne agreed. "It was red and bulbous. Once I heard Mama say to Papa it's because he's too fond of bourbon." At this, Margaret erupted into laughter. Emily heard Lila snicker too.

"Yes. Well, let's forget about Mr. Tate for the moment. Please show me the books he used with you two in your lessons."

"With us three," Margaret corrected. "Lila studies with us."

"Will you mind if I sit in?" the young woman asked, meeting the governess's eye.

"Mind? Goodness, no. I'm pleased, as a matter of fact." Emily stopped rambling before she said something regrettable, as she had with the girls' mother. "All right, let's be seated and take a look at your books."

The morning passed pleasantly as Emily gauged their proficiencies. The girls had solid foundations in English grammar, diction, and penmanship. Margaret and Lila could get by with spoken French but couldn't read or write it very well. Anne had progressed little beyond *merci* and *s'il vous plaît*. She would also require a remedial level of mathematics, whereas the other two were ready for algebra and geometry. All three needed a broader base in literature, and science seemed to have been completely neglected by the imbibing Mr. Tate.

After two hours, Emily stood and announced, "Tomorrow afternoon we'll start a science unit on the edible versus poisonous plants indigenous to this area."

They had been reading from a stack of *Godey's Lady's Books* and looked up with quizzical expressions. "I beg your pardon?" said Margaret.

"You should know which plants are safe to pick when you are in the forest and which things you should never put in your mouth," explained Emily, attempting to stimulate interest in her topic.

"But Matilde usually packs a hamper of refreshments whenever we spend an afternoon on the levee or by the lake." Margaret's tone indicated bafflement in studying such matters.

"Yes, but what if you became lost or stranded in the mountains?" Emily's question hung in the air as three sets of eyes grew round as saucers. Then Lila giggled behind an upraised palm. "Never mind," Emily said, holding up her hands in dismissal. "We'll stop for the day. I'll take the rest of the afternoon to plan my curriculum and course of study."

"Good afternoon." Anne bobbed her head and flew out the door.

Margaret approached the oak writing table where Emily sat. "Good afternoon, Miss Harrison." With a demure tentativeness, she placed her hand atop Emily's. "I'm so glad you've come to our island. I do hope you'll be happy here." After a flash of brilliant white teeth, she too was gone, taking several periodicals with her.

Only Lila remained, silently appraising her. "I'll bring you a lunch tray, miss, and if you like, I can show you around the island later."

"Thank you, Lila. I'd like a sandwich and would very much enjoy a tour." Emily wondered more about her impression on the maid than on the Bennington sisters. Lila had watched her all morning as though waiting for something dangerous to happen. Her mother had probably repeated the story of Emily's cooking attempt that almost burned down the kitchen. "I do hope we can be friends," she added.

"Yes, ma'am," Lila said before vanishing through the door without a backward glance.

Hours later the promised tour revealed much to Emily. Bennington Plantation wasn't really a plantation at all, but more of an elegant subsistence farm. There were apple and peach orchards, fields sown in corn and oats, and a substantial garden behind the kitchen. But no crop appeared large enough to supply more than necessary for man and beast in residence.

Lila stopped the open carriage near the gate to a grassy paddock. Sleek, beautiful horses grazed and frolicked with several new colts. As soon as the girl set the brake, Emily jumped down and ran with her skirt and petticoats clutched in her fist. She loved to run despite her mother's insistence on ladylike behavior at all times. After all, only Lila would witness and she quickly caught up and beat Emily to the fence. Breathless, they climbed up to the top rail for a better view.

"Those are some beautiful horses, Lila. Are they Thoroughbreds?"

"Yes, ma'am, they are. Dr. Bennington's pride and joy."

"Does he race them? I bet they're very fast. I do wish Matthew—he's my intended—could see them. He's particularly fond of horseflesh." Emily couldn't contain her giddiness.

"No, ma'am, there's no place on the island to race. Dr. Bennington breeds horses and shows them off to his friends. But he grows so attached, he seldom sells a foal."

"I would get attached too. And don't call me 'ma'am' when it's just you and me. Please call me Emily."

Lila shook her head. "That would not be right, Miss Harrison. I won't do it."

"Fine. As long as you address me as 'Miss Harrison,' I shall address you as 'Miss Amite.'"

Lila looked both confused and suspicious as they walked back to the carriage. "You may call me whatever you prefer."

Emily inhaled deeply. "Ah, the smell of timothy grass. We grew it in our best pasture. Only honeysuckle is sweeter." Emily climbed into the buggy and took up the reins. After a cluck of her tongue, the horse broke into a brisk trot down the shady lane.

"You can drive a carriage?" Lila gripped the seat with both hands.

"Of course I can. I didn't grow up on a plantation like this. I lived on a small hardscrabble farm where I learned to do most everything." Which wasn't exactly true, considering her cooking abilities. Emily pointed at a low, whitewashed building bustling with activity. "What goes on in there?"

"That's our dairy," Lila said proudly. "We have four hundred head of Jersey cows on the island. We make our own butter and cheese to sell in town, along with any milk we don't need."

"Dr. Bennington has time to run a dairy besides his medical practice?"

"No, the workers run it and take the cheese to Parkersburg on market day. They split the profits down the middle with Dr. Bennington."

Emily's mouth dropped open. "Are those men slaves?"

"Yes, ma'am." Lila reached up to pluck low-hanging leaves overhead.

"He lets them keep the money they earn from *his* milk?"

"Yes, ma'am." Lila looked at her from the corner of her eye.

"What do they do with it?" Emily's questions were starting to sound inane even to her.

"They buy their freedom once they've saved enough. That's what my two brothers did last year." Lila looked at Emily with pride.

"Do they still work here?" Emily pulled on the reins to slow the carriage.

"No'm. They both moved to Cleveland to work on the ore boats. They don't much like being sailors, from what we could figure out from their letters. My brothers don't read or write well, like I do. There's another business on the island too. Dr. Bennington makes whiskey from the five-hundred acres of corn grown here. He takes the whiskey down to Cincinnati to sell twice a year. He keeps all that money, though. He says it's for the lean times when people can't afford to pay their doctor bills. Mama says Mrs. Bennington doesn't know anything about the whiskey, she being a former Quaker and all. Quakers don't look kindly on spirits."

"I'm well aware of that, being a Quaker myself." Emily brought the carriage to a halt. "Hard liquor is produced on this island?"

Lila drew in a sharp breath and pursed her lips. "Have I erred in telling you this, Miss Harrison? Mama will skin me alive if the secret gets back to Mrs. Bennington." She looked uneasy. "You did say you wanted to be friends and all," she added for good measure.

Emily swallowed down her revulsion over a distillery in close proximity. "Your confidences are safe, Miss Amite. Have no fear. How the Benningtons run their personal lives is of no concern to me. I'm an employee here, nothing more, the same as you."

"Yes, ma'am." Lila relaxed against the seat again.

"Did you purchase your freedom, Miss Amite?"

"My father did, a long time ago. I don't much remember." Lila sat up and reached for the reins, which Emily handed over to her. "We'd best get back to the house. You might want to rest before dinner."

"Very well. You've answered enough questions for one day." Truth was, the island wasn't what Emily had expected or the residents quite the demons her mother had described slaveholders to be. *But appearances can be deceiving,* she reminded herself.

"Will you be eating in the kitchen with the young ladies or dining with the Benningtons?" Lila's bright eyes revealed an unspoken third possibility.

"If you're checking to see if I will again attempt to cook for myself, the answer is no. But I don't see why they don't all eat together. My family did. Every family I've ever known eats together at mealtime."

Lila thought before replying. "Miss Margaret is fourteen. Soon she'll be asked to join her parents at the dinner table on a regular basis, but Miss Anne is only eleven. She's much too young to be expected to comport herself that long. She dines with the family only on Sundays and on special occasions."

Emily's inaugural dinner later that evening explained much as to why an eleven-year-old wouldn't be welcome. No one could expect someone that young to sit still for a three-hour meal. Having decided to eat in the kitchen with the girls, she had changed her mind after discovering the heavy vellum card that had been slipped beneath her door while she was out with the maid.

In a spidery script, Mrs. Bennington had written: "Please join us for dinner. Dr. Bennington is looking forward to making your acquaintance."

How could she refuse such a summons from her employer?

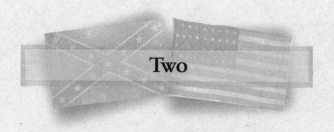

Two

*D*onning her best Sunday dress—peach muslin with a lace collar and cuffs—Emily made an appearance downstairs promptly at seven o'clock, but not a soul was there. Stepping into the lovely dining room, her eyes drifted up to the high ceiling. Hand-carved plaster rosettes encircled a magnificent crystal chandelier that held at least three dozen candles. Another thirty tapers burned in silver candelabras along the windowsills, throwing dancing light and shadows across the room. The red pine floor had been polished to a high gloss with a thick Aubusson carpet beneath the Hepplewhite table. Emily gingerly picked up a piece of Haviland bone china from a place setting. A band of gold trimmed each piece. Emily gasped, having seen such opulence only in catalogs at Miss Turner's school.

"That is a dinner plate, Miss Harrison." Someone spoke near the windows.

Recognizing the taunting voice, Emily lurched in her shoes. "I *know* what it is. I was merely admiring the pattern." She kept her words soft and controlled. She had no intention of letting him under her skin again.

"I believe the pattern is called 'Maiden Bride' or 'Long-Suffering Maiden,' something like that." Alexander came up swiftly and loomed over her shoulder. He plucked the dinner plate from her fingers to examine more closely

His breath on her neck sent tingles up her spine, but flanked by a high-back chair on both sides, Emily was enclosed. "Do you enjoy trapping people on walkways and in between heavy furniture, Mr. Hunt?"

"Ah, you remembered my name from yesterday, Miss Harrison. It does a man's heart good to realize he's not…forgettable." He bent close as he replaced the plate, breathing in her fragrance in a none-too-subtle manner.

"That pattern is called 'Versailles,' Alexander." Mrs. Bennington spoke from the doorway. "I had no idea you took interest in place settings of china." Angling her nephew a wry glance as she entered, she leaned on a cane and the arm of a distinguished-looking gentleman. Her wheeled chair was nowhere in sight. Joshua followed vigilantly behind the pair.

"Good evening, Aunt Augusta." He bowed deeply. "You look lovely this evening, as always."

Mrs. Bennington turned her attention to Emily. "Forgive our tardiness, Miss Harrison," she said with a gracious smile. "I'm glad you decided to join us for dinner." She was dressed impeccably in emerald satin with a heavy jeweled pendant that glittered in the candlelight.

"Thank you for the invitation, ma'am." Emily bobbed her head politely.

Once seated, Mrs. Bennington made introductions. "Miss Harrison, this is my husband, Dr. Porter Bennington. Dear, this is Miss Emily Harrison, formerly of Ohio."

Emily pulled her contemplation of the mysterious nephew to gaze into the watery blue eyes of her employer, her adversary—a *slaver*. She had to admit he didn't look evil. *Don't let appearances deceive you.* She could hear her mother's words ringing in her ears even as she extended her fingers to the genteel man. "How do you do, sir," she murmured.

"Miss Harrison." Dr. Bennington nodded and clasped her hand. "It is a pleasure to meet you." With graying dark hair and a deeply lined forehead, his face was too haggard and weathered to be handsome. Yet his eyes sparkled with compassion, especially as he listened to his wife recount Emily's list of attributes as governess. When she had concluded, he grinned. "Our unschooled daughters have fallen into the right hands. You'll have your work cut out for you to prepare them to be received into polite society. I'm afraid our isolated little island has beguiled us, and our girls will be at a disadvantage in the world." From the tureen presented on his left, he ladled a hearty portion of soup into his bowl. "I join my wife in welcoming you and wish to extend anything that might make your stay more pleasant."

"Thank you, sir," Emily said. *It would be so much easier to hate him if he wasn't so blasted nice.*

Dr. Bennington glanced at his nephew. "Good evening, Alexander. I trust you have introduced yourself to our new governess."

"Good evening, sir. Yes, I made proper introductions on the path to the summer kitchen yesterday."

When Emily remembered Alexander's bare chest, dappled with water droplets down to the waistband of his trousers, she felt a hot rush of color creep up her neck. *Proper indeed.* Emily sensed his gaze as she ladled creamy soup into her bowl. Glancing up, she found her intuition correct. "It's a pleasure to see you again, Mr. Hunt."

"I assure you that the pleasure is mine. My aunt and uncle are fortunate to have someone to squelch any calamites that arise."

Blushing to her hairline, she concentrated on getting soup to her mouth without spilling it on her gown.

"What calamities are you talking about, Alexander?" asked his aunt.

"Didn't you hear? Miss Harrison handily doused a kitchen fire yesterday, thereby saving Matilde's domain from certain ruin."

The soup in Emily's spoon sloshed over the edge onto her dress. "The cook and I handled the situation together."

"Truly, I'm sure she's made her first friend on the island in Matilde." He beamed at her and then focused his attention on her soup stain.

Emily sank lower in her chair.

"Is that right?" asked Dr. Bennington. "Our cook has been with us a long time. I must say, first impressions go a long way with Matilde. Well done, Miss Harrison."

"And your new governess is also a chef, Uncle. I believe she was exchanging recipes with Matilde when the blaze broke out."

"When the *blaze* broke out?" Mrs. Bennington sounded distressed.

"You are exaggerating the story out of proportion, Mr. Hunt. You're making it sound like an out-of-control inferno." Emily set down her spoon. "And I don't wish to give Dr. and Mrs. Bennington false expectations."

"Nonsense. I'm sure you're being modest about your attributes and abilities."

The Benningtons looked perplexedly at each other and then at Alexander. His aunt's face registered suspicion as she narrowed her eyes at him.

"My wife tells me you are betrothed?" asked the doctor, changing the subject.

"Yes, to Matthew Norton of Marietta. He's proudly serving with the Ohio volunteer infantry." Emily straightened her back. "In the Federal Army," she added unnecessarily.

A muscle twitched in Alexander's neck. He opened his mouth to speak, but his uncle's reply was quicker.

"Most of us here in Wood County weren't pleased when Virginia seceded from the Union, myself included. There is little reason to preserve the antiquated institution of slavery, especially in these western counties." Dr. Bennington studied his new employee.

But you do preserve it. You continue to own human beings. Emily's unspoken words hung in the air like a fog.

Clearing his throat, Joshua lifted a lid to reveal an elaborately dressed pheasant on the sideboard. A cornucopia of fruits and vegetables surrounded the roast bird. "A marvelous presentation, Joshua, thank you. You may carve now." Mrs. Bennington's compliment curtailed the uncomfortable moment.

Emily let the matter drop and gave her full attention to the salad course. It wouldn't do to get fired on her second day of employment.

"I picked up a copy of the *Richmond Ledger* in town today," said Alexander, addressing his uncle. "The Gray Wraith has struck again. He made off with a hundred prime cavalry horses with their saddles and tack, besides fifty wagons of food, blankets, and medicine on their way to the Union Army encamped at Warrenton. Begging your pardon, Miss Harrison." He bobbed his head in Emily's direction. "The paper says they masqueraded as a Federal detachment, rode in, and ransacked the caravan without a single shot being fired. The supplies are now in the hands of Thomas Jackson's men in the Shenandoah," he concluded with great enthusiasm. "Begging your pardon again, Miss Harrison."

"Excellent news," said Dr. Bennington. "Those horses couldn't be more essential with skirmishes increasing and recruits arriving to the camps daily. But I doubt Mr. Lincoln's prime stock can compare with your horses, Alexander, or with mine."

Alexander turned to Emily for a reaction, but she was concentrating on a biscuit. She spread butter into each nook and cranny with deliberation. With a shrug of his shoulders, he proceeded to devour an entire pheasant leg. "Joshua, please give my compliments to Matilde. This roast bird is superb."

Joshua's smile revealed a gold tooth. "Thank you, Mr. Hunt." He bowed slightly and withdrew from the room.

"Would you like to try your hand at cooking, Miss Harrison, during your free time?" Alexander handed her a bowl of candied yams. "I'm sure my aunt and uncle will let you experiment on Matilde's day off. They should send in Margaret and Annie as your assistants to develop their domestic talents." His gaze remained on Emily as he took a long drink of wine.

Emily knew he was taunting her, but she could say nothing without offending her employers. So she imagined upturning the bowl of yams over his head, along with the platter of sautéed spinach. The image of sugary juice running down his chin and wilted greens decorating his pristine white shirt brought a smile to her lips. She sipped from her water glass. "I look forward to it, Mr. Hunt, but I'll save the occasion for your next visit that you might enjoy the fruits of my labor."

Alexander raised his glass in a mock toast. "Shall I pour you some wine?"

"Thank you, no. I'm Quaker and don't partake in spirits. I'm surprised you do. Your aunt mentioned you were a Friend."

"I have fallen away, I'm afraid. Too many thees, thys, and thous for my tastes." He nodded deferentially to his aunt.

"Tell me more about this Gray Wraith, Dr. Bennington," said Emily, eager to change the subject. "The Ohio newspapers don't print stories about him."

"Oh, he's very mysterious, my dear." Mrs. Bennington provided the explanation. "He's believed to be a partisan ranger, but no one knows his true identity. His men refer to him only as Colonel. He rides a white stallion in the dead of night with his scarlet-lined cape flying behind him. Very dashing, don't you think? According to the accounts, he carries only a saber, refusing to possess a firearm." Mrs. Bennington's eyes sparkled in the glow of the candlelight.

"My wife has grown more besotted with the Wraith's intrigue than even Margaret. I pray he never rides to Bennington Plantation. I fear I'll lose the love of my life if she sets eyes on him."

Mrs. Bennington blushed demurely. "Oh, Porter, how you do go on."

Emily looked from one to the other but refused to glance at Alexander. *Who is this Gray Wraith wreaking havoc on the Union forces? How dare he steal food and medicine from the very troops Matthew serves with?* The veins at her temples began to throb as her hands turned clammy. She didn't view the matter quite as blithely as the other three. No doubt this was the first of many differences of opinion she would have with Dr. Bennington. Fortunately, Mr. Hunt would soon return to his home. She wouldn't have to deal with his cocky attitude or his forward behavior. The man had the exasperating ability to reduce her to a nervous, skittish doe, with her stomach flip-flopping each time their gazes met.

Finally, the endless dinner drew to a close and she bade them all a good night. But neither Dr. Bennington's complacent view of slavery, nor the exploits of this Gray Wraith, nor even Mr. Hunt's effect on her composure was Emily's chief concern as she climbed the staircase to her room. Someone had slipped a letter under her door from the evening mail packet. Carrying the letter onto her balcony, she could barely make out the address on the dirty, tattered envelope: Miss Emily

Harrison, c/o Bennington Plantation, Parkersburg, Virginia. In the fading light, she read two sentences that would change her life forever:

Dear Miss Harrison, I regret to inform you that Pvt. Matthew Norton of the OVI has fallen in battle in Virginia at the Battle of Bull Run. He died a hero's death, covering himself in glory on the battlefield and into eternity.

She read the words over and over as her hopes and dreams crumbled to dust. A single tear fell on the parchment sheet before it fluttered to the portico flagstones below. Emily gazed over the lawns, gardens, and fields of the plantation that was not much of a plantation at all. In the distance, she saw men and women marching back from the fields in the last rays of sunlight. The sight of slaves salved her wounded spirit, galvanizing her resolve.

"At least I know what to do," she whispered in the humid, enveloping darkness. "My duty to God and my country is clear."

From their well-hidden position in the foliage, twenty men gazed down on the sleeping town, watching with satisfaction as blue-clad soldiers mounted and rode out in formation. None spoke, but they held their reins tightly in hand lest their horses draw undue attention. As the last of their adversaries disappeared into a cloud of dust, the men turned toward their leader.

Sitting tall in the saddle, the colonel didn't move a muscle until the last Yank disappeared into the haze and stillness returned to the hamlet. Then his lips formed a smile as he glanced left and right at his men. "Well, boys, it looks like Ellsworth worked his magic again." Laughter broke the silence as their plan came together. But their leader didn't wait for compliments or backslapping. Spurring his horse, he galloped toward the train station below with a singular purpose and his second-in-command close behind.

"Dawson, ride up the track to the signal flags," ordered the colonel.

"Post the red to make sure the train slows well in advance. Jamison, you and Hobart throw the switch to turn the train into the siding. The rest of you men position yourselves among those trees. Any Yanks traveling with the train will either be in the first car or in the last, so that's where you enter. Be quick, be decisive. Surround and create havoc. Shoot only if you must, but to wound not to kill. Boggs, Turner, follow me."

The men reacted with speed and proficiency. These were no green recruits, no nervous, trigger-happy youngsters eager to throw themselves into battle without thought or care. These seasoned professionals were the elite of trained cavalry, men who had been born to the saddle and who handled weapons with the same precision as their mounts. Yet regular Confederate cavalry they were not.

The colonel ordered his second-in-command to enter the passenger compartment while he directed maneuvers from outside the train. If his unwelcome notoriety grew any larger, the Yankees would move him up their list of priorities. And that would only hamper their cause.

"Good morning, ladies and gentlemen. I am Captain Nathan Smith of the Army of Northern Virginia. This train will be delayed for a brief interval. Please sit quietly, and you'll still be alive when the train pulls into the station." Although the dapper young officer tipped his hat upon entering and smiled during his introduction, his two Colt revolvers left no doubt regarding his intentions. Rangers at the other end of the car leveled their Enfield rifles with the same silent threat.

Well-dressed businessmen, traveling from Washington and points east, looked with contempt upon the intrusion, yet no one twitched a whisker. Their wives and daughters weren't quite as composed. Several sobbed into lace handkerchiefs, and more than one began to pray.

"What do you want with us, sir?" asked a white-haired matron with plenty of courage as the captain made his way down the aisle. She pulled her heavy reticule from the floor to her lap. "Will you take our cash and jewelry?"

"No, madam, I assure you." Captain Smith swept off his hat and bowed. "We're only interested in the provisions on their way to Yankee camps." His smile revealed perfectly straight teeth. "You are in the sovereign state of Virginia, part of the Confederate States of America. You are not home any longer. But I assure you, the colonel has no desire for civilian property." He pointed to the window with a flourish of his hand. A tall man, clothed in a black cloak with a plumed hat pulled low, sat astride a majestic white horse. Fog swirled around horse and rider, increasing the aura of intrigue.

Leaning toward the glass, the elderly woman gasped. "Is that the Gray Wraith? He doesn't appear mortal. I read about him in the papers."

"I assure you, madam, he is flesh and blood." Captain Smith replaced his hat and strode from the car, leaving his men to guard against would-be heroes.

The rangers quickly overpowered a dozen Union soldiers, stripping them of their weapons and leaving them tied up in an empty train car. Along the tracks, the colonel directed the train's unloading with well-honed efficiency. True to the captain's word, the passengers were soon on their way. In less than thirty minutes, the rangers unloaded food, medicine, guns, and ammunition into wagons hidden in the woods. In the last two boxcars they found fifty fine horses with saddles and tack stacked along the wall, plus the unexpected bounty of a Union payroll. After tethering the horses into groups of five, they galloped off before the sun rose high enough to burn off the mist.

"Those boxes contain repeating rifles, Colonel," shouted Captain Smith as they rode out of town. "Woolen socks, buckskin gloves, leather boots, engraved saddles, halters, bridles—this shipment must have been headed to a cavalry brigade, sir."

The colonel glanced at Smith with amusement. Seldom had plunder so excited the man. "That's right, Captain." He slowed his horse on the narrow path, pulled off his hat and ran a hand through his hair. "This bounty will be for Jeb Stuart, not for General Jackson as we had planned. Sheridan's loss will be Stuart's gain," he added, scratching his stubbly chin. He never would get used to the bristly beard he grew prior to a raid. "And Jeff Davis will appreciate that Union payroll, thirty thousand dollars by my estimate."

"To another successful raid and the diminishing of the Mr. Lincoln's Treasury, sir." Smith pulled a silver flask from his pocket and offered a toast to his superior officer.

The colonel stared at the flask momentarily before downing a hearty swig. "I'm just glad we were able to serve our Glorious Cause without killing any of those fool Yankees in the process," he muttered. "Now let's organize the men and send this bounty on its way to Richmond before the Yanks figure out that no division of infantry is marching to Winchester this morning." Both men laughed over their successful deception. Union officers would boil when they discovered they had been tricked. The colonel hoped local citizens wouldn't suffer because of his activities, but they couldn't raid anywhere else. Federal provisions, greenbacks, and horseflesh appeared to be limitless in the fertile area between the Shenandoah Valley and Washington. Their storehouses were like sweet cherries—ripe and ready to be picked. And his beloved Confederacy desperately needed all they could provide.

Rendezvoused with his men, the colonel savored some of the commandeered, spit-roasted Yankee beef. Someone passed around an expensive bottle of bourbon and another of brandy. He allowed his men to enjoy this small diversion in camp while he sipped only strong coffee. One man played a harmonica as another danced a jig. Most of his seasoned soldiers retold the day's adventure over and over until they drifted to their bedrolls. Tomorrow they would return home—to their parents or wives or just to a lonely boarding house in a small town. But tonight they were rangers—brave, accomplished, and famous. And their leader was proud of them all.

Staring into the flames as dampness drew him to the fire, the colonel thought of the winsome, spirited girl he'd met on Bennington Island. Emily Harrison was nothing like the flirtatious women who usually heated his blood and caused his heart to race. He found her peculiarity unnerving, as though she'd ensnared him with a spell. When he wrote to his aunt to inquire about her, he couldn't keep exuberance from his words. How could he become smitten after so brief an encounter? He was no youth experiencing attraction to a pretty girl for the first time.

But as he stared into the fire, the unbidden memory of a different woman crept to mind, spoiling his sweet reverie. With lustrous ebony hair cascading down her back, a small waist, deep violet eyes, and porcelain skin, Rosalyn was more of a vision than creature of this world. But she had been real the nights she gave herself eagerly to him. She had bewitched him with soft lips and tender words spoken in passion. Never questioning the incongruity of their encounters, nor her curious interest in his comings and goings, he had answered her endless queries, boasting of his troops' exploits with shameless bravado. Painfully, he remembered supplying her with information that led four of his men to their graves. As they had lain entwined in each other's arms, warmed by a goose down comforter and expensive wine, she set a trap for his troops—an ambush by Federal cavalry. Because he had foolishly trusted a woman, wives, children, and parents grieved for what could never be replaced. The memory of Rosalyn's deception and his weakness for a beautiful face would follow him for the rest of his life. Never again would he trust a female's lilting voice or warm embrace. One could no more trust a woman than a cobra or rattler. They could sense a man's desire and recognize it for what it was: weakness.

Never again, he whispered into the night, trying once more to forget his shameful past. His parents wished him to marry and provide an heir for Hunt Farms. But what would be left by the end of the war to inherit? He had seen plantations burned to the ground or sold off parcel by parcel to settle debts. What made him think his family would fare any better? War wasn't the time to think about marriage or children or inheritances. No new life would be waiting for him. The Wraith's path was forged. The South was dying a slow, agonizing death, and he had no choice but to see it through. He had no business thinking about any woman…least of all, a Yankee.

Two days later, a tired and dirty Alexander rode the back roads to his home. Having not slept or bathed since before he left and having eaten only what had been packed in his saddlebags days ago, he wasn't in the best of moods. He barely resembled the dashing colonel who had materialized in the mist and then vanished just as quickly. His uniform with the striking red-lined cape had been packed away. It wouldn't help him cross enemy lines to deliver the precious booty—gold, greenbacks, and medicine—to Confederate command posts. The homespun garb of a farmer with a tattered straw hat better served his purpose. No one had stopped his rickety wagon as he made his way along, selling tallow candles and sharpening knives with his grinding wheel. The colonel appeared to be a simple man trying to earn a living instead of the infamous Gray Wraith transferring a fortune to the Cause.

But what troubled Alexander during the waning miles to his tub of hot water and soft bed wasn't his scratchy garments or ill-fitting shoes. Once again, a heated argument had ensued when he had denied his men spoils from their foray. A small amount of plunder always slipped past him. He wouldn't fight Dawson over a few bolts of calico for his wife. And certainly no ranger who needed a fresh horse or additional equipment would be denied. But he couldn't abide with personal gain by his soldiers while the rest of the Confederate Army suffered. They were not thieves. They were not mercenaries. But sometimes convincing his men of that proved impossible.

Lost in thought, he almost rode past the oak-canopied lane to his home. However his horse, tired and hungry like his master, knew the way. Phantom pricked up his ears and quickened his pace, knowing oats and a good rubdown awaited at journey's end. As they broke into a canter, he pulled on the reins and patted Phantom's flank.

"Whoa, boy. Let's not wake everyone." Halfway up the lane, he slipped silently from the horse to walk the remaining distance. As he passed, he checked the bedroom window where his parents slept for signs of movement.

"They're not up yet, sir." A voice emanated from the inky shadows. A very dark and sinewy young man stepped into a shaft of moonlight.

"William, my man, it's good to see you." Alexander slapped his lifelong friend on the shoulder as they entered the cavernous barn. Handing William the reins, he pulled the saddle from Phantom's back.

William carried the plain saddle to the table, placing it next to those embossed with the sterling silver crest of Hunt Farms. "I'll bet it is. I had a feeling you would be back this morn. Beatrice is already up and fixing breakfast. She'll have it ready soon."

"I'm not sure I can stay awake to lift my fork." Alexander cross-tied his horse inside a stall and began currying him.

"See to your own comfort. I'll take care of Phantom." William picked up a second brush.

"Where do my parents think I've been these past two days?" The light from the solitary lantern provided little illumination, but Alexander spotted a smile on his friend's face and a definite glimmer in his eye.

"Well, sir, let's just say I alluded to your getting a bit luckier with the ladies of Chantilly than with cards the night before last."

"*What?*" The colonel's tired face pinched into a scowl.

"To your father, of course," added William hastily. "I spoke of this matter only to him."

Alexander wasn't pacified. "Little is kept from my mother's ears. I believe she has more spies than the Union Army. Now she will lecture me about my sinful ways of card-playing and carousing for some time to come. Was there no other explanation you could have come up with?"

"None that I thought sounded believable." William ducked his head in time to miss a flying brush.

"I'll remember this, William. Someday when you have a fine young wife, I'll find an opportunity to land *you* in the doghouse."

"Me with a wife, sir? Highly unlikely." The two men laughed. They had grown up on this farm and reached manhood together. They were friends, even if one was the son of a planter and the other, a free black employee. "I'll finish Phantom," William said, keeping the large stallion between them. "Your breakfast is probably ready by now."

With a grateful nod, Alexander picked up the brush and tossed it into the basket. "While you work, why not think up possible excuses that don't involve drinking, card-playing, or carousing in cathouses? My mother is peeved with me enough."

The exhausted colonel went to his much-needed food and rest. After breakfast and a bath, he slept like the dead for ten hours—his sleep blissfully void of dreams.

Autumn 1861

Never let it be said that the heart is not a peculiar thing. As quickly as hers had swelled with the promise of new love and the anticipation of marriage, Emily's heart contracted until there was neither pain nor any emotion left. After receiving the letter which ended her newfound status as fiancée, she slogged through her days methodically, as though nothing had happened. Her dear beau, Matthew, was dead, his vitality destroyed in the blink of an eye on the bank of a creek called Bull Run. Yet because he had been little more than a stranger, she possessed few comforting memories. One day she would take up Matthew's sword, but for now she licked her wounds and taught her lessons. Her two students were both well behaved and eager to learn. Though still young, Margaret sensed Emily's profound loss and didn't press for details or offer unsolicited advice. She tried to distract her teacher from melancholia with a warm smile or an interesting piece of poetry. Even little Annie behaved with restraint during the ensuing weeks.

Emily performed her duties as governess with dignity and grace. Yet, when she finally stopped crying herself to sleep at night, numbness washed over her like a fog. While Margaret and Anne rested, she spent her afternoons walking along the river or hiking through the orchard until her legs grew rubbery. She never felt afraid no matter how far she wandered. Nothing could hurt her now. She filled each hour of the day with activity so exhaustion would carry her to sleep at night. She ate her meals in the kitchen with the girls. Or, if they were to dine with their parents, Emily invented excuses to eat with the staff, thus avoiding the Benningtons whenever possible. Though they weren't personally responsible for Matthew's death, she couldn't look on their wealth and not be reminded of a war fought to preserve the institution that created it. Emily ignored the largesse Dr. Bennington extended in his medical practice to both black and white patients. She refused to acknowledge the kindness Mrs. Bennington lavished on everyone she encountered. Like a wounded animal caught in a trap, she longed to hold someone responsible for her pain and misery.

Emily saw only one enemy—the South—with its decadent, privileged society. She read newspaper accounts of battles, privately hoping for Union victories. She followed the bizarre exploits of a partisan band of rangers with interest. Who was this man who made fools of the Union cavalry? Responsible for tremendous financial loss to the Federal war effort, he was nothing more than a bandit. How dare he steal with such impunity? Eventually, this latter-day Robin Hood roused her anger, pulling her from her paralysis as nothing had been able to do.

The Gray Wraith…her hatred of the South's Glorious Cause now had a name.

THREE

*A*dam, life is very different there—in ways you can't see from across the river even on the clearest of days." Emily straightened her back defiantly but kept her voice low.

"Yes, ma'am. I know there's no slavery in Ohio. I think about it all the time." Adam wouldn't look at the schoolmarm who had stopped her horse and then approached him like a swarm of hornets. He continued to mend the fence rails and replace the rotted slats along the north pasture.

"The Ordinance of 1787 established the Northwest Territory as the first government born free in all the world. 'Here no witch was ever burned; nor heretic molested; here no slave was ever born or dwelt.'" Emily recited the litany taught to her by her parents with pride and conviction.

Adam, a man not yet thirty, set down his tools and faced Emily. "Yes, ma'am. I know all about that proclamation, but I also know 'bout the Fugitive Slave Act of 1850. That means I ain't no freer in Ohio than I am here, not as long as slave-catchers with guns and dogs can track me like an animal. I'm no animal here, miss. I may be a slave, but I can work in the dairy when my chores are done. When I save enough money, I'll buy my freedom and my wife's. With signed manumission papers, no slave hunter and his dogs can come after me." He looked her straight in the eye and held her gaze.

"I understand, Adam."

"No, ma'am, you don't. You may mean well, but you don't understand a'tall." Selecting the next slat of wood to nail in place, Adam turned away from her, not rudely but with the concerted effort of a man with a job to do.

"I can help you and your wife reach Cleveland or Fairport Harbor." Emily glanced around before stepping closer. "From there, Friends will put you on a boat to Canada. That's what the Quakers are called—Friends," she added earnestly. "You'll be safe in Canada." *Why is this man behaving like this? So aloof and disinterested. Doesn't he trust me?* "Take the freedom train, Adam. You won't regret it."

"No one can say what we will or won't regret during our lifetime, but I'll think about it. I'll think on it plenty, you can be sure 'bout that. You go on now. I'm grateful for the offer, but you must leave me. This ain't something a man decides on the spur of the moment." With the discussion over on his part, Adam picked up his tools and walked away without a backward glance.

Alone, Emily stood watching him lumber down the dusty road. Was it her? Was there something in her that didn't inspire trust? Adam was the third slave on Bennington Plantation who hadn't jumped at the opportunity of the freedom she was offering. True, after observing island life for the past several months she had to admit slaves weren't abused here. But there was no freedom either for more than half the workers. Dead leaves swirled around her feet, and a cool breeze lifted the hem of her skirt, sending a shiver up her spine. With fall rapidly approaching and her sorrow pushed to the back corner of her mind, she was eager to find a purpose. Yet she'd found no takers for her offer to assist slaves across the river to Ohio. And the reason continued to elude her.

Emily often read aloud to Mrs. Bennington during the afternoon when neither felt like napping. Emily enjoyed the recitations of *Pickwick Papers* and *David Copperfield* as much as her employer. An incongruous bond formed between the two women as they discussed Charles Dickens's bleak outlook on society. Emily offered forthright opinions with growing confidence, while Mrs. Bennington loved to impart Quaker principles into every debate. Although members of the same Christian sect, their backgrounds and experiences had created rather divergent ideas. But both women had abandoned the somber gray dresses and wide-brimmed, face-obscuring bonnets worn by Quakers—Mrs. Bennington because her husband insisted she dress like the fashionable women of her class, and Emily because, after her brief period of mourning, she rebelled against the constant reminder of her loss.

Mrs. Bennington's kindness finally wore down Emily's resolve not to socialize with the family. An additional incentive to accepting the invitation to dine in the grand salon that evening was because her services as chaperone had been requested. Margaret would be attending her first adult affair, while Anne would serve as punch bowl monitor until her bedtime. Guests from Louisville were already arriving and would stay at the mansion for several days. Their neighbors in Parkersburg would float downriver on flatboats to participate in the evening festivities. Lila explained that local dinner guests would also spend the night and return home after breakfast.

"Why are they making such a to-do over an evening meal?" asked Emily as she and Lila laid out the clothes Margaret and Anne would wear. "How can people linger five or six hours over dinner? What can they find to talk about for so long?" She shook her head. "My family always ate supper and returned to whatever they still needed to do that day."

"I suppose it's something you get used to." Lila set out dainty slippers for both girls. "And once you see the number of courses, you'll understand why dinner takes so long. Just don't eat much of any one food." She held up Emily's new yellow silk dress. "Will you wear this one? I can lace you into your corset while the girls are bathing."

Emily blanched. "I don't own such an undergarment, only plain chemises."

Lila stared in disbelief. "Good thing you're as skinny as a bean stalk. Stay here. I'll be right back." She bolted out the door before Emily could object.

She stared at the yellow gown and three daytime dresses, all gifts from Mrs. Bennington. Her employers were pleased with their daughters' progress. Margaret's deportment had improved, and her French was practically fluent. Little Annie no longer stampeded through the upper halls and had stopped sliding down the bannister on her belly. Emily had originally declined the offer of new frocks, but she relented after viewing her meager wardrobe hanging on the clothesline. Due to frequent launderings, sunlight streamed through the faded fabric, rendering the material nearly transparent.

Emily fingered the gown, having never owned anything like it. It was tightly fitted from the bodice down to her hips, where billows of tiered lace cascaded to the floor. Delicate white cuffs set off the pale shade of buttercup, and lace edging accented the deep neckline.

"Hurry, Miss Harrison. Shimmy into this." Lila flew into the bedroom and thrust a stiff apparatus at her. "Miss Margaret outgrew this one before ever wearing it. I'll turn my back."

Emily studied the garment to determine top from bottom and drew it up over her hips. Despite her skinny-as-a-stalk frame, she had to hold her breath to close the hooks-and-eyes.

"Turn around and I'll lace you up. Then I must leave to help Miss Margaret. Shall I send in another maid?" asked Lila, already knowing the answer. All of the other maids were slaves.

"No, thank you." Emily was barely able to inhale as Lila tightened the stays. "I can manage. You run along when you're done. And don't worry about me eating too much. That would be impossible wearing this. I'm not sure I'll be able to even sit down."

Once alone in the room, Emily slipped the dress over her head and struggled to reach the row of buttons in back. Then she lowered herself to the stool before her mirror and pinned her freshly washed hair into a cluster of curls atop her head. Springy tendrils slipped loose to frame her face. Her burnished cheeks glowed, inappropriately suntanned from her walks without a hat. Emily touched rouge to her lips, dabbed lemon balm on her pulse points, and sucked in a deep breath.

On her way downstairs, she caught her reflection in the mirror. She didn't recognize the woman who gazed back.

"Miss Harrison, there you are. I'd like you to meet some of my guests," boomed Dr. Bennington before she reached the landing.

"Good evening, Dr. Bennington." Emily bobbed her head politely. "Perhaps I should check on Anne or Margaret."

"Nonsense, they'll be fine. We don't stand on ceremony on my little island. Relax a bit tonight." He took her forearm and practically dragged her out on the portico. An elderly couple stood alone, sipping iced tea. "Miss Harrison, may I introduce Mr. and Mrs. Hull of Parkersburg. Edwina, Howard, this is Miss Emily Harrison of Marietta."

"How do you?" she murmured, withholding her curtsey at the last moment.

"You'll be pleased to discover they share your views on slavery," said Dr. Bennington. "They feel the institution should be abolished and say so often and loudly at every public meeting and forum they attend." His eyes twinkled, apparently pleased with himself. Then he bowed to the Hulls and disappeared into the throng of guests.

Reluctantly, Emily struck up a conversation with them. "I am pleased to learn there are antislavery sentiments on this side of the river too," she said to Mr. Hull.

"An archaic system that places a few rich planters at the top of society while the rest of us struggle to earn a living!" he thundered. "How can a farmer or shopkeeper compete with free labor?" Mr. Hull made little attempt to modulate his voice. "Young people are hard pressed to find decent jobs if they weren't born with a silver spoon in their mouth."

Emily glanced around uncomfortably. "You speak of economic concerns, but what of the ethical reasons for the institution's abolishment?" she asked.

Mr. Hull blinked like an owl and took a swallow of something brown in a bowl-shaped glass. Mrs. Hull tilted her head toward her. "I'm not sure how much traveling you've done, my dear, but few families in these western counties have been blessed with so much… abundance as our dear host and hostess." Smiling, she nodded in the direction of Mrs. Bennington. "I assure you, slaveholding plantations are rare in this part of Virginia."

"We're forced to suffer to maintain old King Charles's land grants from a hundred years ago," interjected Mr. Hull. "Those created some very rich men among the king's cronies. With no offense toward our friends, the Benningtons," he added hastily.

It was Emily's turn to blink with disbelief. "King Charles should have insisted that the Colonies contain no slavery from the start."

Ignoring her comment, Mr. Hull downed the contents of his odd-shaped glass. "Economies aside, Miss Harrison, what about the principles of states' rights? That's what this rebellion is about, at least here in Wood County. Why should some Yankee in Washington tell us how to live our lives?"

Emily felt the boning of her corset cut into her ribs and breathed with relief when Joshua threw open the French doors.

"Ladies and gentlemen, dinner is served," he announced with a deep bow.

"It was a pleasure to make your acquaintance, sir, ma'am, but I must locate my charges." She bobbed her head and hurried away from the tiresome couple.

She spotted Margaret near the dining room door, looking winsome and lovely in her new gown. "Thank goodness I found you," Emily whispered in Margaret's ear. "Let's find two seats at the far end of the table."

"Dear me, Miss Harrison. We must sit where our name cards have been placed. And I doubt that will be together. Wish me luck at my first gala." Margaret squeezed her hand and then glided into the room without waiting for Emily's wishes, good or otherwise.

She entered at a less enthusiastic pace, trying not to gape at her surroundings. At least a hundred tapers illuminated the beautifully appointed Hepplewhite table. The silver gleamed and the crystal sparkled in the candlelight, reminding her once again of her modest upbringing. As Margaret predicted, the governess and charge had been separated. Margaret sat between two young men, one more simpering than the other. Emily found her name card across from Dr. Bennington and between two slightly older men. Neither was as expensively dressed as their host. During the meal, they attempted to outdo one another with stories of bravado in vain attempts to impress her. Dr. Bennington appeared amused by the attention they lavished on Emily, but she wished to be anywhere but here with these vapid Southern aristocrats. Only when the conversation turned to the Gray Wraith did her interest pique.

"You'll be happy to learn, Miss Harrison, being a Unionist, that the Gray Wraith never harms a hair on a Yankee head," said the older of the two men. "Why, he doesn't even carry a firearm." He nodded his head, revealing a shiny, bald patch of scalp.

"He does carry a saber, but I understand he uses it solely to sever the purse strings of rich businessmen," the younger of the pair added to the great entertainment of all. "More wine, Miss Harrison?"

"No, thank you. I don't imbibe. And I fail to comprehend how being a thief is a noble occupation, gentlemen." Emily kept her voice low with great effort.

"Ah, the difference is that our mysterious Wraith steals food only to feed a hungry army, medicine for the wounded in field hospitals, and clothing to keep our boys in the Shenandoah warm."

"I understand he also steals money from the Federal Army payrolls." Emily's voice rose in agitation despite her desire not to embarrass the Benningtons at their dinner party.

But her table companions didn't seem to take exception. "True enough, Miss Harrison, but your Federal Treasury contains much placed there by Southern planters. You can't really blame the man for wishing to *redistribute* the funds more equitably," the man concluded. Everyone within earshot nodded their well-coifed heads in agreement. Several began relaying stories they had heard of the Wraith's exploits. Everyone but Emily, that is. Red-faced and cross, she sipped her grape juice in an effort to curb her tongue. Even though she refused the constant offer of spirits, she found herself growing light headed before the main course was finally served. Then, thankfully, the political conversation changed over to polite compliments regarding the fare.

Emily picked at the undercooked rib of beef—meat so rare it was still bloody—and enjoyed only the side dishes. The spiced apples and baked squash reminded her of home. Inside, she seethed over the blithe remarks about a cavalier thief. How dare they turn his sinful behavior into a crusadelike cause? Women who idolized the Wraith were

pure fools. *If I knew the man's identity, I would expose him to the authorities,* she mused. He wouldn't look so noble swinging at the end of a
noose like a common thief. Reaching for her flute, she swallowed a
hearty mouthful before realizing someone had refilled her empty glass
with red wine. The wine roiled bitterly in her stomach, yet she dared
not excuse herself from the table. *Drinking spirits…thank goodness my
mother isn't here to see this.*

"I can't blame you one bit, Porter. Selling Bennington Plantation to
an Ohio horse breeder is probably the wisest thing you can do at this
point. Since Virginia seceded, conditions have worsened in this area
for the planter. Why, there's even talk among the rabble that these western counties should break from Virginia. Could you imagine such an
idea? Nothing will come of it, of course, but men of our class will be
more welcome in the East than here. Although I must say, the town of
Parkersburg will be sorry to see your medical practice go." The elderly
man's booming voice cut through Emily's reverie. Her head snapped
around in attention.

"Yes, the Ohioan offered a fair price. I haven't been able to turn a
profit since inheriting the plantation from my father, so I thought I
should sell." Dr. Bennington leaned back in his chair. "I am a physician and not much of a gentlemen farmer."

"That's due to your generous nature, Porter. You don't press anyone
to pay for your services. I heard you let your people keep the profits
from their businesses," drawled an overly made-up woman. "You are
too kind for your own good." She dragged out each word for emphasis
without taking her eyes off Mrs. Bennington seated at the other end
of the table.

"Porter is indeed a charitable man." His wife beamed a smile at him.
"I wouldn't have him any other way."

He lifted his glass in salute. "Thank you, my dear. My hope is that
we will be surrounded by as many caring friends in Martinsburg as we
are here." He drained his glass and held it out for Joshua to refill.

When everyone raised their glass to toast, so did Emily, forget-
ting her flute no longer contained juice. The wine began jangling her

thoughts as she tried to absorb Dr. Bennington's words. "Martinsburg?" she asked in a tiny voice. "You're moving your family to Martinsburg?"

Every head turned in her direction. "Yes, Miss Harrison, right after the Christmas holidays." He smiled patiently at her. "I have sold Bennington Plantation and will move my practice there."

"You're moving east because things have become uncomfortable for slavers here?"

The room grew so quiet one could hear wax drip from the sconces.

"No." His heavy lids drooped, rendering his eyes impossible to read. "I'm moving because doctors are desperately needed in that area. Most doctors in the East have joined one or the other armies, leaving towns frightfully short of medical professionals." Several guests put down their glasses and stared at her with undisguised hostility.

Emily couldn't seem to stop herself. "Your guest just said planters are more welcome in eastern counties than here, where most farms are run without keeping people in bondage."

Ladies reacted to Emily's display of unfeminine behavior with a sharp intake of breath. To be sure, no one present had ever heard a woman speak so boldly before. The gentleman on Emily's right covered her hand with his and squeezed, as though attempting to bring her to her senses. The older man on her left cleared his throat. "Here, here, miss. Do not talk of matters of which you have no knowledge."

"But I do have knowledge of such matters, sir. Mr. and Mrs. Hull confirmed my suspicions about slavery in this area."

"You are correct, Miss Harrison," said Dr. Bennington. "Slaveholding plantations are few and becoming increasingly unpopular here, but that is not my reason for leaving."

"Porter, you don't owe this ill-bred young woman an explanation," interrupted the elderly man. His bulbous nose had grown increasingly pink during the meal. "Isn't she your governess? She should be sent back to the nursery to her charges at once, if not given her walking papers."

More than one dinner guest nodded in agreement. Except for

Margaret. She stared at Emily with wide-eyed horror. And not Mrs. Bennington, either. Oddly, she watched the ordeal with teary eyes, wringing her hands as though frightened of the outcome.

Sipping his wine, Dr. Bennington remained unruffled. "No, Walter. Miss Harrison is encouraged to speak her mind in my house. That's how we are raising our daughters."

Emily regained her composure and looked at him squarely. "I acknowledge that you are an unusually benevolent master, Dr. Bennington, but how can it be just to uproot and move your *people* miles away against their will?" Again, the room grew so quiet she could hear the clock ticking on the mantel.

"I agree with you, Miss Harrison. That is why I signed Deeds of Manumission today for all my workers. They are free men and women, and they can go east with us…or not." He took another sip of wine, but his gaze never left his young employee. "I will resettle in Martinsburg with only paid staff. And I intend to send Margaret and Anne to Europe until I'm confident Virginia is free of hostilities that might threaten their safety."

At long last, Emily was speechless.

Spring 1862

Alexander had always preferred an active, dangerous life. Unfortunately it came with secrets, subterfuge, and deception. From his earliest days at the University of Virginia, he'd told his parents a steady stream of white lies to protect them from the scandal of his brawling, gambling, and carousing with women. He'd been expelled after dueling with another student over a not-so-virtuous lady. Only by luck had the man recovered from his wound and intervened to have him reinstated, following payment of an exorbitant sum of money.

His parents had all but given up hope of children when Alexander was born. He soon became his father's pride and joy and the apple of his mother's eye. But when he grew into a rebellious teenager, James Hunt sheltered his delicate wife from his rowdy behavior. Now that his father had grown old and troubled by a weakened heart, Alexander's web of lies also included him. However, it was no longer schoolyard brawling that would bring shame to the Hunt family reputation. These days he was up to his neck in something that could send him to a Northern prison...or put him at the end of a hangman's noose.

His mother had begged him not to join the Confederate Army during Jefferson Davis's call for volunteers. She insisted he run the plantation due to his father's poor health. Many in his social class resisted the impulse to enlist and fulfilled their patriotic duty in safer ways. Alexander had no desire for the tedium of camp life—the endless drills, marches to nowhere, and the stultifying boredom between battles. Following secession, he yearned to serve his fledging country, but not within the confines of the regular army.

His role as partisan ranger—a guerrilla—hadn't been planned. During one of his frequent rides, he discovered that a Union telegraph office had been set up behind newly drawn battle lines. After Alexander overpowered and tied up the operator, his friend Daniel Ellsworth cut into the circuit using a ground wire. From intercepted messages, they learned of the transport of Confederate prisoners through Loudoun County. Alexander answered messages for the Yankee agent, giving false reports of troop movements to throw off the enemy and inflating Confederate troop numbers before the next battle. With Ellsworth's knowledge of telegraph lines and Alexander's natural military intellect, they began a series of clandestine forays that would eventually make him famous. No telegraph office in the Shenandoah Valley was safe from their trickery. Newspapers dubbed him the Gray Wraith due to his mastery of disguise and stealth. Commissioned in secret by the Secretary of War, Colonel Alexander Hunt walked a fine line, giving his handpicked men the necessary advantage to supply the Army of Northern Virginia. Because they would be nowhere near as effective if his identity became known, he and his rangers returned to their quiet lives between raids. But each day the subterfuge grew harder to maintain.

His parents frequently questioned his absences and were less than satisfied with his evasive replies. Alexander envied his men who returned to wives and children, but despite his attraction to the red-haired governess at his uncle's home, he doubted marriage would ever be his destiny. Not that Emily Harrison would make a suitable wife, Northern or Southern. Pity the poor man who married that sharp-tongued, ill-tempered troublemaker.

On a lovely spring afternoon, as peepers created a frenzied tumult from the pond, Alexander was in no hurry to return to life in Front Royal. Because his father employed well-paid trainers, grooms, and jockeys, besides overseers and field hands to run his horse breeding operation, Alexander never felt essential at Hunt Farms. Only in the saddle in the backwoods did he feel part of something significant. He rode like a true Southern aristocrat after many summers of steeplechase in his youth. He and Phantom were two halves of one powerful whole. And that ability to handle a horse saved him in many close calls during his current identity.

Their last raid hadn't yielded what he had hoped. The Union train from Alexandria contained only grain forage for livestock and a limited amount of rations—no weapons or ammunition, and no military intelligence. But the last boxcar yielded a rare treat—crates of oranges, lemons, candy, and fresh shad. Fish was scarce due to the Union blockade of the seacoast. His rangers carried the provisions back to camp for a fish fry. Like children they cavorted around the fire as grease in the pans spattered, eagerly awaiting the change in cuisine.

After dispersing his troops, the colonel had spent the day scouting new rendezvous locations in the Berryville area. It wouldn't be prudent to keep to familiar haunts. He had learned of a small abandoned barn outside of Berryville, and therefore was surprised to spot a horse tethered to the water trough. *Might be a deserter, but from which side?* Alexander carried no firearm. His mother's instructions on the Quaker way of life had taken root, giving him no desire to take another life. An intelligent man knew other ways to gain the upper hand. Using handholds in the side of the barn, he climbed up the wall to the hayloft window and perched silently over the door, prepared for anyone exiting the barn.

Almost anyone, that is. When the door swung open, he leapt down on the deserter, landing with a mouthful of flaming red hair and a sharp knee to his gut.

"*Ouff*! Get off me, you oaf! Are you some sort of wild beast?"

Hearing a feminine voice, Alexander scrambled to extract himself from a person both female and beautiful. Beautiful, that is, if one found red-faced, scowling women with leaves in their hair and dusty clothes beautiful. At the moment, he did. It was Emily Harrison—the governess who almost burned down the kitchen at Bennington Plantation. The same woman who demanded he cover his chest yet couldn't keep her eyes off of his bare skin. He laughed at the absurdity of meeting her in the remote countryside.

"*You!*" She spat out the word as though it were a distasteful mouthful of castor oil.

"Alexander Wesley Hunt, madam, of Hunt Farms, Front Royal." He bowed deeply before stretching out his hand. "We met last summer at Bennington Plantation. I believe Matilde had just ousted you from her kitchen."

She jumped back, glowering as though his hand were a serpent. "I remember you, Mr. Hunt. Perhaps you will explain why you leaped down on me?" Her voice seethed with venom.

"I humbly beg your pardon." Alexander swept off his hat and ran a hand through his hair. Fortuitously, he wore riding clothes with his uniform packed safely away in the saddlebag. "I thought you might be a deserter looking for a place to hide. Please forgive my indiscretion, madam. Both Union and Confederate scalawags travel this valley on their way home."

While Emily dusted herself off and pulled leaves from her hair, Alexander assessed her appearance. Instead of a riding habit, she wore a summer ensemble more suited to a walk in the garden. His eyes flicked over her briefly before coming back to her face. "Madam, where is your carriage and driver? May I assist you in some way? Are you lost, or did the carriage throw a wheel and you sent your driver for help?"

"Stop calling me 'madam,'" she demanded with a stomp of her foot. "You know very well I'm unmarried. And I do not have a driver, sir."

"Then how did you get here?" He peered around the barnyard with confusion.

"I rode my horse, you simpleton."

"In that?" He pointed to her cotton dress and smock. "Without leather boots or a riding habit?" Then the full impact of her words struck him like a whack to his head. "Great Scot. I believe this is the first time in my life anyone called me a simpleton."

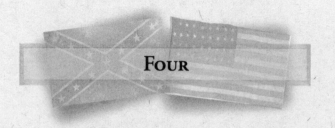

FOUR

mily couldn't tell if Mr. Hunt's shocked expression was due to the insulting word she had just used or her inappropriate attire. "Well, that rather surprises me. And it's none of your business what I wear when I ride, Mr. Alexander Wesley Hunt of Front Royal. If you've finished pouncing on me, I'll be on my way." The masculine scents of leather and shaving balm wafted around her. She remembered meeting the arrogant nephew on the island, but she had no intention of allowing him to intimidate her again. "I am no deserter looking for a place to hide out." She pushed past him. Her tone was dismissive, but he still followed at her heels like a puppy. "Truly, Mr. Hunt, I do not need your assistance. Good day to you."

Spying her new chestnut mare, his attention focused on the horse. "What a beauty! What's her name?" He ran his hand down the shiny flank.

"Miss Kitty. She was a gift from Dr. and Mrs. Bennington." Emily tugged the reins loose from the branch, wishing it wasn't her first time on the new Morgan. Though an experienced horsewoman, she always rode astride as a girl and was uncomfortable with the new sidesaddle. She didn't need this mule of a man seeing her fall on her backside.

"Why such a lavish gift? Did you serve some of your culinary delights at their dinner table?" He winked impishly.

"Must you continue to refer to one accident as though no other thoughts ramble through your mind?" Her breath left her lungs in a huff. "Mrs. Bennington was pleased I agreed to accompany them east, despite the fact their daughters left for Europe."

"With the girls gone, why would my aunt still need a governess?"

"She wishes me to remain in her employ as her personal assistant. Now, as I've answered your questions, you may continue on your way."

He grasped Miss Kitty's bridle. "Humor me with one more, Miss Harrison. How will you mount without a hitching block?"

"Not all women are helpless belles, Mr. Hunt." Emily lifted her foot into the stirrup, grabbed the saddle and a fistful of mane, and hauled herself up. Unfortunately, she revealed an expanse of dainty petticoat lace and quite of bit of stocking above her shoe. She tugged down her skirt, but not before his eyes practically bugged from his head.

"I would feel much better if I rode with you, Miss Harrison," he said, shifting his gaze from her leg to her face. "May I see you safely back to my uncle's home?"

"You may not. Now, please let go of my horse, sir."

"A woman shouldn't be out here alone," he insisted.

With a glare Emily leaned forward in the saddle. "And why not, may I ask?" Her voice dripped with scorn; her jaw set with determination.

"These are dangerous times. Aren't you afraid of running into the Gray Wraith? Rumor has it these woods are his usual haunt."

"I'm not afraid of any *ghost*, Mr. Hunt. I would simply shoot him with my hidden derringer." She quickly straightened her back as the saddle shifted precariously.

"My word, you ride around the county unchaperoned carrying a hidden pistol?" The smirk on his face belied her assertion. "What, may I ask, are you doing here?" He hooked a thumb toward the barn. "You're a long way from…Martinsburg. I believe that's where my uncle moved his practice."

Emily released an exasperated sigh. "I was out riding on this pleasant day and grew fatigued. I spotted this old barn and decided to rest inside."

"I see." Again his tone indicated little belief in her story. "You chose a mice-infested, cobweb-shrouded barn for your afternoon repose? Perhaps bales of moldy old straw for your chaise?" He grinned, revealing white teeth to contrast his tanned, ruddy face. A two- or three-day beard, along with his long hair loose around his shoulders, gave him a feral look.

"You forget, Mr. Hunt, that I'm a simple farm girl, unaccustomed to tapestry-covered sofas. The hay smelled fresh and I saw no mice." Emily picked leaves from Miss Kitty's mane to keep her focus off his well-cut jacket and white shirt, unbuttoned at the neck. A bit of skin showed where his shirt gaped open. Just for a moment she stared at his muscular chest. Then she swallowed hard and forced her gaze upward. Meeting his eye, her stomach twisted into a knot

"Excuse me, Miss Harrison. I forgot that the sight of a man's chest is unsettling for a maiden." He buttoned his shirt with deliberate exaggeration. "Forgive my imprudence."

"I have seen men with their shirts off. That is not what I find unsettling about you," said Emily, acutely aware of her own disheveled appearance. She didn't remember Mrs. Bennington's nephew being so handsome...for a rich, aristocratic Southerner. "I ask you again to release your hold on my bridle."

"I'm reluctant to let you leave with the Gray Wraith prowling the valley. Would you be pleased or terrified if he crossed your path?"

"If I run into the Gray Wraith, I shall shoot him between the eyes and spare the Union Army the task. He is a murdering desperado that even a noose is too good for."

"Goodness, you would shoot an unarmed man without benefit of a trial? Aren't you a Quaker and a pacifist by nature?" He clucked his tongue in mockery.

"Times of war call for extraordinary measures. Some Quakers have enlisted in the Union Army. Anyway, the Wraith probably carries a hidden gun. How else could he accomplish what they say with only trickery and a saber?"

"A hidden gun, similar to your hidden derringer?" Alexander scratched his chin as though pondering the idea. "Women say they would swoon with undying love if they met him, yet you seem immune to his mystique. Ah, but you are a Yankee."

With cheeks aflame, Emily tugged the reins from his grasp. "I have no more time for idle chitchat. Good day to you." Giving Miss Kitty a small kick to her flanks, she took off from the dusty barnyard. Halfway up the path, she stole a glance over her shoulder, powerless to stop herself. Alexander stood with both hands on his hips, laughing at her... again.

Blast it. Shoot the Wraith with my hidden gun? Of all the ridiculous things to say. If I had a hidden gun, I would shoot myself. Of all of the out-of-the-way, abandoned spots she had seen, this had been undoubtedly the most hidden. Now this oaf of a man had not only stumbled upon it, but upon her as well.

Emily rode hard for several hours, pausing twice to rest her horse. She needed time to collect her thoughts and to put some space between herself and the nephew from Bennington Island. Of all the luck to run into him! "What am I doing here, Miss Kitty?" she whispered to her mount. "An area even more loyal to the Southern Cause." Miss Kitty had no answer as they rode down the brick streets of Martinsburg. But what choice did she have? She couldn't have returned to Marietta because another family now occupied her childhood home. In their last letter, Reverend and Mrs. Ames gushed with relief that she had not been fired when the Benningtons moved east. Jobs were nonexistent in the Ohio River Valley, and the elderly couple hadn't offered to take her in while she looked for work.

She was no different than Lila or Joshua or Matilde. Like them, she might be free to go wherever she chose, but an empty belly or thoughts of cold nights without shelter made her willing to move to keep her job. And Lila and her parents didn't seem the least bit unhappy about relocating. Since their arrival, the Amites all but bubbled over with joy to be living in a city instead of on an isolated island. Emily knew she should count her blessings. She had no idea why Dr. Bennington invited her to accompany them after he sent the girls away to school in Paris. Mrs. Bennington had been apprehensive for her daughters, but Dr. Bennington insisted that the girls would benefit from the strict *Maison*

Muguet. For the sake of Margaret and the especially precocious Annie, Emily hoped it would only be for one term as their father promised.

Emily's new role was companion to Mrs. Bennington, whose health had deteriorated during the trip. She seldom walked with her cane, preferring the wheeled chair to get from room to room. She tired more easily now and took frequent naps, so Emily's tasks weren't very strenuous. She would breakfast with Mrs. Bennington after her husband left to attend to his medical practice, and they usually shared lunch in the beautiful back garden. Emily's sole duty was to read to Mrs. Bennington in the afternoon. She poured endless cups of Darjeeling tea and read aloud for long stretches of time. But this was no chore because she loved to hear the words of Sir Walter Scott brought to life.

Often Mrs. Bennington's rheumatism kept her in bed for days. She insisted on using Matilde, Lila, and a hired Irish girl for help, refusing to allow Emily to wait on her. On these mornings, Emily worked for Dr. Bennington in his office. During the afternoon, he suggested she take rides around town to familiarize herself, preferably accompanied by Lila. But often Emily went alone if Lila had other errands. Her jaunts into the countryside proved useful. Using her father's maps brought from Ohio, she marked every safe house owned by Friends or other places to hide runaways. Slowly, carefully, Emily found each one and introduced herself to the owners.

Dr. Bennington continued to be an enigma to her. Southern down to his penchant for bourbon and corn bread, he had freed his slaves and extended his medical expertise to both Union and Confederate casualties, treating both with equal kindness. Both armies alternately either surrounded or occupied the town of Martinsburg, but neither prevented the shipment of medicine to Dr. Bennington's office. He ordered supplies from New York, Boston, and even abroad, never sure what would get through the blockade. Growing grayer by the day, with deep lines around his mouth and eyes, he returned home a tired man. Yet he still made time to share a late supper with his wife or sit by her bedside until she drifted to sleep.

Emily yearned for someone to love her like that, but with her sharp tongue and quick temper, she thought it unlikely. For the first time since leaving home, she felt lonely. She missed her parents and Matthew. He was becoming an ever more distant memory, fading like a fuzzy daguerreotype. Some days she had to open her locket to recall his features. But even as she did, the haughty profile of Mrs. Bennington's nephew would invade her thoughts. How could she be attracted to someone so soon after her loss? What was so special about this man that he could steal away her precious memories?

"Emily? Are you all right, my dear?" The concerned voice of Mrs. Bennington broke through her reverie. Emily's head snapped up at the breakfast table.

"Yes, ma'am, I'm fine. Just a little tired." She managed a weak smile and took another gulp of coffee. *Just a little tired* was an understatement of theatrical proportions. Emily had never been so sore in her life—every muscle ached. Even muscles in places she didn't know contained muscles. Her trip to Berryville yesterday had cost her dearly. Right now she would be happy never to get on Miss Kitty again.

"I daresay you should be tired. Matilde said it was nearly dark when you returned from your ride and that you could barely hold your head up during supper."

"Matilde does love to exaggerate." She refilled her cup from the coffee carafe.

"That she does," Mrs. Bennington agreed, dropping the matter. "So today we will both rest because tomorrow we will be traveling. We've been invited to a grand ball and afterward will stay for a week to visit."

"A trip?" asked Emily, flabbergasted. "But we just settled in a few months ago and you have not been feeling well. What about Dr. Bennington's practice? He can't up and leave his work, can he?" Were these pampered Southerners so jaded they would abandon the sick and wounded for a ball during wartime?

"You are sweet to worry so about others, but I feel stronger today. Even if I must remain in my chair, I'd love a change of scenery. And Porter's work is the precise reason we're making the journey. Apparently there was a battle with more casualties than the army surgeons can handle. Porter will leave at first light to assist with the wounded. We'll follow in the carriage as soon Joshua, Matilde, and Lila can get things ready. The Amites have kin at Hunt Farms," added Mrs. Bennington. She helped herself to a biscuit and spread honey on it.

"Excuse me?" Emily choked out. Her mouthful of coffee almost sprayed her employer.

"I said that the Amites have—"

"Yes, ma'am, that part I heard. What is the name of the place we're headed?" Emily's voice was little more than a squeak.

"Hunt Farms, my brother-in-law's plantation. It's near Front Royal. Of course, it's not likely the fame of a Virginia thoroughbred farm would reach those living in Ohio, but you remember meeting Alexander on the island, don't you?" Mrs. Bennington covertly studied her young companion as she asked the question.

"Oh, Hunt Farms. Of course. I thought I had misunderstood you." Emily cut her fried egg into tiny pieces, her appetite gone.

Mrs. Bennington bubbled with enthusiasm. "It's nice living so close to my sister and her family. I can't wait to see them. Pack your new gowns, my dear. I wish we had time to have special ones made. Everyone within a three-county radius will be at their ball."

"I hardly think it appropriate for me to accompany you, Mrs. Bennington. I'm a hired employee, not an invited guest. I'll spend the evening with Lila."

"Nonsense. You're not a governess while the girls are in Europe. As my personal companion and my *friend*, you will be welcome at any ball I choose to attend." Her statement was matter-of-fact. Mrs. Bennington rose regally to her feet and pushed her chair back from the table. When she focused her soft green eyes on her, Emily knew the matter was closed.

Sweet as she was, Augusta Bennington always got her way.

Mrs. Bennington couldn't wait until the carriage came to a halt before craning her neck out the window. "Rebecca! It's so good to see you."

Emily peeked over the woman's shoulder to study the mansion. It was a rather impressive sight, she had to admit. The house was nothing like Bennington Plantation back on the island. Entirely wood-framed with tall columns and second-floor balconies, it rambled outward from several wings and additions, yet the whole structure had a welcoming elegance. Crepe myrtle, potted bougainvillea, and lattice filled with climbing wisteria gave the home a riotous, overblown feel.

"Augusta, it's been far too long." A woman hurried down the steps to greet Mrs. Bennington, leaving the master of the house to follow behind at a more leisurely pace. Tall and straight backed, Rebecca Hunt had silver-streaked hair and ruddy skin. Bone thin and hawk nosed, she wasn't beautiful like her sister, yet something appealing radiated from her smile.

Emily helped Mrs. Bennington down from the carriage, clutching her arm with one hand and her reticule tightly in the other. "Good afternoon, ma'am."

"Good afternoon and welcome." Mrs. Hunt smiled pleasantly in her direction and then hugged her sister.

The gentleman stepped forward. "I'm James Hunt. You must be Miss Harrison." He extended a smooth hand that had never engaged in hard labor. "I believe you've already met our son, Alexander."

She dipped one knee slightly. "Yes, sir. Thank you for your kind hospitality."

"Not at all. Let me take that." He pulled the bag from her fingers, handed it to a servant, and turned to greet his sister-in-law.

Blessedly, the master's son was nowhere to be seen. Emily didn't like the way her gut tightened whenever Alexander looked at her or the way he twisted her words. He made her feel like an unpolished schoolgirl instead of a trained governess.

"Come, Emily," said Mrs. Bennington. "Rebecca will give us a tour of the main rooms. She's made some changes I'm eager to see." Arm in arm, the two sisters climbed the steps, chattering away. Because Mrs. Bennington had refused her chair today, Emily trailed close behind, ready to catch the woman should she fall.

As she wandered the expensively appointed rooms, Emily remembered her ill-timed meeting with Alexander at the abandoned barn with an uncomfortable flush. This home, deeper in the Confederacy, was a place she could effectively start slaves on their road to freedom. She hoped the master's son had forgotten her perfect spot to hide runaways overnight.

Two hours later, Mrs. Hunt held up her palms, concluding her lengthy explanation of hand-painted wall coverings, imported tapestries, and European furniture. "Enough. Shall we enjoy an informal dinner on the terrace tonight? You're probably exhausted after the trip." She, however, looked as fresh as a spring morning.

"I believe I'll retire to my room," Mrs. Bennington said. She appeared ready to faint. "Please send dinner up on a tray later, something light."

"Will you be joining us this evening, Miss Harrison?"

"No, ma'am. Thank you for the invitation, but I also prefer to relax." She slipped her arm firmly around Mrs. Bennington's waist as they started up the stairs. With the inevitable meal with the Hunts postponed, she was granted a temporary reprieve. After unpacking and resting in her room, she slipped down two flights of servants' stairs to the first floor. Conversation ceased and all eyes turned as Emily entered the room.

"Hello, Miss Harrison." Lila scrambled to her feet. She sat at a long trestle table in the huge, partially underground kitchen. The room was comfortably cool, yet the massive fireplace would make it cozy warm during winter.

"May I join your family for supper?" Emily directed the query to Matilde.

"Yes, if you promise to stay away from the stove." Matilde flashed her magnificent smile. "Sit there, next to my daughter."

Emily complied with both requests. Over the next hour, Matilde introduced Emily to the entire Amite extended family as workers came in to eat and then returned to chores. Relaxing on the bench, she dined on rabbit stew, wilted greens, lima beans, corn bread, stewed tomatoes, and blackberry pie. The Amites were well known and loved by the Hunt Farm workers, both slave and free. Lila introduced her to cousins and nieces and nephews until Emily gave up trying to remember names. After eating their fill, Emily and Lila took a long walk as the sun dropped behind the Shenandoah Mountains. It was peaceful here and beautiful, yet Emily was filled with an odd sense of foreboding long after she told Lila good night and crawled beneath the soft quilt on her bed. Storms and specters filled her dreams as she tossed and turned in the perfect bedroom in the perfect world of Hunt Plantation.

"Miss Harrison. Miss Harrison." A voice pierced her fitful slumber, causing Emily to scramble from her bed. "Mrs. Bennington wishes you to join her for breakfast on the terrace." A voice called through the door.

"Tarnation," she muttered. In a louder voice, she said, "Please tell Mrs. Bennington I awoke frightfully hungry and had breakfast in the kitchen earlier."

The person at the door seemed to be waiting for a better excuse. When none came, the maid said, "Yes, miss. I'll tell her."

Forgive me, Lord, for lying and breaking Your Ninth Commandment. Emily sent up her penitent prayer. *Another reprieve, but how long can this go on?*

Unfortunately, not long at all. Mrs. Bennington sent a note to Emily's room, insisting she join her for lunch on the terrace. Because the ball was that evening, luncheon would be served at two. Emily arrived promptly at the appointed time to find Mrs. Bennington seated with her sister.

"Come sit, my dear. It'll just be us women for the meal. My

brother-in-law left to track down Porter at the field hospital. He'll lend a hand until time to bring Porter back for the evening festivities."

"One could almost forget a war is going on," Emily murmured. Mrs. Bennington nodded in agreement, but Mrs. Hunt slanted an odd expression. Emily concentrated on lunch while the two sisters shared news and gossip about mutual friends. There was absolutely no mention of Alexander during the meal. Perhaps he was estranged from his family and wouldn't be making an appearance. Oddly, she found no relief at the thought. Though he wasn't physically present, the laughing, mocking eyes that had caused her to blush in the barnyard seemed to follow her around her room. Would there be no escaping him, even in his absence?

Finally, Mrs. Bennington struggled to her feet. "Shall we rest, Emily, until time to get ready for the ball?"

After helping her employer to her room, Emily napped for several hours—something unheard of on her parents' farm. Refreshed, she dressed carefully for the Hunt Farms ball. If she was to be of use, she must study her adversaries in this region of white columns and slave-tended fields. The aristocratic manners and genial hospitality of the slave owners couldn't mask their evil, blackened hearts. She grew up poor, but she had also grown up knowing freedom.

Because Lila had the evening off, Emily struggled into her underthings and the ball gown on her own. The deep sapphire color added depth to her pale blue eyes. With tiny pearl buttons down the front and hundreds of pin-tucked folds below the waist, the dress accentuated her slim figure. Slipping on dancing slippers, she pinned up the few stray locks that escaped her chignon. She refused to have her hair done by a slave maid.

No one will be looking at me anyway. She had seen the steady stream of carriages for the past hour, delivering at least one belle and in some cases, several beauties on the arms of their fathers. Each wore a gown more exquisite than the last. A Paris fashion house during the spring shows wouldn't offer such gorgeous selection. *"Consider the lilies of the field, how they grow...Solomon in all his glory was not arrayed like one of these."* For some reason, the Bible's assurance that Christians shouldn't worry about clothes failed to console her. Jealousy filled her heart and eroded her confidence. Just once, Emily wanted to feel pretty, self-assured, and carefree instead of backwoods, unsophisticated, and poor.

Not wanting to be announced at the entrance, Emily slipped up the servants' stairs to the third floor ballroom. The high-ceilinged, palatial space was crowded with revelers. Emily found an obscure spot behind a potted hibiscus to watch the festivities. Couples whirled around the polished marble floor with confidence, as though each fluid movement felt as natural as drawing breath. *Miss Turner's School for Ladies didn't quite prepare me for this*, she mused sourly.

Along the wall conservatively dressed, silver-haired ladies and rakishly handsome aristocrats stood in clusters, sipping from long-stemmed flutes. From her position by the hibiscus, Emily spied her host across the room talking with several soldiers clad in Confederate butternut. As often the case when one stares long enough, Emily locked eyes with Alexander Hunt, who was apparently not estranged from his family after all. He stopped talking and grinned from ear to ear. She glanced left and right to see for whom the magnificent smile had been intended. No one had ever looked at her in such a fashion. Emily felt like a snared rabbit when Alexander bowed to the soldiers and crossed the room.

"Great Scot, it is you, Miss Harrison. I thought I saw that potted plant move. I arrived home just a bit ago and didn't know my aunt and uncle were visiting."

"If you'd been forewarned, Mr. Hunt, would you have leaped down on me from the balcony?"

He threw back his head and laughed. "At the very least, Miss Harrison." His voice turned several heads in their direction.

"Would you be so kind, sir, as to lower your voice?" she whispered.

He furrowed his eyebrows. "Are you afraid I will mention you went riding in a completely inappropriate costume with your petticoats showing?"

Emily bit the inside of her cheek. "No. I simply don't want Mrs.

Bennington to know I had…wandered so far off-track from Martins-burg."

"You were definitely beyond the reach of a casual ride. Some might be curious as to what you were doing. But since the girls are in Paris, I imagine you have much free time on your hands when Aunt Augusta rests." Again he laughed as though greatly amused.

The sound was starting to grate on her nerves. She offered her stern-est, most schoolmarmish scowl.

"Don't worry, Miss Harrison. Your secret is safe with me. I'll never tell a soul you left Martinsburg for the afternoon and somehow ended up in Berryville." Then he added, more to the potted hibiscus than to her, "My uncle said you were a fireball."

"I shouldn't keep you from your other guests and, frankly, I've grown weary of this conversation." She scrunched her nose, sniffed, and turned away.

But he was too quick for her. Alexander trapped her against a pillar behind her with his palms flat on both sides of her head.

"Do I vex you, Miss Harrison? Or maybe I tempt you to do some-thing spontaneous?"

"No, Mr. Hunt, you do not. I like my actions to be well thought out," she snapped, trying not to breathe in his heady scent. Matthew had smelled no different than any other farmer, not like this exotic blend of spicy shaving balm and pomade. She slipped down the pillar and prayed her knees wouldn't buckle from anxiety. "Does this method usually work for you? Do women usually find this kind of effrontery charming?"

"I daresay, more often than not they do."

"Then I shall be a new experience for you." Emily ducked under his arm to escape.

"Wait, please," he begged. "Let me at least sign your dance card. You cannot refuse your host."

"I have no dance card, sir. I don't plan to indulge in dancing."

"Because due to your Quaker religious convictions you never learned how?"

"I didn't say that. Miss Turner taught me the basics, but I choose not to participate in ridiculous frivolity." She picked up her voluminous skirt, but he wouldn't be put off so easily.

He took her arm with a gentle but firm grasp. "My aunt will be crushed when she learns you treated your host with such unwarranted hostility. Were you raised by a pack of wolves, Miss Harrison?"

That was the last straw. Emily rose up on tiptoes to almost be on eye level with him. "My mother raised me to have manners no different than any of these silly Virginia belles."

"Is that so? But a lady would indulge her host in his simple request…"

"Fine, we shall dance," said Emily through gritted teeth. Taking his arm with a gloved hand, she allowed herself to be led into the crowd. Once on the floor, however, she couldn't keep up as he tried to guide her through a reel. She found herself taking extra steps which threw off their rhythm. It was as if her legs were a yard too short or she'd grown a third foot.

When she glanced down at her feet for the fourth time, Alexander put a finger under her chin and lifted her face. "You're too tense and stiff. I know you can dance, so allow yourself to relax. I promise not to bite you." His voice was gentle, his smile no longer mocking.

Emily grew transfixed by his deeply set gray eyes, mesmerized by their fathomless depth. A woman would kill to be blessed with lashes like those. But with a strong jaw, high cheekbones, and sharp aquiline nose, his face held no softness. His features had a hawklike appearance, softened only by his hair falling lazily over his forehead. *Matthew would roar with laughter at his dandified clothing. All he needs is a walking stick to be the perfect fop.*

"A penny for your thoughts, Miss Harrison."

"I was just…admiring your attire, Mr. Hunt."

"Then you must have excellent taste in fashion. I go to a haberdasher and tailor in Winchester who makes my garments before each season. The man is quite good, staying abreast of everything happening on the Continent. One has to be careful not to dress as though this were still the frontier, don't you think?"

"Oh, I certainly do. With the country embroiled in war, we must not forget about style." They whirled effortlessly around the dance floor. What kind of people were these aristocrats? But at least with the distraction of banal conversation her dancing had improved. Her stiffness and self-consciousness disappeared as he held her in his arms. "Tell me, Mr. Hunt. I believe Warren County has become part of the Confederacy, has it not? How is it you haven't been conscripted?" *Or volunteered* hung in the air unsaid, yet even she knew how rude that would be to add.

"Ah, yes, the Glorious Cause. Don't think my heart doesn't yearn to fight with my school chums on the battlefield, but the Confederate government recognizes the importance of Hunt Farms. We supply horses to the cavalry along with a steady stream of grain and grass for horse fodder. I was told to send a replacement to the local regiment while I keep things going here at home. My father doesn't have the strength he once had. With many of our people running off…it was the least I could do."

And so much safer, I would imagine. Why did these Southerners insist on calling slaves "their people"? As though softening the term of possession could change the corrupt, heinous nature of bondage. Emily couldn't believe she was put off by his reluctance to sign up with the Confederate Army. Why would she be angry that a rich, indolent man didn't join the traitorous rebels to fight against everything she stood for? Yet somehow his avoidance bothered her a great deal. When the interminable waltz ended, she pulled away from his embrace. "Thank you, Mr. Hunt."

"The pleasure was mine, Miss Harrison. I assure you."

She left as fast as her dignity would allow. She had to get away from him…she had to think.

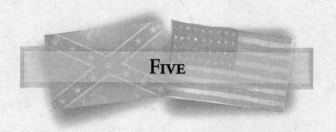

FIVE

Alexander watched Emily depart in a great hurry. What a conundrum she was. She was obviously the woman who had been hiding in a barn in Berryville, his aunt's recalcitrant governess. The woman he had danced with tonight had the same flaming red hair and spattering of freckles across her nose, but in that gown he hadn't been sure they were one and the same until she had scowled at him from behind the potted plant and unleashed her barbed tongue. The woman he baited on Bennington Island and then pounced upon in the barnyard near Berryville looked more like an underfed chicken than the pleasingly attractive swan who had graced his parents' ballroom.

He was familiar with women who flirted—who charmed their way into men's hearts and minds by wielding their feminine powers. Lately Alexander wanted little to do with them because he didn't trust them... and because he couldn't trust himself. He preferred to stay away from pretty faces and stunning figures, from women whose touch could melt icicles in the dead of winter. But this odd creature with her wild hair and long legs like a yearling wasn't like them. Without artifice or an ounce of seductiveness, she couldn't charm a bear to a beehive. Strong-willed and opinionated, especially on topics she knew nothing about, Emily Harrison nevertheless possessed her own sense of grace. Alexander found her dissimilarity to the belles of Virginia oddly appealing.

"Good grief," he moaned. "If that skinny colt looks enticing, I've been away from the ladies of Belinda's too long." He laughed, realizing that this governess living in his uncle's home could come in handy. His parents had begun to question him about his comings and goings. They wondered why he needed to spend so much time away from the farm. The last thing he wanted was to cause his parents worry. If he struck up a courtship with Miss Fancy-Bloomers, he would have an excuse to be away for days at a time. Martinsburg and Front Royal weren't exactly around the corner from one another. Because there was no chance of Miss Emily Harrison bewitching him with her charms, this little Yankee could come in handy indeed.

Emily didn't slow down until she was out of the crowded room of overdressed, perfumed peacocks. At the door an elderly servant approached from his assigned station. "May I bring you a wrap, miss?"

"No. If I wished for a wrap, I would get one myself," she snapped, but regretted her words the moment they left her mouth. The poor man looked as though he'd been slapped.

"I beg your pardon. That wasn't what I intended to say. I meant I have no desire to be waited on by slaves."

"Yes, miss," he said, lowering his gaze to the foyer floor. His expression registered distress and bewilderment.

Emily felt ashamed. Lately, she couldn't control her words or her temper. Offering a weak smile, she hurried through the door. Once she was out on the expansive verandah, she inhaled the cool night air and began to relax. Jasmine and honeysuckle—two of her favorite scents—wafted on the breeze. She closed her eyes and imagined herself back home in Ohio, listening to the foghorns of steamboats passing on the river. Strains of another reel drifted through the open windows, but she concentrated on the calls of the whippoorwills and nightjars. Tree frogs and crickets added to the evening symphony she found so comforting.

And she needed some comfort. Her behavior with Alexander left her far from calm and relaxed. How could she enjoy dancing after being raised a Quaker? How could she enjoy being held in another man's arms so soon after Matthew's death? Shamelessly, she savored the attention she received in the beautiful ball gown, secretly delighting when a man's head turned in her direction. Restless and confused, she began to pace. When she reached the length of the verandah, she discovered that the wide porch wrapped around the house. Turning the corner, she sought peace and quiet in the cool shadows, far from the conviviality of the ballroom.

But here the night music wasn't the tumult of insects calling for mates or the tinkling laughter of coy belles. Emily heard sounds both distinctly human and decidedly angry. She cocked her head to focus her attention with every nerve. Voices emanating in the direction of the slave cabins waxed and waned. Some unfortunate soul was receiving a browbeating, of that she was certain. Listening to the verbal tirade, Emily's breath caught in her throat as her stomach soured. She couldn't discern the hateful words, but the meaning was clear…and far more frightening at night than in the light of day. Her previous musings about dancing and pretty ball gowns vanished.

A memory crept insidiously to mind of another warm summer evening long ago—a memory of men emboldened by darkness and fueled by alcohol. She closed her eyes, trying to force that night back to the past where it held no power over her. Damp with perspiration, Emily heard someone holler in a clear voice: "I'll teach you to sass your betters." She gasped, paralyzed where she stood for several moments. *I'll teach you to sass your betters?* Daring not to breathe, she waited uneasily for the next harangue. But it did not come; she heard nothing but the pounding of her own heart. Soon the sounds of crickets and tree frogs filled the air. Indoors, the musicians struck the chords of the next dance for couples young and old.

Emily exhaled a weary sigh. She hadn't come south to wear fancy silk dresses with embroidered slippers, or sip champagne under twinkling chandeliers, or recite the sonnets of Shakespeare to her employer while drinking cups of tea. And she certainly wasn't here to be held in the arms of a rich Virginia planter, no matter how handsome.

Suddenly the breeze turned chilly. Crossing her arms over her chest, Emily wished she'd accepted the butler's offer of a wrap. "I can be useful," she whispered. "And you, Alexander Hunt, will be useful too." Emily smiled. *At least there's certainly no chance of me falling in love with you, Mr. Hunt. You don't possess an ounce of the gumption or conviction of*

Matthew Norton. You can keep your beautiful manners, expensive clothes, and gracious dancing. I can be coy like your belles if need be, but once I have you in the palm of my hand, you'll be too smitten to notice a few less people around the place.

"Good morning, Miss Harrison." Alexander's voice boomed through the open doorway. "Are you famished for breakfast? You missed the midnight repast."

Emily had waited in the kitchen until Mrs. Bennington came downstairs, hoping to avoid being alone with him that morning. She assumed any man worth his salt would have gone to his business concerns or at least to chores around the farm. She should have known better than to expect a lazy aristocrat to rise early. "Good morning. I don't believe I am hungry."

"Emily, please join us," summoned Mrs. Bennington from the dining room.

"Yes, ma'am." She sighed as she tried to step past him, but he blocked her path.

"You refused breakfasting with me, but acquiesced to my aunt?" he asked, furrowing his brow.

"I cannot refuse my employer or her hostess. Please excuse me, Mr. Hunt."

Alexander stepped aside and then followed her into the dining room.

Emily couldn't believe Mrs. Bennington was up this early. Was this the same woman who slept past ten each morning, took breakfast on a tray, and never appeared downstairs before noon? "I noticed your wheelchair still remains in the back of the carriage. You're managing nicely with your two canes."

"Truly, I am. The reunion with my favorite sister has done wonders for my health." Mrs. Bennington beamed at Mrs. Hunt.

"I am your only sister." Mrs. Hunt winked over her porcelain cup.

Emily peered at one and then the other as her heart swelled. There was a sparkle in her employer's green eyes. Years had fallen away from her face in the comfort and ease of Hunt Farms. Emily hadn't planned to grow fond of Augusta Bennington, but she couldn't help herself. "Dr. Bennington will be pleased with your improved health when he returns," she said, sampling sliced peaches in heavy cream. "I didn't see him last night at the ball. Was he detained at the field hospital?"

Mrs. Hunt shook her silvery head. "James was unsuccessful in persuading Porter to attend. 'Men are dying here for lack of care,'" she said, mimicking Porter's voice. "'And you wish me to come home, put on a penguin suit, and waltz around a ballroom as though things were normal?' James volunteered to help until it was time to dress for the ball. Porter found plenty of nonmedical tasks to keep him busy." Mrs. Hunt clucked her tongue. "Even with the help of convalescing soldiers, they are still so understaffed." She nibbled a piece of toast daintily.

"Dr. Bennington spent the night in a battlefield field hospital?" asked Emily.

"He sleeps for a few hours on a pallet in the corner of the surgery tent. He hasn't eaten properly or slept in a decent bed in days." Mrs. Bennington delivered this news in a whisper.

"I hope the casualties will soon taper off."

Dr. Bennington continued to confound Emily. People had been simpler in the Ohio River Valley—they were either good or not.

Sipping her tea, Mrs. Bennington studied her companion. "Let's change the subject. My nephew would like to take you for a ride on this absolutely beautiful morning. I think it's a wonderful idea. That would give me time to catch up on gossip with my sister." She reached for Mrs. Hunt's hand.

"I'll have to see if I have the time." Emily couldn't look at Alexander, who had remained uncharacteristically quiet during the meal. Clutching her cup with both hands, she stared into her coffee as though life's mysteries were about to be revealed in its depths.

"Did you two run into each other at the ball last night, my dear?"

"We certainly did, Aunt Augusta," Alexander said before Emily could reply. "Miss Harrison graced me with not one but three dances, although her dance card was practically full when I found her hiding in the hibiscus."

Emily's head snapped up. What blatant lies. "I was observing, not hiding—merely curious because Quakers don't attend balls." When no one spoke, she amended her thoughtless comment. "Begging your pardon, I meant Ohio Quakers don't dance."

"No offense taken," murmured Mrs. Hunt, fixing her gaze on her son.

Alexander beamed a most ingratiating smile. "I appreciate that you lowered your standards for my sake, Miss Harrison. What good are rules if they can't be broken?"

The two sisters exchanged a glance.

"Alexander used to be a practicing Quaker before he fell in with the wrong crowd during his college years." His mother's gray eyes twinkled with mischief. "Front Royal has a small Society of Friends if you would like to attend meetings, Miss Harrison. Perhaps you can convince my son to join you."

Alexander leaned back in his chair. "I'll give that some thought, Mother, right after the war is over." He fixed Emily with his steely eyes.

"Alexander takes the convictions of pacifism very seriously," said Mrs. Bennington. "That's why he refrained from joining the Confederacy."

Pacifism or fear of the enemy's bullets? Taking deep breaths to regain control of her temper, Emily concentrated on crumbling a biscuit on her plate.

"Aren't you feeling well, my dear?" asked Mrs. Bennington. "You have barely said half a dozen words and eaten little more than biscuit crumbs."

"I feel fine, ma'am. A little tired perhaps." Remembering her manners, she shook away her personal opinions. "Thank you, Mrs. Hunt, for your gracious invitation to the ball last evening. And thank you, Mr. Hunt, for rescuing me from the potted plant. I enjoyed our dance."

"Rest assured that the pleasure was mine." Dabbing his chin with his napkin, he straightened in his chair. "What do you say to that ride after breakfast, Miss Harrison? But I must insist you wear suitable riding attire. We're not the wild frontier here in Warren County. We don't permit ladies to mount their own horses and trot off with petticoats flying and lace bloomers showing the way they do in dime novels."

Mrs. Hunt stopped eating and stared at her son as though he'd gone mad. "Alexander, *what* has gotten into you? Why would you say such a thing or, for that matter, read such trash when we have a library filled with classics? To my knowledge you haven't bent the binding of a good book in quite some time." She didn't sound pleased with his topic of breakfast conversation. "And I have several riding habits Miss Harrison can use if she forgot to pack hers. That is, *if* she chooses to ride with a boorish man like you." Smiling at Emily, Mrs. Hunt rose from the table, her breakfast complete, but she offered her son a look of tacit disapproval.

"I believe I will ride this morning. It will give me an opportunity to exercise Miss Kitty. And thank you again for your generous gift, Mrs. Bennington." Emily spoke with her most gracious tone of voice. She'd overheard enough witless belles last night to know how society ladies talked. "I'll see you this afternoon, ma'am. Mrs. Hunt, thank you for the delicious breakfast and for the loan of riding clothes. I will go change." She rose with as much dignity as she could muster and strolled from the room.

Unfortunately, the sound of Alexander's laughter followed her halfway up the stairs.

Emily changed into a rather snug riding habit, high leather boots, a deep green felt hat, and kid gloves. Before leaving her room, she plucked out the ridiculous feather sticking up from the hatband and left it on the dressing table, along with the riding crop. Having never cropped a horse in her life, she wasn't about to start now. Outside on the front steps, she spotted two men lounging in the shade of a live oak, each holding the reins of a saddled horse. She strode toward them feeling jaunty in her borrowed clothes, never having owned anything of this quality in her life. The boots alone would cost a month's wages.

"I was beginning to think you changed your mind, Miss Harrison." Alexander pushed away from the tree as she approached and bowed low. "I must say you look delightful in my mother's clothes."

Her cheeks flushed pink. "Must you be so irritating on a day as lovely as this?" Scratching Miss Kitty's nose, she turned toward the tall, muscular black man holding her reins. "I am Miss Emily Harrison. How do you do?"

"Very well, thank you, ma'am." He swept his hat from his head and bowed.

"Excuse my manners," said Alexander. "Miss Harrison, this is William Tyler, my right-hand man and trusted friend. William, this is Aunt Augusta's companion. Miss Harrison hails from Ohio but now resides in Virginia, making Martinsburg that much fairer a city."

"Ma'am." William nodded before replacing his cap.

"Are you a slave, Mr. Tyler?" Emily asked without preamble.

Momentarily flummoxed, William hesitated before answering. "No, ma'am, I'm a free man of color employed by Mr. Hunt. But come to think of it, it's been so long since my last increase in wages that perhaps I should check my papers to make sure I read the fine print." The two men exploded into laughter.

Emily failed to see the humor, but she refused to be baited into displaying any fits of temper. "I can mount without assistance, thank you." She lifted her boot heel into the stirrup and swung up effortlessly into the sidesaddle.

Alexander moved behind her, perhaps in case she fell on her backside. Then he mounted his huge, spirited stallion in one fluid motion and turned the animal around with the barest of nudges. "I keep telling you, William. Once you stop landing me in the doghouse with my mother regarding my absences, then we'll talk salary increases. Shall we be off, Miss Harrison?"

"I'm as ready as I ever will be." As they cantered down the oak-lined drive, she couldn't help noticing Alexander was an imposing presence in the saddle. His well-cut jacket and starched linen shirt were rather conservative compared with his dandified outfit of last night.

"Are you admiring my riding attire, Miss Harrison?" he asked, noticing her perusal.

"I am, Mr. Hunt. You look quite at home in the saddle. And in regards to clothing, a country girl like me prefers these less formal occasions." She aimed a gloved finger at his stirrup. "Your boots certainly have received far more wear than I would expect from a gentleman farmer."

"You are right. They are worn down to the soles. In wartime few leather goods are available in stores, and I would certainly never deprive a Southern cavalryman of footwear. Besides, I'm not half the gentleman you imagine me to be, Miss Harrison." When the Hunt Farms tree-lined lane met the county pike, he spurred his horse and sprinted off at full gallop, not looking back once. Alexander and his stallion soon disappeared from sight around the bend.

Of all the rudeness! But Emily wasted no breath on recriminations without an audience. She pressed her heel against Miss Kitty's flank, and the mare bounded down the dirt road. In the sidesaddle, Emily couldn't grip with her thighs as her father had taught her so many summers ago. She bent low in the saddle, gripping the reins and clinging tightly to the animal's silky neck. Heat radiated from the beast's skin as they galloped across an open field in pursuit of the stallion. Scattered, craggy apple trees indicated this had once been an orchard, though it was now well beyond its productive days. Despite the fact she was hanging on for dear life, Emily made no attempt to slow her horse. It felt wonderful to have the wind in her face and her hair streaming behind her. Mrs. Hunt's chic fedora bounced against her back, with only knotted ribbons preventing it from becoming lost forever. Emily held her breath as Miss Kitty leaped fallen logs and shallow streams. Her stomach rose once or twice into her throat, but after a while she abandoned herself to the delicious taste of freedom.

Breathless and flushed, Emily and Miss Kitty eventually caught up to the two males as they slowed their pace to a walk.

"Well done, Miss Harrison. Phantom tried his best to lose you, but apparently we have met our match." Alexander slipped from his mount and grasped Miss Kitty's bridle as she pranced restlessly under a shady cedar.

"Miss Kitty has a smooth gait and is very responsive to even an unfamiliar rider. But why did you extend an invitation if you didn't wish to ride with me?" She patted the horse's neck and flashed a wounded expression.

"Come now, my little Yankee, I was joking. Of course, I wanted to ride with you." He offered his hand to her.

Emily ignored it and slipped effortlessly to the ground. "Once again I don't find your humor amusing." Spotting a small stream under a stand of pines, she headed in that direction.

Alexander tied their mounts to a low branch and quickly caught up to her. "Had you no rascally brothers to tease you while growing up?" He grasped the elbow of her jacket. "Please don't be cross with me. If you pout, I won't share the picnic Beatrice packed." He danced around like a schoolboy trying to win favor with a treat.

Emily settled herself demurely on a fallen log in the shade. "I'm not hungry, Mr. Hunt." She dabbed a tiny bead of sweat from her lip. "So you needn't perplex yourself with whether or not to share your lunch." Her voice was melodic and refined, although on the inside she wished she could wipe the smug look from his face. "And I assure you, I'm *not* your little Yankee or anyone else's."

Alexander plopped down on the riverbank and stretched his long legs over the edge. "Forgive me, Miss Harrison. My mother was correct at breakfast—I'm a complete boor, unfit to spend an afternoon with gentle souls. My grandmother once described me as 'a mule in horse harness.'"

"Sounds like your granny was an astute judge of character."

His shout of laughter sent a flock of birds on to a quieter location. "She was at that. I still miss her." He glanced at her over his shoulder. "If you give me another chance, I will try to change." Rising to his feet, he sauntered toward her with exasperating confidence, plucking a buttercup along the way. "What do you say?" He offered it as a peace token.

Emily gazed at the flower and then the man. "I'll give you the rest of the afternoon." Close as they were now, she found him more handsome than ever. True, his nose was too prominent and his chin a bit severe, yet his eyes were mesmerizing and his smile lit up his face. Of course, people with abundant wealth had that much more to smile about. She accepted the flower and sniffed it. "I don't know why people smell wildflowers. They almost never have much scent." Emily tossed the buttercup into the tall grass.

"It's a natural reaction." He lowered himself to her log. "We anticipate a sweet fragrance despite our previous disappointments."

Suddenly, it seemed to grow cloyingly warm under the shady cedars and pines. "Tell me how your skin became so suntanned," she asked, desperate for benign conversation. "I wouldn't think you had that many outdoor chores at Hunt Farms."

He moved closer on the log. "You'd be surprised how much work I do on a given day." Suddenly, he took hold of her chin.

"What do you have in mind, Mr. Hunt?" she asked as her breath caught in her throat.

"Only this." Alexander leaned over and kissed her. Without asking her leave, he tilted his head and simply kissed her.

Shivers shot up her spine. Her legs went numb, her palms grew clammy, and her stomach turned a somersault—all a reaction from one little kiss. She might have toppled from the log if he wasn't holding her face steady.

"What are you doing?" she squeaked.

"I'm kissing you, Miss Harrison." Their lips hovered an inch away. The space between them filled with enough energy to move boulders.

"Is that why you brought me out here? To catch me off guard and steal a kiss?"

"Not *a* kiss. I intend to steal several." His last word became muffled as his lips pressed down on hers with intensity.

Her stomach took a second tumble until she placed a hand on his chest and pushed. When he lifted his head, she said, "Stop! Is this your best attempt at civilized behavior?" She turned away and straightened her skirt in a dignified manner.

"I beg your pardon, Miss Harrison, but it's your effect on me. You have my sincere apology." He stood, bowed, and then headed toward the horses.

For a short while Emily feared he would mount his stallion and leave her alone on the creek bank. She waited, trying not to hold her breath, as he dug into his saddlebags.

He returned carrying a cloth sack. "I promised to share lunch and I must keep my word. That is, if you have forgiven me." He snapped open a checkered cloth, spread it across the grass, and then dropped down to his knees.

"There are new things to forgive every moment. But yes, I have, mainly because my appetite has returned."

"I'll take whatever grace you might extend." He set out slices of cheese and ham on a linen napkin, along with a cluster of grapes and a pickled egg for each of them. Pulling out the cork of a flask, Alexander offered her a drink.

"No, thank you. I don't care for spirits. And you shouldn't lower your practically nonexistent inhibitions."

He laughed and took a long draught. "Don't worry your pretty head. This is only sassafras tea. Your virtue is safe for the remainder of the afternoon." Leaning back against a tree trunk, he ate a rolled slice of cheese and ham, the kisses they had shared apparently forgotten.

Emily wasn't so fortunate. The piece of cheese she sampled stuck in her dry throat. "May I have that, please?" She took the flask and drank half its contents to wash the cheese down. After that, she limited herself to the egg and grapes because gagging wouldn't be appropriate after a kiss. Her first since Matthew's death. Alexander's kisses was nothing like the few clumsy, embarrassing kisses she'd shared with Matthew during their brief courtship. Surprisingly, she felt not guilt or remorse. After all, this was business.

She sipped more tea and cleared her throat. "Thank you for lunch. I'm glad you decided to share with me."

"You're quite welcome." He leaned back on one elbow. "Tell me how you learned to ride like that. Your seat is superior to any woman I know."

Emily considered her answer. "My father taught me. He hand raised a mare from birth so she would be gentle, and then he gave her to me on my fifth birthday. I rode bareback until my father could afford a used saddle—astride, of course, not sidesaddle. Girls weren't sissies where I grew up. Eventually, I could beat almost everyone in town in races—boys included, I might add."

"Astounding. I can picture you racing across the meadows with your pigtails flying."

"Yes, well, those days are gone. We all grow up and must put child-hood behind us." Emily rose to her feet. "Shall we continue our tour of your estate, sir? At a slower pace, if you don't mind."

Amazement registered on his face. "Of course, but I'm surprised you still wish to be in my company after my unwanted advances." He swept the remains of their lunch back into the sack. His tone was exas-peratingly hard to decipher.

"Should I have slapped your face with indignation? Is that the femi-nine behavior you anticipated?" Emily hid her trembling hands behind her back on the way to Miss Kitty.

"I can't seem to anticipate a single thing around you." He steadied her arm as she mounted.

"It was just a kiss, Mr. Hunt. Not my first and certainly not my last. But I will ask you to refrain from future bold gestures until certain that the affection is mutual." She tugged her reins free and cantered off, try-ing to ignore the effect his touch had on her.

For the remaining afternoon they rode at a leisurely pace. He pointed out pasturelands that contained more fine horseflesh than Emily had ever seen in her life. In addition to the Thoroughbred blood-line, Hunt Farms owned Arabians, Standardbreds, and Narragansett pacers, besides the requisite draft horses and Tennessee walkers for

farming. Fields of hay, oats, and sweetgrass covered the hills and valleys for as far as the eye could see. Behind the mansion he presented a
kitchen garden that took her breath away. Every vegetable Emily knew
and many she'd never heard of grew in tidy rows, surrounded by mesh
fencing to keep out rabbits. There wasn't a weed or a mealy bug to be
found. Around the other side of the house she discovered an expansive flower garden.

"I'd wondered where all the lovely flowers came from. I don't think
I've been in a room yet without at least one fragrant bouquet." She
stood up in the stirrups to view hundreds of roses, giant dahlias, dai-
sies, and arbors filled with climbing vines. "My, Mr. Hunt. One can do
wonders on a plantation with a huge *slave* labor force," she said spite-
fully, remembering her own spindly, weed-choked attempt at horti-
culture.

Alexander stared at her. His magnetic gray eyes had turned icy. "I'm
sure that's how it appears, Miss Harrison." He spoke in a bitter voice.
"But half our workers are *free* and remain here by their own choice."

"Why only half? Why not grant freedom to the rest?" Emily shifted
on the uncomfortable sidesaddle.

"My mother and I wish it were that simple." He focused on the
Shenandoah Mountains in the distance. "My father inherited everything you see from his father and so on, back to an original land grant
from King Charles. My father has the Hunt family honor to uphold,
as well as the responsibilities of the estate. This is his culture—the way
he was raised—the way you are a product of your parents' values."

"My parents' values could never include keeping people in bondage."

"Nor does my mother's or mine, for that matter." Alexander met
her eye. "We cannot change my father's mind overnight, but he has
instituted Uncle Porter's plan whereby slaves can earn money to purchase their freedom. That's why half our workers are free. We also teach
our slaves to read to prepare them for the future—a practice against
the law in Virginia."

"Why should men have to buy something that should be their God-given birthright?" Emily's voice raised up a notch.

Alexander lifted his chin and rolled his eyes. "I should have known you would make no attempt to understand. Yankees see things only one way—their way. Let's change the subject, shall we? Suffice it to say things aren't as simple as your small, narrow mind would like them to be."

"My…small…narrow…mind?" She repeated his words as her face flushed a shade of scarlet. *He finds me dense and ignorant?* Kicking Miss Kitty's flank, Emily took off toward the barns as her eyes filled with tears. She didn't stop until she reached the cool interior of the stable. Slipping from the horse's back, she cross-tied her mare and dragged the infernal saddle from her back.

"Let me rub down your horse, miss." William appeared at her side carrying an expensive leather bridle with silver buckles and nail-head trim.

"No, thank you, Mr. Tyler. I'm used to doing my own chores. If I could borrow one of your brushes, I'd be much obliged." She patted her horse's sweaty flank.

William's gaze scanned her riding clothes—or rather those belonging to Mrs. Hunt. His expression changed to one of mortification as he hooked the tack on a peg on the stall wall. "Ladies don't do barn chores at Hunt Farms. If someone were to see you, I could lose my job."

Exhaling slowly, Emily contemplated her options and found none. "Thank you, William. I am in your debt." She retreated until she tripped over the saddle she'd carelessly discarded. She flailed clumsily before catching her balance, and then she hurried from the barn before Alexander came in. At least the Lord granted her that small blessing.

Once she was within the private confines of her room, Emily paced the floor trying to make sense of her afternoon. Try as she might, she couldn't deny she had enjoyed his kisses. After all, she was a grown woman and not a child. It was normal to be flattered by a man's attentions, especially an attractive man like Alexander Hunt. Despite his arrogance, she found his off-kilter humor and self-assurance appealing. Apparently, she wasn't any more immune to his patrician features and raw-boned power than vapid Virginia belles. Emily attempted to generate guilt over his boldness, but she could not. Matthew had grown fuzzy in her mind. He was a bittersweet memory, his loss no longer triggering the pain it once did.

Alexander provided an invaluable entrée into his world. If he were her beau, no one would question her. A small dalliance with the master's son would open doors for her that even her relationship with the Benningtons could not. And she wouldn't have to fear falling in love as she had with Matthew. How could she respect a man who had paid someone to take his place on the battlefield so he might stay far from the horrors of war? And without respect, there never could be love.

"I'll teach you to sass your betters." Every time she remembered those words, she was spurred to action anew. She would set her small, narrow, Quaker mind on one goal—to convince each slave she encountered to take the first step on the Freedom Road.

Six

Alexander would have loved to take back his words the moment he spoke them. Her scornful remark had crawled under his skin and settled in his gut. She had prodded and provoked him. But losing his temper with an abolitionist schoolmarm was the last thing he wanted—especially because he agreed with her on most counts. How could she possibly understand that his father, as kind and generous as any man, came from another era? And frankly, he was tired of judgmental Yankees. Did they think God reserved His grace solely for them? He'd seen tenement slums and company housing up North. Freedom could get mighty cold during the winter.

Slumping into a chair, Alexander decided not to follow her. What could he say to undo the damage? Better to give the woman a wide berth for the rest of the day…and maybe the remainder of her visit. But something cautioned that would be hard to do. He'd seen her tears as she rode away, evidence that he'd hurt her feelings. What happened to the sassy firebrand? Had the vim and vinegar all been an act or was this?

Emily Harrison wasn't like the other women he knew. The ladies at last night's ball were lovely creatures, but they played demure games to move poor fools around like pieces on a chessboard. The women he knew would merely murmur, "Dear me, it's growing warm in here," if their gowns were on fire. Their hearts contained not one genuine emotion. Emily possessed neither their shrewd wiles nor their artifice. This afternoon, with her cheeks reddened from the wind and her hair a tangle down her back, she had still looked beautiful. Unlike other ladies, Emily didn't fret endlessly over her appearance. What thoughts crossed her mind by day and what did she dream of at night? Did she ever yearn to be held in the dark? Alexander forced those thoughts from his mind. Miss Harrison had been gently brought up, even if it was in an Ohio River frontier town. During their ride he had gone too far and offended her. Apparently, he spent too much time in the saddle with his rangers and was no longer fit for polite company.

Feeling lower than a flea-ridden dog, Alexander couldn't sleep that night. After tossing and turning in his hot room, he finally rolled out of bed, slipped on his trousers, and strode from the airless room onto the welcome cool of the verandah.

"Women," he muttered. "Confound them." Yet he couldn't block out the memory of their unpleasant parting. Why should two kisses on the riverbank create so much torment? He'd stolen more than kisses from willing belles in the past. The ladies of his social circle expected certain liberties and suffered no pangs of guilt the next day. And the women of Middleburg, although certainly not ladies, enjoyed sharing their charms with him. Once or twice, they even refused his coin. But today had been different. Emily had reacted like a wide-eyed school-girl. Aunt Augusta had told him snippets of her past history. How well had she known her unfortunate fiancé before he'd been killed in bat-tle? Had her parents arranged a match between two strangers—people who had only shared shy glances over a church pew on Sunday morn-ings? Her life in Ohio must have been difficult after her parents had been killed. Why hadn't the mysterious beau married her before enlist-ing in Mr. Lincoln's army? Maybe he had second thoughts about some-one who disdained the sidesaddle, could never remember her hat, and expressed her opinion at every opportunity.

Emily was cheerful, patient, and caring while tending his aunt. Aunt Augusta spoke of the young woman's wit and intelligence, but in his presence she avoided meeting his eye, blushed profusely, and fidg-eted. Although she dressed like a schoolmarm, Alexander suspected she would kick off her high button shoes and run barefoot through the meadow if no one was around.

Sleep would now be more elusive than ever. As it was pointless to return to bed, he took the stairs to the garden for a solitary walk. Yet even the flowers reminded him of Emily. Passing beneath her dark-ened window, he swore he smelled lemon verbena floating on the air. As the first streaks of dawn colored the horizon, he turned his thoughts to more troubling matters. He had overheard her questioning Beatrice and the maids about their life on Hunt Farms. He'd heard her ask his mother about the religious background of their neighbors. Why would she be so curious about life on a plantation—the very thing she held in contempt?

Heading to the horse barns, Alexander was determined to work off his fascination with a woman so patently wrong for him. Emily was a stubborn Quaker, a holier-than-thou Yankee who thought herself superior to dissipated Southerners. And *that* would never change, no matter what he said or did.

Having slept like a baby, Emily awoke to a new day feeling refreshed. Her pique with Alexander had ebbed and then faded altogether. After all, she probably *was* narrow minded, but she absolutely refused to consider the other side of the matter of slavery.

She had missed dinner last night due to a feigned headache. Lila had been concerned and peppered Emily with questions: *Why are you so upset with Mr. Hunt? What did you two argue about?* The young maid had become her first true friend. Yet Emily couldn't explain what they had disagreed about. She hoped they could get past the comments of yesterday. She couldn't put Alexander to good use if their romance fizzled out due to her hot temper.

This morning, Emily dressed quickly and then hurried downstairs to arrive first in the dining room. Or so she thought.

Alexander stood sipping coffee by the tall windows. "Good morning, Miss Harrison. I picked you these myself." He held out a massive bouquet of day lilies and mountain laurel. "They grow wild by the fencerows. Please forgive my thoughtlessness yesterday. If anyone can be narrow minded, it is I."

"Let's not speak of our argument again. Mrs. Bennington would probably fire me if she knew how I behaved toward you." She accepted the bouquet with a smile. "These are beautiful, Mr. Hunt. Thank you."

Pouring a cup of coffee, Emily remembered her grandmother's advice: *Spread the honey on thick, and then watch the bees swarm around you.*

"My lips are sealed, and you're welcome." He sat down with his coffee.

Setting the flowers on the sideboard to be put in water later, she took a seat on the opposite side of the table. "Your farm is beautiful. I meant to tell you that yesterday. It's a tribute to hard work and your love for the land."

He nodded graciously. "Tell me about your home, Miss Harrison. I've seen Ohio only from the banks of Bennington Island."

"A fertile valley looks the same on both sides of a river." She carefully avoided the essential difference between the two states. "My father farmed fifty acres outside Marietta, planted mostly in corn and hay. We owned four cows, a dozen chickens, two horses, and a pair of goats, but I never figured out why." She grinned at the memory. "The male was the orneriest billy on earth, and our nanny never produced an ounce of milk."

"Tell me about your mother." He leaned back from the table.

"My mother raised a huge garden and had a small orchard. She put up the best peach preserves in the county, with blue ribbons from the fair to prove it. She took first place in the apple pie competition more times than naught."

"What was her secret?" Alexander studied her from beneath lowered brows.

Emily glanced around as though looking for eavesdroppers. "She picked the apples a bit early and then sweetened them with honey. They would remain firm instead of mushy like those of her competition. I will expect you to keep that secret under your hat," she whispered.

"I promise." He solemnly drew an *X* over his heart. "Do you share your mother's joy in the kitchen?"

"I'm afraid not. I didn't inherit a fraction of her abilities. I once roasted a goose to charred oblivion. Downright unrecognizable, I'm afraid."

"You're young. There's still time to learn. I admire your high regard for your mother. No Southern woman would ever admit to inferior domestic skills, even though most probably possess far less than you."

"I see no reason for deception. We are what we are. Don't you agree, Mr. Hunt?"

"Unquestionably." He drained his cup and lifted the carafe to refill it. "Sounds like you had a happy childhood in Ohio."

It was a statement, not a question, but Emily felt obliged to confirm. "Yes, I enjoyed my childhood. I climbed trees, skinned my knees, and rode my horse bareback through the woods. My mother and I picked blackberries in July, but I would eat more from the basket than ever landed in a pie. My father taught me to swim in the river and how to skip stones. We waved at the passing riverboats and made up stories about traveling to places like St. Louis or Memphis or New Orleans."

"And what would you do, Emily, if you visited one of those places now?" Alexander spooned fried eggs and crisp bacon from the platter offered by Nathaniel.

She glanced at him, taking a small portion of food. Yesterday, stolen kisses, and now he used her given name without permission. "What would I do? First, I would go to a fancy shop where the dresses are already made and try on each and every one. I'm tired of looking at patterns and bolts of fabric, trying to imagine what a dress might look like. Next, I would seat myself in a fine restaurant and order every dish I've never heard of. Then I would walk down a street of fine homes and peek in their windows to see how they live." Emily felt a blush crawl up her neck. She set down her fork to hide her shaking hands.

"You would look in people's windows?"

"That's what I do in Martinsburg whenever I take a walk." She clamped her mouth shut, unsure why she had just bared her soul to a son of wealth and privilege.

"Why?" He sounded truly perplexed.

"I'm not spying on them. I like to see the color of their draperies, which portraits hang on the walls or what furnishings they own." She ate a forkful of eggs with melted cheese and tomatoes, waiting for him to laugh.

But he did not. "Rest assured, those people are no happier with their fine possessions than your family. They just have more to dust." He watched her over the rim of his cup. "What happened to your parents, Emily?"

Although she had been enjoying the meal, she set her fork and knife on the plate. "They were killed in an accident. My father used to race his horse down the road along the river. It was the only reckless thing he ever did. One day the axle broke and his buggy lost a wheel. My parents were thrown to their deaths a few miles from home." Her eyes filled with tears, but she refused to cry. "Because the farm had a mortgage, I had no choice but to sell it and look for employment. The Benningtons were the only family in the area that could afford paid help." She leaned back in the damask chair. "You now know the entire dismal story of my uneventful life." Her tone took on an unwarranted defensiveness.

"Dismal, yes, but not unusual. Death surrounds us. It pervades our lives insidiously, forcing us to make decisions and do things we normally wouldn't. You've done well for yourself since your parents' deaths. I'm sure they would be proud of you." Downing the last of his coffee, Alexander tossed his napkin on his plate.

"How has death pervaded your life?" she asked, taken aback by his declaration. Wasn't this a man whose life remained unchanged while war raged all around him? "What regrettable decisions have you made?"

"I didn't say I regretted anything." He stood and pushed back his chair. "Let's go to town, shall we? Apparently, the rest of the family wasn't hungry this morning."

"You forget, Mr. Hunt, that I'm a paid employee of Mrs. Bennington. I don't share with you the liberty of spending the day as I please." Rising from the table, she shook the creases from her skirt. "If you'll excuse me, I'll go check on her."

"As you wish." Alexander bowed deeply as she left.

Emily found Mrs. Bennington on the verandah outside her room. A tray with empty dishes indicated nothing was amiss with her appetite. "Good morning, ma'am. How are you feeling today?"

"I'm feeling fine, dear, never better. I'm catching up on my correspondence to the girls." Mrs. Bennington smiled up from her chaise. "Rebecca and I heard that you and Alexander had a spat. We thought it best if we gave you time to patch things up." She sounded conspiratorial.

Emily's eyes grew round as saucers. "We didn't exactly have a spat, Mrs. Bennington, merely a difference of opinion. I hope I haven't overstepped my bounds by arguing with my host. You have my sincere apology, ma'am. I hope you'll extend my regrets to Mrs. Hunt."

"Nonsense. No apologies are necessary. Alexander can be stubborn as a mule and far too accustomed to getting his own way. The belles of the Shenandoah Valley wouldn't disagree with him even if he stated the earth was flat and Christopher Columbus was a madman."

"Do you suppose he prefers women who behave like that?" Emily asked in a timid voice.

Mrs. Bennington pondered a moment. "I don't know. I suspect it's all he's ever experienced. Men seldom give women's opinions much thought unless forced to. That is how it is with Porter, or at least how it used to be," she added with a wink. "You and my nephew quarrel because you're both the same—stubborn, willful, and opinionated. But you could settle him down and give him direction."

Emily stared at her. "I doubt that I could give him anything but indigestion." But just for a moment she imagined being married to him. In her dreamy vision, she was held securely in the crook of his shoulder, cherished and protected, while he whispered unceasing endearments in her ear.

"Speaking of Porter," said Mrs. Bennington, pulling Emily from her daydream. "I have a favor to ask of you and Alexander." Mischief shone in her green eyes.

"What kind of favor?" Emily tensed with a growing sense of doom.

"Porter hasn't been home in days. James said the work at the hospital isn't diminishing. Battlefield casualties continue to pour in, while contagious disease spreads through the troops. He must be out of clean clothes by now." She straightened in the chaise. "I would like you two to ride to Front Royal with clothes and the food Beatrice prepared, plus a crate of medical supplies that arrived from Alexandria. I have no idea what Porter has been eating. But knowing him, it's probably the same thin soup and hard biscuits as the soldiers."

Emily's dread solidified into a lump in her stomach. She had no desire to spend more time with Alexander than necessary. Ideas were taking hold which had no place in a Quaker woman's mind. "Couldn't Alex—Mr. Hunt travel alone? I feel I've neglected you since our arrival, Mrs. Bennington. Perhaps we could read this afternoon over tea."

"Nonsense. Besides, Alexander might lose his way. I doubt he leaves Hunt Farms very often. I would feel better if you accompanied him. Then you could also provide a more accurate description of hospital conditions. My brother-in-law's reports are designed to spare me worry over Porter. Please, Emily?"

Of course, she had no choice. Within the hour she changed into the oldest traveling outfit with the most unbecoming bonnet she owned. There was no reason to wear a good dress when she'd be bouncing over rough roads.

Matilde and Beatrice had been busy all morning cooking and baking an assortment of nourishing food for the hospital. Emily and Lila carried hamper after hamper out to the buckboard, along with sacks of bandages and boxes of brown-wrapped medicine. When they arrived with their final load, they found Alexander hitching two Percherons to the wagon. Emily stared at him with interest. His breeches had been tucked inside tall boots and his jacket forgotten. Sweat had rendered his shirt nearly transparent, the damp linen outlining every muscle of his back and shoulders.

Unfortunately, Lila witnessed her perusal. "Give me that basket before you drop it in the mud." She hissed in Emily's ear. "You're about as subtle as a new bull in a March pasture."

Emily hid behind her new fan—another gift from Mrs. Bennington.

"Miss Amite, I have no idea what you mean. I was wondering why Mr. Hunt hitched draft horses instead of regular stock."

But Lila's attention wasn't on the horses or Mr. Hunt, for that matter. William had ridden into the stable yard, reined in inches from his employer, and bent his head to speak in hushed tones. Tall, rangy, rugged William—Lila stared at him with no more restraint than Emily had showed. She'd seen Lila and William exchange surreptitious looks and shy smiles before. Emily pulled her gaze from the men long enough to turn toward the wagon. Lila selected the same precise moment to heft her basket of baked goods, cracking Emily resolutely in the head.

"Excuse me, Miss Emily. I beg your pardon," said Lila.

"Excuse me, Lila. The fault was mine."

"No, miss, if I hadn't—"

"Excuse *me*, ladies," interrupted Alexander. He tapped a rolled piece of paper on the palm of his hand. "I'm afraid there's been a change of plans, Miss Harrison. You won't be accompanying me to the field hospital after all."

"But Mrs. Bennington insisted that I go along." Emily protested as though just noticing his presence.

Alexander held up a gloved hand to silence her. "Aunt Augusta has no concept of battle lines or Union troop activities. Skirmishes around Winchester have spread to the outskirts of Front Royal. It's not safe for you to leave the farm. I simply won't allow it."

His tone brooked no further discussion. His flirtatious manner with bating witticisms and playful winks was gone. His face had paled, and tiny lines around his eyes and mouth stood in stark relief. "I'll ask you both and the rest of the family to remain indoors. Do not ride around the farm, Emily. It wouldn't be prudent. Please assure my aunt that Uncle Porter will receive the food and medical supplies." Donning his jacket, he swept his hair back from his brow and bowed without his usual swagger. Then he strode to his stallion, mounted, and galloped from the yard without another word.

William pulled the last hamper from Lila's grip. Then he climbed aboard and drove the loaded wagon down the Hunt Farms lane, while the two women stood in the dust-roused yard, staring in silence long after they were gone.

"What do suppose that message was about?" asked Lila. "It seems to have ruffled some of Mr. Hunt's feathers."

"I don't know, but I would give next month's pay to find out."

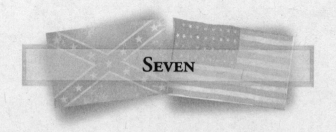

SEVEN

*A*lexander sent William to the field hospital to deliver the supplies, while he rode his stallion hard toward Millwood. While he was squandering time courting a skinny Yankee schoolteacher, his men had apparently gotten themselves into a fine mess. "Sakes alive," he muttered, pulling the rolled note from his breast pocket. He reined in his horse sharply and read the brief words once more. "*Come at once to the stand of pines. Yours are on their way north. N.*" Tearing the sheet into small pieces, he scattered them to the wind before spurring Phantom on.

Farm fields gave way to a hardwood forest on the eastern bank of the Shenandoah River. Unnoticed by most passersby, an odd cluster of pines grew not far from the trail, providing Alexander with a safe spot to meet his men. He found Nathan Smith waiting in the cool shade and looking very nervous.

"Captain." Alexander addressed Smith without smiling.

"Colonel." Smith snapped a salute to his superior before proceeding with his explanation. "I had no knowledge of this, sir. You have my word. Dawson and a few others got it into their heads to do a little ranging on their own."

"Go on," Alexander gritted between clenched teeth. His anger and frustration spiraled as the story unfolded.

"They decided to bust into some storehouses in Winchester last night. For some fool reason they didn't think the Yanks would be watching too closely. They overpowered a few guards and filled their saddlebags with chewing tobacco, whiskey, coffee—whatever they could get their hands on."

A vein pulsed in Alexander's neck, and his hands involuntarily tightened on the reins. Smith paused, as though uncertain if he should continue.

"Go on, Captain. Give me the full story."

"Then the men decided to fill a wagon to haul away. I believe, sir, they planned to sell the supplies to our own sutlers."

Pure rage coursed through his veins, but Alexander said nothing.

"By the time they found a wagon and loaded it, an entire Union regiment had surrounded the storehouse. Our men were so busy with their bounty that they never saw the Yanks until time to move out. They rode right into a perfect ambush—"

Alexander held up his hand. "I've heard enough. Just give me the numbers."

"Three dead, sir, two wounded, along with seven captured."

"*Twelve* men rode out on their own without my orders?" asked Alexander, stunned.

"Yes, sir, but we might be able to get them back. A short while ago, Ellsworth tapped into the telegraph line at White Post. He heard that our men will be on the Winchester and Potomac train bound for Harper's Ferry this afternoon. From there, they'll be transferred to a Yankee prison."

"Isn't that exactly what they deserve, Captain?"

"Yes, sir."

"Those dozen men behaved like common outlaws, not like soldiers fighting for the Cause."

"Yes, sir."

"Am I expected to jeopardize the rest of my men—men who follow orders—to free nine who pursued their own interests and not those of the Confederacy?"

"Yes, sir. I mean, no, sir." Smith stammered.

An uncomfortable silence filled the glen.

"Have you sent word to the rangers?"

"Yes, sir, I have." The two men locked gazes for a long moment. "They appear to be arriving as we speak." They could hear the sound of horses splashing through shallow water.

"Very well," he said, returning the salute of his second-in-command.

He spurred Phantom toward the river. No further discussion was necessary. The colonel had no choice but to free the captured men.

By three thirty, a solitary man in shabby clothes rode into the sleepy train station at Charles Town. He slid from his swayback nag, sat down on the rails, and pulled off a boot to rub his toes through holes in his sock. When the station dispatcher walked outside to inquire of news, he assumed the man was a farmer waiting for the afternoon train.

"Haven't you heard?" asked the farmer, squinting into the sunshine.

"Heard 'bout what, son?"

"They captured the Gray Wraith outside Upperville."

"You don't say!" exclaimed the dispatcher. "I have a sister living in Upperville. Why, that man ought to have been hung long ago. I hope the scoundrel gets his just desserts now." He practically danced across the platform.

"Oh, I'm sure he will." Nodding agreement, the farmer carefully replaced his boot, as though he had all the time in the world.

Soon the telegraph operator wandered outside to see why the dispatcher was prancing around like a fool.

The colonel rose from the tracks, stretched to his impressive height, and shrugged off the tattered coat. At that moment, Nathan Smith stepped around the corner of the station with his Colt revolver leveled at the two Winchester and Potomac employees. Thirty of the colonel's best men surrounded and seized the station without a single shot being fired. The rest was child's play. With the telegraph operator tied up and the dispatcher making his usual, but forced, appearance on the platform, the unsuspecting train pulled into Charles Town like a fish on a hook. Rangers blocked the tracks with logs to prevent the train from exiting the station in reverse. Other men climbed aboard and quickly subdued the engineer and conductor. The green Union recruits guarding the captured rangers made a wise decision to surrender. The colonel liberated the nine soldiers who had acted on their own, along with six thousand dollars of cash from the express agent.

"Take nothing from the civilians," Alexander said to his men as he moved through the train car. "Ladies and gentlemen, as soon as we recover those who belong to us, you'll be on your way to Harper's Ferry. Have no fear."

Ladies eager to escape the battle raging around Winchester comprised most of the passengers. Judging by their lapel buttons, some were loyal to the Union, and some were loyal to the Confederacy. "Would you like to search my bag?" asked a woman in black. She held open her cloth satchel.

Alexander paused to scan her young face—a widow at such a tender age. "No, ma'am. I have no desire to peek into ladies' purses or examine their trunks. A Southern gentleman would never do such a thing. And *you* have certainly sacrificed enough." He tipped his hat and then jumped down to the platform. A journalist sitting nearby jotted notes in his spiral notebook, and thus the Gray Wraith's notoriety continued to grow.

But notoriety was the last thing on the colonel's mind. Once safely rendezvoused for the evening, he called his troops to formation before allowing fires to be built or supper prepared. With little regard for regular drills and army procedures, forming ranks was something he seldom did. But that was part of the reason he faced this situation now.

"Captain Smith," he ordered. "Call the names of those involved in the unauthorized raid. Men, if your name is called, step forward and offer justification for your actions." A sour taste crept up Alexander's throat into his mouth, but he swallowed it down.

A few of the nine rangers offered weak excuses for their participation. Others stared at the ground, perhaps ashamed of their behavior. And one silently glared at the colonel with unmistakable, ill-concealed hatred.

"You men have disgraced the honor of a soldier," said Alexander. It was so quiet one could hear birds drifting to sleep in overhead nests. "It's not my intention, nor will it ever be, for this regiment to profit by our efforts to procure goods for the Confederate cause." He enunciated each word slowly and deliberately as his anger built. "Any man who doesn't agree is free to leave and join the regular cavalry or the infantry—or become a renegade outlaw if he so wishes. But I will not tolerate acts of thievery for personal benefit."

He stepped forward until he was inches from the men lined up before him. "I liberated you from your fate in a Yankee prison camp out of recognition for past service, but you men are dismissed. Take your personal weapons, your mounts, and whatever bounty is still in your possession and get out of my sight."

Not one man chose to stay and argue, to plead his case or beg for reconsideration. Perhaps because the colonel's expression indicated he might disregard his resolve to do no bodily harm to others.

That night, Alexander had no appetite for supper after the men had left. He knew the majority of his men were good soldiers—their commitment to the South was no less than his own. He also knew they were itching to go out on another raid. Certainly Lee's Army of Northern Virginia could use additional supplies. With his scouts already gathering intelligence, tomorrow he would lead them on a foray. But tonight his soul was troubled. Twelve men had disobeyed orders. A fine line separated a band of thieves and partisan rangers. He could think about little else as he rode the countryside selecting their next target with his second-in-command. Nathan Smith knew him better than any other man. The success of their effort to aid the Confederacy depended upon the Union Army not focusing too much attention on them. And that surely would change if a mission turned into a bloodbath.

They rode long and hard around a moonlit Clarke County to choose their next fatted calf. The ride did wonders for the colonel— Alexander was starting to feel like himself again. But Smith grew weary. "Unless you're planning to sleep in the saddle, I suggest we find somewhere to bed down. I'm bushed." He scrubbed his face with his hands.

"You're right, but we're too far from camp to return before dawn." After consulting his map, Alexander stretched up in the stirrups. "We're just outside of Berryville. I recently came upon an abandoned barn during one of my rides. We'll rest the horses and sleep there. That will also allow the men a chance for revelry without their commanders."

They found the narrow path leading to the old barn without too much difficulty. Before they reached the barnyard, Smith raised a gloved hand and pulled his horse to a stop. "Whoa. There's someone down there, Colonel."

Alexander guided Phantom to the edge of the woods on a tight rein so as to make no unnecessary noise. They stared at thin streams of yellow light between the weathered slats of the barn. A single horse had been tied to the hitching post. "It can't be!" he hissed.

"What?" Smith strained to see in the shadowy moonlight.

"I must examine that horse." For the second time that day, Alexander felt his blood pressure rise. They secured their mounts and then crept silently into the yard for a closer look. Smith followed on the colonel's heels with his Colt drawn.

Even in the poor light Alexander recognized the fine lines and well-tended coat of Miss Kitty. "Confound it," he muttered as he motioned Smith back to the woods.

"What is it, Colonel?"

"It's the blasted horse of our houseguest, Emily Harrison."

The captain looked thoroughly confused.

"You met her, Nathan, the night of the ball. She was that skinny gal in the blue gown with flaming red hair. When I danced with her, she nearly crippled me, for goodness' sake."

Smith looked at him as though he'd taken leave of his senses. "Yes, I remember—your aunt's governess. Why would her horse be here?"

"I don't know, but I'm about to find out." Fury got the better of him as Alexander strode toward the door.

Smith reached out and grabbed his arm. "Wait, sir. Let's think about this a moment."

He glared at Smith. "Why don't we ask her what foolishness she's up to?"

"You told me she was from Ohio. That makes the lady a Yankee. How well do you know her? She could be up to mischief and your sweet aunt and uncle are none the wiser. Anyway, if you go marching into the barn dressed like that, she'll have no question as to who you are."

Alexander glanced down at the gray officer's uniform, his scabbard and sword, and his scarlet-lined cape. He hated to admit it, but Smith was right. She would take one look at him and his identity would no longer be a secret. "Maybe it's not Miss Harrison inside. Maybe a deserter stole her horse from our barn." His heart yearned for a logical explanation. "Let's take cover in the brush off the trail."

Captain Smith stared at him quizzically, but the matter was soon out of their hands. Inside, someone extinguished the barn's lantern. Then they heard the door open and close with a thud. Miss Kitty began to prance as the mysterious rider struggled to get on her back. The rider, swathed in a hooded cloak, patted the horse's flank before heading up the path. As luck would have it—for the colonel, not for Miss Emily Harrison—the moon emerged from the clouds and the wind blew back her hood as the rider passed their hidden position.

Neither man had any doubt as to the identity of the fair-skinned, auburn-haired woman sitting astride in the saddle. At the top of the hill she spurred her horse toward Front Royal and vanished into the shadows. Alexander was left staring into the night with a clenched jaw and wrath emanating from his eyes like sparks from a bonfire.

True to his word, Porter Bennington returned to Hunt Farms the following evening, haggard and ten pounds thinner. Upon his arrival he went straight to the farm pond with a bar of lye soap and scrubbed himself until his skin was nearly raw. Mr. Hunt's valet scurried around with towels and fresh clothes, not knowing quite what to make of someone bathing in the pond. The doctor instructed the servant to burn the clothes worn in Front Royal and to tell no one. Later he joined his family at the dinner table eager to hear about what he'd missed at the ball. For the remaining years Augusta and Porter would spend together, he never spoke of his days at the hospital following the battle of Winchester, despite her attempts to coax him. It remained an experience he would never forget. The unspeakable carnage he witnessed and treated—the aftermath of what men did in battle—would stay with him always. He no longer viewed the Southern cause as glorious. Neither side could possibly receive God's grace with boys as young as twelve dying on the battlefield.

Porter's nephew did not attend his reunion dinner, however. Alexander had mysteriously disappeared and still hadn't returned to Hunt Farms. No one seemed to know where he'd gone. Emily was also absent. She had complained of a piercing headache and excused herself for the remainder of the day. Because light or sound made the jarring pain worse, she had asked not to be disturbed by anyone.

Lila certainly didn't disturb her because she knew Emily was not cloistered in her room with a cool cloth pressed to her forehead. She wasn't in the house at all. Lila didn't like lying—it wasn't how she'd been raised. But she would even break the Commandment about bearing false witness to help Emily. Lila spent the day in the basement kitchen helping her mother in order to keep from running into Mrs. Bennington or Mrs. Hunt. That evening she sat alone on the back steps listening to hoot owls and crickets, unable to sleep until Emily safely returned. So many things could go wrong. This close to the front lines, armed patrols stopped and questioned everyone. Or Emily could simply lose her way on unfamiliar roads. When Lila finally spotted her friend riding up the drive, she breathed a sigh of relief and ran to open the stable door.

Emily quietly entered the barn, dismounted, and then pulled the saddle from Miss Kitty's back. She startled upon noticing Lila in the shadows. "I'm so glad to see you." Emily threw her arms around Lila breathlessly. "I was so scared, Lila. I didn't think it would be so dark on the roads. I know how absurd that sounds, but I thank God that Miss Kitty was able to find her way home."

Lila hugged her fiercely. "It doesn't sound absurd. Of course you were scared. Any normal person would be, but I'm proud of what you're doing."

A stable boy crept from the shadows and silently took the saddle from Emily. He placed it on the shelf and began rubbing down the sweaty horse. "Thank you, Jack." Emily nodded her gratitude. "Did Mrs. Bennington or Mrs. Hunt get suspicious?" she asked Lila.

"Nope, not that I could tell. I stayed out of their way today."

"What about Alexander? Did he inquire about me?" Her voice faltered.

"No, he's not home from Front Royal yet. William came back alone with the empty wagon."

"Is that so?" Emily didn't like this news one bit as they left Miss Kitty in Jack's capable hands. "I'd better get upstairs before someone notices me gone. Good night, Lila. Sweet dreams." But Emily's dreams were anything but sweet as she tossed and turned for most of the night. The next morning she overslept and found her employers already in the dining room.

"Good morning, Miss Harrison," greeted Dr. Bennington.

"Welcome back from Front Royal, sir. I'm sure you're glad to be home. Good morning, Mrs. Bennington, Mr. and Mrs. Hunt." Smiling politely, she nodded at the other three. When she noticed Alexander had not yet come down to breakfast, her smile faded.

"Yes, Miss Harrison, I am," said Dr. Bennington. "If your headache is better, I have a favor to ask of you."

Hiding her confusion, Emily filled her plate with biscuits and sausage gravy. "I feel fine this morning, sir. How can I help?"

"I must cross the lines into Frederick to buy medicine. Our surgeons are frightfully low on laudanum, quinine, and chloroform. I heard apothecaries there have it for sale, and because I treat as many Union soldiers as Confederate, the people of Frederick shouldn't mind selling to me."

"Oh no, Porter," interrupted his wife. "You've just gotten back. You'll be no use to the wounded if you drop over dead yourself." Her strong words reflected her anxiety.

"Don't worry yourself, my dear." He reached over to pat her hand. "I will deliver the supplies to the field hospital and then return to here. The enlisted doctors have the situation well under control now."

"How can I help?" asked Emily.

"I would like you and Lila to visit my office in Martinsburg and load up a list of things." He produced a folded sheet and placed it on the table. "Because Lila often assisted me on the island, she should be familiar with most of the items. But I don't want the two of you traveling alone. James, can you spare someone to drive them?"

"I would send Alexander, but he's off on one of his jaunts." Mr. Hunt shook his head. "I'll send William. He can be counted on to conduct the ladies safely to Martinsburg and back."

"Thank you. I'm in your debt." Dr. Bennington pulled his plate of breakfast closer.

"Nonsense, and I'm coming with you. If medicine is for sale in Frederick, I will be the one buying it. I can't let you earn all the laurels while I sit around on my backside. How would that look to my wife?"

"In that case don't forget your wallet. We'll buy all they have available." Dr. Bennington smiled at his brother-in-law with appreciation.

Emily finished her breakfast in silence, only vaguely aware of table conversation. She had sworn not to help the Southern cause. She was determined to use her employment solely for her Underground Railroad purposes. But how could she refuse Dr. Bennington, especially as the supplies could as easily save the life of a loyal Unionist as a Rebel? Then her lips curled into a smile as her mind crafted the perfect solution. The Bennington mansion in Martinsburg would be empty except for a few slaves. But it would be fully stocked with food for their benefit and in anticipation of the family's return. Who was to say their trip to his office couldn't include a stop at the barn in Berryville? Emily couldn't stop grinning. This would be easier than she hoped with only one problem. William wouldn't do as their driver. As Alexander's valet, William was loyal to him. She couldn't trust the man to keep quiet about odd things he might see. Judging by the stable boy's behavior last night, Jack would be a better choice. She would wait until the last minute and insist upon him, giving William no opportunity to argue.

There was nothing quite like a perfect plan.

Emily's plan, however, proved far from perfect. William put up a fuss when she chose Jack instead of him. "He doesn't know the roads well, Miss Harrison, because he seldom leaves Hunt Farms. What if you and Lila get lost?" William crossed and uncrossed his arms. "Mr. Alexander is not going to like this. No, ma'am. He's not going to like this a'tall."

"I appreciate your concern, William, but I insist on Jack. Mr. Hunt will need you here when he returns from his trip." Emily refused to budge, even though William continued to mutter as he walked away.

Mr. Alexander doesn't have a say-so in the matter. Unfortunately, Lila also thought taking Jack was a bad idea.

"Why can't William go?" she pleaded. "Jack is a skinny runt of a man, not much older than a boy. What good is he if we find ourselves in a scrap?"

"Stop and think about this." Emily set her valise in the buggy. "William probably won't like the idea of two people disappearing during Mr. Hunt's absence. He's loyal to him. He'll try to stop me, or at least tell Alexander when he returns. This is serious, Lila. I could be arrested and jailed."

"I know it's serious. I could get in trouble just for being with you. But just because William is free black like me doesn't mean he won't help a widow and her child reach freedom." Lila crossed her arms, mimicking William's posture.

"I've made up my mind and refuse to take the chance," insisted Emily. "You only prefer William's company because you fancy him. Please climb aboard. We need to go."

While Jack held the reins and Lila sulked, Emily plotted their route from Front Royal to Martinsburg via Berryville on her map. Although Jack seemed a nice young man, he couldn't read or write and was indeed unfamiliar with the roads. But on the other hand, he didn't raise an eyebrow as a twenty-year-old woman and her month-old son crawled into the storage compartment of the buggy. Before dawn, Emily had checked the space to be sure it contained enough cracks for air. Then she stowed the woman and her son inside and left their canteens of water and hampers of food under a tarp.

Lila had learned from the kitchen staff the name of a likely candidate for their first attempt at setting someone free. Widowed the previous spring from a yellow fever epidemic, the woman refused to marry any suitors who presented themselves. Annabelle had no parents or siblings at Hunt Farms, either slave or free, and few friends. Emily had approached the woman during one of her nightly walks near the slave cabins. Although at first reluctant to talk, Annabelle worried she would be sold to another plantation and possibly separated from her son. She possessed few skills to earn money to purchase her freedom. Being sold to another plantation was a fear she shared with the entire slave population.

"I've got nothing holding me here," she whispered to Emily during their initial meeting. "I heard winters up north are cold and free Canada is nothing but a wilderness, but I ain't takin' a chance of ending up where they beat folks. Most plantations ain't run like this one." Annabelle had locked eyes with Emily. "I have someone worth living for... even if it means dying. Gabriel is gonna grow up free." She hugged the boy to her heart, and at that moment her destiny with Emily had been decided.

"Annabelle?" Emily lifted the lid and peered into the compartment when they reached the barn refuge just before dark. "It's safe to come out."

The thin, tall woman clutching her precious baby slowly unfolded her stiff spine. But she made no complaint about riding in a confining box. She climbed down on shaky legs and looked around like a scared rabbit. "Where we at?"

"We are outside of Berryville. We brought plenty of food. We'll eat and then sleep in the loft. But we'll build no fire—it could attract attention. We'll start for Martinsburg at first light."

Annabelle nodded. "Thank you, ma'am."

"Please call me Emily."

"No, ma'am. I won't." Her discomfort ratcheted up a notch.

Lila stepped forward. "My mother sent a bag of nappies for your boy. Tomorrow we'll arrive at the Bennington house in Martinsburg. We have supplies to pack up there, but when it gets dark we'll take you to a spot on the Potomac River. Quakers will take you across into Maryland, but you won't be alone. Other Quakers will take you up the Conococheague River into Pennsylvania—a free state."

Emily pulled a map from her valise. "Once you are in Pennsylvania, follow this to a safe house in Chambersburg. A Presbyterian couple will shelter you and give directions for the next leg of the journey." She pressed the paper into Annabelle's hand. "Travel at night and follow the North Star if the night is clear. Remember, the handle of the drinking gourd points to it. Sleep during the day, because the rivers are patrolled by slave-catchers. If you need help, approach the Methodist or Presbyterian parson or a Quaker. Don't trust anyone else, Annabelle. These are hard times. Folks receive a fat bounty for turning in runaways."

As they stood in the fading light, Annabelle studied the map and traced the route with her finger. "I know what's at stake, but why you doin' this—helping slaves you don't even know?"

"Because I was raised Quaker." Emily knew this wasn't the time to wax poetic about her religious upbringing.

"This is the only chance you and your son will get." Lila added practical advice as she and Emily unpacked the buggy. Jack unhitched the team and tied them to the water trough. Carrying the water canteens, Emily led the group into the barn where clean straw bales lay everywhere.

"You free?" asked Annabelle of Lila. She stared at Lila's fashionable clothing suspiciously.

"I am. My father purchased my freedom and my mother's when I was little." Once inside, Lila pulled sandwiches from the hamper and passed them around.

"I never saw black folks wearin' clothes like that." She pointed a disdainful finger at Lila's outfit.

"I am a maid for two young women. Because they never wear outfits longer than one season, they give their old clothes to me." Lila passed around fruit and sweet breads from the hamper.

Annabelle's eyes nearly bugged from her head. "They wear clothes less than a year and don't want them no more?" Following Lila's nod, she asked, "They the ones who taught you to talk so fancy?"

"They are." Lila bit daintily into an apple.

"Doesn't that just beat all—your pap havin' enough money to buy folks and you dressin' like you got someplace to go." Annabelle laughed and then settled on a hay bale to nurse her son, turning her back discretely on the others.

Later, while the baby slept soundly in Annabelle's arms, the four exchanged stories, their tales bridging the gap between people from very diverse backgrounds. Although Emily had little in common with them, she shared a few of her own joys and sorrows. Then they packed up the leftovers and went to sleep, filled with hope for the future.

As the travelers slept soundly on the soft straw matting, outside someone spent a fitful night watching the barn. William had followed them to learn why Miss Harrison dismissed him in favor of Jack. Alexander had given him emphatic orders to keep an eye on Miss Harrison and protect her in his absence. Scalawags and deserters from both armies roved the area, foraging and pilfering. Now William wondered if there had been another reason for the request. Did Alexander suspect the governess of something? Tonight William wished he hadn't followed the buggy. He had no reason to be untrustworthy to the Hunts. Despite their bantering, Alexander paid him a very good salary, allowing him to purchase the freedom of his siblings.

Besides, Alexander had been his friend since they were small boys climbing trees and getting into mischief. Alexander trusted him and treated him with respect, plain and simple. William had grown uneasy when the buggy turned off the pike to Martinsburg toward the east. It didn't take long to figure out where they were headed. Alexander had told him the story about stumbling upon Miss Harrison at an abandoned barn and leaping down from the hayloft door. Then she had ridden off in a dither with her frilly bloomers showing. The two men had laughed over the woman's bizarre antics.

Because he knew the Yankee was up to something, William wasn't surprised when a woman and child climbed from the compartment behind the front seat. It also didn't surprise him who the woman was. Annabelle had been dismally unhappy at Hunt Farms since her husband died. Although he wanted to see Annabelle and her son free, he didn't like Miss Harrison deceiving the Hunts to obtain that freedom. He knew Alexander grew fonder of the governess each day. William contemplated his own deception if he returned and said nothing.

If ever he wished he had stayed home and minded his own business, this was the time.

EIGHT

lexander wasn't in the best of moods. First, he'd been forced to discharge nine men from service because they had acted irresponsibly and without orders. Then he'd observed Emily leaving an abandoned barn in the middle of the night. What in the world could that mean? Did she have a lover? Had his aunt forbidden her to see some unsavory suitor and so she stole away to meet him while the Benningtons slept? If so, then why had she accepted his kisses at their picnic and flirted during breakfast if her heart belonged to another?

And what did it matter anyway? He had a bevy of women eager to please him. At least half a dozen would accept his hand in marriage if he asked. But he had no wish to ask, not since this scrappy Yankee had gotten under his skin. He could close his eyes and see the golden glints in her hair, smell its clean piney scent, and almost feel the silky strands between his fingers. He adored her throaty laugh, straight from the belly, and loved how she looked at Aunt Augusta with compassion and tenderness. *The way she might gaze upon me someday.*

Feeling the stirrings of desire, he shook his head to squash the daydream. He had no business hoping for a relationship with her. She was his aunt's governess—a woman who rode horses with her petticoats showing. Whatever reason took her to that barn last night, she hadn't been honest with him. He had trusted a sweet face and gentle touch before and had been tricked. Now he would live with the knowledge that men died because of him for the rest of his life. He wasn't about to make that mistake again.

And who had time for courting? The Confederate victory at Winchester hadn't been the end of hostilities they had hoped for. The trounced Union forces hadn't gone home, leaving them in peace. They pulled back to lick their wounds and wait for new recruits to fill their ranks. And new recruits would surely come, while the bottomless well of Yankee provisions never ran dry. Richmond, on the other hand, couldn't adequately supply Stonewall Jackson's Army of the Shenandoah Valley or Lee's Army of Northern Virginia. Soldiers needed nourishing food, warm clothes, and good boots as well as ammunition and horses to replace those killed in battle. The Southern well hit bottom long ago.

The colonel and his second-in-command led a handpicked company of fifty men on a three-day raid of Union storehouses. Ellsworth tapped into telegraph offices to falsely report rangers attacking outposts first in Alexandria and then heading up into Pennsylvania. Next he reported the Gray Wraith wreaking havoc west of the Shenandoah Mountains. He placed them everywhere except where they planned to be. The rangers liberated hundreds of horses, a vast quantity of provisions, and thousands of Union greenbacks for the Confederate Treasury. They netted so much that Jeb Stuart's cavalry had to assist with distributing the spoils. But the colonel saw no end to the war in sight—no imminent day when hostilities would cease. He could only do his duty to the Confederate Cause, relieved to have done so thus far without killing anyone. He hadn't broken the Sixth Commandment, but he'd broken plenty of others instead.

Bone tired but proud of his men's accomplishments, Alexander headed toward the beloved fields of Hunt Farms. He was eager to taste Beatrice's cooking again, to soak in his copper tub until his skin was wrinkled like a prune, and sleep beneath the soft quilt in his own bed. Most of all, he anticipated a reunion with his aunt's governess. Try as he might, he couldn't get her out of his head. Emily's face was the last thing he saw when he fell asleep at night and her scent of lemon verbena seemed to hang in the air when he awoke each morning. She was dishonest at the very least, and Alexander knew what came from trusting a deceitful woman. Maybe she would have an explanation for her behavior in Berryville and maybe she wouldn't. But he couldn't stay away from her if his life depended on it.

Grinning with happiness, Emily stretched like a cat in her luxurious room at the Bennington mansion. *I hope you're proud of me, Mama.* For the first time in a long while she had accomplished something. After they arrived in Martinsburg, they sent the maids to town on errands and hid Annabelle and Gabriel in the attic to rest for a few hours. Then during the night while Jack and the maids slept, Emily and Lila moved Annabelle to a secret landing on the Potomac River, known only to those on the Underground Railroad route. Long before dawn, Annabelle clumsily embraced Emily and Lila, and then she boarded a flatboat headed upriver to freedom. She carried cloth bags of food, spare clothes, and diapers; a canteen of water; and their heartfelt prayers. Emily and Lila stood on the riverbank until the boat disappeared into swirls of fog and mist. A slave and her son would soon be safely in Pennsylvania, sheltered by a Chambersburg couple, fellow Quakers like her parents. The young mother's tears were all the thanks Emily and Lila needed.

But Emily wasted no time patting herself on the back. She jumped out of bed and dressed quickly, allowing Lila another hour of sleep. Downstairs in Dr. Bennington's tidy office, she gathered and packed up the medical supplies from his list. As she worked, thoughts of betrayal crept to mind to ruin her good mood. Her employers and hosts would consider her actions stealing—the theft of property. But what right did they have to own slaves? She hadn't stolen their money or a horse. Annabelle and Gabriel were human beings. She'd been taught that no Christian would keep another in bondage. Yet the Hunts and Benningtons also considered themselves devout Christians, the same as her. And the Benningtons trusted her, treating her more like a family member than an employee. This odd incongruity niggled in the back of her mind as they loaded the buggy and left Martinsburg, heading toward Front Royal.

As Jack snapped the horses into a brisk gait, Lila stretched out on the backseat. Emily studied the map, directing their route on back roads. She was eager to deliver the medical supplies to the hospital and then return to Hunt Farms. At least Dr. Bennington's humanitarian efforts saved lives on both sides. She wondered if Alexander had noticed that the young woman and her baby were missing. How much contact did he have with *his people*? Or would he only concern himself with the financial loss they represented?

But that wasn't why she yearned to see him. She remembered his bouquet of mountain laurel and day lilies. He had picked her favorite flowers and inquired about her family as though truly interested in her life in Ohio. For some inexplicable reason Emily wanted him to like her, despite their insurmountable differences. Alexander was like a shiny apple just out of reach. He was also everything her parents despised—rich, lazy, and without valor. Yet one glance from him sent shivers up her spine. Could he help that he'd been born to wealth and privilege? No more so than she could help being poor. Back and forth her mind battled until a headache was the only conclusion.

"Welcome to Front Royal," Jack drawled as the buggy turned up a chaotic thoroughfare. Men on horseback, carriages filled to capacity, and buckboards loaded with supplies dashed in all directions.

The thoroughfare was so rutted with potholes that Emily had to set her jaw to keep from chipping her teeth. Brushing back a lock of hair, she tried to smooth the wrinkles from her skirt. "We must have hit every bump in the road. I feel as though I've been dragged behind the buggy inside of inside it."

"Days don't get much hotter than this." Lila dabbed beads of sweat from her brow. She leaned forward between them for a better view.

"Jack, stop at that laundry house." Emily pointed at the sign swinging in the breeze. "Lila and I need to wash up and change our dresses before looking for the hospital." Ten minutes later, only marginally refreshed, the young women climbed back into the dusty buggy.

"We won't have trouble finding the hospital." Jack angled his head at a row of ambulances heading north on Main Street. They followed a steady stream of walking wounded to a makeshift building on the edge of town. Rows of white tents covered every inch of side yard, while bloodied men leaned against a picket fence, patiently awaiting their turn.

"I see Dr. Bennington and Mr. Hunt." Lila pointed at two men unloading a wagon. Soldiers with bandaged heads and arms carried wounded toward the back door. Jack pulled the buggy alongside a row of ambulances.

Emily jumped down as soon as the wheels came to a stop. "Dr. Bennington, we're here."

"Praise the saints!" he cried. He transferred his patient to the arms of an orderly. "There's been another battle. You're not a moment too soon." He began digging into the cartons before Jack could unload them. "I see you found everything I asked for. Thank you, Miss Harrison. Army surgeons have run out of gauze dressings, and mercury spirits are pitifully low. With the medicine we purchased in Frederick, doctors should have enough until shipments can get through the lines." Dr. Bennington pulled items from the packing boxes like a child at Christmas.

"Don't just stand there gawking." Mr. Hunt said to Lila and Jack. "Grab a carton and carry these supplies inside."

Emily helped unload as well. Thankfully, orderlies intercepted them at the door to accept the supplies. From what Emily saw and heard in the hospital yard, she had no desire to venture inside. The coppery smell of blood hung in the air, while cries through the windows made her heart ache. Wounded men lay everywhere, moaning in pain or begging for water. Without space inside the hospital, they waited their turn with the surgeon outdoors. Some men lay so quietly Emily knew they were dead. One could practically see their poor souls hovering before they left the earthly world forever. Emily hurried back to the wagon for their canteens. Jack soon found a bucket and dipper to speed up the process. For hours she and Lila went from soldier to soldier to offer cool drinks or swab a fevered forehead. Jack helped the soldiers unload the wounded, and then he ferried endless buckets from the well to Emily. At sunset, she crawled into the buggy to rest with Lila right behind her. Neither spoke, equally upset by what they had seen.

Soon thereafter, Dr. Bennington and James Hunt arrived. "We're finished here for today, Miss Harrison." Dr. Bennington spoke softly, his voice barely above a whisper, yet his presence nearly startled the wits out of her.

"And the rest of the wounded—what will become of them?" Emily waved her hand over a sea of bloodied uniforms.

"Another batch of army doctors has arrived to help. Mr. Hunt and I have been relieved of our duties. Let's have dinner at the inn before we start back to Hunt Farms." He sounded incredibly weary as they headed to the trough to wash.

"Absolutely not, sir." She stepped down from the buggy to follow him. "I'm not fit to dine in town. My only wish is to return to Hunt Farms and take a bath."

Dr. Bennington seemed temporarily speechless as water dripped from his hair onto his shirt. Mr. Hunt was first to react by bursting into laughter. "You don't say," he said. Grinning from ear to ear, Mr. Hunt assessed Emily's appearance. "You look no worse than anyone else. This is wartime, Miss Harrison."

"Even so, sir, I am out of fresh clothes." Emily stared from one to the other, perplexed as to their amusement.

"As you wish, Miss Harrison. You may return to Hunt Farms," said Dr. Bennington. "Tell my wife and Mrs. Hunt we will follow shortly. Go straight to your *bathtub*," he added, laughing as though helpless to contain himself.

Emily could hear the men's snickers all the way back to the buggy. "I fear the strain and fatigue has made them hysterical," she murmured to her friend.

"That's not why they are laughing." Lila jumped up next to Jack in front, allowing Emily the back bench.

"Then what, pray tell, was so funny?" Emily waited to inquire until they were well away from the hospital grounds.

"A lady *never* refers to taking a bath in the presence of a gentleman who isn't her husband." Lila arched an eye brow and spoke as though addressing a child.

"Oh, tarnation," replied Emily.

"And a lady would never admit her appearance wasn't fit to dine in society," said Lila.

"Is that so?" Emily's voice lifted an octave.

"Yes, that's so. Even if it's true, a lady wouldn't draw attention to the fact."

"That's just plain silly. I'm hot and tired and don't care about society's rules right now."

"And a lady never says *tarnation*," Lila added under her breath.

"Are you finished now, Miss Amite?"

"Yes, Miss Harrison. I believe I am." Lila folded her arms across her chest and stared straight ahead.

Emily noticed tiny crinkles forming around Lila's eyes as she bit her lip with determination. "Well, tarnation, Miss Amite. I din't know nothing 'bout that, since I'm just a backwoods Yankee from the North."

"Yes, miss, that much is apparent." Both women then laughed until their sides ached and tears streamed from their eyes. After their horrific day, it felt good. And it felt even better to be headed back to Hunt Farms…for reasons that had nothing to do with bathtubs.

"Come in." A knock at the door roused Emily to her senses. She had nearly fallen asleep, lulled by hot steamy water and a warm fire in the hearth. It was still too warm for evening fires, but the maid insisted when Emily decided to bathe in her room.

"Are you still in that tub?" Lila came in carrying a long-stemmed glass.

"Yes, and I'm never coming out." Emily shut her eyes against the intrusion.

"This might change your mind." Lila set the drink down on a stool next to the tub. It held only an inch of pale yellow liquid.

"What's that?" she asked, intrigued by the bubbles. "You know Quakers don't imbibe in spirits."

"It's champagne, not spirits. The French drink it like water. Aren't you even a little curious?" Lila set a stack of towels next to the stool and began sorting through dresses in the wardrobe.

"Champagne is just a fancy type of wine." Emily stared as tiny bubbles rose to the surface and burst. She'd never seen the beverage, only read about it in books. After another moment, she picked up the glass and downed the contents in one swallow. A very unladylike burp followed the gulp.

"Goodness, Miss Emily. You're not supposed to swig the stuff like buttermilk." Lila dropped the dress she'd been inspecting on the bed. "You sip it a tiny bit at a time, especially as this is very good champagne." She demonstrated with the empty flute.

"How would you know that, Lila?" Emily slouched deeper into the bubble bath. "Is that where the rest of it went—you *sipped* on your way upstairs?"

Laughing, Lila reached into the tub to splash her. "No, I didn't. There wasn't enough or I might have. I learned about vintage wines from my father, who was trained by Dr. Bennington. This particular brand would be served only to treasured guests, not some neighbor stopping by to chew the fat."

"Vintage is wasted on me since I wouldn't know the difference." But Emily savored the last drops remaining on her tongue.

"Mr. Hunt said if you want more, you must come downstairs."

"Mr. James Hunt?" asked Emily. She remembered her embarrassing comments outside the hospital.

Lila pulled a vellum envelope from her pocket. "No, Mr. Alexander. And you knew very well which Mr. Hunt I meant."

"Is that for me?" Emily reached for the letter.

"Now, that's two Yankee questions so far." She held the envelope just beyond Emily's reach.

"*Yankee* questions? How dare you, you little imp." Emily sent a wave of water over the side of the polished copper tub. Suds formed small pools on the polished floor. "Now look what you made me do."

Lila jumped back in the nick of time. "I'll leave the note here to hurry you along." She set the envelope on the mantle. "Read it at your convenience and call me when you're ready for me to tighten your laces." She left the room in a fit of giggles.

"Wait until I get my Yankee hands on your scrawny neck!" Emily called after her. A moment later she stepped from her bath and wrapped herself in a thick towel. It took only three strides to reach the envelope and less than two seconds to extract the note.

> *Dearest Emily:*
>
> *Please join me for a late dinner on the terrace. I have missed your sunny disposition these past few days and wish to make up for my inopportune absence.*
>
> *There is also something I need to ask.*
>
> *A.H.*

Emily reread his fine slanted script three times. With each reading her heartbeat quickened. She flew behind the painted screen to don her corset and chemise as her mind reeled with what to wear, what to say, and how to act. Lila had laid out a gown Emily had never worn— a gift from Mrs. Hunt. "*Très chic*," Mrs. Hunt had declared when she'd drawn the gown from the box. Emily doubted she had enough *élan* to carry off a piece of couture. The pale yellow dress with white lace over-lay revealed her shoulders. After wrestling with her corset, she called for help.

Lila materialized like a specter. "I wondered when you'd give up try-ing to lace yourself up."

"All this trouble for supper on the terrace," she muttered. "I could just as easily eat a sandwich in my room." Nevertheless, within a half hour Emily was gowned, powdered, and perfumed.

Lila gathered her damp hair into a cluster atop her head, wove a yellow ribbon through the curls, and drew out several tendrils to frame her face. "Look at that. I'm getting pretty good with your thick hair." Lila took a jar of henna clay from the vanity drawer.

"Stop. Cosmetics would make my mother turn over in her grave." Emily spoke in a whisper, even though they were alone in the room.

"Or she would say you're too pale for your own good." Lila dipped her finger into the jar and touched Emily's cheeks lightly, and then she dabbed lemon verbena at her throat and wrists. "Done. Now go before the man comes to his senses." Lila pulled Emily off the stool.

"Comes to his senses?" Emily grabbed her empty glass and stuck her tongue out at Lila on her way to the door.

"Very ladylike. Be sure to do that tonight." Lila winked impishly.

Busily plotting revenge on her friend, Emily didn't consider what awaited her on the terrace. But once she stepped outside, she realized Lila had purposefully distracted her. Otherwise she might have bolted like a doe caught in crosshairs all the way back to the banks of the Ohio River.

Bathed in moonlight, the terrace looked like something from a childhood dream. The china, silver, and crystal goblets sparkled like diamonds on a small wrought-iron table. A vase of white lilies of the valley sat on the table, while a bottle of champagne and a single flute waited on the flagstones. These things caught Emily's attention one by one. Like a child unable to take in the full splendor of a Christmas tree, she focused on one thing at a time. She took a step onto the terrace and sensed someone's gaze on her. Turning, Emily spotted Alexander lounging against the balustrade with his legs crossed at the ankles. Her breath caught in her throat, and a tight knot formed in her stomach.

"I'm pleased you chose to join me tonight, Miss Harrison." Relaxed and at ease, he folded his arms over his chest and smiled.

"A person does need to eat, and my usual dinner companions are still in Paris." Emily crossed the flagstones as though walking on hot coals. "I do hope the girls return soon." She set her glass down on the table, glad she remembered to return the empty flute.

"Have you come for a refill?" He closed the distance in a few long strides.

"Yes, I have. I don't think a single glass will hurt, although my Quaker pastor might not agree." She forced herself to look at him.

"I'll write to Paris tomorrow and request a case be put aboard the next ship bound for Virginia." He filled both glasses with the bubbly liquid. "Besides, the Bible states that only drunkenness is an abomination to the Lord."

"I didn't take you for a man well versed in Scripture." Accepting the glass, Emily trembled as their fingertips brushed.

"Then you assumed incorrectly. I studied theology at the University of Virginia, besides rhetoric and philosophy. However, that seems a lifetime ago when I was younger and a more…idealistic man. The last few years would have undermined the most resolute of faiths."

Emily decided not to ask how war would affect someone not actively serving. "What about the Federal blockade of the coastline? Won't they intercept any shipments from abroad?" Immediately she regretted the question. If their courtship was to mask her clandestine activities, maybe she shouldn't speak of war at all. And if she was truthful, she yearned to enjoy one night without dwelling on present circumstances.

"Some of my best friends own nimble blockade runners. If this vintage is to your taste, your wish is my command." He held up his glass in salute and then drank half the contents.

"Don't waste your money. I wouldn't notice the difference." She sipped daintily, studying him over the bubbles. His knotted cravat hung loosely over a white linen shirt, open at the neck. He wore no frock coat, only an unbuttoned waistcoat. Taut chest muscles pulled at the fabric of his shirt when he leaned one palm on the table. Unnerved by his close proximity, Emily took a long drink and fought back a sneeze from the effervescence.

"You look beautiful, Emily." Alexander's eyes never left hers. "That gown is stunning. Or perhaps the dress is a worthless scrap of cloth but found redemption worn by you." He finished the rest of his glass.

She sipped before replying. "Your former assessment is correct, Mr. Hunt. The dress is a gift from your mother. Does she usually do things like that?"

"Do things like what?" Without warning, he brushed back a lock of hair from her cheek.

Emily pulled back from the intimate gesture yet didn't object. "Lavish expensive gifts on one of her sister's employees?" Again she lifted the glass of liquid gold to her lips.

"I suspect it was your relationship with me that occasioned the gift."

She blinked several times, even though the sun had long since set. "Is that so? I wasn't aware we had a relationship, Mr. Hunt."

"Perhaps it was just my mother's wishful thinking...and mine." Reaching for her face again, he caressed her cheek with his fingertips.

Emily jumped like a startled rabbit. "Why do you behave so boldly, sir? I thought I'd been invited to dinner, not to my seduction. I am famished, to be sure." Her voice remained even, feigning calmness she didn't feel. Part of her wanted to put this presumptuous rooster in his place even as another part wished that his caresses would never stop.

"I beg your pardon." Alexander grinned lazily, refilling both flutes. "I'm sure you are hungry. It was a long trip to Front Royal and then home. My uncle is indebted to you." Pulling out her chair, he motioned to unseen servants.

Emily seated herself in the voluminous skirt, petticoats, and cumbersome hoop. Her mouth dropped open as food began to arrive. Joshua materialized on her right with a platter of roast beef, biscuits with honey, slivered beans, baked apples, and corn in sweet cream. Emily filled her plate and immediately regretted taking so much. Virginia society ladies didn't load their plates like Ohio farmwives.

Alexander didn't seem to notice, for he heaped his plate even higher. They ate in companionable silence for a few minutes, soothed by the familiar sound of peepers and crickets in the fields beyond the verandah. Restored by the food and mellowed by the champagne, Emily relaxed for the first time in his presence. Her glass had been refilled once, so she dared not drain it again. She pushed it beyond reach so as not to be tempted by the delicious bubbles. Alexander told amusing, homespun tales of growing up on a vast plantation. She laughed easily. Some childhood tribulations remained the same regardless of your class or circumstances. Because courting him was an integral part of her ruse, she didn't flinch when he dabbed honey from her lips with his finger.

But when he stuck his finger in his mouth and licked off the stickiness, her sense of propriety returned. Flushing, she lifted her napkin to remove the rest.

"Allow me." He spoke softly and then leaned across the table to kiss her. But as fate would have it, he couldn't quite reach. Their lips hovered inches apart.

The gesture so hypnotized her, Emily did what any red-blooded woman would do. She bent forward and closed her eyes. Her minimal effort proved sufficient. His lips covered hers, and then she felt his tongue trace the outline of her mouth for any remaining honey. Emily's heartbeat amplified to a roar in her ears. Only her palms flattened against the table kept her from falling off the chair. She breathed in his scent and savored the kiss like a delicacy long denied.

Take hold of yourself, she thought after a moment. Drawing back, she straightened her back and glanced around as though waking from a dream.

"How about a walk, Miss Harrison?" he asked in a slow Southern drawl. "That is, if you're finished with dinner."

"Yes, let's walk. I couldn't eat another bite if my life depended on it. I hope you don't think me uncouth, but I've never tasted food this delicious."

"I would never think such a thing. Women should have healthy appetites. But I distracted you before you put a dent in your meal."

"My corset stays will thank me for walking away." She bit her tongue, certain that "corset stays" were on Lila's list of inappropriate conversation topics.

The moon, just above the tree line, illuminated steps down to a pebble path. He guided her into a garden cloaked in shadows, both mysterious and strangely welcoming. Once away from the house, Emily felt anticipation race through her blood like a tonic. *Why shouldn't I kiss him? Matthew is dead and so are my parents. Whom am I saving myself for? No one is left to be disappointed in me.*

"What do you think of our wisteria?" Alexander ducked under a bower formed by thick, woody vines. "My great-grandfather planted it soon after building the house with cuttings he carried from his ancestral home in Hampshire." Clusters of purple flowers formed a canopy above their heads, their fragrance almost intoxicating.

Emily tilted her head back and inhaled deeply. "I've never seen anything so lovely."

"Nor have I." Not waiting for permission, he brushed her lips with the softest of kisses.

She arched up on her tiptoes and returned the kiss, feeling heat radiate from his chest. Any other day she would have been mortified by her behavior, but not today. These weren't like the schoolyard kisses she had shared with Matthew. While her insides roiled with trepidation, an electric jolt ran from her belly to her knees. Then he wrapped his arms around her and drew her head to his shoulder. She allowed herself to be enfolded as she whispered his name into the fabric of his shirt.

"Alexander."

NINE

lexander came to his senses first and drew back. "Forgive me, Miss Harrison. I meant no disrespect. And I don't wish to take advantage of your situation, especially because we're in the midst of a war." He held her at arm's length.

"No disrespect taken, but I thought you were calling me 'Emily.'"

He lifted her chin with one finger. "You wish me to use your given name?"

"Yes, at least when we're alone...like now."

"Are you certain about this?" He wanted no misunderstanding.

"Yes, I'm quite certain we're alone." She whispered, smiling up at him.

"No," he said, flustered. "Are you saying you welcome my advances?"

She looked around with amusement. "There's no one here but you, Alexander. You must have been the one kissing me."

"Confound it, Emily. Take this seriously. I'm no farm boy playing games."

"I seemed to have changed my opinion of you. It is a woman's prerogative." She stretched up and kissed him fully on the mouth. "Maybe I'm falling in love with you."

"In love with me? Most days you act as though you don't even like me. This must be the champagne talking, not our prim Miss Harrison. Tomorrow you will feel differently and regret everything you have said and done tonight."

"I assure you I won't, but we should go in before we're seen."

His smile warmed her heart. "No one is home to see us. My mother and Aunt Augusta went to a neighbor's, and my father and Uncle Porter haven't returned from Front Royal."

"We are alone?" She sounded childlike, not like the kissable woman of the past few minutes.

"Have no fear, Emily." He tucked a curl behind her ear.

"I'm not afraid. But if no one is home, I would love to see the rest of the house, not just the public rooms on the first floor." She clasped her hands behind her back. "I'm curious as to what you keep behind closed doors."

He laughed, infected by her enthusiasm. "We'll take the back stairs to the gallery. With any luck the servants won't see us sneaking through the French doors."

"And tell Mrs. Bennington," she whispered, already skipping across dew-dampened ground. She grinned at him over her shoulder. "I don't think I could face her over breakfast if she knew I had been upstairs alone with you."

Alexander hurried to catch up with her on the path, and then they ran up the steps to the second floor without pausing. He peeked down the hall in both directions. "So far no one has seen us. There will be no wagging tongues tomorrow." He threw open the door to every guest room so she could peer inside. When he opened the carved, double doors of the last suite, Emily pranced inside like a yearling on the first warm day of spring.

"My goodness!" She exclaimed, pivoting in the center of the room. "I've never seen a grander room or one more spacious." She studied the room's appointments in awe before moving to the balcony. "There's even a chaise for sleeping outdoors on warm nights with a breakfast table overlooking half the Shenandoah Valley."

"Come now, Emily." Alexander joined her in the doorway. "Surely you've seen boudoirs more luxurious than this."

"I assure you I have not. And that is the most amazing piece of furniture I've ever seen." She pointed at the canopied bed, high off the floor and surrounded by thin muslin to allow breezes in and keep flying insects out. The bed created an enclosed nook with plump pillows, an embroidered coverlet, and a soft goose down tick. "How does one get on this thing?" Without waiting for an answer, she took a running leap and threw herself onto the bed.

"My father purchased the antique abroad, in Italy I believe."

Enjoying her naive exuberance, Alexander remained in the center of the room.

"A person would sleep well here. It's nothing like the narrow, lumpy cot I had in Ohio." She stretched out languidly like a cat, her arms above her head.

"Indeed, but there is a conventional way of getting on and off." He slid a three-step platform from under the bed skirt.

Sitting up, she leaned over the edge almost far enough to fall. "Is that so?" She ignored the steps and slid off the bed with a thump.

Alexander followed her around the room as she continued her perusal, offering a story to go with everything she touched. It felt as though he viewed the bookcase, upholstered easy chair, mahogany writing desk, and washstand for the first time too.

"Havilland china." Emily tapped the pitcher with her finger. "I recognized the pattern from Miss Turner's *Godey's Lady's Books*. Thank goodness I'm not a total boor."

"Knowledge of such matters is highly overrated, especially in wartime."

"There isn't one but two armoires, along with two highboys." She walked to the fireplace and ran a hand over the mahogany mantle. "And someone has laid a fire for the next cool evening. This room must be reserved for a very special guest—a person who travels with an enormous amount of clothing."

"The room isn't for guests, Emily. It's mine." He waited for her reaction.

She pivoted on the Oriental hearth rug, her face turning the color of a ripe tomato. "Goodness, Alexander! Why didn't you tell me sooner? I never would have invaded your privacy in such a fashion." Emily stood stock-still, as though paralyzed.

"You've invaded nothing. I'm pleased to show you my home. I've taken God's generosity for granted until viewing it through your eyes." He bowed from the waist. "I require no privacy—inspect all you like." Within a moment of uttering the words, he realized the folly of his statement.

Emily marched to one of the highboys and opened the carved doors, smiling mischievously. "My father only owned one suit, one hat, two pairs of work trousers, and half a dozen shirts. Let's see how many you have." Her eyes grew round at the number of coats, jackets, and waistcoats, with a stack of neatly pressed trousers on one side and piles of starched shirts on the other. There were winter woolens, summer cottons, starched linens, uncountable cravats, and at least a dozen pairs of braces hanging from pegs. "My, your wardrobe is vaster than the sum total my parents and I owned in our lifetimes." She stepped back, staring. "How in the world do you pick what to wear each day?" Emily ran her hand down a full-length robe. "Is this exquisite material Chinese silk? I've read about the fabric."

"My valet helps me make selections, and yes, that cloth was imported from the Orient."

She pressed the smooth silk to her cheek. "I would remain in this robe all day and refuse to get dressed."

"Emily, why don't we view the artwork in the morning room? There are some—"

"Please let me continue. I'm fascinated by your wardrobe." In the other armoire were more practical garments. Cotton shirts, cowhide breeches, tall leather boots, and a collection of straw hats perched on the top shelf. "Ah, clothes useful to a gentleman farmer." She was about to close the doors when one garment caught her eye—a long coat of butternut wool with distinctive gold braided epaulets adorning the shoulders.

"Are you sure you wouldn't care for some tea? That roast beef has left me thirsty." He crossed the room in three long strides, trying to draw her away in a gentle but deliberate manner.

She wouldn't budge. "This is a Confederate officer's uniform." She pulled out the garment for a better look.

Alexander walked back to the armoire as a sour taste rose up his throat. "It was a gift from an old friend—an impetus to induce me to join the Glorious Cause. I'm afraid it didn't work."

"I read somewhere that Richmond is short on uniforms for soldiers.

Perhaps the gentleman would like to have it back." She spoke in a soft voice.

"The former owner…is dead, Emily." Alexander shut the wardrobe and took hold of her hand. "Let's not talk of him or fabrics or clothes."

"Forgive me, Mr. Hunt." Suddenly she shook her head as though waking from a nap. "I have overstepped the boundaries as a governess, along with your hospitality. I will return to my room now." She curtsied with the innocence of a child. "Thank you for supper."

"You have no boundaries, but why don't we adjourn to—"

But she had already left the room and vanished down the steps. All thoughts of kisses in the garden were apparently forgotten.

Alexander shut his bedroom door as memories of Emily creeping from a barn in the dead of night returned. With the Federal Army camped not twenty miles away, had she been sneaking out to meet a Yankee lover? Shrouded in her cloak, alone but apparently unafraid, she hadn't seemed shy or helpless that night. He should have asked her to explain herself when he had the chance instead of falling prey to her sweetness and beauty.

What a cool, clever actress you are, Miss Harrison, but two can play your little game of intrigue.

His lips thinned to a narrow line as his jaw clenched. After pacing the length of the gallery for an hour, he still couldn't figure her out. Long ago he would have prayed for guidance, sending his troubles heavenward. But he'd since given up expecting help from God. With this conundrum as with all others, he was alone.

Exhausted, he finally crawled into bed for an hour of rest. But his troubled sleep did little to refresh or restore. Phantoms filled his dreams, those of the past and those yet to come. And a red-haired nymph, wearing a dark cloak in the dead of night, danced through them all.

Emily didn't sleep much that night either. She awoke in the dark with a start, momentarily confused by her surroundings. When she recalled each sweet kiss and tender touch, a blush filled her cheeks and warmth spread through her belly. Drawing the quilt up to her neck, she savored the memory of the most enchanting evening of her life. Alexander—tousle-haired, dreamy-eyed, and honey-lipped—a dream that had swept her up and carried her away. Emily laughed at the absurdity of kissing him in the garden as though they were characters from a dime novel. But Alexander wasn't a dream or a storybook character. He was a man of flesh and blood, one she had considered her enemy not long ago. *Did I really say I might be falling in love with him?* Remembering her heat-of-the-moment confession, she pulled the covers over her head.

"Never drink champagne again," she moaned aloud.

Then she recalled something odd he had said as well: *I don't wish to take advantage of your situation, especially because we're in the midst of a war.* What an odd comment from someone who bred horses far from the horrors of the battlefield. Matthew would never return to make her his bride, to build a home for them. She was no longer an engaged woman with a future. The fact they were in the midst of war was the reason she sought an evening of human companionship.

Throwing back the covers, she scampered to light the mantel lamp. But halfway across the floor she paused as a bolt of lightning shot through her head. Pressing her fingers to her temples, she slumped into a chair, the sharp pain a reminder of the champagne. Surprisingly, she felt no pangs of guilt for kissing Alexander at dinner or in the garden. Would this bold behavior become normal for her after a lifetime of proper decorum? She hoped not, but the man seemed to have changed everything.

"Alexander." She whispered his name in the dark bedroom, as though testing the sound of it for the first time. "Alexander Wesley Hunt," she said with a Southern drawl. "Alexander Wesley Hunt of the distinguished line dating back to the Mayflower Wesley Hunts." She said that in a British accent, making the words sound the way Miss Turner would have said them, and then giggled. Emily knew she was acting like a girl with her first schoolyard crush, but she hadn't felt like this about Matthew. She'd never experienced these emotions before.

Wrapping a shawl around her nightgown, she walked onto the verandah. No one stirred outdoors—even the servants were asleep at this hour. She climbed the steps to the upper gallery, treading mouse-like past each dark bedroom until arriving at the one she knew to be his. The French doors were ajar to catch the evening breeze, and a kerosene lamp had been left burning, it's wick trimmed low. Careful not to make a sound, she sidled to the doorway for a peek. She'd never seen a sleeping man before other than her father, who snored loud enough to wake neighbors a mile away.

But a view of Alexander curled under the embroidered coverlet, shrouded by muslin, was not to be. His room was empty. Only a tangle of bed sheets, wadded into a ball, indicated someone had been there earlier. Boldly, Emily crept into the room, knowing that she could be discovered and questioned at any moment. Then she would be fired and sent back to Ohio without references or prospects of employment. Yet his room drew her like a moth to a flame.

Is this what love did to a person—made one reckless enough to trespass into another's private domain without invitation? She glanced back at the open doors with a shiver, but she didn't run this time. Instead, she lifted the lamp from the table and padded over to the armoire where she'd seen the Oriental robe. What would silk feel like next to her skin? Was she brave enough to try it on? But when she reached for the robe, she noticed that the butternut uniform with brass trim and tassels was missing. Emily turned up the lamp and thumbed through the hangers to no avail. The gift from a dead childhood friend, an impetus to join the Glorious Cause, was gone.

An odd frisson of fear snaked up her spine. Closing the highboy, she returned the lamp to table and hurried from the room. She paused on the balcony, hidden from below by entwined grape vines, and clutched her shawl tightly around her shoulders. Darkness shrouded the world, the eastern sky yielding only a hint of dawn. In the garden, owls called to their mates, while bats swooped in their eternal quest for mosquitoes. Emily crept toward the top of the steps and then froze at the sound of a scraping latch. Squinting in the direction of the noise, Emily watched a tall, powerfully built man lead his horse from the barn. Clad in dark clothes and high boots, he stopped at the water trough. If he hadn't allowed his horse to drink, she never would have learned the identity of the nighttime rider. In the moonlight, she recognized the profile of Alexander and his horse, Phantom.

Where could he possibly be going at this hour? Is he bound for the bed of another woman because I permitted only a few kisses?

Emily leaned precariously over the rail and glimpsed the butternut uniform with shiny brass buttons and a strangely plumed hat. Had she not been infatuated and consumed with female jealousy, she might have drawn a different conclusion from his attire. She watched until he mounted his horse and rode away, vanishing into the inky night. Then she returned to her own modest accommodations, not wishing to remain in a rake's room another moment longer. As a tear slid down her cheek, she knew she had seen all she needed to see. How foolish she had been to believe he could love a woman like her.

"I'll teach you to sass your betters."

You have your secrets, Alexander, and I have mine. Now I won't feel so guilty with what I plan to do.

"Colonel, sir!" Captain Smith snapped a salute as his superior rode into a misty clearing in the forest.

Alexander was late. He had selected the midnight rendezvous at their last parting and now it was several hours past. As he reined in Phantom, forty rangers stopped what they were doing and gave him their attention. Those assembled were his best and most trusted. He wished he could greet each man personally, but time was precious. "Gentlemen, dawn lies within the hour and there is much to do, but I need a moment with Captain Smith." He offered his men a rare smile and then nodded at his second-in-command. He swung off his horse, handed the reins to the nearest soldier, and then walked to the smoldering fire. Nathan Smith followed at his heels. The men around the fire stepped back to give them some privacy.

"What have you learned, Captain?"

Smith handed him a cup of coffee. "Our scouts have been gathering intelligence for the past several days, sir. Meade's army has moved from Centerville and is camped outside Warrenton."

Alexander grinned at the news. "They are very close. The Yankees are coming to us this time."

"I believe they're planning to stay awhile, sir. A wagon train left the depot at Gainesville and is headed this way. Supply wagons have been coming down Warrenton Turnpike all day and night." Smith gestured toward the west with a gloved hand.

"You don't say. I haven't seen you this excited in a long time." The colonel slapped his adjutant on the back. "Are you telling me no troops guard this delectable string of wagons?" He sipped the steaming, bitter coffee.

"I'm afraid we're not that lucky, sir. They set up a cavalry screen for a ten-mile perimeter around their camp, and have cavalry riding alongside the wagons with infantry guards too."

"Is that so? Sounds like they expect us, Captain." He finished the coffee with another gulp.

"Yes, I believe they do. Why don't we fool 'em and ride up Pennsylvania Avenue in Washington to pay old Abe a social call? I doubt they're expecting us there."

Alexander scratched his new growth of chin whiskers as though pondering the idea. "Do our scouts have any idea what's in those wagons? We'll get mighty steamed up if we risk our lives for more bolts of calico."

Captain Smith grimaced at the memory of one of their less fortuitous raids. "They have horses for sure—fine cavalry stock and mules, lots of mules. Plus whatever's inside the covered wagons."

"How many animals?"

"At least a hundred. Maybe a hundred and fifty."

Alexander threw his coffee grounds into the fire and walked from the ring of light into the dense woods. Smith knew better than to follow him, but he didn't have long to wait. It never took the notorious Gray Wraith long to hatch a plan. That was one of the reasons Alexander was so good at what he did. Within minutes he emerged and began kicking dirt onto the fire. "Break camp, Captain. We're riding to Salem. We'll hit them tonight after dark."

No other explanations were necessary. Whatever they needed to know would be made clear to them when the time was right. After the last man swung into his saddle, they followed their caped leader to the west with complete faith. For several hours the rangers picked their way single file through spiny brambles and new growth forest, swatting at mosquitos and sweating from the heat and humidity. Finally, when the overgrown path joined a dirt road used by local farmers, conversation became once again possible.

Captain Smith brought his horse up to ride beside the colonel, leaving the men a short distance behind. "Did you ask her?"

"Ask who what, Captain?" Alexander knew what Smith inquired about, but he had no desire to discuss the matter.

"Ask that governess what the devil she was doing in Berryville. She was a long way from Hunt Farms, but maybe not so far from her Yankee friends."

Alexander shot him a cautionary glare. "No, I did not."

"Confound it, Alex, why not?" His adjutant leaned forward in his saddle, expecting an answer.

"Let it go, Nathan. The woman is no spy," he growled. Then he softened his tone to his most trusted friend. "The subject didn't come up because we were engaged in other activities."

This took Smith, not quite as quick-witted as Alexander, a moment to digest. "Good grief, man. You mean you took that *Yankee* to your bed?"

Alexander's arm shot out to grab Smith by the sleeve, nearly pulling him from his horse. "Watch your tongue regarding Miss Harrison or I'll thrash you right here. She is a lady, whether a Yankee or not."

Smith righted himself in the saddle. "Easy, man. I meant no disrespect. I was just curious as to what she was doing at that barn."

Alexander released his grip on Smith's sleeve. "Remember what curiosity did to the cat."

"What's gotten into you?" Smith glanced over his shoulder. "I haven't seen you this vexed since the schoolmarm caught you kissing Margaret O'Brien. Didn't she make you sit on the girls' side of the room for a week?" He reined his horse to a slower pace.

Alexander clenched down on his back molars. "We're not schoolboys anymore, Captain. I'll find out why she was in Berryville in due time. In the meantime, hold your tongue in matters regarding Miss Harrison. Now drop back and ride with the men." He spurred Phantom and surged ahead down the narrow road.

He had much to think about—the raid they would undertake this evening and that red-haired governess, the one he'd vowed to keep his distance from. His anger was more with himself than with his inquisitive adjutant. *Have I lost my mind?* With no end to the hostilities in sight, he was in no position to lose his heart to a woman. Defeat could come at any time from faulty information or a simple miscalculation of enemy strength. His troops were always outnumbered. Only their tactics of surprise, subterfuge, and quick escapes had allowed them to prevail thus far. If he were captured, he would be sent to a Northern prison or the gallows. He didn't need someone to worry about other than his aging parents. He ground his teeth at his reckless loss of control. Why had he kissed her at supper and again in the garden? Was the Quaker schoolteacher from Ohio simply a challenge? Had he become that much of a dissipated scoundrel? No. She had wormed her way into every waking thought as well as his dreams.

Yet the fact remained that she was a Yankee, raised in a household where slavery was an abomination, not a mere philosophical debate. How far would she go if her antislavery convictions were as strong as his love for the Glorious Cause?

Would she be willing to sacrifice as much as he was?

Would she be willing to sacrifice *him*?

More importantly, would she sacrifice his men? Alexander didn't fear of his own death, but he wouldn't jeopardize the lives of his rangers again. An image of the traitorous Rosalyn soured his stomach, banishing his pleasant thoughts of Emily. How stupid he had been. Some women would say or do anything to get their way. For the remainder of the ride to Salem, a single question plagued him. *Am I a fool to trust a woman again?*

The wagon train heading to the Union encampment from the Gainesville depot turned out to be well guarded indeed. However, Alexander's scouts reported troops and artillery mainly at the front and rear, leaving the center relatively unprotected. The undertaking was now possible, but still not easy. Even if they attacked from the side, teamsters driving the wagons could easily alert the regiments of troops. But the colonel knew just the diversion to use. He sent Dawson and eight men dressed in Federal uniforms to masquerade as a cavalry unit on provost duty. The imposters arrested the Union officers guarding the middle and ordered the wagons to fall out of line. Then the rangers surrounded the teamsters, tethered the horses and mules, and confiscated several wagonloads of food before the rest of the caravan knew a thing. And without a single shot being fired. The colonel then delivered the animals and provisions to the Confederate troops in the Shenandoah's foothills.

When the Gray Wraith's troops finally returned to one of their secret camps, they had much cause for celebration. They had relieved the Federal Army of approximately twelve thousand dollars' worth of replacement mounts and procured a feast of delicacies for their supper. That night they dined on smoked fish, fresh oranges, sweet potatoes, rice, and pickled beans. They passed around a bottle of brandy saved from the crate delivered to Confederate officers. Spirits soared among the men around the campfire…all but those of their leader.

Alexander picked at his food. When Captain Smith passed him the bottle of brandy, he refused to imbibe. Spirits only weakened his willpower and lowered his inhibitions. He knew too well what happened when he gave in to pleasure. Not wishing to eat, and not eager to sleep for fear a dark-haired siren or a red-haired governess would haunt his dreams, Alexander did something he hadn't done in a long time. He crept off into the forest, lowered himself to his knees, and began to pray.

No lives had been lost in today's mission. Divine Providence had again intervened, sparing the lives of his troops and the enemy alike. Divine Providence had bestowed favor on a man not entitled to grace. The least he could do was express his gratitude.

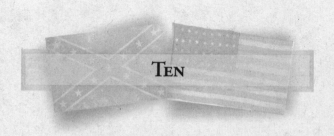

TEN

athan Smith was not a happy man either. Normally easy-going, he had been raised a gentleman. Although his family wasn't as prosperous as the colonel's, he had been denied little while growing up. And a gentleman learned never to show anger when it could be avoided. Rarely had any man raised his ire like this, and never had he been so angered by a woman.

Shortly after Alexander walked into the woods, Nathan rode out of camp. He didn't wait for the beef roasting on the spit, even though the aroma made his mouth water. He packed beans, salted pork, two oranges, and a full bottle of whiskey into his saddlebags despite the colonel's aversion to strong spirits in camp. *"Whiskey makes intelligent men do stupid things"* was the colonel's favorite expression. He allowed only fruit brandy or an occasional cask of wine. But what the colonel didn't know wouldn't hurt him. And right now the colonel wasn't exactly Nathan's favorite person.

He didn't appreciate being pulled from his saddle and threatened with a thrashing. What if one of the rangers had ridden up and overheard their argument? The last time he and Alexander resorted to fists during a disagreement they had been sixteen years old. They had vied for the affection of the same girl at a summer fair. The end result of their altercation had been two bloodied noses; one blackened eye—his, one split lip—Alexander's; and plenty of torn clothing that got them both in trouble. And the girl in the middle shared her picnic with Jake Finley, throwing salt into their wounds.

That woman had been a redhead too. *What is it about freckle-faced carrottops and Alex?* The Bennington governess was too skinny—all knobby knees and bony elbows with no bosom to speak of. Women should be soft and well-rounded.

Taking a hearty swig of whiskey, Captain Smith spurred his horse away from camp to let things cool off with the colonel. The foray in Salem couldn't have gone better. Now he needed to drive the image of Emily Harrison from his mind. He couldn't allow her to come between himself and the person he respected the most. How could a woman cause such problems—and a Yankee, no less? If women were ladies, they should look pretty, smell nice, and not talk too much. But this governess from Ohio was no lady, regardless of how much schooling she had. She came from a hardscrabble farm on the wrong side of the Ohio River. Her Quaker sodbuster father probably hadn't saved two dollars during his entire life.

Smith reined his horse to a walk and took another deep pull of whiskey. Not just a Yankee but a Quaker. Something jangled in his liquor-sodden mind, something he'd overheard at home. Their overseer spoke of someone stirring up the field hands with talk of freedom in the North. None of his house servants said much when he questioned them. He figured it was rumor. Now he wasn't so sure.

"Is that what you're up to, Miss Harrison?" he whispered to the enveloping darkness. "Showing slaves the path to Freedom Road? Why, you meddlesome little troublemaker. Don't you know what we do to your kind in Virginia? I would happily tie you to a tree and deliver the twenty lashes myself." Smith gritted his teeth, remembering Emily sneaking from a barn in the dead of night.

He spurred his horse and rode hard toward Middleburg, eager to spend some of his gold and celebrate. While the colonel had been occupied, he'd taken a thousand dollars off a Union teamster. He had no intention of giving it to the Confederate Treasury. He would buy time with the feistiest girl at Belinda's or play poker in the upstairs room reserved for favored customers. His friend should be with him tonight instead of pining over that governess. The colonel had once enjoyed a glass of well-aged bourbon or a game of cards in Middleburg. Now he wouldn't go near the place since that raven-haired woman had tricked him.

Smith clenched his jaw with the memory of Rosalyn. How he would have loved to get his hands around her creamy neck, but she'd left town before he could show her what happens to Yankee spies. He shifted in his saddle as the sleepy town of Middleburg came into view. Spurring his horse again, he rode hard to the freshly painted front door of Belinda's as the cheap whiskey churned in his belly.

Maybe Emily Harrison was an abolitionist who had come to fire up the slaves with tales of the land of plenty up North, and maybe she wasn't. Maybe she was a sister-under-the-skin to that other temptress, Rosalyn.

"Watch your tongue regarding Miss Harrison or I'll thrash you right here." Alexander's words still rang in his ear. He needed to be sure about this Yankee before casting aspersion on her sterling character. Nathan didn't have many friends. The few he had were now dead. Arguing with the colonel had vexed him more than he cared to admit. He would bide his time. He had to be certain. That scrawny governess had already caught the colonel's eye. He had to stop her before she wormed her way into his heart.

I'll find out what you're about, Miss Harrison. You can rest assured of that.

Emily roused from sleep at the sound of barking dogs and a sharp, piercing scream. Bolting upright in bed, she peered around the dark room but could discern nothing amiss. On a sweltering midsummer night the curtains barely stirred in the still air. Then she heard it again—a woman's shriek—and she knew with certainty it belonged to her mother.

Emily crept to the window overlooking the backyard and the river beyond. With a shaky hand she parted the muslin and peered down on horror she couldn't possibly understand. Men holding burning sticks high above their heads moved in and out of the shadows. Why didn't they just get the lanterns from the barn? More men arrived on horseback as people seemed to scurry in every direction at once. The whicker of a horse drew her to the side window, where a rider trampled her mother's prized flower garden. Who in the world had knocked down their picket fence? And why would her parents have a party the evening before the Sabbath?

Icy fingers of dread clawed her neck as she dropped the curtain back in place. This was no party. But Emily wasn't about to hide in her room like a baby. She dressed in the calico skirt and blouse her mother had pressed for church and crept down the stairs to the living room. "Mama?" she called. Padding to the front window, she called again, "Mama?" Through the wavy glass came only men's muffled shouts and the whinnies of frightened horses. Then she heard wood splintering as something crashed in the back of the house. Emily ran to the kitchen and found the door wide open—something her mother never allowed. *"Are you letting every moth, mosquito, and cricket take up residence?"* Her mother's favorite expression ran through her head as Emily began to shiver. Seeing the door gone from the hinges frightened her more than the men dancing in the backyard.

"Infernal slave-lover. Stinkin', lousy slave-lover." Loud voices pierced the night from the direction of the bonfire. *Slave-lover?* There were no slaves here. The preacher at the meeting house said there never had been slavery in Ohio. What were these men talking about?

Emily inhaled a deep breath and stepped onto the back porch. She heard her mother's voice but couldn't see her amid the smoke. Then she spotted her father by the barn with his arms tied around a tree. He looked to be giving the oak a big hug. While she watched, a fat man hit her father on the side of his head. The man wore a black hat pulled low on his forehead. "We'll show you what happens to meddlesome slave-lovin' abolitionists!" he yelled.

Bile rose up Emily's throat as the man pulled out a large hunting knife. Did he intend to stab her father? She stared, dreading what she would see but unable to look away. The man sliced through her father's shirt and yanked it down around his waist. He cut through the braces holding up his britches, too.

"Stop, I beg of you." Her mother's pleas pierced the din in the yard. "We didn't mean you people any harm. Please, leave us in peace."

"Didn't mean no harm?" Another man carried his burning stick toward the sound of her voice. Now Emily could see her mother clearly. She still wore her nightgown with her bare feet sticking out from beneath the hem. Mama never let people see her bare feet, insisting they were big as a mule's.

"Didn't mean no harm?" mimicked the man. "You steal someone's property, property he paid good money for, and you say you didn't mean no harm?" He moved the torch closer to her face.

"Go in the house, Martha!" hollered her father in a voice that was barely recognizable.

"Yeah, go in the house, *Martha,* unless you want some of this yourself." The fat man flourished his knife through the air.

"I beg of you, we're good Christians just trying to help the downtrodden," pleaded her mother. "Have some compassion, sir."

"Quakers make me sick. You only spout Scripture that suits you." The thin man shifted his torch close to her mother's face. She cringed helplessly from the flames. "Whatever happened to 'Thou shalt not steal'? What about 'Thou shalt not covet that which is thy neighbor's'?"

"We don't covet slaves, sir. Slavery is an abomination before the Lord."

Even with her tender years, Emily knew this was not the right thing to say.

"Nowhere in the Good Book is slavery described as an abomination!" he shouted. "Slaves are supposed to obey their masters." He loomed toward her mother again with his torch dangerously close. Martha Harrison could step back no further—a ring of men had closed in behind her.

"Martha, do as I say. Go in the house!" Her father's desperate pleas came too late.

The black-clad man dragged Mama by the arm to the same tree to which Papa had been tied. Emily yearned to holler; she wanted to make the men stop, but instead she could only watch from the porch, stupefied.

"I will teach you, Martha, what happens to thieves. Because that's all you two are—stinkin' thieves."

"Please, sir, we'll pay for your loss. Tell us how much those slaves were worth and we'll pay you."

The man with the hunting knife stepped forward, but the thin man didn't release his grasp on Mama's upper arm. "Pay us for what they're worth?" He laughed with cruel mockery. He turned his head to gaze left and right. "Look around, boys. Does this rundown farm look like they have fifteen hundred dollars sitting in a coffee can on the shelf?" Several men guffawed and slapped each other on the back.

"Because that's what the young buck and his wife were worth to the man who hired us. A thousand for the man and five hundred for the woman—more if she was carrying a youngin'. Then you're looking at eighteen hundred dollars for sure." He grabbed Mama's face by the chin. "You got that kind of money in your cookie jar, you Yankee abolitionist?"

Sobbing hysterically, Mama made no effort to knock away the man's hand.

"I didn't think so." Thin man sneered and shoved her mother backward. She would have fallen if the crowd hadn't prodded her upright.

"Stop pushing my mother!" A voice rose above the clamor created by rabid men and skittish horses. The voice belonged to Emily. "Stop that right now!"

For a moment they did stop and turned to stare. No one had noticed a little girl on the porch before. No light filtered from the house to illuminate the spot where she watched the terrifying goings-on. But Emily knew her father was in trouble and a horrible man was pushing her mother. No one ever pushed full-grown women.

Everyone looked at the skinny, red-haired little girl in faded calico and laughed.

Then things began to happen fast. The ring of men parted while the thin man tied her mother to the tree. Emily breathed easier when the other man shoved the hunting knife back into his belt. But her relief was short lived. A man on horseback handed down a whip, the likes of which she'd never seen before. Then the thin man started to whip her father. Emily heard the whip crack and her father scream. Never before had she heard such a pitiful sound. Again and again, he bellowed in agony each time the whip struck bare skin. No one tried to stop the man with the black hat. Instead onlookers formed a circle and shouted hateful words.

Emily ran from the porch, straight into the arms of a burly man in a long coat. He swung her up and tucked her under his arm like a feed sack. Her bare feet dangled a foot from the ground as he carried her back to the house. No matter how she pleaded or sobbed or pounded on him, the man held her tight and took her away from the devilish activity at the tree. On it continued—her father screaming, her mother weeping, the men shouting, the dogs barking.

There was nothing left for Emily to do but scream too. So that's what she did, until not another sound could issue from her throat...

"Miss Emily!"

Someone was calling her name and shaking her like a rag doll.

"Miss Emily, wake up!"

She opened one eye, terrified she would see the thin man or the fat man or the man in the heavy coat. But it was none of them—it was Lila. And she was shaking the stuffing out of her.

"Stop, Lila. I'm awake." Emily sat upright in bed, rubbing her eyes to drive away the horrific nightmare.

"Goodness, I thought the devil had you. I couldn't wake you up." Lila released Emily's shoulders and began dabbing her forehead with a hankerchief.

"Something just as bad," she replied. Emily peered around the room. Five black and two white faces were staring at her—all of them very concerned.

"That must have been quite a dream, Miss Harrison." The serene voice of Mrs. Bennington commanded her attention. She stepped forward and touched Emily's forearm. "Are you all right, my dear? Your screams scared the entire household."

"It sounded as though you were being murdered in your bed," added Mrs. Hunt.

"Nightmares can be quite vivid," said Mrs. Bennington, angling her sister a wry look.

"I apologize for creating such a fuss." Emily drew the quilt to her chin.

"Shall I have a cup of tea brought to you, or perhaps a brandy to settle your nerves?" asked Mrs. Hunt.

"I am fine, really. It was just a bad dream. And no to the brandy, Mrs. Hunt, but thank you just the same." She slowly regained her manners along with her composure.

The servants gave her another peculiar perusal before filing out of the room. Embarrassed, Emily could only imagine what she had been raving. Tears filled her eyes. The dream had been so vivid, so real, as if that horrible summer night in Marietta was happening all over again. She hadn't suffered that nightmare in years and had prayed she never would again.

Mrs. Bennington smoothed the hair away from her face as she probably had done to her own daughters over the years. "I'll have Lila stay the rest of the night with you. I'm just down the hall should you need me."

Who is supposed to be taking care of whom? Emily smiled at Mrs. Bennington. "Thank you, ma'am, but I'll be fine. It was only a bad dream."

After further murmurs of comfort, the ladies went back to their rooms. Lila remained, closing the door after everyone left. "Goodness, you can make a lot of noise for one skinny gal." She perched on the edge of Emily's bed.

Emily didn't want to go back to sleep. "It's nearly morning. Let's take our pillows and quilts out to the balcony to watch the sun rise."

Huddled close together without speaking, they waited for the first pink streaks to appear, followed by bands of rose and bright orange. The glorious sun rose above rolling pastures, heralding another perfect day in western Virginia. Emily was glad to see dawn because phantoms and ghosts would be held at bay. Lila didn't press her to talk about the nightmare.

As her friend dozed in the warm morning air with her head on Emily's shoulder, Emily had time to think…about the dream and about her behavior last night. She had practically thrown herself at Alexander. He was a slaver—no different than the men who had flogged her father and left him unconscious at the feet of her hysterical mother. Those bounty hunters had destroyed fences, trampled the vegetable patch, set fire to the barn, and then ridden to the river ford whooping and hollering.

Martha Harrison had not known what to do first, whether it was to try to put out the barn fire, comfort her eight-year-old daughter, who had just witnessed depraved brutality, or tend to her husband's lacerated back. Emily's parents never talked about the bounty hunters and forbade her to speak of them. With his wife's herbs and salves, Robert Harrison's back eventually healed, but he never worked his fields without a shirt or swam in the river again, no matter how hot the day. No one would bear witness to his shame. After that night, he was a changed man until the day he died.

Emily's thoughts rambled between her parents' ordeal to her fateful night with Alexander. The two events, separated by years and circumstances without parallel, somehow seemed connected. She felt ashamed, as though she'd betrayed her parents. Would they be proud of a daughter being held in the arms of a man without honor? She blushed as she remembered his smile, his touch across the dinner table, and their kisses in the bower. He was not the man for her no matter how special he made her feel. He had left in the middle of the night, dressed in the uniform of a dead soldier, for who knew where. This was all a game to him, one she could never win.

Virginia belles might have the leisure to ponder flirtations and indiscretions, but Emily had work to do. She gently slipped away from her sleeping friend and marched to the bath to scrub every inch of her skin until nearly raw. Then she dressed in a plain black skirt with white blouse and pinned her hair into a severe chignon. By the time she emerged from her dressing room, Lila had disappeared.

"Good morning, Mrs. Bennington," Emily said as she slipped into the chair opposite her employer in the dining room. "Forgive my tardiness, ma'am."

"I didn't know you were up. Breakfast seems to be served at all hours of the morning." Mrs. Bennington poured a cup of coffee and passed the carafe to Emily.

"Where are Mr. and Mrs. Hunt? Are they not up yet?"

"They are up and have gone out. A bit of a mishap, one might say. Two of their people seem to have misplaced themselves." Mrs. Bennington studied Emily over the rim of her cup, her expression never wavering.

Emily almost sprayed the table with coffee. She swallowed down the mouthful and bravely looked the woman in the eye. "Two people are missing? Who are they?"

"A young widow and her child. The woman worked as a field hand, so I doubt you would have run into her."

I'm about as subtle as a starving man at a banquet. Maybe my next job should be a professional poker player on a riverboat. Emily glanced at the door, expecting Robert E. Lee himself to appear and drag her off to prison...or slave-catchers like those who had crossed the Ohio River to tie her to the nearest tree. "A young woman and child? Perhaps they're on an errand to a neighboring plantation. Maybe they're delivering garden produce or baked goods from the kitchen."

"I'm sure it's something like that. Rebecca asked the house servants if they had any ideas. She is concerned about the young woman. There have been skirmishes in the area, with deserters from both sides roaming the countryside." Mrs. Bennington paused, as if waiting for some reaction, but Emily didn't respond.

"Apparently the woman has been unhappy since her husband died last spring. If she has run off, she could cross paths with dangerous bounty hunters. Who knows what kind of unsavory people are out there?"

"I'm sure she will turn up." Emily reached for a biscuit, forcing herself to swallow a small piece.

"Do you think so? Something tells me the Hunts will never see Annabelle and little Gabriel again. We can only pray she's in a safe place." Mrs. Bennington drained her coffee and set down the cup with a clatter, scrutinizing Emily with her lovely green eyes.

Emily set down the biscuit and folded her hands in her lap, unable to meet the gaze of the woman who had sheltered her, trusted her, and befriended her. If Mrs. Bennington had even a shred of doubt, she didn't any longer.

"Perhaps we have disrupted the Hunt household enough." She set her fork on the side of her plate. "We shouldn't overstay our welcome. Besides, I'm eager for Porter to return home, where he'll keep regular hours. There'll be quite a lot for him to do in Martinsburg with doctors running off to join the army." Mrs. Bennington rose from the table and laid her small white hand on Emily's shoulder. "Will you help me pack my things?"

"Of course." Emily downed her coffee and struggled to her feet.

"Before you come upstairs, please inform the Amites of our plans to leave as soon as possible. I've already sent a message to Porter at the hospital."

Emily looked into the woman's unruffled face and forced a smile. "Yes, ma'am. I'll tell Matilde and then join you in your suite."

"Thank you." She swept from the room, leaving a cloud of lavender behind.

I am so undeserving of this woman's kindness and protection. Rebecca Hunt is her sister, her blood kin, while I'm only an employee. If it were the last thing she did, Emily would find a way to make this up to her employer.

She knew Mrs. Bennington knew she was taking a thief back to Martinsburg. For that Emily was grateful, but she couldn't wait to be gone from Hunt Farms.

"They're out looking for Annabelle and Gabriel."

Startled, Emily turned to find Lila right behind her. She'd been so preoccupied with packing she hadn't heard her come in. "I know," she said quietly. "Well, they won't find them."

"No, they won't, but Mr. Hunt is in a lather."

"He has lots of other slaves." She focused on folding undergarments and setting them in the trunk.

"He's in a lather because young Mr. Hunt has gone off again. 'He's never around when I need him,' I heard him tell William. He searched for Annabelle all day yesterday. William said Mr. Hunt won't hire slave-catchers since he can't trust them."

Emily huffed out her breath. "Perhaps you and I shouldn't concern ourselves with the doings of this plantation so much. We'll be leaving today. By the way, have you seen my gold locket? I can't remember when I took it off, and I can't find it anywhere."

"No, I haven't seen it." Lila wouldn't be put off so easily. "William knows what we did," she whispered.

"*What?*" Emily's voiced cracked, betraying her overwrought nerves. William was Alexander's trusted personal employee.

"William knows what you and I and Jack did on the way to Martinsburg." She explained as though Emily were a simpleton.

"How do you know that, Lila?"

"Because he told me." Lila began folding the skirts and blouses Emily had strewn across the bed.

Emily had enough of Lila's evasiveness and grabbed her by the shoulders. "Tell me what you know."

Lila sat on the bed and crossed her arms. "William followed us when we left here. He watched us take the turnoff to Berryville."

"Why would he do that?" Emily slumped into a chair, finding it difficult to breathe.

"Because you picked Jack over him and he doesn't trust that rascal. And because..." Lila's voice faltered as she lost some of her exasperating self-confidence. "William has had his eye on me since...well, forever." Lila stared at a flower on the wallpaper, chewing her lip.

"Is that so? Is there something wrong with the man? You know, not quite right?" She tapped her temple with her index finger.

Lila shot her a mischievous look. "He probably got stung by the same bug that bit Mr. Hunt." She waited for Emily to catch her meaning.

But Emily said nothing as she returned to the bureau drawers.

Lila followed at her heels. "Mr. Hunt told William to look after you while he was gone. That's the other reason why he followed us. And he told me about your dining on the terrace and then taking a moonlit stroll in the garden with Mr. Hunt."

"How could he possibly know that?" Emily demanded.

"I asked him that. William said there wasn't much that went on he didn't know about." Lila pulled the stack of underpinnings from Emily's hands. "Why didn't you tell me about Mr. Hunt? I didn't know you were sweet on him. I thought you hated him. You sure had me fooled." She gave Emily a sidelong perusal.

"Apparently I fooled myself, but don't change the subject. What about William? Will he turn us in for aiding runaways? We could land in a lot of trouble."

"No." Lila answered without a moment's hesitation. "He said he felt sorry for Annabelle because she was so unhappy. But he doesn't want to see more people disappearing. He said the Hunts are good people, and you should do your work anywhere but here." Slamming the trunk lid, Lila put her hands on her hips.

"That won't be a problem. We're leaving."

"I told him I wouldn't help you at Hunt Farms. He said fair enough." Then Lila began waltzing around the bedroom as though at a ball. "Beatrice said he always asks questions about me whenever he's in the kitchen. He's been real nice to my ma, and Beatrice saw him talking to my pa." Lila clamped her hand over her mouth to stop rambling.

"Why, Lila Amite. If I didn't know better, I would think you were sweet on William." Emily feigned a Southern drawl.

"Maybe I am a little...curious. But it won't do me a bit of good

because we're going back to Martinsburg today. I don't know when I'll
see him again." She plopped down on the bed and dropped her head
into her hands.

Emily plunked down beside her and settled her arm around her
shoulders. *I don't know when I'll see Alexander again,* she thought. And
somehow, she wasn't quite so happy about leaving Hunt Farms.

ELEVEN

The infamous Gray Wraith and his Rebel Rangers were a perfect terror to the Yankees. They moved silently under the cover of night, struck swiftly, and usually took only what they could carry. They fed the Confederate Treasury with a steady stream of gold and greenbacks, and the cavalry with replacement horses for those killed in battle. They knew the Shenandoah Valley and the flatlands to the east like the backs of their hands. The rangers were familiar with every road, bridle path, farm trace, bridge, river ford, and observation point in a six-county radius. The men had grown up in these remote valleys, hunting and fishing in the isolated bogs and ponds. They could creep up on an enemy camp, eavesdrop on a conversation, and leave with the information without the pickets hearing more than a rustle of leaves.

The press loved their larger-than-life reputation. Northern newspapers described them as rogues operating within the limits of decent society. The rangers stretched but didn't break wartime codes and traditions, unlike the bushwhackers of Missouri, whose barbarous acts had been described in detail across the country. Even Northerners viewed them more as romantic Robin Hoods than dangerous desperados like their Western counterparts. Women pored over their bloodless exploits as they would yellow-backed novels, with any reproach directed at the Union Army's inability to catch them.

Southern papers portrayed them as dashing cavalrymen, living lives filled with romantic intrigue. Many a belle fell asleep dreaming of the notorious Gray Wraith carrying her away on his magnificent white steed. Local townsfolk willingly fed and sheltered the rangers, considering it their duty to the war effort in the same vein as knitting socks or rolling bandages for the hospitals.

Prior to the war, many wealthy rangers had failed to develop any self-discipline whatsoever. Because slaves did most of the work, these honorable gentlemen grew to manhood with time and money on their hands. Their parents seldom frowned on indolence. It was accepted for these upper-class gentlemen to spend their days drinking, racing horses, chasing women, and spending money lavishly. Although most were churchgoing men, their behavior would have shocked most Northern Christians.

Gambling was widely accepted among Alexander's peers. They bet on everything from palmetto bug races to the outcome of an election to who would be appointed the next Yankee commander. Almost every tavern provided card games and billiards in which debts of thousands of dollars were amassed in a single evening. Professional gamblers roved through Southern towns stripping more than one plantation heir of a significant part of his fortune.

Although most churches frowned on drinking, pastors often overlooked indulgence by the rich. Some plantation masters sipped something alcoholic from sunup to sundown, remaining in a mildly inebriated blur. The blue-blooded aristocracy was allowed leeway in their romantic pursuits too. Women were expected to remain virtuous until marriage but men were not. Brothels could be found in most Southern towns, unheard of in New England villages.

The rangers, many from aristocratic families, carried their undisciplined ways into their brand of cavalry. Whereas the regular Confederate Army fought battles separated by boring stretches of camp life, rangers could stalk their enemy, strike an unprotected underbelly, and still stay close to home. They enjoyed adventure and glory while avoiding the tedium of camp life. Only the Gray Wraith prevented them from disintegrating into a mob of plunderers.

Rebecca Hunt's strong Quaker upbringing didn't permit dissipated behavior in the Hunt household. Although she served spirits at dinner parties or balls at the insistence of James, drunkenness wasn't tolerated. Neither was gambling, swearing, and certainly not visiting fancy houses. Alexander didn't have much trouble growing up under her rules. Although newspaper accounts depicted the Gray Wraith as the leader of a band of rakes, nothing was further from the truth. His goal was simple: assist the beleaguered Confederacy to the best of his abilities. He harassed the Union Army by disrupting communications and thereby dividing their strength before a battle. He aimed to appropriate every provision he could from their railroads and supply wagons without personal advancement or financial gain. But each day it grew harder to maintain discipline among his troops. With increasing frequency he noticed soldiers with fancy clothing, new expensive weaponry, and flashing rolls of bank notes around the campfire.

On this summer day, Alexander wasn't a happy man. Lately his satisfaction from serving the Confederacy had become tangled with conflicting emotions. It didn't help that he was in love with a Unionist. He'd finally acknowledged to himself that he'd been smitten by a Yankee schoolteacher from Ohio—one who may have stolen away to meet another man in Berryville. Why had she responded to his kisses if she loved someone else? Fool. He was a stupid fool. Alexander knew only too well that a woman could feign passion she didn't feel. Rosalyn had professed love for him while plotting the deaths of his soldiers. Refusing to listen to Nathan's warnings, Alexander desperately wanted to believe Emily wasn't like Rosalyn. Yet, in his heart, he knew the truth. Why had he allowed himself to become caught in her web of deceit?

Alexander ground his teeth. Once he returned to Front Royal, he would demand to know whom she'd met that night in Berryville. He would give her a chance to explain her behavior. But one thing was certain—she must never learn his identity or what he did when he left Hunt Farms. He would never risk the safety of his rangers again.

He rode hard to meet Smith and Ellsworth at a small farm outside of Warrenton. The reunion went well, his argument with Nathan long forgotten. Because his rangers had attracted so much attention lately, Alexander dismissed his troops for this particular sortie. Armed with reports from well-paid scouts, they had reliable information on the movement of enemy troops in the Shenandoah Valley. Wearing Federal uniforms procured in their last raid, the three men slipped through Union lines and headed for the telegraph office at the railroad depot.

"Good afternoon, sir. What news have you heard?" asked the colonel, disguising his Southern accent.

"Not much, sir." The telegraph operator barely glanced up from his keys. "Only that that confounded Wraith marauds on this side of the mountains with a cavalry of two hundred."

"You don't say." Smiling, the colonel sank into the opposite chair. Smith and Ellsworth lounged against a wall in the small, cramped office.

"I do say, sir. That madman is cutting lines, tearing up train tracks, burning bridges, and taking hostages as we speak. He's nothing but a ruthless guerrilla. If he were here right now, I would show him what we do to guerrillas like him and Quantrill." In a surprising show of bravado, the paunchy operator drew a long-barreled Colt from his drawer. He flourished it before the nose of the curious, bearded officer.

"He's taking hostages? Are you sure about that, sir?" The colonel knew his notoriety went far and wide, yet false reports of callousness raised his ire like nothing else.

"Yes, sir. He stopped a trainload of invalid soldiers and civilian merchants with women and children. He held the train captive for hours until ransoms could be paid for the passengers' release."

A muscle twitched in the colonel's jaw, but he kept his voice steady. "When did all this take place?"

"Yesterday. The Gray Wraith released the train just this morning after he got paid his blood money."

"Is that so?" The colonel leaned close to the barrel of the revolver. Then, faster than the operator could blink, Alexander snatched the weapon from his hand, spun it around, and stuck it in his belt. "If I was in Winchester this morning, how could I possibly be here in Warrenton talking to you now?"

The operator pondered for a moment and then paled considerably. He drew in an uneasy breath. "I see your point, sir. I didn't mean any disrespect."

"Then I suggest you not repeat tall tales to complete strangers." Lowering his voice to a whisper, Alexander loomed inches from the man's face. "In the meantime, kindly hand over your code book and recent dispatches to my associate." He nodded in the direction of Ellsworth.

Paralyzed with fear, the operator stared mutely at the legendary rebel. Smith and Ellsworth cocked their revolvers. "Did you not hear the man?" barked Smith.

"Yes, sir." The operator snapped out of his trance and provided Ellsworth with everything necessary to transmit erroneous information to telegraph offices in every direction.

The three rangers, without firing a shot, sent the Union Army on a goose chase of epic proportions. It was all in a good day's work, but it gave Alexander little pleasure anymore.

"Slow down, Miss Emily," Lila pleaded, hanging tightly to the side of the wagon.

"If we slow down, we'll never make it to Berryville by dark." Emily didn't take her attention off the strong draft horse careening down the narrow road at breakneck speed. "And I have no desire to spend a moonless night in these woods." She bobbed her head toward the overgrown swamp, filled with snakes and insects of every size and shape. "That wouldn't make for a comfortable evening. We couldn't move ten feet into these stunted pines, thorny Hawthorne bushes, and blackberry briars."

Lila gazed into dense, moss-hung branches and nodded. "I agree, but if we throw a wheel, we'll have a hard time explaining why we're stuck out here. This is *not* the road back from Harper's Ferry."

Emily tugged on the reins, slowing the team. "You're right. I'm just eager to be done with this. Dr. Bennington said the Union Army has taken Winchester and are encamped all around it. That's not far from here." A shudder ran from her shoulders to her feet.

Lila gave her an odd look. "Why are you so worried about running into Yankees? I thought you were a Yankee yourself."

"I don't wish to encounter soldiers from either side. Both would demand explanations as to what we're doing out here. And the less said about that, the better."

"We wouldn't fool anyone that you're a lady out for a drive with her personal maid," huffed Lila. "Not when you insist on driving the wagon yourself. No mistress would ever do such a thing."

"That's another reason to finish and head back to Martinsburg, but you have a point." Emily begrudgingly handed the reins to Lila.

It wasn't the possibility of running into Union pickets or Confederate scouts that concerned Emily. Her steady stream of lies to Porter and Augusta Bennington had begun to take their toll. She also worried about involving Lila in her personal mission, and that the amount of food they gave the runaways wouldn't be adequate for their trip north. When the wagon rounded the final curve and began the steep descent into the barnyard, Emily breathed a sigh of relief. Both women were so tired they didn't notice trodden weeds or fresh hoof prints in the dirt.

Emily jumped from the wagon and hurried into the barn, leaving the door ajar in order to see.

"Hello? Hello?" she repeated. "I am Miss Harrison from Martinsburg. I received a message from Mr. and Mrs. Brent." With the name of the previous safe house, she heard a slight rustle in the dark. Emily squinted, trying to focus in the thin light. To her surprise, an ancient black man with pure white hair and a deeply creased face stepped from behind the bales.

"Yes'm, I'm Jacob and this is my wife, Ruth." The man had to be eighty if he was a day.

"How do you do?" Emily watched as he helped an equally old woman to her feet. Her arthritic fingers curled around a walking stick, and a white film covered her right eye. Seldom did slaves their age wish to make the journey to a new life in an unknown land. The woman gazed at Emily for a long moment.

As though reading her mind, Jacob explained, "They were gonna split us up. Send me to Richmond to be the daughter's driver and not let my wife come with me." He patted Ruth's hand with tenderness.

"Nobody gonna split us up 'cept the Lord in death. And that only be for a short while." When the barn door opened, Jacob moved protectively in front of Ruth.

Lila led the Percheron inside. "Looks like rain. He might break loose and bolt if we get thunder." Lila stole sidelong glances at the couple as she cross-tied the horse and broke open two bales of hay.

The couple gawked at the well-dressed black woman.

"S'pose you haven't seen too many free people of color. Where y'all from?" Lila used country dialect to try to put them at ease.

"We've seen freemen, but none looked like you." Jacob rubbed his bristly chin. "We escaped a tobacco farm in the Carolinas."

Emily still wasn't sure what to say in these situations. Her parents never prepared her for face-to-face encounters. "This is my helper and friend, Miss Amite. We're both recently from Martinsburg, but formerly of Parkersburg in the western counties of Virginia." The couple turned their attention from Lila back to her, their expressions increasingly anxious.

"Now that you have made proper introductions, we can all fill out our dance cards for the ball later," Lila whispered under her breath to Emily and rolled her eyes. "In the meantime I'll fill the water buckets."

Emily wrinkled her face into a scowl. "Speaking of which, I had better start dinner." She headed for the wagon with Lila on her heels.

"I'll fix dinner after I get water. You can make our guests comfortable for the night." Lila set down the buckets and retrieved the hamper from the wagon.

"Don't be silly, Lila. You already unhitched and fed the horse, so it's my job to cook. We split work down the middle, remember?" Emily pulled the hamper from Lila's hand.

"The horse was no trouble. I insist you let me make supper." Lila huffed like a riled hen.

"What will they think if I let you do all the work?" Emily spoke softly so the runaways wouldn't hear.

"Would it better be if they thought a white woman was trying to poison them?" Lila tugged at the hamper straps with both hands.

"Poison them? I can cook just as well as you." Emily straightened her spine to be half a head taller than Lila, therefore gaining an illusory advantage.

"You certainly cannot cook better than me. You nearly burned my mother's kitchen to the ground on Bennington Island."

"I did *not* nearly burn your mother's..." Emily's voice trailed off when she noticed the couple in the doorway. They stared as though facing two madwomen.

Then Ruth broke into a laugh, revealing a mouth with few lower teeth. "Why don't y'all let me do the cookin' since I've had the most practice?" Clucking her tongue, she walked to Emily and held out her hand.

"Thank you, Ruth." Emily gave the woman the hamper.

Assessing Lila's fashionable outfit once more, Ruth made another clucking sound as she crossed the barnyard toward her husband. Jacob had already uncovered a fire pit and limped off to find kindling.

"If we're not careful, they're going to run away from *us*," Emily said to Lila as they each picked up a water bucket. Soon they had all gathered enough twigs and branches for a cook fire.

Ruth proved to be the best choice of chefs. In no time, she diced an onion for the pot of pinto beans that had been soaking all day. Jacob picked a basket of greens behind the barn, which Ruth wilted atop the beans as they simmered. Lila gathered windfall apples beneath a scraggly tree, while Emily set out a loaf of Johnnycake and jar of sweet tea from the hamper. An hour later, Jacob carried the pot inside the barn and they settled themselves on the floor.

Jacob bowed his head. "Lord, thank You for brungin' us thus far and for the meal we are 'bout to partake."

After everyone murmured "Amen," Lila filled bowls with the steaming beans. Emily watched the couple as they ate, slowly due to poor teeth. They talked little, quaking nervously each time a bird stirred in a rafter nest or the wind whistled through cracks between the boards. Emily gave up trying to initiate conversation and ate in quiet companionship. She had been a silly, naive woman to think runaways, who had lived vastly different lives, would find any common ground with her.

As the moon appeared low in the eastern sky, Jacob doused the fire, Lila washed the tin plates, and Emily repacked the wagon. Then Jacob helped Ruth up onto the hay bales and covered her with a tattered patchwork quilt. "God bless you, miss," he said to Emily.

"And you. Sleep easy, Jacob. You're safe here."

He met her eye, his eyes yellowed from age. "No one is safe in this world. Our future is in God's hands, but I thank ya just the same." He crawled up next to his wife, propped their sack of garments for a pillow and promptly fell asleep.

Truer words were never spoken. Emily listened to their muffled snores long into the night, envious of the trust and love they shared. They had made an irrevocable decision. They would forge ahead, risking everything to stay together. Wisdom must come with age. This couple had no need to lie or deceive each other. No need to be anything other than what they were. Without knowing the future or their fate, they trusted the Lord and rested in the sweet shelter of the other's love. Nothing else in the world seemed quite as precious as that.

At first light Lila fed the horses, Emily hitched the wagon, and the foursome left the Berryville barn. Emily felt oddly tranquil, as though the couple were already safely in Pennsylvania and she were home in bed. Her serenity was misguided at best, because Alexander's valet knew about this location. Suddenly, a horse and rider appeared as the steep path from the barn joined the road. The Thoroughbred reared and pranced, startled by the huge Percheron.

The man struggled to settle his horse. "Why, you're Miss Harrison, are you not? What a surprise. I've had my eye on this place hoping to catch some Yankee deserters."

"I am, sir," she sputtered. "But I'm afraid you have me at a disadvantage." Emily couldn't place the fastidiously dressed man with tall equestrian boots. As he apparently knew her, she prayed to make the connection before saying something foolish.

"Captain Nathan Smith of Red Oak, fourteen miles to the west. My family has a plantation outside of Winchester." He swept off his hat, revealing a thick head of blond hair tied back with a leather cord. With broad shoulders, a short beard, and a well-trimmed moustache, he wore the expression of a man pleased with himself. "A pleasure to see you again, Miss Harrison."

Emily vaguely remembered their acquaintance. "Could it have been the June ball at Hunt Farms where we met, sir?" She tried to sound relaxed even as her gut roiled. This man was one of Alexander's rich, slaver friends. Huddled in the storage box behind the seat were two runaway slaves, and the hamper and cooking pots bounced around in the back of the wagon. That fact alone might draw Captain Smith's attention.

"Indeed, it was." Smith stared at Lila for a long moment before looking again at Emily. "Yes, the June ball. I'm sure of it. I don't believe you honored me with a dance, Miss Harrison." Leaning from the saddle, Smith stretched out his hand. "You must promise to rectify that on the next occasion."

Emily stared at his hand until Lila nudged her with a foot. "Of course, Mr. Smith." Emily leaned forward to shake.

Instead of shaking, he kissed the back of her gloved fingers. "I look forward to that dance and will hold you to your promise."

"You must be a friend of Mr. Hunt." Emily tugged her hand back.

"Yes, for a very long time. Since we were young boys." Though Smith smiled, his eyes remained cold. "There is little happening in Alex's life that I'm not a part of or at least aware of."

Emily flushed but refused to let this rooster nettle her. "Is that so? Truly, I would think a man would have plenty in his own life to occupy his attention." Again, Lila's foot tapped hers in warning, but Emily paid no heed.

His laughter resembled a snort. "Of course, I only meant we had much in common and took each other into confidences." Smith fastened his focus on Lila once more.

"Tell me, Miss Harrison. Why are you driving the wagon while your slave sits at her ease watching the scenery?"

Lila shrank lower on the bench beside her. "Miss Amite is not my slave, Mr. Smith," said Emily. "She is a free woman of color. I would never own a slave." Emily didn't try to hide her repugnance.

"Oh, that's right. I remember Alexander mentioning you were from the North." He uttered the last word as though spitting poison. "Pray tell, what is a Yankee woman doing on a back road in Clarke County, with the Union Army camped not ten miles away?" His glare was frightening. All cordial pretention had disappeared.

Emily stiffened with alarm. He suspected her of spying? If he thought her a Union spy, he might search the wagon and discover the elderly couple. Of course, people who assisted runaways were fined a thousand dollars and jailed for six months, but spies were hanged. That thought crossed her mind in the seconds following Smith's insinuation. But she couldn't let him send Jacob and Ruth back to slavery.

"I know nothing of the whereabouts of Union camps, sir. I am running errands for Dr. Porter Bennington of Martinsburg. We came from Harper's Ferry depot, where we picked up medical supplies. Now we're on our way to Front Royal's hospital. We spent the night here because we were waylaid and didn't reach our destination by nightfall. You might not be aware, but Dr. Bennington is a physician—"

"I know who Porter Bennington is," he snapped with impatience. "I just can't believe he would send his governess and a maid to deliver anything this close to enemy lines."

He was right. Dr. Bennington never would. Now that Winchester had fallen into Federal control, he wouldn't allow her to get this close to the fighting. "I'm not sure he realizes. You know Dr. Bennington. All he thinks about are his patients. That's why Miss Amite and I volunteered to pick up the shipment." Emily beamed a smile and prayed it didn't look as false as it felt.

"Yes, well…" he stammered. "Because this is a day for good deeds, I will accompany you to Front Royal to assure your safety."

"But you are dressed as a Confederate soldier, sir. You'll be shot on sight by Union pickets. We have the white smocks of the Sanitary Commission." Emily dug in her valise by her feet and pulled out a garment. "We'll be able to cross the lines unimpeded while wearing these." She offered another bright smile.

Lighting a cheroot, Smith took a great deal of time to mull that over. "Well, Miss Harrison, I would be remiss in light of your friendship with Alexander if I don't accompany you at least part of the way." He grabbed the halter of her horse as the wagon began to lurch forward, and then he pulled the reins from her hands.

Emily blushed a shade of scarlet. Had Alexander discussed her with this peacock, perhaps over an evening cigar? "As you wish, sir." Her new beau spread gossip after a few kisses in the garden? She would use that to her advantage.

After several miles, Captain Smith tossed the Percheron's reins to Lila. "Good day to you, Miss Harrison. I look forward to our next meeting." He tipped his hat, spurred his horse, and rode off in a cloud of dust.

Lila exhaled an audible sigh. "Whew, you sure do have the gift of gab. That man was too confused by your story not to believe you. But I didn't like the way he looked at you or at me," she added in a soft voice. "I know what that look means. My mama warned me about bad intentions before I even knew what went on between men and women. You had better give that dandy a wide berth."

"I'm not sure how much he believed." Emily dabbed her forehead with a handkerchief as a shiver ran up her spine and took back the reins. "But don't worry. I intend to stay far away from Nathan Smith of Red Oak Plantation."

Soon her thoughts drifted to a tall man with gray eyes, strong hands, and warm lips she would never forget. Their moonlit supper on the terrace had meant something to her. She had fantasized about a new life in which she was cherished and loved. She was hopelessly misguided—hopeless and helpless to do anything about it.

If she hadn't been pining for love and romance, she never would have turned north at the crossroads heading toward Charles Town. In keeping with the tale she'd spun, she would have headed toward Front Royal until absolutely certain the audacious captain was long gone. But Emily's mind had been on Alexander and little else.

The cocky Confederate officer, astride his stallion, followed the two women for several miles. He didn't know what to make of the situation. He hadn't believed a word Emily had said, yet if on the outside chance she was telling the truth, any affront would get quickly back to the colonel. When their wagon turned north instead of south toward Front Royal, he spat on the ground. "You lying Yankee." Seething, Smith ground down on his back teeth.

"I will enjoy seeing you brought to your knees, Miss Harrison, along with your black friend who fancies herself a lady. This might prove rather interesting, indeed."

TWELVE

*A*unt Augusta? Aunt Augusta!"

Mrs. Bennington awoke in her chaise in the back sunroom. "Alexander, what a pleasure to see you in Martinsburg," she said. "Joshua built a fire in the stove on this unusually cool day, and I'm afraid I nodded off." Sitting up, she stretched out her arms to him.

"The pleasure is mine, dear aunt." He kissed her cheek and rubbed her hands between his.

"Where are James and Rebecca?" She peered around his shoulder. "Are your parents with you?"

"No, ma'am. I rode up alone just to see you."

"Do you think you can fool me so easily?" Augusta rose to her feet and rang the bell for the maid. "I believe you came to see Miss Harrison." She tapped one elegant finger against her cheek. "But I'm always glad to see you. Let's have tea while you tell me the news."

Alexander plopped down in a chair near hers and stretched out his long legs. "You know me too well."

"I doubt that, nephew. Anyway, Emily walked to town on some errands and to get some air. The poor thing read to me all afternoon until I yawned rudely in the middle of her book." Her smile erased years from her face. "Since we've been home she taught me the game of hearts and I've taught her to play whist. I don't know what I would do without her. Porter insists on keeping the girls in Europe until this matter is settled."

"This *matter* is a war, dear Aunt. Uncle Porter is wise to protect his daughters. I had to evade several Union patrols on my way here. That is part of the reason why I came. Martinsburg will soon be in Federal control. There's no way around it. Neither Robert E. Lee nor anyone else can spare the troops to protect the city."

"But the railroad is how we get medical supplies for Porter's practice." Augusta wrung her hands.

"That's exactly why the Yanks want this area. And there's not much we can do to stop them, considering local sentiments."

Augusta nodded her head gravely. "I've heard the same news from Porter. Many of the town's residents show Union loyalties. On the outlying farms, more than half of the families want to return to the Union. They are too poor to have ever owned slaves in the first place. Because the crops are being destroyed by constant skirmishes, their survival depends on peace being restored."

"I heard that a vote will soon be taken in the statehouse. If rumors are true, counties west of the Alleghenies and here along the Potomac will leave the Confederacy." Alexander couldn't hide his sorrow.

"What? I can't believe it." Augusta slumped onto the chaise.

"That's what is being reported in the newspapers. These counties will secede from Virginia and form a new Union state, West Virginia." Alexander began to pace the room. "If that happens, you and Uncle Porter cannot remain in Martinsburg. You won't be safe from Yankee reprisals. You must come to Hunt Farms for the duration of the war. In fact, my parents insist that you not wait any longer." He crossed the room and took hold of Augusta's hands. "Come back with me now and stay for Christmas. Then we can see what happens after the vote."

"What about Parkersburg and our dear little island? Will they also return to the Union?"

"Most assuredly if the other western counties vote to secede."

"I must talk this over with your uncle. Porter will be heartbroken." She closed her eyes, fighting back tears.

"I stopped at his office first and have already spoken with him. Uncle Porter is packing his equipment. He asked me to be the one to tell you."

"Then it is decided." Augusta's voice faltered as she rose to her feet. "Now, I must see about dinner. It won't do to serve bacon and boiled potatoes when my favorite nephew comes to call." She sounded normal, but her gait suggested the news had grieved her sorely. At the door she paused. "I cannot comprehend this, Alexander. The world seems to be spinning out of control. When it finally stops, nothing will be the same."

He met her gaze solemnly. "I won't insult you by saying everything will be well. Only God knows the future. We must leave it in His capable hands."

A tiny smile lifted the corners of her mouth. "Good to hear you say that, nephew. Lately I feared you had lost your faith." She disappeared down the hall to the kitchen.

Walking to the sideboard, Alexander spotted the decanter of brandy. Instead, he chose to pour a glass of lemonade from a waiting pitcher. He sank onto the hearth chair with his drink to ponder the future. Warmed and mesmerized by the fire, he didn't hear the parlor door open and close until a familiar voice broke his reverie.

"That is not his horse, Lila. Just because a white stallion is here doesn't mean it belongs to Mr. Hunt."

Hearing Emily's voice, Alexander's heart leaped. He smiled at the memory of wild hair flying around her head and crinoline lace peeking beneath her hem.

"It is too, Emily. That is exactly the horse we saw at Hunt Farms, and now it's tied up out front. I just hope William is with him."

He slouched lower in the high-backed chair, recognizing the distinctive voice of Lila Amite and her perfect Queen's English. *Lila Amite is sweet on William?* This was an interesting tidbit of news.

"What would he be doing here?" asked Emily. "There are Federal troops everywhere. He's not senseless enough to cross Union lines."

"Oh, I can assure you, Miss Harrison, I am." Alexander stood up, stopping both women in their tracks. They turned toward him simultaneously, their mouths hanging open. "Would you care to warm yourselves by the fire? There is a bit of a chill in the air today, don't you think?" He downed the rest of his lemonade in one long gulp.

"It's quite rude to eavesdrop on conversations, Mr. Hunt." Emily's tone was crisp as she marched into the sitting room. "I would have thought you'd learned your manners by now."

"Eavesdropping wasn't my intention. I was enjoying the fire when I heard voices in the hall. I'm pleased to see *you* again too, Miss Harrison. Good afternoon, Miss Amite," he added with a nod at Lila.

"Good afternoon, sir." Lila bobbed a quick curtsey. "Perhaps you can forget what I said about William?" She pulled Emily's coat from her hands and disappeared down the hallway.

"Thank you, Lila," Emily said toward her retreating back.

"You look as though you're blindfolded and standing before an executioner, Miss Harrison."

"I'm not the least bit afraid of you." Emily gingerly took a step in his direction. "What brings you to Martinsburg?"

"Why, I've come to see you, of course. That night we shared dinner changed the course of the planets for me."

Emily glanced over her shoulder at the doorway. "Please don't make light of such matters, especially if we might be overheard."

"I'm not making light of anything, I assure you." He closed the distance between them and took hold of her chin. "I was disappointed to find you gone when I returned home. You left without even the briefest letter of explanation."

"It is you who owes me an explanation." She pulled from his grasp and stepped around the chair, as though to place a barrier between them. "I couldn't sleep after our eventful garden stroll. I paced the verandah and watched you ride off in the night. Perhaps to visit someone else?"

"I didn't leave to go to another woman if that is what you are implying." He refilled his glass at the sideboard. "I had pressing business at first light that was a good distance away. You take me for a man of leisure, but Hunt Farms needs income to survive." Alexander held out a glass to her.

Emily shook her head. "Absolutely not. Spirits are the reason I ended up with you in the garden. What if someone had seen us kissing so indiscreetly that night? I would have been dismissed."

"No, you would not have been. My family knows of my affection for you, Emily." He walked over to her, leaned over the chair back, and kissed her forehead.

"Then they are aware of something I am not." She held up her hand to stave off interruption. "And of something I don't wish to encourage. My behavior was a mistake, a lapse of judgment that won't be repeated. I don't dally in romance as a casual pastime the way you and your compatriots do."

"My compatriots? What an odd choice of words."

"You Southerners turn love into a sporting event. Why, I would bet you and your friends wager on romantic conquests."

"You are the one making a wager on love, Emily."

A blush rose up her neck. "That was an unfortunate choice of words, nothing more."

"For a woman who has spent little time in the South, you certainly have strong opinions about how we live our lives." Alexander's agitation grew by the moment.

"I believe I've seen enough to form an opinion. One doesn't have to wallow in the barnyard. A person usually gets the general idea from a whiff and a glance."

He threw his head back and laughed. "That is how you view our life at Hunt Farms…of my parents and me…as pigs wallowing in mud?"

Emily drew in a strangled breath and lowered her eyes. "I beg your pardon. I have no wish to insult your parents, sir. They showed me nothing but kindness during my visit."

"Then your only desire was to insult me?"

"Yes. I mean, no. Again, I chose my words poorly. What I'm trying to say is that our divergent backgrounds make the possibility of a liaison impossible."

"Whew, that was a mouthful! You truly are a schoolmarm from head to toe." Alexander downed the rest of his lemonade. "I'm not sure I understand. Do you mean you find me unappealing?"

"No, Mr. Hunt. I—"

"That you thought our dinner on the terrace was a crushing bore?"

"No, but—"

"Perhaps you find my family to be porcine curmudgeons that repel you upon every acquaintance, totally inappropriate for a woman of your tender sensibilities?"

"Mr. Hunt, please allow me to speak for myself!" she hissed. Then, taking a deep breath, she said, "I find your family endearing, dinner with you more pleasurable than I could have imagined, and you to be…reasonably attractive."

"Then what seems to be the problem?"

"Only that when I'm in your presence, I can't seem to get a word in edgewise. That would not make for a satisfactory relationship!" Emily's voice was close to a roar.

Suddenly, they heard someone clear their throat in the doorway. Mrs. Bennington leaned against the doorjamb for support. With her hand over her mouth, she appeared to be stifling giggles.

"Forgive me, ma'am," murmured Emily. "I didn't mean to raise my voice in your home."

"Think nothing of it. Alexander often affects people that way. I've noticed it on several occasions before." Straightening from the doorjamb, Mrs. Bennington leaned heavily on her cane.

Emily hurried forward to take her arm. "Please let me help you."

"I only wished to let you know Porter has returned and dinner is about to be served." She pulled away from Emily's support. "Thank you, my dear, but I feel strong today." She stepped into the hallway and then paused to look back. "Alexander, please escort Miss Harrison to the table if you can promise to be on your best behavior. Stop tormenting her. You really can be a thorn in one's foot."

He smiled. "I will put forth an extraordinary effort to be polite, despite my natural predisposition." He held out his forearm to a much paler Emily. "Under those terms, may I have the honor of escorting you to the dining room?"

Emily waited until assured her employer was out of earshot before speaking. "How can you make light of this? She overheard us arguing. I am mortified—no other word describes it. Now she knows of our flirtation. I could simply die of shame right here on the spot." Indeed, her face had taken on a deathly pallor.

" 'Tis a natural thing for two people to fall in love. It happens all the time. My aunt is aware of human inclinations. She's borne two fine daughters if you recall."

"Stop changing the subject." Emily stomped her foot. "I don't wish to lose my position over your folly. This sort of thing doesn't happen *all the time* to me."

"That could be what's causing your discomfort. Taking moonlit strolls arm in arm, kissing in hidden alcoves, and sneaking away to be alone is much like riding a horse. If you get thrown, the best course of action is to climb back up and give it another try." He took her hand, placed it on his forearm, and clamped his hand securely over it. "Shall we hurry along? My stomach growls for sustenance."

"It doesn't happen to me because I do not allow it." Emily enunciated as though speaking to a small child. "And I most assuredly won't get back on this particular horse."

"We'll just see about that." When they were a few paces from the dining room, he stopped and lifted her chin with one finger. "Soon it will be unsafe for my aunt and uncle to remain in Martinsburg. If you stay in their employ, and I certainly hope you do, you will be moving to Hunt Farms. Perhaps then you will gain a better understanding of our lives and will see things more objectively."

As she tried to pull away he tightened his grip and his eyes grew serious. "And if you come, Miss Harrison, I expect you to return my parents' hospitality with like behavior, and do nothing that could cause their ruin." He released her face and they entered the dining room for what proved to be an interminable meal—the Benningtons' last in Martinsburg.

Alexander had much to mull over during his long ride back to Front Royal. *Riding off in the middle of the night to meet someone else?* She thought he'd ridden off to another woman. What kind of depraved soul did she think him? He could never do such a thing, not since meeting her. He hated all the lies and deception, first to his parents and now to Emily. But what choice did he have? He couldn't tell her the truth. No matter how sweet her face or how tender her lips, she was a Yankee, born and bred. And this Yankee was up to something. The memory of her emerging from that barn in Berryville was embedded in his mind. Yet he still hadn't demanded an explanation for her behavior. A part of him, deep and hidden, didn't want to know.

Emily had never been to a harvest ball, at least nothing remotely like this. Because many guests had come from afar, the event would be an all-day affair and would carry into the next day as well. An afternoon picnic was planned on the lawn with games set up for both ladies and gentlemen. Small boats, kites, and ponies would entertain the young guests under the watchful eyes of their nannies. Silent, uniformed servants set up long trestle tables in the shade and would place delicious delicacies on them throughout the day. Guests could partake of food and beverages whenever they chose. Ladies usually napped in the late afternoon, while gentlemen could find coffee and brandy in the cool interior of Mr. Hunt's study. A light supper would be set out on the back portico for anyone hungry, and then the ball would begin at nine o'clock. A formal dinner would be served in the dining salon at midnight. Thereafter, revelers could dance until dawn, retire to guest rooms if they wished, or begin their journey home. A meal would be served at noon in the dining room for guests who had stayed overnight.

With amazement Emily watched families arrive in handsome broughams throughout the morning, while young men rode in on fine steeds. Wagons followed behind carrying grooms, valets, and maids, along with the trunks of formal attire for the partygoers and pastries and wine for their hosts. Neighbors who had come to Emily's home had worn one outfit the entire day, and their gift to her parents was usually a bowl of snap beans. As buggies stopped at the front steps, Emily greeted the new arrivals and then carried food down to the cool, subterranean kitchen. Maids arranged pastries and canapés on silver trays, which had been accented with fresh flowers or sprays of ferns.

Trays would be brought up to the appropriate luncheon, supper, after-ball dinner, or breakfast.

"How do these women manage to keep such slim figures, considering the number of meals served during social events?" she whispered to Lila as they carried down another rum cake.

Lila rolled her eyes. "These ladies don't eat much, Emily. They pick a little at this or taste a little of that." Lila demonstrated using two fingers and an imaginary food. "They never eat until they're full."

"What happens if they sample something they really like?" Emily slipped a strawberry tart from a tray. She broke it in two, popped half into her mouth, and then held out the other half.

Lila glanced around to make sure no one was watching and then popped it in her mouth. "Doesn't make any difference if they think it tastes like heaven itself. They would never eat much and risk being thought of as common folk." Lila pressed the backs of her fingers to her mouth. "I didn't mean any offense."

"None taken. That sounds wasteful and silly to me, putting out an array of food for people to just push around their plates with a fork. That's not what the Lord intended." Emily slipped a layered petit four off the tray. This time she wasn't so lucky.

"And the Good Lord didn't intend for you two to be gobbling up sweets down here." Beatrice's booming voice nearly lifted them from their shoes. "Shoo, Miss Harrison. The picnic is out on the lawn. Lila, your mama needs help at the tables." The cook shook her long white apron at them with a scowl.

"Doesn't it bother you that you must work today while I'm permitted to behave as a guest?" asked Emily on their way up the steps. "We are both paid employees."

Lila pulled the petit four from her friend's fingers and devoured it in two bites. "Not in the least." She skipped off toward the buffet.

But it bothered Emily. Even if this had been Lila's day off, she wouldn't have been allowed to mingle among the guests and enjoy the festivities.

After a short search, Emily found Mrs. Bennington walking the grounds with a woman wearing an outrageous hat. It was broad-brimmed in a bright shade of blue and had several ostrich feathers sticking from the ribbon. Lifting two glasses of lemonade off of a waiter's tray, Emily carried them to the ladies. "Good afternoon," she murmured in a musical tone. "Are you thirsty?"

"Ah, Emily, there you are. Let's sit somewhere in the shade." Mrs. Bennington pointed toward the rose garden.

Emily waited until both ladies were seated on a bench before handing them their drinks. Because the bench was only large enough for two, she plopped down on the grass at their feet...and noticed their shocked expressions too late. The back of Emily's stiff hoop caught beneath her, causing the front to tip up and display her lacy petticoats and the bottom of her pantaloons. Mrs. Bennington merely chuckled, but the lady with the monstrosity of a hat almost fainted. Because the dress was so snug, Emily was trapped on the ground, unable to get the hoop out from beneath her.

Then, without warning, two strong hands hooked under her arms to hoist her upright, free from the clothing. "There you go, Miss Harrison. Did you lose your balance and take a tumble? Nasty things—hoops. You really can't sit down in them, can you?" Alexander steadied her with one hand and brushed grass off her backside with the other, adding to the shock of Mrs. Ostrich Feathers.

"Thank you, Mr. Hunt, for assisting me." Emily slapped his hand away from her dress. "Yes, I lost my balance, but I'm fine now." She desperately tried to recover her dignity. He was so close she could smell his shaving soap.

Alexander rested his hand on the small of Emily's back. "Wasn't it a Yankee who invented the hoop, Aunt Augusta?"

"No, I believe the gentleman was a Parisian. Please take Miss Harrison to get something cool to drink. She looks a bit peaked. And remember what I told you about tormenting people." His aunt smiled fondly at him.

"It would be my pleasure." He winked at her and then bowed to the other woman.

"Excuse me, please, ma'am." Seething, Emily bobbed her head and retreated to the house with Alexander on her heels.

"Emily, hold up there before you take another tumble. You had better spend the remainder of the picnic in my company. That way I can be certain you won't throw yourself prostrate into the clover and not be able to get up. That fetching new dress came all the way from Paris, didn't it?" He sounded quite amused with himself.

She stopped and gazed down at her attire, still dotted with bits of grass. "Your mother ordered this gown from France? I'm shocked by such an expensive gift. I had no idea."

"Yes. She respects your wish not to wear anything made by slave hands, even if most of our household help are now free workers."

"Why would she do such a thing and pay such a dear price for a gift to her sister's governess?"

"Maybe because she suspects you are more to *me* than her sister's governess." Alexander leaned over and kissed her lightly on the mouth.

His kiss was more like a caress than a kiss, but the bottom fell from her stomach just the same. "Please...someone could see us." Emily glanced around. Sure enough, several young women strolling between the house and pond had witnessed the kiss. A middle-aged couple stopped in their tracks and stared openly.

"And what if someone does? I am their host. My behavior is above reproach."

"I forgot you've had more experience with these types of theatrical performances."

He crossed his arms. "I'm no thespian. That kiss was an honest expression of my affection for you."

"But you've shocked the guests with your forward behavior. Kisses on the lawn without benefit of a parasol for privacy must be curtailed." Emily tried to infuse merriment into her words.

Alexander glanced toward the pond and then the house. He spotted the women watching them and whispering behind their fans. "I see what you mean, Emily. You have captured the competition's attention. Soon we'll have ladies throwing themselves down on the lawn in great numbers in hopes of being rescued by their host." He laughed with amusement.

"Then they would be mistaken, because I'm nothing more to you than your aunt's governess. And I assure you, Mr. Hunt, that is all I ever will be." Her cheeks flushed as she remembered her behavior a few minutes ago.

She then walked away with a swiftness that belied the constriction of her attire. She lost herself in a sea of guests milling down the portico steps onto the lawn. For some inexplicable reason, she would have given anything not to look silly in front of his refined friends. How she appeared to these vapid aristocrats had never mattered to her before. But it mattered dearly to her now. Her knees felt weak and tears prickled her eyes, but she held them back.

The last thing she needed was to start crying.

"And I assure you, Emily Harrison, you will become much more than that, and maybe as soon as tonight." Alexander muttered under his breath.

Why he kept chasing after a woman who continued to spurn him remained one of life's mysteries. He had wealth, success in business, and the respect of men from the highest level in the Confederacy. Almost any belle present would welcome his attentions and be happy to allow him to court her. But it was this prideful Yankee's esteem he coveted and couldn't seem to earn. She remained an elusive mystery beyond his reach...one that could very well lead to his undoing.

Admittedly, Emily adored the new gift from Mrs. Hunt. Back in the refuge of her room, she took off the dress to pick off the remaining blades of grass and dab at a small stain with a damp cloth. The beautiful garment was a confection of white organdy dotted with blue flowers, with a wide white collar at the neckline and a matching sash at the tightly fitted waist. It was the dastardly hoop that had caused trouble. Emily hung the dress back in her meager wardrobe and stretched out on the chaise by the open window. It felt strange to be back at Hunt Farms. They had packed their belongings and Dr. Bennington's medical equipment into two wagons and the carriage and left Martinsburg within two days of Alexander's visit.

He had left immediately after the agonizing dinner, according to the report by the self-appointed spy, Lila. Alexander had noticed Lila peeking from the curtains and waved farewell. He had tipped his hat and called, "I'm sure William will join us in welcoming your return to Hunt Farms."

For once, she had been speechless, and Emily had a good laugh at her expense. At first they both had been so happy to be back with the Hunts, but now Emily wasn't so sure. She wasn't strong like her mother. She could easily fall prey to Alexander's attentions. Though she knew she could never mean anything to him, she was drawn to him like a bee to nectar. Here in his Front Royal plantation, she felt like a guest, not an employee. And Mrs. Bennington, for some odd reason, seemed to encourage that. She rarely let Emily read to her anymore or help with dressing or lend a hand with personal correspondence. With so little for her to do, she begged Dr. Bennington to allow his daughters to return from Europe. Their recent correspondence indicated they missed their parents sorely. And the endearing letters they sent to her attention made her heart swell with joy. She needed something to occupy her time when not helping refugee slaves along their path to freedom. Too much time on her hands allowed only one thing: daydreaming about Alexander, a man who could never be her husband, no matter how tender his kiss or how soothing his touch.

"What are you doing lounging around in your petticoats?" Lila flounced into the room delivering her ball gown, freshly ironed.

"Growing restless and ravenously hungry. I plan to load my plate with every delicacy we sampled down in the kitchen." Emily fanned herself in the airless room.

Opening the French doors, Lila pulled the filmy muslin drapes for privacy. "Why didn't you eat at the picnic?" She arched an eyebrow.

"After delivering drinks to Mrs. Bennington and her friend, I sat down in the grass and couldn't get back up. I'd forgotten about the hoop and had to be hoisted to my feet by Mr. Hunt." Her throat tightened with the memory of her humiliation.

"Pray tell me you're teasing." Lila stared with round, disbelieving eyes.

She shook her head. "I made a spectacle of myself and worse, I ran away from the picnic without a single morsel to eat."

"That is so like you—worrying about your stomach instead of your dignity." Lila rolled her eyes as though disappointed with a naughty child. "I'll draw you a bath."

"I was embarrassed, true enough, but I refuse to allow anyone's opinion of me interfere with getting some good vittles." Laughing, Emily felt the afternoon's tension drain away. "I intend to dance at the ball tonight and have a delightful time." She waltzed around the room with an invisible partner. "I will eat my fill of everything I want. After all, I don't give a fig what these Southerners think of me."

"Who are you trying to convince, me or you?" asked Lila, reentering the room. "And who are you dancing with? Have you gone addlebrained from the heat?"

"I am dancing with myself. And don't fear for my sanity. I feel it returning as we speak." She whirled around Lila several times.

Lila furled a suspicious brow. "What are you up to?"

"Nothing, but I'm starving. What do I wear to partake of supper on the terrace? Do I stay in a day dress or put on my gown? Goodness, because the sun is starting to set, perhaps I must start in the day dress and then run back upstairs and change the moment the sun slips below the horizon. These aristocrats certainly have complicated rules dictating the sun's progression."

Lila peered around the room. "Have you been quaffing spirits? Let me smell your breath." She grabbed Emily's wrists, leaned close, and inhaled deeply.

Emily sniffed. "Lila, I am sober as a Quaker preacher, who would never approve of that gown." She placed her hands defiantly on her hips.

"But you must wear the ball gown to supper. Don't worry about the location of the sun when you make your entrance. Just try not to fall into the punch bowl because I'll be too busy to pull you out and dry you off." She turned her back to Emily to shake out the pleats in the gown.

Emily grabbed her around the ribcage and squeezed. "What will you be busy with? Tell me, tell me." She shook Lila like a rag doll when the girl remained mute.

Finally Lila faced her. "Seeing that today is William's day off, and I'm finished after helping with supper, we're going to take a wagon ride and have a picnic down by the river, just him and me."

"Just he and I will picnic," Emily corrected, enjoying every minute of this. "Does your mother know?"

"No, but Papa does because William asked his permission." Lila's face glowed in the lamplight, radiating joy.

Emily hugged her again. "This sounds serious. Don't you run off and get yourself hitched before I get back from the ball."

Lila giggled like a schoolgirl but then sobered. "Quick, jump into that tub I poured for you. I want to help you into this gown, hurry down to the kitchen, and then get out to William before he changes his mind." Both girls broke into fits of laughter.

Emily was very pleased for her friend. At least one of them had a bright future.

As pretty as the dress was for the picnic, the ball gown took her breath away. It was pale peach brocade embossed with tiny cream-colored rosebuds. A dropped waist formed a V-shape in front with a bustle in back with layers of silk. The tightly fitted bodice made the dreaded corset a necessity. The skirt flowed out from a hundred tiny pleats at the waist with a small, discreet hoop. A beautiful cluster of fabric roses accented the neckline, and the lace sleeves, lined with peach silk, ended in points at her wrists.

She felt like a princess when Lila laced her into the gown. Though it must have cost a fortune, she hadn't considered refusing the gift for even a moment. Pride was one of the deadliest of sins. Emily shook her head to forget her preacher's warning. *Just for tonight, I want to feel beautiful.* Inside the dress box were matching copper-colored slippers and grosgrain ribbons to weave through her hair. Lila pinned some of Emily's thick hair into a cluster of curls atop her head and then let the remainder cascade freely down her back. This was not the fashion, not the accepted style, but Emily liked the effect when she stared into the pier glass. She dabbed a touch of russet rouge to her lips and cheeks and almost didn't recognize her reflection.

The skinny, scab-kneed girl with tangled hair and sweaty forehead was gone.

The person gazing back was a woman and at least for one night... a lady.

THIRTEEN

lexander! Alexander, over here."

Alexander looked around a sea of tables set across the lawn for the hailing voice. He spotted Quincy Daniels and smiled. Quincy, a longtime friend of his father's, was an owner and trainer of racehorses and an excellent customer of Hunt Farm yearlings. But when Alexander saw Quincy's daughter, Samantha, seated with him, his smile faded. Holding his supper plate aloft, he navigated through the crowd, most of whom greeted the son of their host graciously.

"Good evening, Quincy. Samantha." He bowed to the gentleman and accepted the outstretched hand of Miss Daniels, brushing a kiss on the back of her glove.

"Good evening. Sit with us, my boy. What a lovely spread your parents set out for supper. I can't wait to see what they will serve for the midnight feast," effused Quincy. His girth indicated the robust man enjoyed his meals very much.

"Father, please don't go on so. Mr. Hunt will think we've come all this way just for the food." Samantha's low voice drawled with cloying sweetness. She smiled, displaying large teeth that brought to mind a surly brood mare he'd once owned. Alexander also noted that Miss Daniels probably loaded her plate bountifully in the privacy of her home, judging by the fit of her dress. Though she was an attractive woman, he always felt uncomfortable in her presence, much like a rabbit under the keen gaze of a hawk.

"Not at all, Miss Daniels. It gives my family great pleasure when our guests enjoy the repast." Smiling at Quincy, Alexander dug into his own plate of cold sliced ham, pickled eggs, and crisp julienned vegetables.

Samantha lifted a dainty forkful to her mouth. "Mmm, I believe this is the most delicious ham I've ever tasted. Do you think Beatrice would share the glaze recipe with our Maggie?" She fluttered long dark eyelashes.

"Of course," he replied, amazed she remembered the name of their cook. He had to be careful with this one. It was no secret that Quincy Daniels, a widower, sought a husband for his daughter. Alexander ate several more forkfuls of supper as he glanced over their heads at the new arrivals. He searched the crowd for Emily, something he had been doing ever since she vanished that afternoon.

"Don't worry, my dear. Mr. Hunt knows the real reason I'm here." Quincy pulled three glasses of champagne from a waiter's tray for them. "I would like to buy any worthy horse stock that's for sale before the Yankees confiscate every last one in the Shenandoah Valley." Daniels raised his glass in salute before downing half the contents. "I hear they've retaken Winchester." His voice rose in anger.

Alexander set his glass out of reach. "True enough. I have it on good information that a Union brigade has camped not twenty miles from here." He pushed aside his plate as well, his appetite vanishing.

Samantha raised her glass. "Gentlemen, let's not speak of military encampments. We're here to celebrate a good harvest." She moved to clink glasses with Alexander and then frowned. "Is something wrong with your champagne?"

"I've lost my taste for the stuff." He rose to his feet. "But you are absolutely right. We shouldn't bore you with matters such as horseflesh or the war. Quincy, why don't we take a walk to the barn? I have several horses to show you." Remembering his manners, he bowed in her direction. "I hope you'll honor me with a dance tonight, Miss Daniels."

"It would be unkind to deny my host, sir."

Alexander and Quincy never reached the stables. They were stopped by an endless number of guests, all eager to share a story or offer a toast to the two wealthy men. Most others hadn't fared so well. Their faded silks and frayed cuffs told tales of vanishing fortunes and lost social position. None could have afforded a ball even half as lavish. In fact, many were close to foreclosure on their vast land holdings. Crops ravaged by the war, the loss of manpower due to runaway slaves, and the steady devaluation of Confederate currency had created hardship in most households. Perhaps seeing Quincy Daniels and the Hunts renewed their hope for the future after the Yankees gave up and went home. That night, the revelers consumed much food and imbibed whatever limited spirits were available to mask their unease. Everyone present was keenly aware General Grant's huge Army of the Potomac waited just a dozen miles to the west.

"Begging your pardon, sir." A servant interrupted a couple's lament over missing cattle. "Your parents request your presence in the receiving line."

"If you'll excuse me." Alexander bowed to the pair and stepped away. Conversation with them had begun to irritate him. And he had not seen Emily since this afternoon. Why she so vexed him, he couldn't say. She would never fit into his world, yet lately it seemed he didn't fit into his world anymore either. Only with his rangers did he feel he belonged. With his men he found purpose—a cause greater than himself.

Alexander remained in the interminable receiving line until the last guest filed past. Then he threw himself into a whirlwind of hospitality, dancing with belles and matrons alike, each one more pleasant and amenable than the last.

"One doesn't have to wallow in the barnyard."

One dark-haired beauty brushed against him several times during their waltz while constantly wetting her upper lip as they danced. When he returned the young lady to her parents' table, her fingers lingered far too long on his arm, her eyes speaking of things they should not.

"A person usually gets the general idea from a whiff and a glance."

No matter which woman he danced with, he couldn't stop Emily's words from troubling his thoughts. Something was wrong with him, and he didn't know what it was until he danced with Samantha Daniels.

"You are quite the subject of conversation this evening behind the ladies' fans, Alexander," Samantha drawled close to his ear.

"Is that so, Miss Daniels? Why would that be? Did I step in something out near the barn?" He smelled her heavy, cloying perfume and yearned for a breath of fresh air.

She looked shocked but recovered quickly. "No, I don't believe so. It was the kiss you bestowed on that tutor, or whoever the woman is, that has the ladies in a dither," she whispered conspiratorially.

"Truly? It wasn't much of a kiss that it should generate such interest."

"I didn't think so either," she eagerly agreed. "I told the ladies you simply felt sorry for the girl." Samantha flashed a honey-sweet smile as they whirled around the room.

"Why would I feel sorry for Miss Harrison?" Finally, she had his full attention.

"Because she made such an unfortunate spectacle of herself, of course. I told them you were such a gentleman you would never allow someone to embarrass themselves so thoroughly without trying to relieve their distress." She looked pleased with her magnanimity. "Even if the person was just a domestic."

Without knowing how to react to that in a manner that wouldn't cause his parents to faint or Quincy Daniels to demand a duel, Alexander threw his head back and laughed. "I assure you, Miss Daniels, I never kiss out of pity." He remembered Emily in a heap of petticoats on the lawn, and there was nothing piteous about the image. She looked more appealing in disarray than any pampered belle here. "Excuse me," he murmured the moment the waltz ended. "I see someone I must greet."

He bowed and headed downstairs to his father's study. Inside a dozen men milled about, smoking cigars and sipping something stronger than champagne. Alexander had yet to see the domestic in question, though he kept his eye on the staircase to the upstairs rooms. *Emily is probably on her way to the Federal camp for a late night foray.*

"Drink, sir?" A waiter offered a tray of cognacs.

"No, thank you. Kindly bring me a glass of lemonade." This was yet another effect the Yankee had on him. He'd lost his taste for spirits with a Quaker back in his life.

The Yankee in question had problems of her own. By the time she struggled into the corset, gown, and necessary accessories, most of the guests had left the supper tables and made their way indoors toward the ballroom. However, her growling stomach demanded that she not miss another meal. She fixed herself a plate from the buffet and found a solitary table under the emerging stars and fiery light of Venus. A pleasant waiter brought her a glass of spring water when she declined the champagne. While she ate and drank in solitude, a hundred people competed to be seen or heard only yards away. Emily ate every bite of the delicious ham and crisp garden vegetables. Tonight's fare was far more pleasing to her palate than the Hunts' usual heavy dishes. Beyond the terrace, night sounds from the fields and river began their crescendo to compete with the orchestra's first chords inside the grand house.

Drink no champagne tonight. You know what happened the last time you indulged. Emily tried to banish thoughts of that night, but the memory of Alexander's kisses crept insidiously back. "You didn't get all dressed up to sit here pining over a man," she muttered to herself. Then she rose to her feet and marched toward the house, her emotions waging a war of contradictions. She was excited but wary. She didn't belong with the revelers, but a part of her wanted to belong. Most of all, Emily yearned to see Alexander.

The massive front door stood ajar, allowing music to waft into the night while people thronged in. She paused on the threshold, transfixed by the crowd. They milled in and out of every room on the main floor and lined the entire grand staircase. Where did all these people come from? The jewels and gowns were magnificent, though few dresses looked new like hers. Some styles may have been dated, but each gown highlighted the particular charms of the wearer. Glamour and opulence radiated from floor to ceiling.

"We meet again, Miss Harrison." Snapping from her perusal of fashion, Emily found herself face-to-face with Nathan Smith.

"Mr. Smith, what a pleasure to see you again." Smiling politely at Alexander's friend, she tried to step past him toward the staircase.

"The pleasure is mine." He blocked her path. "Please allow me to escort you to the ballroom. I believe you promised me a dance during our last encounter." His eyes flickered down her gown, pausing rudely at her expanse of décolletage.

She felt like a horse having its teeth examined by a potential buyer. With no quick retort for such audacious behavior, she found it difficult to look him in the eye. "I have not forgotten, sir." Emily stared at a flower in the wallpaper behind him.

"Perhaps you'll honor me with the first dance." He proffered his elbow.

"As you wish." She flushed, grasped his arm, and climbed two flights of steps to the third-floor ballroom. They paused in the doorway to catch their breath. Hundreds of tapers in chandeliers, wall sconces, and windowsill candelabras cast light and shadow across the highly polished mahogany floor. Small tables with dainty chairs lined the walls, where guests could rest between dances and sip punch or champagne. Fastidious waiters refilled glasses, while small children waved peacock feather fans to relieve the room's unseasonable warmth. Unfortunately, with the receiving line long finished, the Hunts were nowhere in sight. As Emily and Nathan entered the huge ballroom, already crowded with dancers, the orchestra began to play.

"A reel. My favorite," said Emily. "Let's dance this one, Mr. Smith." A reel would allow her to study him from a comfortable distance. Although not unattractive, he possessed a dissipated appearance, like a gambler who had staked his fortune on a crooked game of cards.

"I hope your errand for Dr. Bennington went smoothly," he said when the reel brought them together. "I didn't like leaving you in unfamiliar territory, especially as you were unfamiliar with the roads in that area." He clasped her hand tighter than necessary.

She lifted her chin. "You needn't have worried, sir. We found our way and arrived back to Martinsburg by nightfall."

"You don't say. Then I must stop racing Thoroughbreds, Miss Harrison, and start putting my money on Percheron draft horses."

His false laughter chilled her blood. He apparently hadn't believed her story that evening, yet for some reason he wasn't calling her out. Why he took such interest in her, Emily couldn't fathom. Then she remembered their meeting on the Berryville road. She was certain Nathan Smith had been wearing a Confederate officer's uniform, yet this evening he wore formal attire. The invalid Rebel soldiers attending the ball all proudly wore uniforms. Emily assumed Smith, like other aristocrats, had paid a replacement to serve in his place. Perhaps she wasn't the only one lying tonight. This man might prove to be dangerous after all.

"Thank you, sir," she murmured when the reel ended. She bobbed her head and pulled free from his grasp. Whatever his parting comments were, she didn't hear as noisy couples separated and found new partners. Halfway across the dance floor, Emily glanced back at him. He remained motionless where she'd left him, glaring at her with evil intent.

"Miss Harrison, do you have room on your dance card to humor an old gentleman?"

She gratefully greeted her employer. "I would be honored, Dr. Bennington, as long as you promise not to withhold my pay envelope if I tread on your feet." Candlelight sparkled in his pale blue eyes, bloodshot from long hours, little sleep, and squinting to read without his glasses. Seeing him in immaculate evening clothes, she could imagine the person Mrs. Bennington had fallen in love with. Emily was filled with daughterly compassion for the man who had taken her into his home.

"Tread all you like," he said. A smile lifted his usual beleaguered features. "Your wages are safe."

Dr. Bennington waltzed her around the ballroom with effortless grace and ease. He shared charming vignettes from his years as a small-town doctor, treating cranky hundred-year-old patients and once, Margaret's pet pig.

Emily laughed with abandon. "It sounds like you miss your daughters."

"I do, indeed. I've written them twice a week, every week since they left for school in Paris. I have no idea how many letters have gotten through the blockade. Maybe they haven't seen a single word, but it still soothes my soul to write them." His watery eyes glanced away.

Sweet memories of her own father made Emily's heart ache for Porter Bennington. But before she could formulate a suitable reply, James Hunt swept her away.

"I believe this dance shall be mine, Miss Harrison." Mr. Hunt pulled her into an unfamiliar, three-step that left her breathless and desperate for something to drink.

"Allow me to rescue you from my father before you faint dead away." Alexander appeared holding out a cup of punch.

"Thank you," she said, accepting it appreciatively.

"Let's move out of the way." He led her toward a potted plant. "I believe you're well acquainted with this hibiscus."

"Ah, my favorite hiding spot." Sipping the cool drink, she studied him over the rim of her glass. In his formal attire, Alexander was handsomer than any man in the room. His smoky gray eyes stood in stark contrast to the golden tan of his cheeks. Clean shaven, he looked like a rogue from the dime novels Miss Turner disdained. Even a lock of hair had fallen across his brow, adding to his cavalier charm. At his side, she felt like an Ohio farm girl in borrowed clothes and affected airs—exactly what she was.

"A penny for your thoughts, Emily." He leaned a shoulder against a post.

"I was thinking how nice you look tonight. Is that proper?" She blinked several times. "Would any of these Virginia belles make mention of that?" Emily's voice contained a note cynicism.

"Thank you for the compliment. And I don't give a horse hair what any of the belles would say." He lifted her gloved hand to his lips for a kiss. "I care solely about your opinion." His second kiss landed on her forehead. "And while we're on the topic of appearances, yours takes my breath away. I watched you dance with Nathan and Uncle Porter and then my father, boiling with jealousy. I want you to dance with no one else for the rest of the evening." His lips found their mark on hers, stifling her protests.

Emily pushed hard on his chest and stepped back, stunned by his boldness. "Please, Mr. Hunt, not in front of your parents and their guests."

"What are you afraid of, Emily?" His soft words cut deep.

"Nothing. Everything. I don't know, but I don't feel like dancing anymore." Overwhelmed with insecurity, she ran from the room like a child. She couldn't explain her immature behavior if her life depended on it. She'd been so eager to see him. Now she had to get away. Emily didn't slow her pace until she was down two flights of stairs and out of the mansion. Breathless, with a heart ready to burst, she halted on a narrow path that wound through the garden. For several minutes she breathed deeply. When her eyes adjusted to the dark, she recognized the row of slave cabins where she'd met Annabelle and her son. That seemed so long ago. Picking her way between the ruts, she heard no voices lifted in conversation or song through open windows. The cabins were either dark or contained a single candle burning in a glass jar.

As Emily neared the end of the lane, the rumblings of a chant caught her attention. She hurried to the pasture fence, which enclosed an open field of beat-down grass and apple trees stripped clean of fruit. She saw in the distance the fenced horse pastures of Hunt Farms. Behind her two cats hissed among the slave cabins, displeased with her trespass. For a moment, Emily contemplated running pell-mell back to the ball until she heard the sound of laughter floating on the air. Inhaling a deep breath, she stepped over downed fence rails and picked her way between the briars.

Ahead several men played tunes on reed flutes, while others kept rhythm by slapping sticks together. Old women sat cross-legged on the perimeter of the circle beating on overturned buckets with spoons. They created a din that surprisingly added depth to the strange music. Men and women danced inside the circle, and children played tag, darting in and out between the adults. Emily's heart began to pound, keeping pace with the music's beat. Three lit torches, stuck in the dirt, provided illumination. The sight of the torches turned her stomach queasy, resurrecting painful memories of Ohio. *I don't belong here.* But when she turned to go, two smiling little girls stopped her. One stuck out her hand, surreal in the quavering light of the fire, but Emily reached for it. The hand felt soft and sticky, like every child's.

"Don't be afraid, miss. Nobody's gonna bite you," said the little girl.

Emily laughed as she was pulled toward the circle of light. With bobbing heads and flailing arms, the dancers moved with carefree abandon. No regimented reels or dainty waltzes where a misstep meant a bruised toe. They danced not in couples and not alone— people seemed to be dancing with the entire group as bodies weaved, skirts swung, and petticoats rustled in the warm night air. Some dancers had closed their eyes, chanting and swaying as though in some sort of trance. The two little girls' dance resembled a game of hopscotch.

Emily stepped closer to the fire, where she could watch the revelry unnoticed. Under the trees were tables laden with platters of corn on the cob, roast potatoes, various cheeses, and baskets of corn bread. A small pig rotated on a spit above a cook fire. People milled around the buffet wearing a wide variety of attire. Several young ladies were smartly dressed, perhaps the personal maids or nannies of visiting guests with their charges already asleep. Emily spotted the livery of coachmen and valets, along with the attire of horse trainers and groomsmen. Some people were barefoot in the rough, homespun garments of field hands who tended crops or the extensive vegetable gardens. Milling around wooden benches, arriving and leaving as duties dictated, the party-goers possessed an infectious camaraderie.

With music unlike any she'd ever heard, Emily's hips began to move with a mind of their own. When a banjo added a twang to the tune, she closed her eyes and swayed, utterly hypnotized by the beat. No longer did she feel too hot, too clumsy, too backward, or too anything.

"Miss Emily Harrison, have you come to do some real dancing?" A voice cut through her mesmerized stupor.

Emily's eyes flew open. Wearing her best dress, Lila stood before her with William. His arm was draped lightly around the young woman's shoulders. "What are you doing here?" Emily asked.

Lila giggled. "Look around. What are *you* doing here?"

"I grew bored with the indoor party and thought to have me a look-see." Emily feigned a not very convincing drawl. "I thought you two went on a picnic."

"Done and over with. It's time for dancing." Lila shook her head. "Oh, excuse my manners. Do you remember William, Miss Harrison?"

"Yes, I do. How are you, William? Did Miss Amite eat you out of a full week's wages?" she teased.

William didn't know what to make out of her question. "I am fine, ma'am. And no, Miss Amite ate only a normal amount of food." He peered from one woman to the other.

Lila narrowed her eyes and placed her hands on her hips. "Did you come out here because you fell in the punch bowl?" Lila's head swiveled from left to right, assessing Emily's gown.

"No, I stayed far away from the punch bowl so as not to take any chances." Emily held out her skirt for inspection.

"Did Beatrice chase you away with a broom for eating the whole buffet?" Lila arched one eyebrow.

She shook her head. "Absolutely not. I ate like a delicate bird."

After a single *harrumph*, Lila took Emily by the hand. "Come on then, let's dance. You'll not be a wallflower here too."

Emily complied, knowing she couldn't withstand Lila's formidable will once the woman's mind had been made up. And truth be told, she wanted to dance—not in the shadows but with everyone else—experiencing the fullness of life. Without hesitation Lila pulled her into the center of the circle where dancers moved in and out of the torchlight. At first Emily swayed to the tune of the flutes, letting her shoulders dip while her hips swayed slightly. As she danced, the music seemed to fill her with energy. Her head felt light as her mouth went dry. When she opened her eyes, Lila was dancing not two feet away with her knees bent low, shaking her reed-thin body. William hovered nearby with his arms crossed over his massive chest. He neither danced nor sang, but watched the two of them like a sentinel to make sure no one got too close.

If anyone found the sole white face odd or unsettling, they made no mention of it. Emily relaxed in the torchlight, stepping in a square pattern as though inventing her own waltz.

"I thought you didn't wish to dance anymore, Miss Harrison." Alexander's unmistakable voice cut through the warm night air.

Emily turned toward the direction of the sound. "I changed my mind." She tried to peer through the smoke, shielding her eyes from flying sparks.

He leaned against one of the ancient apple trees with his shirt collar open and his cravat undone. "Perhaps it was only me you didn't want as your partner."

Lila also stopped abruptly, as though Matilde had caught her stealing cookies. "Good evening, Mr. Hunt." Lila hid behind the considerable bulk of William. Everyone else continued to dance but cleared an open pathway for the master's son.

"Are you spying on me, Mr. Hunt?" Emily asked. She marched to the tree with her hands balled into fists.

"I am, but please don't let me interrupt. I'm glad you're enjoying yourself at my festival."

"Your festival—this is your party too?" She stared at him, perplexed.

"Of course it is. We throw one festival for our friends and neighbors and another for our workers. We want everyone to celebrate the culmination of a good year and give thanks for the harvest."

"Even the slaves, Mr. Hunt?" She hissed the words as not to be overheard.

"Yes, the slaves and even…the governesses." When he pushed away from the tree, firelight reflected in his dark eyes. "I followed you to make sure you were safe. And because I was curious as to what you planned to do. I loved watching you dance, by the way." He sighed heavily. "But as usual, you view my family's motives as something evil. I'm sure you can find your way back to the house, Miss Harrison. You found your way here easy enough." With that, he disappeared into the shadows.

Emily was speechless. Then she bolted after him. She circled around the dancers, away from the smoky torches and curious onlookers, and down the path between the cabins. As she had anticipated, he stepped from the thicket just ahead of her on the path. "Where are you going, Alexander? I thought you came to dance." Emily reached for his arm as she caught up to him.

"No, I've had enough dancing for the rest of the season. I came for you, but that was my mistake." He shrugged off her hold and stalked toward the garden ahead.

Emily, with considerably shorter legs, had to run to keep pace with his long strides. "Please don't hurry so. I can't keep up."

He pivoted on the spot. "How do you like it, Miss Harrison? I learned the rude little trick of running away from you."

She bumped into his hard chest. Struggling not to pant like a dog, she steadied herself with both hands. "I don't care for it now that the shoe is on the other foot." Emily pressed a hand to her throat, willing her heart to slow down. "I apologize for my former behavior and promise…not…to…do…it…again." The words came in fits and starts as she gasped for air. Goodness, her corset was tight.

His features softened. "Please don't faint on me. Several ladies have already done so this evening. And I'm plum out of smelling salts." Supporting her elbow, Alexander helped her to a bench near an overgrown patch of mountain laurel and crepe myrtle. "Sit and catch your breath. I'm certain you'll resume despising me once your wits return."

Emily sat down on the stone bench and fanned herself with her new fan—another gift from Mrs. Bennington. "I don't despise you, Alexander. Right now, I reserve that emotion for myself. I'm truly sorry for the way I behaved. I felt lonely and out of place, and I took my insecurity out on you."

He sat down beside her and slicked a hand through his hair. "Just when I thought I finally figured—"

Whatever he'd meant to add was lost. Emily wrapped her arms tightly around his neck, interrupting his dialogue. Then she kissed him fully on the mouth as a rush of heat shot through her veins. "Thank you for following me, Alexander. I secretly hoped you would." Her words were a bare whisper against his lips, even though they were alone.

He pulled back slightly to study her. "Why do you insist on seeing my family as devils? Truly, many slave owners are, but I assure you my father is trying to deal with the land and the people he inherited the best he can. I agree that no one should be owned, but he is just a man without horns or tail."

"I'm starting to realize life may not be as simple as I grew up believing." She released him but snuggled up against his side, feeling warmth radiate between them. "But tonight I have no wish to debate the South's reliance on slavery or banter society's ridiculous rules of etiquette." Emily ran her fingers up the muscles of his chest where his shirt clung to his skin.

"If you don't wish to spar, what would you like to do, my little Yankee?" He pulled up a weed and tickled her nose.

Stifling a sneeze, Emily closed her eyes. "Let me think." The smell of rain hung in the air along with the sweet scent of bougainvillea. Heat lightning streaked the sky in the distance, and a rumble of thunder foretold a coming storm. "What I should do is go up the back steps to my room. I've lost my hairpins and ribbons, so my hair has come down in a hopeless tangle. My coiffure is rather improper for a ball, no?" She winked as she sat up to work her fingers through her long hair.

He pulled her hand to his lips and kissed her fingers. "You look beautiful with your hair across your shoulders. Now tell me, what do you *wish* to do?"

Emily sat in the fading light of faraway stars and listened to the notes of a waltz drift through the ballroom windows.

"I would like to dance, out here in the garden, with you." She rose with a stately bearing learned from Mrs. Bennington.

Alexander bowed low and offered his hand. "Then that is what we will do. We shall dance for the rest of the night or for the rest of our lives if you prefer. I love you, Emily Harrison." His murmur carried on the breeze as lightning lit up the sky.

But she heard him clear and true. She knew it was an honest declaration, not spoken in a moment of passion, but coming from a hidden place deep inside him.

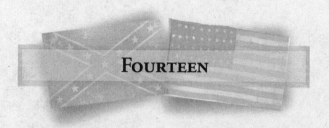

FOURTEEN

*N*athan Smith downed the contents of his glass and refilled it again from the sideboard decanter. The bourbon failed to assuage his ill temper as it usually did. Nothing had gone right that evening.

The insipid Daniels girl deserted him after only a few kisses. After two interminable waltzes, Samantha had followed willingly when he led her away from the ballroom and up the stairs. She'd giggled as they entered a guest room at the end of the hall. But when he tried to lift her skirt, she slapped his hand away like an annoying mosquito.

"Sir, I believe there has been a misunderstanding." She pulled from his embrace and flounced out the door of the stuffy room.

His attempts to seduce two younger, more naive belles yielded the same unsatisfactory result. In one case the father of the girl, and in the other case, a brother, kept a keen eye on them to make sure their reputation remained unsullied. Even a scrawny Irish maid from Fredericksburg spurned him, raving that "her intended beau wouldn't be likin' his gal spoonin' with the master" when he asked her to walk in the garden. His luck hadn't been this bad in a long time.

The high-and-mighty master of Hunt Farms had barely talked to him all evening other than to set the time and place of their next foray. That he would do with his usual efficiency, making sure the rangers arrived knowledgeable about the plan and expectations. Alexander had been cordial but too preoccupied to share a brandy with him after concluding their business. *When had he become a teetotaler?* Smith knew whom Alex's eyes searched for across the crowded ballroom. But the outspoken governess had disappeared after her obligatory dances with Porter Bennington and James Hunt. She couldn't have gotten away from Alexander soon enough, that much was clear.

Smith tossed back his bourbon as he stared out the library window.

He could see the dancing firelight of the slaves' festival in the distance. Movement in the garden beyond the portico caught his attention. Squinting through the wavy glass, he witnessed a kiss between William, Alexander's valet, and that maid of the Benningtons. How sweet their kiss—brief, chaste, tender. What was her name—Linda or Leah? Her name didn't matter, but he recalled the ripe figure filling out her dress the day he ran into the Yankee. Then William tipped his hat, bowed to the maid, and disappeared down the path.

William is a gentleman, Smith mused. *But you don't need a gentleman, little miss. What you need is someone to introduce you to the pleasures of life.* Setting down his empty glass, he moved swiftly out the front door and down the steps. When Lila turned to reenter the house from the portico, Smith intercepted her. He grabbed her wrists. "Good evening, miss. Forgive me, but I seem to have forgotten your name. We met on the road to Front Royal, or wherever you and Miss Harrison were headed that day."

Lila reared back, perhaps from the smell of whiskey. "It's Lila, sir. Lila Amite." She attempted a half curtsey, difficult with constrained wrists. "Now, if you'll excuse me, my parents will be wondering why I'm not in yet." She kept her voice level and calm.

"What's your hurry? I'm happy to see you, Lila. Aren't you just a lit'l glad to see me too?" He heard the slur in his words.

"Yes, sir, a pleasure to see you again. But I must return to my quarters before I cause my father undue worry."

Smith tamped down his irritation that a maid possessed better language skills than him at the moment. "Well, if it's a pleasure to see me as you say, you won't mind giving me a lit'l kiss." He covered her lips with his before she had a chance to respond.

Recoiling from the whiskey vapors—or perhaps his kiss—she tried to step away. But he stopped her with two strong hands that pinned her shoulders to the wall, and then kissed her again. "That wasn't so bad, was it? If you would just relax, you might find this enjoyable." His gaze raked over her from head to toe. "You are a beautiful woman, Lila. We should get better acquainted while you're at Hunt Farms."

Without warning, she stomped down on his instep. "Ow! Why, you—" Crying out in pain, he released his grip.

"Lila, is that you?" The door to the first-floor kitchen swung open. Joshua Amite stepped out in his long nightshirt.

"Yes, Papa, it's me. Mr. Smith was inquiring about food, so I explained where a late night meal can be found." With that, Lila bolted down the steps into the kitchen and pantries without a backward glance.

Joshua peered at the man before giving him a clipped, "Good night then, sir." The butler bowed deeply and closed the door in his face.

Smith was left in the dark, feeling angrier than he had in a very long time.

Lila didn't slow down until she was into the hallway of rooms reserved for domestic servants. Miraculously, the kitchen was empty, uncommon on an active plantation like this during the harvest festival. She struggled to compose herself before her father caught up to her. Her heart pounded so hard she feared it could be heard.

"Why are you so out of breath, girl?" Joshua sounded both concerned and exasperated.

She gazed into his soft brown eyes. Even standing barefoot with his gray hair wild, her father still maintained utter dignity. "I have been running, Papa. We had a race back to the house from the bonfire." She hated lying to him, but what else could she say?

"Lila, you are too old for footraces. You don't see your mother picking up her skirts and galloping across the yard, do you?"

Actually, she had seen her mother doing exactly that more than once on Bennington Island. But her father looked so weary, Lila simply shook her head. "No, Papa. Tomorrow I promise to be a perfect lady from sunup to sundown." She leaned over to kiss his grizzled cheek.

"See that you are. Good night, daughter. Sleep with sweet dreams."

Joshua entered the room where her mother already lay snoring and closed the door.

Lila was alone—alone to catch her breath and collect her thoughts. And she had a lot to think about. How in the world could she avoid a friend of Mr. Hunt's for the entire time she was here? Entering the room she shared with Mrs. Hunt's maid, she undressed without lighting a candle and slipped on her nightdress. She stretched out on her cot and closed her eyes, but sleep wouldn't come. A bad feeling had crawled up her spine and taken hold, no matter how she tossed or turned.

Alexander stood for several minutes outside a bedroom window, watching Emily sleep as peacefully as a child. Her hair spilled across the pillow like a copper shawl, almost obscuring her soft features. She slept on her side with her knees bent. One hand clutched the coverlet, and the other cradled her sweet face. When he crept into her room and kissed her brow, she didn't stir. Alexander couldn't remember a night when he hadn't stared at the ceiling for hours. Although he would give half his fortune to sleep so soundly, his sweet dreams ended when he became a ranger. And this morning was no exception as he crept from her room. Back on the gallery, he paced from one end to the other plotting their next mission. But it wasn't their upcoming attack on a Union supply train that confounded him. It was the woman just beyond the French doors—the one who occupied an ever larger place in his heart. He knew full well he was a fool to let emotions control his actions.

But Emily was no Rosalyn. Raised by Quaker parents, she might not have grown up cultured and refined, but she had learned honor and trust. *Does she love me or am I only deceiving myself?* When he made his earnest declaration in the garden, she had uttered nothing in return. He would have given anything to hear those three words from her. She appeared surprised by his confession but then returned his kiss with an ardor to match his own. Wasn't that what women excelled at—playacting? Didn't they charm their way to wardrobes filled with new gowns, larger mansions, and excursions abroad? Beautiful women quickly learned that the path to a man's heart was *not* through his stomach.

Pausing at the balustrade, he gazed over moonlit wheat fields recently harvested. The tasseled heads of a few missed sheaves waved in the warm evening breeze. A lump rose in Alexander's throat. There was nothing more beautiful than land in the fertile Shenandoah Valley. He loved the woodlots filled with game and songbirds, the pastures covered in wild flowers in the spring, and the majestic Blue Ridge Mountains to the west. This plantation, purchased by his grandfather with inherited wealth, grew dearer to him each day. The Hunt family fortunes had dwindled over the years because running a business for profit had never interested his father. Now the war would surely take what little James Hunt had left. The Glorious Cause certainly demanded all of Alexander's time and most of his money. Duty had become his sole motivation in life, demanding every waking moment…until he met Emily.

Now he was in love with a woman hiding something, a woman whose affections ran from cold to hot and then back again, a woman who disagreed with everything he said and was annoyed with everything he did. Emily Harrison wasn't someone who could be trusted, and yet watching her sleep had stirred something primeval inside him. The lure of her vulnerability was overpowering. He was helplessly smitten, and that realization afforded him many more sleepless nights to come.

But at the moment, Emily Harrison wasn't the Gray Wraith's chief problem.

Several miles away, five civilian homes went up in flames as their occupants watched helplessly outside. Although unclear where the order had originated, a Union cavalry regiment burned the farms of families suspected of harboring or aiding the Gray Wraith and his Rebel Rangers.

Although General Philip Sheridan didn't approve of burning

homes, he had instituted a plan to destroy crops and livestock that sustained the rangers in the Shenandoah and fed the Rebel Army in general. Sheridan had also ordered the arrest of any able-bodied males less than fifty years old suspected of being guerrillas. He had sent a unit of cavalry to the Berryville area, where they filled twenty wagons with civilians and incarcerated them in Charles Town. And he organized a company of his best soldiers to hunt down the Gray Wraith. Sheridan's men had developed friendships with citizens loyal to the Union. They relied on children and slaves to provide directions and serve as guides. Union soldiers dressed in Confederate uniforms had tried to infiltrate the area and gather intelligence. But even when they apprehended a ranger, they couldn't discover the whereabouts of the Gray Wraith. No matter what they threatened, no one would reveal the identity of their revered hero.

Over the summer, as Union counterspy activity increased, the Gray Wraith had changed how he conducted business. He never revealed his plans until immediately before the foray. He and his men slept outdoors under the stars so not to jeopardize the homes of his supporters. Despite their tremendous effort, the Union cavalry failed to snare its prey. That is, until Charles Mimms walked into General George Meade's headquarters and announced, "I know where you can find the Wraith."

Charles Mimms had been born in Virginia and lived his whole life in the small town of Aldie. Recruited by the rich planters' sons who had been his childhood friends, Mimms had been proud to ride with the rangers. But greed for the spoils of war eventually replaced pride as his motivation. He saw no need to turn over everything they confiscated to the Confederate Army, not when he'd risked his life to get it. At first, Mimms held back small items or an extra saddle or weapon to sell to Confederate sutlers. Then U.S. mailbags became a sought-after prize because they often contained Federal greenbacks. His love of the Confederacy paled beside his lust for money. With each new foray, Mimms rode with the troops solely for the bounty.

That is, until he was dismissed one shameful evening outside of Winchester.

With eight others lined up like naughty schoolboys, the arrogant colonel had humiliated those who had participated in the ill-fated raid on a Union warehouse. Of course, a rich planter's son could afford to hand over everything to the Glorious Cause. He'd never gone to bed hungry or grown up in a tenant shack with a father who drank all the time. His mother hadn't taken in dressmaking to put food on the table.

It was so easy for a wealthy man to be noble.

At least the colonel had sprung them from the train bound for a Yankee prison. But to dismiss them without a second chance? That wasn't something Charles Mimms could ever forget. After getting tossed out of the rangers, he had no desire to join the regular infantry or cavalry. Their six-dollars-a-month pay was laughable. Besides, he'd had enough of taking orders to last a lifetime, and now he possessed only one goal: to cut the invincible Gray Wraith down to size.

Mimms had found a more than receptive audience with a commander of the Union forces.

The morning after the ball, Emily awoke to the sound of knocking. Sitting up, she stretched lazily until the sound of her name cut though her sleepy fog.

"Emily." A male voice repeated in a hushed tone.

Then she jumped out of bed and pulled on a robe over her nightgown. "Alexander?" she asked, tightening the belt around her waist. She opened the door an inch as though afraid of what lurked on the other side.

"Good morning, my little Yankee. I trust you slept well." He leaned against the door frame, already dressed in tight breeches, tall boots, a pressed linen shirt, and a fitted waistcoat. Only his cravat remained loose around his throat.

Emily opened the door wide and glanced down the hallway in both directions. "Here, let me help you." She reached for his cravat, but unfortunately created a knot that wouldn't release no matter how she yanked or twisted.

"Never mind. Go back to sleep, my love. I'm in a hurry. I'll have William tie it on the way to the barn." He kissed her forehead tenderly. "I hope to return by nightfall. Try not to forget me while I'm gone." Then he turned and vanished down the stairs.

"Wait," she whispered. "I have something to tell you." She took two steps into the hallway but was too late. The man was already gone.

Emily turned and went back into her room, closed the door, and sat down on the edge of the bed. Emptiness filled her, a void she'd never experienced before. Where was the self-assured woman who had danced with the workers while the guests attended a lavish ball in the house? Where was the woman who had chased after her hosts' son, and then danced with him and kissed him in the early morning hours? That woman had vanished with the dawn, and she didn't care for the weakling left behind one bit.

My little Yankee, indeed.

Emily tiptoed to the window, hoping not to see anyone for a long time. But luck was not on her side.

Lila sat on the balcony, reading the paper at the small table. "Thank goodness. I thought you would never wake up." Her voice contained a note of pique. "Come have some coffee." Lila filled two cups with a stern expression.

"Thank you," said Emily, sipping the strong brew.

"Well?" demanded Lila.

"Well, what? I thanked you for the coffee."

"You know very well what. What happened after you left the bonfire?"

"Lila, you are too young to act like my mother. But maybe I'll oblige you just this once." Emily refilled her cup from the carafe on the table. "I caught up with Mr. Hunt in the garden, apologized for my behavior, and then we danced in the moonlight." Emily tried not to smile.

"Just the two of you dancing outside?" Lila's eyes widened. "What if Mrs. Bennington would have seen you?"

"Maybe nothing or maybe I would have been fired." Emily answered with little concern.

"But why? I thought you didn't even like him." Lila squinted at her as though some strange creature.

"I don't, but I seem to have fallen in love with him." She grinned over the rim of the coffee cup.

Her friend rolled her eyes in disbelief. "You sure changed your mind in a hurry. I'm taking your gown to the laundry before the grass stains set. I know you must have fallen down once or twice." Lila scrambled to her feet. "And you'd better bathe and get down to the terrace. Mrs. Bennington has already asked about you this morning. That tub of water is cold because you slept in so late." Lila left the room shaking her head.

"Thank you for drawing my bath." Emily followed her through the bedroom and climbed into the tub as soon as Lila left the room. Cool water might help her think, providing she remained until her skin was wrinkled and her lips had turned blue. How could she explain her odd behavior to Lila when she didn't understand it herself? By the time she dried off, the only thing she was certain of was she loved Alexander Hunt despite every impulse cautioning against it. He had pledged his love to her. He had spoken the words women yearned to hear.

So why is it so hard to believe he could love a woman like me? And would he still love me if he found out the truth?

The remainder of the day dragged interminably. First, she had to endure luncheon on the terrace with guests who had stayed overnight. At least Mrs. Bennington sat beside her, but she kept stealing curious glances at her.

"Ma'am, is there butter on my nose or something else amiss?" asked Emily in Mrs. Bennington's ear. "I do wish to make a better impression than yesterday on the lawn."

Her employer laughed. "Your nose is fine, dear. And don't worry about the impression you made. You seem to have garnered more jealousy than one woman can handle for a harvest ball." She whispered conspiratorially while smiling like a cat.

Emily froze. "I don't understand what you mean."

Mrs. Bennington bobbed her head toward the other end.

Emily gazed down the table and spotted Samantha Daniels frowning. The two young ladies sitting with her were glaring as though their shoes fit too tight. Emily opened her fan to hide behind. Finally, the silly thing served a purpose. "I don't remember those women, Mrs. Bennington. I don't believe I did anything to offend them."

"Of course you didn't. Don't give them another thought." Mrs. Bennington patted her hand and then cut into her fish fillet. "Eat your lunch, Emily. You'll need to keep up your strength for the rest of the day." She nodded at the women at the far end.

Mrs. Bennington's advice proved wise, indeed. There were walks in the gardens—vegetable, floral, and herbal—followed by carriage rides around the property and then tea in the shade of live oaks. The guests were apparently in no hurry to go home. Finally, when Mrs. Bennington retreated to her room for a nap, Emily went to hers to hide. She'd endured the entire day without seeing Alexander.

Dinner was equally exasperating. Why did these people take three hours to eat their food? If this was the life of the well-heeled aristocracy, she had no desire to gain *entrée*. Seated next to an elderly gentleman with poor hearing, she attempted to carry on a lively conversation. She finally gave up trying to make herself understood and smiled sweetly at everything he said. On her right sat a young man of about seventeen who attempted to impress her with tales of horsemanship.

Alexander arrived with his father after the first course had been served and sat at the far end with several visiting horse breeders. Other than receiving a warm smile cast in her direction, she had no contact with him. Afterward, the men headed to the library for cigars and brandy, while the ladies retired to the parlor for dessert. Emily could neither eat another morsel of food, nor spend another minute in the company of these women. Excusing herself, she nearly ran to her room.

Pacing the floor, she tried to invent an excuse to interrupt Alexander with his business associates. Unfortunately, nothing rational occurred to her. Instead, things she should have said out in the garden flowed through her mind like a river. She had so many chances for honesty and had taken none. Exhausted, she slipped into bed with his tender confession ringing in her ears. *I love you, Emily.* When she eventually drifted to sleep, her dreams offered no respite. She envisioned Alexander striding down a misty path with her in futile pursuit. Of course, even in the dream she was unable to speak her mind because the phantom remained just out of reach. Waking with a start, she threw off the quilt and returned to the balcony for another promenade. At this rate her slipper soles would wear paper thin by Christmas.

From the balcony Emily spotted Alexander marching toward the barn, weaving in and out of the mist. Was he real or merely another phantom? Raindrops on her nose and cheeks brought her fully awake. This was no dream. The man she desperately needed to talk to was blissfully alone. Wasting no time, she scampered down the gallery stairs, heedless that only a shawl protected her from the downpour. Rain quickly soaked her nightdress and matted her hair into tangles down her back, but she sloshed on through puddles that chilled her bare legs and ruined the hem of her nightgown. Like in her dream, her legs felt heavy, as though she moved underwater. Never had the distance to the barn seemed so far.

She had to tell him he wasn't an ogre but the most attractive man she'd ever met.

Maybe she would also mention she'd been narrow minded and judgmental.

She might even muster the courage to tell him the truth—that she loved him.

With her blood pounding in her ears, she tried to slide open the heavy door. It barely moved two inches, but it was enough for her to see inside. A single lantern hanging from a low rafter provided poor illumination. Alexander wasn't alone after all but deep in conversation with his trusted friend and valet, William. Neither man had heard the door open.

Dread inched up her spine as she craned her neck to listen. Shivering as her rain-soaked shawl hugged her body, Emily couldn't hear a word they said. But what she saw spoke volumes. As he spoke, Alexander donned the uniform coat of an officer—the memento of a long-dead friend from his childhood, with its double row of gold buttons, stripes on the sleeves, and stars at the collar. Next he strapped on a sword and scabbard and pulled on long buckskin gloves. Realization struck her like a mule kick. Alexander was a colonel in the Confederate cavalry, not a gentleman farmer who remained safe while his friends and neighbors marched off to fight and die. Yet the biggest surprise was yet to come. As cold rain sheeted off the barn eaves and ran down her back, Emily watched William open a scarlet-lined cape for Alexander and then hand him a wide-brimmed, plumed hat. As he mounted a huge white stallion, she saw that he wore no holster or pistol.

Alexander wasn't just a Rebel officer, but the notorious Gray Wraith. This was the man who had foiled countless Union maneuvers to deliver clothing, food, and medical supplies to the Army of the Shenandoah. He was the one who provided Confederate infantry with desperately needed shoes and blankets to separate themselves from the cold ground. This man had transferred thousands of dollars from the Union to the Confederate Treasury without even carrying a firearm. This information should have made a dyed-in-the-wool Yankee very angry, but somehow the knowledge made Emily love him all the more.

She jumped back just as the barn door swung wide. Alexander rode out and disappeared into the rainy night. Blessedly, neither man noticed her behind the door clutching her shawl, trying not to shiver to death. No one suspected that a Unionist had learned the truth. Emily waited until certain William had returned to his quarters before creeping back to hers.

Sleep would come no easier now. She hadn't done what she'd set out to do. She'd made no late night confessions to the man she loved. And the knowledge of Alexander's true identity didn't change her heart one bit. They were both living counterfeit lives.

FIFTEEN

*E*mily, wake up." Lila shook her gently. "Why is your night-gown wet?" She picked up the cast-off garment from the floor.

"I fell in the river. Go away, Lila. It can't possibly be time to get up yet." Emily buried her head deeper under the quilt to protect her eyes from the streaming sunlight.

"The river? You walked all the way to the Shenandoah River in your nightgown? Have you lost your mind?"

"Yes. If that is what you came to ask me, you have your answer." Emily gripped the edge of the covers tightly as Lila pulled them from the bottom of the bed.

"I already knew that. The reason I came is to get you up. I thought Yankees were supposed to be industrious, while we Southerners were the lazy ones."

"You heard wrong and have it backward." Emily's words sounded muffled from under the feather pillow.

Lila stared at the lumpy form beneath the quilts with arms akimbo. "I'm out of insults to raise your dander, so I'll try a different approach." She plopped down on the bed. "If you tell me what you did with Mr. Hunt after the ball, I'll tell you about the kiss I got from William." Lila bounced up and down on the edge.

Emily pushed away the pillow and sat up, not pleased in the least. "Lila Amite, I have no desire to admit to what we did that night. A lady does not discuss delicate matters. You'll have to find out for yourself when you grow up."

"When I'm all grown up like you? Is that why you went searching for him last night and fell in the river?" Lila sashayed away from the bed with exaggerated drama.

"How do you know I looked for him last night? Lila, you must promise you won't speak of my sneaking out. Not to William, not to anyone." She jumped out of bed and caught the young woman by her shoulders. "It's of upmost importance."

"Your reputation is safe from my wagging tongue. Now get yourself down to breakfast." Lila tapped her nose with a finger, as though remembering something. "Mr. Alexander will be there. I saw him return this morning while helping in the kitchen."

Emily flew to the wardrobe. "Why didn't you say so earlier, you goose?"

"Maybe I had something—or someone—on my mind." Lila filled a porcelain cup with coffee from the carafe on a tray. "I'll set this next to the tub and return later to help you dress."

"Don't trouble yourself. I'm not wearing a corset today or anything else that must be laced up. Enough is enough."

"Suit yourself. At least you're still skinny." Lila left shaking her head with damp nightgown in hand.

Emily bathed, donned her peach calico dress, and was downstairs in thirty minutes—a record time for her. "Good morning, everyone." She smiled as she entered the dining room. "Please forgive my tardiness."

Dr. Bennington, Mr. Hunt, and Alexander stood as she reached the table. Mrs. Hunt and Mrs. Bennington were already at their usual places. Fortunately, the lingering guests had finally all gone home.

"You are not tardy, my dear," said Mrs. Bennington. "We've just started. It was a good morning to sleep in."

"I trust you slept well, Miss Harrison," said Alexander with a wink. Deep lines creased his forehead, and blue-black smudges beneath his eyes indicated he'd had no rest the previous night. His tousled hair was badly in need of a haircut, while a two-day-old beard darkened his cheeks.

Studying him over the rim of her cup, Emily thought he looked wonderful. A surge of electricity snaked up her spine even as her stomach flip-flopped. With a face so rakishly handsome, she yearned to lean across the table and kiss him—in front of the Benningtons and his parents. Only the fear of overturning a candelabra and burning down the house kept her seated. "I slept blissfully well," she lied.

"Breakfast, Miss Harrison?" Joshua presented two platters at her side.

"Everything looks wonderful, thank you." Despite the abundant array, she took only a small amount of eggs, a slice of ham, and one piece of toast. She declined the potatoes with onions, fried tomatoes, and poached pears.

"Is something wrong, Miss Harrison?" Alexander asked. "Aren't you feeling well?"

"I'm feeling fine, sir. Why do you ask?" She ate a dainty forkful of eggs.

"I'm concerned about your paltry amount of breakfast. The thing I appreciate about Yankee women is that they know how to enjoy a good meal." Alexander beamed at her.

His uncle and father laughed, his mother frowned, and Aunt Augusta spoke in an admonishing tone. "Alexander, are you nettling Emily already?" Mrs. Bennington had assumed the formidable role of Emily's protector in the alien land.

"I am, Aunt Augusta. She had the pluck to escape during the ball without giving me a single good night kiss. After she had promised." He grinned as though he finished the last of the bonbons.

Emily nearly choked on her dry toast. How could he tease her after they had shared many garden kisses, especially in front of his parents? She shot him a glare that had little effect.

"Why would Emily wish to kiss you? She struck me as having far more sense than that." Mrs. Hunt lifted her coffee cup in salute.

Alexander pushed away his plate. "A promise is a promise, and I intend to hold Miss Harrison to hers."

"Enough talk of kisses," said Mr. Hunt. "That Fredericksburg horse broker gave me a copy of the *Washington Post* yesterday. Listen to this marvelous article about the Gray Wraith. It describes his rangers as 'such intangible demons and devils that when they scatter into the mountains, the tracks of their horses disappear into the mist.'" He laughed wryly. "The Yankees are terrified of the man. One news story reported him having dinner with war correspondents at the Henry

House in Alexandria wearing a disguise. He supposedly paid for every-one's meal and then gave them each a box of cigars. Another story has him in Culpeper the very same day cutting up the Warrenton railroad."

"Maybe he is a ghost if he's capable of being in two places at the same time," mused Mrs. Hunt.

"Perhaps so, my dear. In a third story he's wreaking havoc at another location. They reported he raided Mercersburg, Pennsylvania, where he captured several hundred cattle and drove them back into Virginia as though this were the Great Plains." Everyone burst out laughing. Everyone that is, but Emily.

"Sounds like the Wraith is planning quite a barbecue," drawled Mrs. Hunt. "I do hope we receive an invitation."

Emily peeked at Alexander. An expression of amusement had lifted the corners of his mouth. He didn't seem the least bit uncomfortable with their topic of conversation.

"Oh, they will catch up with him eventually." James scooped more eggs from the platter onto his plate. "And when they do, they will hang him. Considering what the rangers have stolen, the Union cav-alry are mad as hornets. The Wraith has made the Yankee generals appear mighty foolish on more than one occasion."

"*Hang him?*" Emily was unable to keep quiet another moment. "Why would they do that? I read that he's never taken another life, and he doesn't even carry a gun. When he commandeered a train from Washington, the ladies aboard stated he behaved like a true gentle-man." Inhaling a breath, she clamped her mouth shut.

The three Hunts and two Benningtons were all staring at her.

"If I didn't know better," said Dr. Bennington with great mirth. "I would swear our Miss Harrison has become smitten with the legend-ary Wraith."

"The North might as well concede defeat now if their women start falling at the man's feet. It's bad enough that Southern ladies fall asleep with visions of a caped cavalier swooping into their bedrooms at night." Mr. Hunt fluttered his arms in batlike fashion.

"James, that is not true. I could never tolerate a man who *swoops*." His wife gently patted his hand.

Mr. Hunt smiled at her fondly. "For now my place in your heart is safe."

Emily couldn't let the matter drop. "But his aim is only to feed and clothe the hungry Army of the Shenandoah and supply medicine to the field hospitals. With the Union blockade of the ports, little has gotten through. Patients and soldiers are suffering desperately."

"That is all well and good, Miss Harrison, but they will still hang him if given the opportunity. This story reports he relieved a Yankee paymaster of one hundred seventy-three thousand in greenbacks and turned the money over to Jefferson Davis. That's quite different than food and medicine. If they don't hang him, they'll surely ship him to the worst prison in the North. They have commissioned special units of cavalry to do nothing else but hunt down the Wraith and his rangers. It seems to be only a matter of time." Mr. Hunt folded the newspaper and set it aside.

"Do you consider him an American Robin Hood, Emily?" asked Alexander, joining the conversation. "No wonder you ran away without giving *me* a single kiss. You're smitten with a phantom. I'm sure if you met the man, you would find him dirty and utterly disreputable." He leaned back in his chair and watched her from across the table. "I've read that he's crawling with lice."

"Alexander, that is enough!" scolded his mother. "What's gotten into you? You bait poor Miss Harrison mercilessly. Why wouldn't she fall in love with a ghost when men her own age behave like boors? Lice. I declare."

Emily had enough of the topic and rose unsteadily to her feet. "I assure you that I am not in love with any ghost." Her voice cracked. "If you'll all excuse me, I must catch up with my correspondence." She nodded politely at the Benningtons and left the room on shaky legs.

She so desperately wanted to say *I am in love with your son, Mrs. Hunt.*

But she hadn't. Another opportunity lost. Now she might never get the chance again. He had left last night on one of his late night forays. Now his long periods of absence made sense. There wasn't another woman. The Grand Lady of the South was Emily's competition, and she could demand the greatest sacrifice of all. Alexander had told Emily that he loved her, but what did that mean during a war that refused to end? According to newspapers, a net was dropping on the rangers of the Shenandoah Valley. The powerful Union Army, the same that Matthew had died for, was closing in on the man responsible for supplying the Rebels with so much. The same man she was in love with. And there wasn't a thing she could do but bide her time.

"Pssst, Miss Harrison." A voice called from the gnarly tree at the edge of the upper gallery. Emily stood but saw no one. Left with her book and tea, she had dosed off in the chair after Mrs. Bennington and Mrs. Hunt had retired to their rooms for their customary naps.

"Miss Harrison." The small voice of a child drew her close. A very dark boy had climbed up the crepe myrtle and clung precariously to a thin, spiny limb. He couldn't have been more than eight with close-clipped hair and luminous black eyes.

"You're going to break your neck, young man. What are you doing up here?"

"I got a message for you, miss. Not 'spose to tell it to no one else." The thick waxy leaves and shiny clusters of berries hid his location from anyone passing below.

Emily heard the branch creak ominously. "What message? Tell me quickly and then get down before you fall."

"The wind blows from the south today. You're 'spose to come to Upperville to the Thompson Farm on the Little River Turnpike as soon as you can. Tonight best of all, miss."

She knew instinctively what this meant and shuddered. After what she just learned, she needed time to sort things out. "It must be tonight?" Emily wondered how much this child knew about her involvement in the Underground Railroad.

He nodded. "What say you? I got to get back to my ma. She's delivering honey to Miz Beatrice." The branch creaked again under his weight.

She knew there was no time to question him further. "Tell your mama I will come."

The child climbed down and disappeared into the cool subterranean kitchen. Emily stood for several moments pondering her course of action. *I must find Lila. She will know what to do.*

Unfortunately, she didn't. Lila wasn't eager to give advice that could put Emily in danger. Lila had heard that a pregnant runaway was hidden in the Thompson root cellar, which was sixty miles from the Pennsylvania state line. The woman had left a master who spent his days in an alcoholic haze after his wife and children died from cholera last spring. The rest of the slaves had already run off, but her pregnancy had prevented her from joining them. Now the master vented his rage on the few slaves left on the dilapidated plantation. She had no choice but to leave to protect the life of her unborn child. Lila's heart ached for the woman, but her heart these days belonged to William. And he was very much against Lila helping on the Underground Railroad. The authorities would treat a free black woman harsher than a white Yankee if she were caught. To her relief, William watched her comings and goings like a hawk since the unfortunate encounter with Nathan Smith.

"What are you going to do?" asked Lila as the two women walked toward the Shenandoah River in the cool breeze of late afternoon.

"I must go and help her." Emily answered without much enthusiasm. "The woman wishes to give birth where her child will be born free. We won't let her get caught and returned to a cruel master after she's come this far. I'll slip out tonight and take her to the Potomac, where she can cross into Maryland. She'll be that much closer to Pennsylvania." Details popped into her mind, one by one. "But I can't think of a reason to pay a social call in Upperville. It's too close to Federal lines. The Hunts would never let me go."

Alexander. . .would he still profess his love if he knew what I was up to?

"If you're going then I am too." Lila spoke with determination.

"No, you're not." Emily's tone brooked no discussion. "I'll ride to the Thompson farm with an extra horse and one of your dresses for the runaway. We'll have to reach the crossing by dawn. If we're stopped, I'll say she's my maid and we're fetching the doctor for Mrs. Thompson. How could I explain having two maids along? Then I'll ride back here and pray I'm not seen returning at that hour—with an extra horse, no less." The plan, for whatever it was worth, knitted together while they walked in fading sunlight.

"Leave the horses in the brooding shed. I'll have Jack fetch them back to the main barn later. And I'll take care of distracting the family with a little help from William."

"Thank you." Emily wrapped her arms around Lila's shoulders. "Say a prayer for the runaway—and another for me."

Lila hugged her long and hard. "I'll be saying more than one. You can count on that."

Emily ate dinner with the Hunts and Benningtons that evening as usual. Alexander was absent. For this small grace, she was grateful. Considering their breakfast conversation, his parents knew nothing about Alexander's late night activities. And with her mission to rescue a pregnant runaway ahead of her, Emily was afraid to speak in fear of revealing one of her many secrets. *"What a tangled web we weave when first we practice to deceive."* One of her mother's pet expressions ran through her mind over and over. What hope did their love have when lives were built on lies and deception? With a heart heavy with shame, Emily tried to focus on the dinner conversation.

"They say a vote will be taken soon in the Virginia legislature," said Mr. Hunt, greatly agitated. "Many of the western counties want nothing more to do with this war or the Confederacy. If presented with no alternative, they will leave the Commonwealth of Virginia."

"Perhaps it's only the ravings of a few hotheads," said his wife in a soothing tone. "Cooler, more rational minds may prevail, and Virginia will remain intact."

Mrs. Bennington shook her head. "I'm not so sure, Rebecca. I remember the sentiments of our former neighbors in Parkersburg. This powder keg has been simmering for a long time."

"You can't expect people to fight and die for slavery when little of it exists west of the Shenandoah Mountains." Dr. Bennington scraped his hands down his face.

The young governess paid little attention to their politics as she pushed food around her plate.

"My dear, is something wrong with your dinner? Or have we upset you with our conversation?" Mrs. Hunt asked as she turned a concerned face in Emily's direction.

"Neither, ma'am, but I have little appetite. I've been nursing a headache all day. If you don't mind, I will retire to my room." She pushed back her chair.

"Of course. I'll have Lila send up a tea of white willow bark." Mrs. Bennington patted her arm as Emily walked past her.

Along with the tea, Lila delivered a parcel of food from the kitchen and one of her loosest frocks before she vanished back down to the kitchen. There was nothing left for Emily to do but wait. Wait and worry. And think about Alexander. Were they so different? He fed, clothed, and cared for Southern soldiers. Would he understand her need to lessen the suffering of runaway slaves?

Finally, the house grew silent as darkness fell. The sisters were most likely doing needlework by the parlor fire, while their husbands continued their debate regarding Virginia over brandy in the study. Most of the workers, both slave and free, had completed their tasks and were enjoying dinner in the kitchen downstairs or in cabins out back. Emily dressed in dark colors and then plaited her hair into a long braid before tucking it beneath a riding hat. Creeping from the house, she had no trouble reaching the barn unseen. She tied the cloth bag of food and the extra dress to the saddle horn, along with the reins of the other mare, and mounted Miss Kitty. She avoided a sidesaddle because she would have to ride hard and fast to reach Upperville in a little over two hours. With the moon to light her way and the sounds of crickets and peepers to comfort her country ears, the ride exhilarated Emily.

She arrived at the Thompson farm just after ten o'clock, thankful for the smoothness of the journey thus far. This was a safe house in the Underground Railroad—kind people dedicated to helping slaves find their way to freedom. But the sight of three Thoroughbreds tied to the hitching post nearly stopped Emily's heart. The saddles bore the insignia of the U.S. cavalry. Emily hid Miss Kitty and the extra horse in the barn and knocked timidly on the kitchen door.

"Mrs. Thompson? It's Miss Harrison," she whispered with a queasy stomach.

"Come in, come in, Miss Harrison. I'm just having a cup of coffee." The woman held the door wide. "My husband has guests in the parlor—three Federal officers." She added with great pride. "Those are their horses tied outside." She conveyed this information without a moment's hesitation. After all, Emily was not only a Yankee but a conductor on the Underground Railroad. Surely, she could be trusted.

The serenity Emily had experienced during the ride vanished. She hadn't given the Thompsons much thought—they were simply anti-slavery Christians who helped runaways reach the North. The realization that they were also Union sympathizers, actively assisting the Federal Army camped nearby, hit her like a bolt of lightning. It was one thing to help a pregnant runaway escape slavery, but quite another to be in a house of informants. As she sipped coffee in Mrs. Thompson's comfortable kitchen, she was shamed by the love and trust received from the Benningtons and Hunts. When her thoughts turned to Alexander, a deep flush crept up her neck. *Just exactly who am I?* But as she stared into the grounds at the bottom of her cup, no easy answer came.

"Are you a Quaker, Miss Harrison?" asked Mrs. Thompson, refilling their cups with fresh coffee.

"Yes, ma'am, I was—am." Emily looked everywhere in the room but at her hostess's face.

"We're Methodists. I couldn't abide no organ music or singing in church like the Quakers, but you're very brave to be doing this, miss, and at such a young age. You'll get your just reward."

"Yes, ma'am, I'm quite certain of that, but I'm surprised there's still such need after Mr. Lincoln's proclamation."

Mrs. Thompson clucked. "It doesn't take effect till January. Besides, do you think those Georgia slavers are going to pay much attention?"

Emily shook off a frisson of anxiety. She couldn't keep from glancing toward the parlor. Two Union officers paced back and forth, while a third sat with Mr. Thompson before the hearth.

"Don't worry about them. They'll not trouble you any. The officers are here to discuss important matters with Mr. Thompson."

Emily grew more uncomfortable by the minute. She felt like a traitor. How was that possible? She was a Unionist to the core who hated the institution of slavery, despite who she'd fallen in love with. "I brought along an extra dress," she said, rousing herself to task. Emily drew Lila's gown from her bag.

The hospitable Mrs. Thompson set a plate of cakes in front of her. "Take a moment to refresh yourself, my dear. You still have quite a night ahead of you. I'll get our refugee prepared to go." She picked up the dress and headed for the door.

Emily breathed a sigh of relief when the woman disappeared, leaving her alone. The strains of male voices wafted from the parlor. It wouldn't hurt to listen for a minute. *After all, I am a Yankee, aren't I?* She crept silently to the doorway.

"We won't have to worry about him much longer." The words of one soldier drifted through as she hid by the doorjamb.

"Is that right? He's been cutting up this county and others around it for the entire war. What makes you think you can catch him now?" The booming voice came from a burly man identified by his wife as her host. Mr. Thompson was middle-aged, stoop-shouldered, and balding. Emily took an immediate, illogical dislike to him.

"It appears he made an enemy," said a mustached officer, leaning back in his chair. "Apparently, he discharged several rangers for filling their pockets with plunder instead of turning it over to the Confederacy. The Gray Wraith is a man of strong principle," he added sarcastically. The other two broke into peals of laughter.

"I fail to see the humor," said Mr. Thompson.

"One of the men discharged turned up at General Meade's headquarters. He'd ridden with the Wraith from the start." The officer paused, grinning at the others. "For a small price he described the man's hideouts and habits. This mysterious Wraith keeps to himself and has few vices, but he enjoys a once-a-month poker game at the home of Thaddeus Marshall in Middleburg. We've had our eye on that town for some time. Those citizens are very loyal to the Cause. They would lie to the Maker himself to save the rangers. Apparently, Mr. Marshall is the Wraith's uncle and, from what we can gather, Marshall only has one nephew—Mr. Alexander Hunt of Hunt Farms, Front Royal."

"That's not possible." Thompson shook his head like an ornery mule. "That family is the richest in the area. Why would the son of an aristocrat like James Hunt involve himself with pillaging? You think this former ranger can be trusted?"

Emily's heart pounded so hard she feared it would be overheard.

"Yes, we believe he's telling the truth. These blue-blooded aristocrats have a barrelful of *honor*." He spat the word as though something shameful. "We'll keep the man in the stockade pending the outcome. He'll be paid one way or the other depending on the reliability of his information. He was mad as a wet hen when they locked him up." The other officers stopped pacing long enough to refill their glasses at the sideboard.

"So we have it on good authority the Gray Wraith will be in Middleburg tomorrow night." The officer finished off his own drink. "He won't slip away again. Once he's captured, the raiding of our trains and wagons in the area will cease. If we can stop him from supplying the Rebel Army, we can end this war that much sooner."

Tomorrow. The word turned Emily's entire world upside down. Alexander did have an uncle living in Middleburg. She'd heard him joking with his father how Uncle Thad could bluff at poker better than a riverboat charlatan. With the Yankee cavalry waiting for him, Alexander would be walking into a trap. She stood with her head on the doorjamb, unable to move for several moments. Then she shook off her paralysis and left the warm kitchen.

Moments later, she located Mrs. Thompson and introduced herself to the frightened, pregnant slave anxious to be out of Virginia. Wearing Lila's dress, the woman climbed onto the horse. Emily mounted Miss Kitty and then accepted a bag of provisions from Mrs. Thompson. If anyone told her a month ago she would feel anger toward a fellow member of the Underground Railroad, she never would have believed it. But Emily had no time to mull over her change in attitude. She had to deliver this woman safely into the hands of the next conductor and get herself back to Front Royal.

And pray that she wouldn't be too late to warn Alexander.

Like most towns in the original thirteen colonies, Middleburg had been laid out in a symmetrical grid pattern with blocks relatively the same size.

The opulent home of Thaddeus Marshall occupied almost all of one block, with a small hotel on one corner and the Episcopal Church facing the street to the rear. Arriving guests descended from their carriages at the ornately wrought gate and then strolled through formal gardens to the Marshalls' front door. The stone path wound through manicured boxwood, bowers of clematis and ivy, along with peach and pear trees. Their garden and small orchard created a veritable Eden within the city. The mansion, built on the back property line, resembled an Irish manor house with double chimneys at both ends and tall, symmetrical windows. Circling up three stories, a carved walnut staircase dominated the impressive foyer. The Marshalls used the main floor for their lavish balls and receptions, preferring not to climb to the third floor. To the right of the parlor were the dining room and Mr. Marshall's study.

Alexander and his rangers arrived at the Marshall home for their
beloved poker game. Alexander usually accepted his aunt and uncle's
hospitality and stayed overnight. Guest bedrooms and quarters for
household staff could be found on the third floor. It was not unusual
for his officers to share rooms in the house after their card games, while
another dozen soldiers bunked in the stable loft or other outbuildings.
On warm summer nights some men spread their bedrolls under fruit
trees or in the grape arbor, where they could inhale a sweet fragrance
as they drifted to sleep.

Such was the case on this warm night in late fall. The poker games—
penny ante in the parlor and higher stakes in the library—broke up
around midnight. Alexander, Nathan, and several other officers feasted
on cold fried chicken and sweet corn with Mr. and Mrs. Marshall in
the kitchen. With sandwiches in hand, the other rangers sang on their
way to their bedrolls in the garden. Alexander felt uncommonly con-
tent with the world on this November night. After a flush of hearts in
the final hand, his wallet was richer by ten dollars. His men were ready
to ride to Culpeper at dawn to relieve a supply train of horse feed. And
he had just finished a delicious meal with his aunt and uncle, who
never missed an opportunity to badger him about his bachelor status.

"If you wait any longer, nephew, the only women left who will have
you will be my age." His aunt shook her finger in warning.

"If she's half as lovely as you, I will be a happy bridegroom." His
usual reply brought a blush to his aunt's cheeks.

"You go on upstairs now. You're talking nonsense." Mrs. Marshall
wrapped up the last piece of pecan pie and tucked it into his saddlebag.

Watching her, Alexander felt an odd surge of emotion. Everything in this woman's life had changed drastically, yet she still worried
whether he would marry a nice girl.

Emily Harrison was a nice girl, despite the fact she'd been born
north of the Mason–Dixon line. Her words at breakfast yesterday
morning kept running through his mind, providing another measure of contentment. She had actually defended him—defended the
Wraith, at any rate. *"His aim is only to feed and clothe the hungry Army*

of the Shenandoah and supply medicine to the field hospitals." "When he commandeered a train from Washington, the ladies aboard stated he behaved like a true gentleman." A true gentleman. He smiled at Emily's conclusion. Would she be so eager to save the Wraith from the hangman's noose if she knew his true identity?

Alexander kissed his aunt's papery cheek, shook his uncle's hand, and then climbed the stairs to the third floor. After stretching out on his narrow bed, he listened to the men's banter through the open window. Soon the garden below and hallway of guestrooms quieted as men fell into deep, long-overdue sleep. But he couldn't shake thoughts of Emily from his mind.

You have given your heart to the enemy, Miss Harrison.

But then again, so have I.

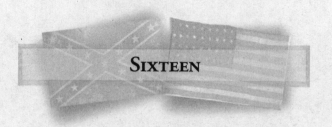

Sixteen

Emily enjoyed no dreams the night she returned from the Thompsons', pleasant or otherwise. The ride from the river ford where the young woman crossed into Maryland had been tortuous. Without a moon to light her way, she had gotten lost twice and hadn't arrived back at Hunt Farms until late morning. She left the two horses in the brooding shed as instructed and walked the distance to the house sore and famished.

"There you are! I thought you would never get back." Lila popped up from the hedges into Emily's path with her usual zeal. "I had to tell so many lies as to why you weren't at breakfast. I don't like bearing false witness."

"I'm sorry, Lila. I made a wrong turn and ended up in Bluemont. Let me rest for a few hours. I'm too exhausted to talk." Stepping around her friend, she entered the warm kitchen.

"No, first you need to eat." Lila pulled a linen napkin from a plate of sandwiches on the table.

"I'll take one up to my room, but don't let me sleep more than a couple of hours." A yawn muffled her words. Emily headed up the back stairs eating her sandwich with eyelids that refused to stay open. Inside her room, she stripped off her sweaty dress and dropped it on the floor. Slipping between her silk sheets, she fell instantly to sleep. When she awoke, it took her several moments to regain her bearings. Someone had drawn the curtains and set out a fresh basin of water and stack of towels.

Jumping out of bed, Emily splashed water on her skin until her senses returned. Then she scrubbed every bit of road dust from her face and arms.

Without knocking, Lila marched into the room with another ewer.

"I was just about to shake you." Peering at the dirty water, Lila threw it out the window and refilled the basin from her pitcher.

"Why didn't you check if someone stood below on the lawn?" Emily lowered her face into the cool water.

"No one is about this time of day." Lila leaned one hip against the bedpost. "When will you tell me what happened?"

"What I will tell you is how wonderful this feels." Emily pressed a soft towel to her face. Then she recounted an abbreviated version of Mrs. Thompson and the pregnant runaway, including the plot to capture the Wraith in a trap. "Now I must find Alexander. Time is of the essence."

Lila dug her hands into her apron pockets. "Mr. Hunt isn't here. I saw him ride out a few hours ago."

It took Emily a moment to absorb the news. Then her knees buckled and she collapsed on the polished bedroom floor. Without hesitation, Lila hauled her to her feet. "Oh, Lila, how long did you let me sleep?" Emily finished drying off and tossed the towel toward the hamper. "If I don't stop him, Alexander will walk right into a trap."

"That William—he never breathed a word about this. He always helps Mr. Hunt cover his tracks." Lila yanked a fresh dress from the wardrobe.

Emily shimmied into clean clothes without bothering with a corset. "I must find Mr. Marshall's home in Middleburg to warn him."

Lila fumed as she pacing the floor. "William knows the way. He's gone there many times with Mr. Hunt—"

"I must see William at once!" Emily pulled on her boots and sprinted toward the balcony door.

"What should I tell Mrs. Bennington?" asked Lila, following close behind on Emily's heels.

"Make up any tale you wish after I'm gone. You should be getting good at it by now."

Although William tried everything in his power to dissuade her, Emily refused to listen. The two of them rode hard to Middleburg, arriving a little after midnight. As they stood on the street behind the Marshall mansion, holding the reins of their lathered horses, they considered their next move. The stillness of the neighborhood offered hope she wasn't too late. "Thank you, William, for accompanying me. I never would have found Mr. Marshall's home on my own."

"Mr. Alexander ain't gonna be happy about you coming."

"You let me worry about Mr. Alexander. He and his men are in danger. The Union cavalry knows about this house."

"I'll go speak to him while you wait here. We don't know what we'll find beyond that gate."

"No, I will do this. Alexander will ask how I came by this information. I must tell him the truth. I must tell him everything."

"Yes, miss, I'd say it's time." Worry creased William's brow. "You gonna tell him what you were doing in Upperville?"

Emily's head snapped around. "What do you know about Upperville?"

"I know what you were doing there. Lila told me all about the Underground Railroad."

"Lila told you? The more people who know, the less safe the route will be."

William crossed his arms. "You think I would blab about that? But I didn't give Lila much choice. When I saw you leave with an extra horse, I was all set to follow you. She stopped me and told me where you were going. When people are fond of each other like me and Lila, they tell each other the truth."

The implication was as subtle as a red hat on a mule. "I know that… or at least I'm figuring it out. That's why I'm going inside, so let's stop arguing."

"No need to argue. We're both going, Miss Harrison." After William tied their horses across the street, they entered the garden through an arched gate. Emily stayed close to him, trying not to make noise on the stone path. However, they hadn't gone ten paces when the *click* of a gun being cocked stopped them cold. With weapons drawn, Confederate rangers quickly surrounded them. Others who'd been asleep under the trees staggered up from their bedrolls.

"Well, look who we have. What do you suppose a Yankee schoolmarm is doing here?"

Emily froze at the voice of Nathan Smith.

Unseen thus far, William stepped into the moonlight. "It's me, Captain Smith, William—valet to Mr. Alexander. I need to speak to him right away."

"I know who you are," snapped Smith. "What's this about? Why have you brought this woman here?" He glared at Emily with ill-concealed contempt.

"It's more like she brought me, sir." William added an uneasy laugh. "She wants to talk to Mr. Alexander. Says it's personal in nature." Taking Emily's elbow, he tried to lead her from the circle of soldiers.

"Hold up there. How dare you turn your back on me? State your business. Then I'll decide whether it's important enough to tell Colonel Hunt in the morning." The icy tone of his voice brooked no further discussion.

"Begging your pardon, sir. If you'll give me a minute to explain." William took a step closer to Smith, intervening dangerously.

Seizing her opportunity, Emily bolted down the path and disappeared into the dark.

"Stop that woman and bring her to me!" shouted Smith.

With surprising courage she sprinted up the steps before the soldiers could give chase. Once she was inside the house, she ran smack into an ancient servant with a full white beard and a completely bald head.

"*Ouff.* Who are you, missy? Why are you calling on the Marshall House at this hour?" With indignation, the butler tugged down the hem of his waistcoat.

"I'm Emily Harrison," she replied quickly, knowing her name would mean nothing to him. "I must speak with Mr. Alexander Hunt at once."

The elderly man stared, bewildered. "Why did you call at the back door, Miss Harrison, and at such an indecent hour? If you come back tomorrow at eight o'clock, you can talk to the Marshalls and Mr. Hunt at breakfast."

Exasperated, she grabbed the butler's thin shoulders. "This is urgent! Where is Mr. Hunt?" Her voice rose in agitation. Overhead, she heard people stirring as they awakened.

The butler recoiled. A strange white woman placing her hands on him was more than he could handle. "Master Hunt sleeps on the third floor, the first room at the top of the steps."

"Lock the door. Don't let those soldiers inside." Emily ran headlong through the house and up the stairs as though familiar with the mansion. Heavy boots sounded on the porch along with men's angry voices. She didn't slow down until she reached the top of the third flight, although it felt as though her side might split open. When she threw open the first door on the left, she heard a gun cock for the second time that night.

"Emily! What in heaven's name are you doing here?" Alexander sprang from the bed. With his suspenders down and his chest bare, he stepped in front of a soldier dozing in a chair. "Put that away." He pushed the gun barrel to the side.

"As you wish, Colonel," said the guard, rising clumsily to his feet. He tucked the weapon into the waistband of his trousers.

"You could have been shot bursting into a room like that." Alexander grabbed Emily by the arms.

"I thought the Gray Wraith had no need of firearms." She averted her eyes from his chest, momentarily flummoxed in a room reeking of stale cigar smoke.

"This is war, Miss Harrison. My soldiers carry guns even if I choose not to." He shook her like a naughty child. "Answer me. Why have you come? You could have been killed by Union pickets or by my guards watching this house." He lowered his voice but didn't lessen his grip. "I can't believe you traveled from Front Royal alone." Oddly, he made no mention of her reference to the Wraith.

"I'm not alone. I rode with William." With nowhere else to look, Emily gazed into his gray eyes.

"*William*? I'll skin him alive for bringing you here. It's not safe—"

"William didn't bring me," she interrupted. "I came because I had to talk to you."

"Whatever you had to say could have waited until I returned. You're in great danger this close to Federal lines." He smoothed her hair back from her face and rubbed a smudge of dirt from her nose.

"No, Alexander, it couldn't have waited because you're the one in danger—you and your men." Emily tried to tuck the lock into her braid. Through the open window they heard the thundering hooves of approaching horses. Then she screamed as the bedroom door banged against the wall.

Nathan Smith and six rangers entered with guns drawn. Alexander shifted in front of Emily protectively. "What's this about, Captain?"

"Yankees have us surrounded! That woman you're soft on led them here." Glaring at Emily, Smith cocked his long-barreled Colt.

"Holster your weapon, Captain Smith." Alexander strode to the corner window and drew back the curtain. In the garden below, blue-coated soldiers marched up the path as though in a regimental parade, while horses whinnied and men shouted on the street.

"I did no such thing," she said, not as forcefully as she would have preferred.

"Someone told them we were here." Every drop of blood drained from his face as the colonel donned his coat and strapped on his sword and scabbard.

Then the crack of gunfire pierced the night. "What is happening?" she cried, trying to peer around his shoulder.

"Men are dying, that's what. My soldiers are being shot down like dogs." Alexander spat the words as though bitter to the taste.

"Lord, have mercy." Emily watched a ranger level his revolver at a skinny bluecoat no more than twenty years old. Without firing a shot the boy crumbled to the ground.

"Death shocks your pacifist sensibilities?" Smith sneered. "This blood is on your hands, Quaker."

"We have to get out of here." Alexander pulled Emily from the window. With a firm hand around her waist, he pushed her toward the door. "Dawson, down the back stairs!"

Smith blocked their exit. "She's coming with us? After she betrayed us and led the Yankees to your uncle's home?" His eyes narrowed into slits as spittle collected in the corner of his mouth.

Emily mustered every bit of strength she had left. "No! I came to warn him—"

"Warn him? How could you know about the ambush if you hadn't tipped them off in the first place?" Smith aimed the barrel of his Colt in the direction of Emily's heart.

Drawing his sword, Alexander shouted with no uncertainty, "If you point your gun at her again, I'll cut off your arm! We'll sort this out later. Now move, Captain!" He pushed Emily through the doorway with Smith following them in a rage.

They took the three flights of stairs so fast Emily stumbled several times. Each time Alexander caught her with a strong grip. At the bottom they found themselves in the servant's hallway to the dining room with the other rangers who had been sleeping in the house. No one seemed to know which way to go. Shouts could be heard in the kitchen, while something battered against the front door.

"This way," whispered Alexander. "Into the winter kitchen." He opened a trap door that was used by servants to carry up food. Steep steps descended into blackness, but the rangers hurried down them without hesitation. Alexander prodded Emily to follow the last man and then pulled the trapdoor closed. They halted on the steps as voices in the hallway sounded above them. At the bottom soldiers clustered, waiting for their eyes to adjust to darkness.

"Our only hope is there." Alexander pointed at a narrow shaft of light penetrating the dusty windowpanes. "The root cellar's outside door. Quickly, men, slip into the garden one at a time. The shrubbery is dense here. If you don't make a sound you may not be seen." He motioned the first man up the steps.

Emily crouched on the dirt in the gloom, watching the men take their turns.

"I was a fool." He spoke softly only to her. "I thought I could make a difference by supplying our desperate troops from your bloated army. It was like taking candy from a babe until greed got in the way. Now we have blood on our hands like every other soldier." Alexander gazed everywhere but at her.

"You're a man who valued human life and tried serving his cause without bloodshed. That doesn't make you a fool." Emily patted his arm.

"That kind of man has no place in war." He shrugged off her touch. "My grandfather fought King Charles to free Virginia from England's tyranny. How could I face my father if I sat idly by and did nothing? How could I face myself?" Pain radiated from his face as his last soldier vanished from sight. "It's time to go, not the time to be discussing the merits of my behavior." Muttering an oath, Alexander grabbed her arm and hauled her up the mossy steps into the November air.

There was uneasy silence on this side of the Marshall house as they wound their way through the garden. "I swear I didn't betray you," she whispered.

"We have no time to discuss your behavior either." He tightened his grip as they ducked and bobbed their way to the stable.

Once through the door into the dim interior, Emily released a sigh of relief. William stepped from behind a stall wall with their horses' reins firmly in hand. "I can't believe you're both safe," said William, shock evident on his face.

"No one is safe yet." Alexander unceremoniously hoisted Emily up on Miss Kitty's back like a sack of grain. "Take Miss Harrison and get out of here."

"Yes, sir." William mounted his own horse, wasting no time. He wrapped Miss Kitty's reins around his saddle horn.

Leaning precariously from the saddle, Emily grabbed a fistful of Alexander's coat and clung tightly. "Why won't you believe me?"

He removed her hand like a thistle burr and pushed her back into the saddle. "My men are surrounded by Federals, so I'm too busy to decide what part you played. But you have lied to me from the start. Why should I believe you're telling the truth now?"

His expression rendered Emily speechless. She *had* lied over and over. But it never mattered before…because she hadn't loved him. What could she say? *I'm sorry? I'll never lie to you again? I love you?* What hollow incongruities those words sounded like now.

Captain Smith appeared in the stable doorway, leading Phantom by the reins. Smith never took his eyes off her, hatred boring into her like needles. In one fluid motion, the colonel mounted the huge stallion. Emily opened her mouth to speak, but Alexander smacked Miss Kitty's flank. The horse bolted through the doorway with her rider clutching fistfuls of mane for dear life. As the Gray Wraith melted into the moonless night, Emily and William flew down the streets of Middleburg to the railroad station. At the depot they followed the tracks in the general direction of Hunt Farms, the report of gunfire growing weaker with each mile.

Neither spoke until the horrible sounds faded away behind them. Any of those bullets could have found their mark in the colonel, who everyone now knew to be Alexander Hunt. Throughout the night they rode, dozing fitfully in the saddle until a cold rain began to fall. Then Emily awoke with a start, and she glanced around at an unfamiliar world—one she had no place in. With little else to occupy her time, she prayed all the way back to Front Royal. She prayed that Alexander hadn't been shot and had escaped safely from Middleburg. She prayed the Federals wouldn't burn the Marshalls' home.

But if he had escaped, what then? She'd seen his expression when he slapped Miss Kitty to send them on their way. It was not the look of a man in love.

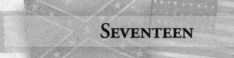

SEVENTEEN

*lexander, will you not listen to reason?" Smith's voice rose into the crisp, early morning air.

They had ridden hard and made camp miles away from the blood-bath of Middleburg. Some of the rangers who had managed to get away met up with them on the road. They were now sleeping close to the fire, exhausted from the fight and flight. The colonel had no idea what had happened to the rest of his men. He feared they had been captured or killed on the pristine, manicured grounds of his uncle's home. "I'm listening, Nathan, but you know nothing for sure."

"*Someone* told the Yankee cavalry who you were and where you would be. For heaven's sake, that governess led them right to us."

"How would she have known where I would be last night? I didn't tell her."

"She showed up with that black valet of yours. He must have told her and then brought her to Middleburg after they sent word to the Yankees."

Alexander kicked a fallen log into the fire. "You're wrong. William would die before he would betray me, and I him."

"You are too gullible." Smith hissed between his teeth. "Our entire regiment has been splintered due to that cunning, red-haired Quaker and your valet. William is a black man, a former slave. Do you really think he wants to see the South win this war?"

"William would never put my life in jeopardy or the lives of my soldiers!" Alexander shouted, not appreciating the way his captain was addressing him. They had been friends before the war. Now they circled each other with fists clenched and teeth bared, neither of them backing down.

"How could you be so sure that Harrison woman wouldn't hand you over? Did you ever bother to ask what she was doing that night

273

in Berryville? Or are you so smitten it slipped your mind? She has bewitched you for her own purposes."

"Shut your mouth, Captain. You've bedded trollops for so long, you place every woman in that category." Alexander began to rethink his vow not to harm another man.

"Think rationally for a minute, Colonel. That's all I ask." Sitting down on a log, Smith ran a hand through his long hair. "If you're correct about William not betraying you—and you could be, at that—then consider this. I saw Miss Harrison and her maid leaving that same barn a few weeks back."

Alexander felt his blood pulse against his temples. According to rumors among the men, Smith had a penchant for inflicting pain on women. He hated the thought of him anywhere near Emily. "You've been watching Miss Harrison behind my back?" he asked, stepping away from the fire. "You dared to speak to her?"

Smith nodded. "When I accidentally discovered them while scouting, I asked what they were doing. Miss Harrison said they were delivering medicine to Front Royal from the depot in Harper's Ferry. That it had gotten dark, so they holed up in the barn until morning."

"What does that prove? Uncle Porter often sent Miss Harrison and Lila on such errands until I convinced him it was unsafe." Alexander glared at his second-in-command with ill-concealed contempt.

"Let me finish. I offered to escort them to Front Royal, but they refused. So I followed for a distance to ensure their safety." Smith forestalled his commander with upraised palms. "When the ladies reached the crossroad, their wagon turned north toward Boyce, not south to Front Royal. Miss Harrison lied about what she was up to."

Alexander pondered the information without a flicker of emotion crossing his face.

Smith snapped, gesturing wildly like a madman. "She was headed to the headquarters of the Second Corps, encamped not ten miles away."

"She could have changed her route to Boyce for fear of one side or the other confiscating her supplies." Alexander offered an alternative explanation for her actions in a cool, matter-of-fact tone.

"She's a spy, an informant who's probably warmed plenty of Yankee beds while laughing behind your back. I should have forced the truth from her when I had the chance in Berryville."

The colonel closed the distance between them in two strides. Before Smith could react, Alexander's fist had crashed into the man's face. Blood flew everywhere as the punch broke Smith's nose. Alexander drew back to strike again, but two of his soldiers restrained his arm. Smith landed a blow before soldiers restrained him too. The colonel barely felt the impact to his chest. All of his frustration over their botched mission, along with the interminable war, had been poured into that one punch. He might have killed Smith if their shouts hadn't roused his rangers to intervene. Yet what would that have changed?

"Stay away from her or I will kill you," he shouted, shaking off the soldiers' hands. "Do you hear me, Captain? If you as much as come near her..."

He took a deep breath and tried to calm down a little. *Doubtful that anyone within five miles didn't just hear me.* If Union patrols were searching for the scattered rangers, their melee would alert them for certain. The colonel faced his men, who clustered at a safe distance. "Mount up. We need to break camp and separate. Dawson, douse the fire and take half the men into the hills by southern roads. Stay out of sight for several months. Don't even *think* about going home until all of this dies down. Federal patrols will be watching the roads. Because they know who I am, they'll figure out who most of you are soon enough."

"Yes, sir." Saluting, Dawson started kicking dirt into the fire.

Alexander turned back to Smith, still restrained by two men. His eye had already begun to swell shut, and bright blood stained his white shirt. "Captain Smith, you will take the other half due west. If any of you are captured with me, you will be hung for sure. You'll have your best chance of survival if I'm not in direct command. You men fought bravely tonight and made me proud. You've been a credit to the Confederacy. May God keep you safe until we are reunited." He offered a final salute to the soldiers who until that night had served him without bloodshed.

Captain Smith didn't return his salute like the other soldiers, but at least he mounted up and did as ordered. No one questioned where the colonel was headed or when he would call their regiment together. No one dared.

Once they had broken camp, Alexander rode off in the early hours of dawn. He'd had enough of this war. After his fistfight with Smith, he no longer recognized the man he'd become. Heading deep into the Shenandoah Mountains, he paused only long enough to rest his horse. He hadn't slept in two days and wouldn't until that night. The road he traveled finally thinned to a narrow mountain trace he knew no Union cavalry would find. Only locals knew about and used these paths for hunting or visiting their kin. Every road went nowhere—exactly where the Gray Wraith wanted to be.

Alexander spotted a low-hanging spruce tree close to a patch of late fall grass. With his horse watered and tethered on a long rope to graze, he wrapped himself in his blanket and immediately fell asleep until the following midday. He dreamed of rangers with wild flashing eyes firing point blank at Union cavalry and of his men dying on Uncle Thaddeus's blood-stained lawn.

His dreams were also filled with a red-haired woman whose laughter still echoed in his ears. Emily reached for him in the dream and called his name, her scent of lemon balm soothing like an elixir. With her hair spilling across her shoulders like a lion's mane, she'd splashed through a shallow stream with bare feet and her skirt clutched in one fist. As she beckoned, the woman seemed a blinding brightness in his dark world of death. He followed her to a secret grotto where only pure light could penetrate. He wanted to cling to her, but she stayed just beyond his grasp. Like a drowning man in a turbulent river, he struggled. Then she vanished with the morning mist.

Alexander woke tangled in his blanket. Casting off the heavy wool, he scraped his face with his hands to rid himself of the dream.

Unfortunately, he couldn't forget memories of Emily quite so easily. She would haunt his waking thoughts as well. Had she and William safely reached Front Royal? Was that even where they were headed? Or were Smith's accusations correct—had she led the Yankee cavalry straight to Middleburg? His heart ached from worry and frustration. Struggling to light a fire in the damp woods, Alexander refused to believe Emily would betray his men. He'd watched her catch moths to release outdoors before they died in a candle's flame. If she had such compassion for the smallest of God's creatures, could she think so little of His greatest? No, despite her politics and headstrong will, he was certain Emily would never cause the loss of so many lives.

Alexander had pledged a long time ago to never trust a woman again. His men looked to him for more than orders during a skirmish. They expected their commander not to endanger them unnecessarily in areas where battle lines changed frequently. If his faith in Emily had been misguided, then he was the one responsible for the debacle at Middleburg.

The following months passed in a blur. Alexander spent his time in the mindless activity of building a shelter—one he knew he would soon abandon—just to keep busy. He worked long days fashioning a lean-to from small trees, weaving pine boughs tightly together for the roof. The matting kept out all but the hardest of rains. He foraged for corn for his horse in a wide circle, returning to his camp each night. The supplies carried in his saddlebags had dwindled quickly, and food for himself was scarce. But it was his empty heart, not his empty stomach, that plagued him. Often when sleep refused to come, he would stare into the campfire remembering something Emily had said, or how she tossed her hair, or the petulant stamp of her foot. And of her words? More to the point, the words she hadn't spoken at the harvest ball. He had earnestly professed his love, and she had stared at him with her cat-green eyes saying nothing. Despite his good intentions, despite his vow made long ago, he realized he'd fallen in love that night…hopelessly, irrevocably in love.

Could Emily ever love a Southerner as she had loved her betrothed? One thing about the dead—memories of them improved with the passing of time.

And what of Smith's accusations? It just wasn't possible that she was a spy. She couldn't manage to remember a sunhat to keep her nose from burning. Emily had risked her own life to save his in Middleburg. She had ridden into a hornet nest of trigger-happy soldiers from both sides. If she'd wished to betray him, she could have given his whereabouts to the Yankees and remained far removed from the consequences. No, he didn't believe Smith's loathsome assertion, but he would never learn the truth hiding in the mountains. He could ponder and surmise from sunrise to sunset with none to hear his ramblings but birds and an occasional curious fawn. With the Union cavalry still searching for him, he must bide his time. Then he would face her and listen to her side of what happened in Middleburg that night, besides her two mysterious trips to Berryville.

And pray his trusting heart hadn't been fooled again.

News of the ambush of the Gray Wraith and his rangers spread across western Virginia almost before William and Emily returned from Middleburg. That fateful night, Emily dropped from her horse into Lila's loving arms, more exhausted than ever before in her life. She couldn't remember climbing the stairs to her room, or undressing, or slipping between the cool, pressed sheets in her room at Hunt Farms. She remembered nothing until she awoke at midday with Lila looming above her and commotion throughout the household.

"Wake up," demanded Lila, pulling back the top sheet. "You must pack your things and then help Mrs. Bennington pack hers. I need to help pack the kitchen and pantry."

Emily rubbed sleep from her eyes and struggled upright. "Where are we going?" Gratefully, she reached for the cup of coffee on her bedside table.

"Both Mr. Hunt and Dr. Bennington are moving their families from Hunt Farms to a safer area. There's no time to spare." Lila flew around the room opening drawers and armoire doors. "Because everyone now knows the identity of the Gray Wraith, the Yankees will soon be here searching for him. We aren't that far from the Federal camp. Dr. Bennington said the Yankees might retaliate if they don't find Mr. Alexander or his rangers." Lila dumped a pile of dainties onto the bed.

Emily staggered to her wardrobe, pressing her fingertips to her temples. "How can we pack up a house this large?"

Lila pulled Emily's trunk from the closet. "We can't. Everyone is to take only their most cherished possessions, plus all the provisions from the cellar that will fit into the wagons. Mr. Hunt has already left with a tether of horses to turn over to the Confederate cavalry. He's keeping only his prized stock and a few pregnant mares." Her expression turned sympathetic toward the plantation owner. "He'll be able to start over someday."

Emily washed her face and dressed quickly. "What about the workers, Lila, slave and free? Mr. Lincoln's edict doesn't take effect until January."

Lila upended a drawer into the trunk. "Mr. Hunt invited his free house staff to move to Richmond. Beatrice, Jack, and a few others accepted. Plus William, of course." She angled a grin in Emily's direction. "He's leaving behind the slaves with food and a small stipend of cash. He gave each of his stable workers a horse to make their way north."

Emily yanked dresses from the closet. "Will they go north with a battle raging all around us?"

"Most of them will. They'll take their chances. But some have families in the area, so they will probably still be here when the Hunts return, no matter how long it takes."

Emily stopped packing to reach for Lila's hand. "Richmond is the heart of the Confederacy. Why not Martinsburg? And what about your family?"

She shrugged. "My parents are paid good wages. They will move wherever their jobs are. Dr. Bennington said their house in Martinsburg is probably overrun by soldiers, now that Berkeley County seceded from the state of Virginia and rejoined the United States."

"What about Bennington Island? Your mother loved living there."

"She would have no job on Bennington Island. Who knows what the new folks are like? Maybe they cook for themselves or maybe that house burned to the ground." Lila shrugged her shoulders. "Mama won't like living in a noisy, crowded city, but she would like joining former slaves living in tents even less. Everything is changing. Now, please, Emily, we must hurry."

Everything changed for Emily too. Within twelve hours they left Front Royal in a slow caravan of buggies, wagons, and tethered horses and journeyed to Richmond along roads ruined by the constant movement of troops and artillery. Hampered by horrible weather, the trip took weeks as they joined hundreds entering a city already filled to capacity with freed blacks and homeless whites whose farms had been destroyed by the advancing Federal Army. Richmond also teemed with invalided soldiers and deserters from the Rebel Army.

A cold rain was falling on the slick, cobbled streets of Richmond where they finally arrived that dreary December day. James Hunt's widowed Aunt Harriet graciously took them in, opening her faded mansion to both families along with their staffs. Harriet Cabot had little to share with her guests, however. The Federal blockade of the port effectively halted all shipments into the city. And what little still grew on the surrounding farms had to feed a lot of hungry mouths. Food was scarce in Richmond, and what could be found cost dearly. Long lines formed each morning in front of the bakery and green grocers. Matilde joined the queue each day to barter with something they had brought from Hunt Farms.

SPRING 1863

Emily looked out from the parlor window on a bleak city of privation. Spring seemed to have bypassed this part of the world, despite what the calendar indicated. Yet the Benningtons and Hunts went about their business with the same rectitude that had always graced their lives. Dr. Bennington arrived at the sprawling Chimborazo Hospital on the outskirts of Richmond before dawn each day. A larger hospital had never existed in the world, yet it proved inadequate for the constant flow of sick and wounded, both Confederate and Yankee. Mr. Hunt moved his valuable horse stock to a rented stable on the James River, where he continued to buy and sell on a limited basis. Dignified Mrs. Hunt and quiet-mannered Mrs. Bennnington set about turning the run-down residence into a comfortable home for the two transplanted families. With plenty of room in her three-story mansion on Franklin Street, Mrs. Cabot appreciated the attention she received more than the physical help with chores. All but one of her slaves left following the effective date of the Emancipation Proclamation. The loyal maid who had remained wasn't able to do more than cook simple meals for two old ladies and wash their frayed dresses in a tub on the porch. They acted more like sisters than employer and servant, fretting about each other's aches and aliments.

Emily was troubled by more than adjustments to a city in turmoil. Recriminating memories of past actions followed her around the house like Mrs. Cabot's tabby cat. She wasn't the same fiery abolitionist who had left Ohio two years ago. Her conviction that slavery was an evil that never should have come to the New World remained the same, but now that it had been abolished, she saw that the newly freed had few choices open to them. Many joined the tent camps of burned-out refugees from the surrounding farms. The first step had been taken, but a permanent solution in the ravished South was obviously years away.

No, what changed for Emily had been brewing for a long while. She was in love with Alexander. Of that she was certain. No one had ever touched her heart as he had, not even Matthew. She had judged him to be a shallow, vapid aristocrat and overlooked his kindness and integrity. Alexander and his family weren't like others in the privileged class of inherited money, land, and power, yet she had judged the Hunts with her preconceived biases. Shame over her past deception filled her with sorrow. Had she shared even one honest conversation with Alexander? Perhaps a woman lacking honor could not recognize it in others.

The lesson had cost her the only man she had ever loved. How stupid she had been. He might have overlooked her lack of sophistication, but who could overlook manipulation and trickery? Telling herself the end justified the means, Emily had borne false witness many times. She had stolen from him and from his family. Alexander would have freed his slaves if they had been his to free. He would have given her what she wanted if she'd asked. But she never gave him the chance. Now it was too late. The look he gave her inside the stable of Marshall House said it all. *I do not trust you. And I can never love a woman I cannot trust.*

EIGHTEEN

The rain had dwindled to a drizzle when Alexander, tired beyond measure and sporting a heavy beard, rode into the Hunt Farms stable yard. Traveling by night with only moonlight to guide him, he had circled around Front Royal to the east in case cavalry patrols still watched the roads from the mountains. Not having seen a newspaper or heard military reports in several months, he didn't know if Union troops had found more important matters to occupy themselves. But he couldn't stay away from home a moment longer even if Yankee cavalry camped in the orchards and Union officers dined at his mother's Hepplewhite table. He also couldn't stay away from Emily any longer. He needed to talk to her, to hear what she had to say. He owed her that much. Even if he left his beloved Shenandoah Valley for the remainder of the war, he had to gaze on her sweet face one last time. He owed himself that.

Reining Phantom to a halt outside their largest horse barn, Alexander felt an uneasiness hanging in the air like a mist. Nothing seemed as it should. The stable doors swung back and forth in the breeze, banging each time upon a rusted hasp. Dead leaves swirled across a barnyard no one had swept in weeks. Wiping rain from his eyes, he stared in the direction of the house that had been his home since birth. He'd heard tales of Yankee vindictiveness, of burning the homes and businesses of people suspected of aiding rangers. What price had his parents paid for having sired the Wraith? But when the moon broke through the cloud cover, the outline of the house appeared before him unscathed.

Alexander dismounted to inspect the stable and barns first. Every single horse, mule, cow, and laying hen was gone. The Union Army had confiscated every piece of tack and equipment they could carry—his father's lifetime of hard work. On his way to the house, he noticed that the flower garden had been trampled and the vegetable plots picked clean. Not a cabbage, squash, or carrot remained. But the absence of any human life felt the most ominous. No one seemed to live or work at Hunt Farms anymore. Alexander entered the house through the front door, removed his hat ridiculously from habit, and then walked through one dusty room after another. Most of the massive, heavy furniture remained, but the chairs, paintings, silver, crystal—anything valuable and easily carried off to be resold—were gone.

Where were his parents and the Benningtons? And where was Emily? He prayed she had returned with William from Middleburg and was with his family.

Alexander opened the door at the far end of the center hall to gaze over his father's abandoned pastures and fields. In every direction, the once-fertile land had been stripped clean and beaten down. Not even a crow perched on forlorn branches in between meals of fallen corn kernels.

Suddenly, the distinctive sound of a chair scraping across wood lifted the hairs on the back of his neck. Someone was in the house, directly below him in the winter kitchen. Drawing a long-barreled Colt from his belt, he silently made his way down the narrow interior steps. Carrying no firearm on his ranger forays was one thing—he endangered no one but himself. But returning to Hunt Farms without a weapon, the infamous home of the Gray Wraith, was unthinkable. He would have no way to protect his parents...or Emily.

At the bottom of the dark steps, his boot caught on a broken tread and sent him flying. Someone jumped up from a pallet close to the dying fire. Others stirred and fought to extract themselves from their blankets. Were deserters living in the cellar of his home? "Identify yourself and state your business!" he shouted. Then he leveled his gun at the man moving toward him.

"Mr. Hunt?" said a tenuous voice in the dark.

Alexander struck a match to put a face to the familiar voice. Someone close to the hearth lit a tallow candle. The flickering light revealed the weathered face of their best horse trainer.

"Ephraim?" he asked, jamming his gun back into his belt.

"Yes, sir, it's me. We're livin' down here to look after things the best we can." The face of Ephraim's wife, his mother's seamstress, stepped into the yellow pool. One by one, four children rose from the floor to join her side.

"Hello, Mr. Alex," said Fanny. She hefted the smallest child to her hip.

He stared at one and then the other. "Where is everyone? Where's my family?"

"They're gone, sir, gone to Richmond to your Aunt Harriet's. Your pa said I should tell you that, but nobody else. So far, you're the first who asked. We hid when those soldiers came. They made an awful racket."

"And made a mess too," added Fanny. "I cleaned up best I could, but I can't fix what's broken." The woman whom he'd known most of his life smiled at him shyly.

"Thank you. I'll see that you're paid for your work. I'm just not sure when that will be." Unsure what to do, Alexander awkwardly extended his hand to Ephraim.

The former slave shook it heartily. "Sit by the fire, sir, while my wife fixes you somethin' to eat. It ain't much, but whatever we got we'll share."

"Much obliged," Alexander said, feeling like a guest in his own home. "Tell me everything you know, Ephraim. Leave nothing out." He ran a hand through his shoulder-length hair.

"Not much to tell, sir. Mr. Hunt and Dr. Bennington packed up whatever they could carry in the wagons. Then Mr. Hunt roped most of his best horses together and gave the rest away. He gave me that paint Morgan, but the soldiers took her." His mouth pulled into a frown. "Mr. Hunt told us they were going to Richmond, where it would be safer for the womenfolk." Ephraim waited for this to be absorbed.

Alexander exhaled a sigh. "Then my family wasn't jailed by the Yankees."

"A couple freemen who had been gettin' paid went to Richmond. Most everybody who had been a slave just run off. Your ma gave them a little money and told them to take food and whatever their pockets could hold." Ephraim lowered his voice to a whisper. "Some are still here, hidin' from the army in the woods. They are scared the Yankees will force them to join up. They don't wanna get shot."

Fanny handed him a cup of the weakest chicory coffee he'd ever tasted, but he nodded his appreciation. "My father should have signed papers giving folks their freedom long ago," Alexander said quietly.

"Yes, sir, he should of." Ephraim poured himself a cup from the pot on the hearth. "But he gave away almost as many horses as he took, plus food and clothes too."

"Your ma gave the women blankets, cook pots, all kinds of things." Fanny interjected, slicing off a piece of dark, crumbly bread. "She divided her purse money between the women too."

Alexander forced himself to meet the woman's eye—a woman his family had held in bondage. Shame filled his empty gut. Shame and regret. "Where did they go, all of our people?"

"They ain't your people no more," said Ephraim with pride. "Most went north to try to find kinfolk. Some said they were going west. A few are still livin' out in their old cabins until they make up their minds where they're goin'. They do some trappin' to eat and hide from the soldiers."

"Why are you still here, Ephraim?" Alexander asked softly. "You're free. You could have left anytime."

Ephraim pulled on his beard sagely. "Oh, we'll go one of these days, but I ain't got a place in mind right now. Until I figure it out, might as well stay and look after things for a spell."

Handing him the bread and some slices of cheese, Fanny nodded in agreement.

One question still remained. Alexander swallowed hard before asking. "What about my Aunt Augusta's governess? Did Miss Harrison accompany my family to Richmond?"

Having little contact with house staff, Ephraim looked confused. "Can't say yay or nay, sir. I was packing the feed wagons before they left." He looked to his wife, who simply shrugged.

"Thank you, Ephraim, Fanny. Stay as long as you wish." Giving them permission for something they had done for months seemed ridiculous. He quickly finished his meal, drank down the rest of his coffee, and then said, "I'm going upstairs to sleep in my room if the bed's still there."

"Oh, it's still there, but you won't find a sheet or a blanket nowhere. Best to sleep in your clothes." Fanny peered curiously at his outfit, which obviously had been slept in for some time as she handed him a stub of a tallow candle.

As he wandered up two flights of steps, weary beyond description, his home felt desolate and alien, but at least no one had taken a torch and burned it to the ground. "Thank You, God," he whispered in the darkness. Stretching out on his bed, he wrapped himself in the same tattered blanket he had carried from the mountains, but sleep refused to come. Troubling questions plagued him until dawn. Why would Emily go with the Benningtons to Richmond? Wouldn't she have sought safe passage back north with help from the Yankee Army? If she were a spy, she needed the governess subterfuge no longer. And she needed him no longer.

Either way, she must hate him knowing his true identity—a man who wreaked havoc on her beloved Union Army. Alone in his cold, damp bedroom, Alexander had only the memory of a few stolen kisses to keep him warm. Tomorrow he would head for Richmond. And he would not rest until he knew the truth.

Autumn 1863

The sunlight warmed his already overheated skin as Nathan Smith walked back to his boarding house. However, his spirits needed little buoying up. After many months of evading Yankee patrols determined to capture the legendary Rebel Rangers, he finally felt safe to walk the streets of his country's new capital—Richmond. His visit to the

Confederate War Department had gone well. The Secretary of War not only received him but listened intently to how a Yankee had ingratiated herself into the lives of the Benningtons and Hunts. People of their class never would have suspected someone like her. Possessing high moral standards, they assumed everyone else was of the same ilk.

Nathan inflated only minor parts of his report, exaggerating a bit here and embellishing a bit there to blame the Middleburg fiasco on that red-haired wench. True, he had no proof that Miss Harrison reported the movement of Confederate troops through the Shenandoah, along with their strength in numbers to the Yankees, but she was up to no-good. He was certain she'd led the enemy to the Marshall House that horrible night. Many of his compatriots, his lifelong friends, were moldering in their graves instead of riding beside him.

The fact that Colonel Hunt had protected her grated on Nathan sorely. But he couldn't blame Alex—the man was a babe in the woods when it came to women. This wasn't the first time a female had wormed her way into his heart and gained a foothold. Nathan enjoyed a romp between the bed sheets too, but Alex failed to realize women couldn't be trusted. They would say anything to get their way. So he boiled quite a stew at the War Department and then dropped the skinny governess into the pot. Now Emily Harrison would get her just reward.

Thanks to her, the Union government knew the Gray Wraith's identity. The Southern newspapers had portrayed him as a hero, pointing out that his social position hadn't prevented him from serving the Cause. Some of the rangers who escaped the Middleburg trap joined the regular cavalry, praising their former commander to anyone who would listen. The rest disbanded and scattered to the four winds. Their handpicked band could no longer slip across enemy lines to raid horse stockades or commandeer a trainload of supplies, disappearing into the woods like mist. The plunder Nathan had reaped from sutlers' wagons while the colonel had been occupied was especially missed by his family. Their plantation hadn't turned a profit since long before the war. With his side venture gone, Nathan felt the financial pinch. Confederate pay envelopes were too small and too infrequent to support those with healthy appetites. The commission he'd been offered in the regular cavalry held little appeal. Officers' pay was little more than a foot soldier's. And a captain's rank placed a man in a perfect location to be shot during battle. Not an appealing proposition. His glory stemmed from being a ranger, not dying for the Glorious Cause.

All this because of a woman.

Losing the colonel's respect and friendship had been the hardest to bear. Emily Harrison had destroyed everything for Nathan. He would enjoy watching her swing from a rope outside Castle Thunder—the price for treason. When she confessed her crimes to spare her neck at the gallows, Alexander would thank him for his diligence. With men of the home guard soon on their way to Franklin Street, that Yankee governess wouldn't be sitting so high and mighty much longer.

"It was rather hard at first, Miss Harrison, to make ourselves understood." Margaret Bennington explained in her cultured voice. "The nuns and other students had never heard French spoken with a Southern accent before. When we would ask someone at table to please pass the bread, they would stare and ponder the question. Then they would pass the jam," she added with tinkling laughter.

"When I requested a new sliver of soap, I received an extra towel," said Annie. Perched on the arm of her sister's chair, she was eager to fill in the details about their stay in Paris.

Emily looked from one of her newly returned charges to the other with joy. She had missed Margaret's gentle spirit, along with Annie's dauntless enthusiasm. She wasn't good at sipping tea or taking leisurely walks in the garden once they ran out of materials to repair the mansion. While abroad, Margaret had matured into a charming young lady and no longer required a governess. That would soon be the case with the younger Bennington daughter as well. Shaking off her sorrows, Emily leaned forward in her straight-backed chair. "Tell me more. Don't leave out a single thing."

Margaret smoothed a tiny wrinkle from her skirt. "Once, when I told classmates I would meet them on the Champs Elysees at half past three, they went there promptly at noon to wait. I apparently lacked something in my pronunciation." Margaret reached for Emily's hand. "How I wish you could see the Rue de Rivoli—so many lovely shops. And the Cathedral of Notre Dame took my breath away."

"Perhaps someday I will. For now, I'm so happy you're home…and that you found us in Richmond at your great-aunt's."

Annie picked up the narrative. "Papa wrote to say it was time we returned to Virginia. He said we would be safe in the capital of the Confederacy, so he sent money to the school and documents with official stamps in the sealing wax. Sister Maddy took us by train to the port and put us on a ship bound for Baltimore. We could get through the blockade there. We were only delayed twice during the train ride south." She beamed with pride over her father's cleverness.

"Mama is glad to have us home," said Margaret. "She and Aunt Rebecca plan to restore Aunt Harriett's house to its former beauty. I've never seen her with so much energy." Glancing over her shoulder, she dropped her voice to whisper. "Do you think we're safe in Richmond, Miss Harrison? We saw some loathsome sights coming from the train station."

"According to the papers, the Army of Northern Virginia is nearby. Robert E. Lee promises he'll never let Richmond fall into enemy hands." Emily cringed at her wording. How could she refer to President Lincoln and the Union Army as the enemy? "We shall trust our future to the Lord and worry not. Now, tell me your plans, Margaret. Will you still make your debut this winter despite the war?"

The young woman's smile faltered. "Why bother? What kind of social season will there be with the men gone to war?"

"Or dead." Annie stated the obvious fact everyone had been thinking.

"Hush, now. Don't speak of such things." Emily admonished, resuming her role as governess.

"She's right, Miss Harrison. Who is left to one day ask Papa for my hand? I will die a spinster, perhaps living in one of the attic rooms above." Margaret gestured toward the ceiling.

For a brief moment, Emily couldn't help but pity the girl. Despite poverty and hardship everywhere, Margaret had once looked forward to her first social season with no concerns other than finding suitable gowns for each ball. Or maybe where her future husband would take her to live—city townhouse or country estate?

Margaret's voice broke into Emily's woolgathering, "…here I am going on and on when we brought you gifts from Paris."

Annie scampered into the hall and soon returned with two boxes covered with pastel tissue.

"You shouldn't have done such a thing. Money is scarce these days and shouldn't be wasted." When Margaret's smile faded again, Emily quickly amended her response. "But since you already have, I can't wait to see what has sailed across the ocean."

"Open mine first." Annie handed her the smaller of the boxes.

Emily tore off the wrappings and extracted a crystal flagon. "A bottle of perfume!" She unscrewed the silver cap and sniffed the stopper. "Oh, my. It's heavenly." Emily dabbed her pulse points as Miss Turner had taught her.

"Open my gift," Margaret said, her face lighting up in anticipation of her governess's happiness.

Emily undid the ribbons and pulled up layers of tissue. "Books," she said as her throat clogged with emotion. "The latest works by Alexandre Dumas. I will treasure these." She lifted one to inspect and then clutched it to her chest. There were six leather embossed volumes, printed on the finest quality velum. "I thank both of you. I've never received lovelier gifts."

Margaret squeezed her hand. "Perhaps you could read aloud to us in the afternoons, the way you did on Bennington Island."

"I will, whenever I'm not needed elsewhere." Emily blinked back her tears. "Tell me more about the French because I probably never will go to Europe."

Margaret happily obliged. "They were very nice but peculiar in

some ways. They ignore most vegetables but eat sweets in vast quan-
tities. They drink red wine with every meal except breakfast, and sip
strong coffee from tiny cups." Her fingers indicated the diminutive
size.

Annie shook her head, sending her long curls flying. "One day I
asked Madame why she didn't buy a real cup—one that would hold
more. She said that simply wasn't done."

"Perhaps you can send her one of ours as a token of your appreciation." Emily's suggestion sent the youngest Bennington scurrying
from the room.

After watching her go, Margaret turned toward Emily with a somber expression. "I'm so glad you came to Richmond with my parents.
I would miss you sorely if you had returned to Ohio."

Emily drew in a deep breath to steady her nerves. "And I would
miss both of you, but someday I must go back. Ohio is my home. It's
where I belong." The words echoed falsely in her ears. What was left
for her there? She had no friends, no family, not even her self-righteous
ideals to pack in the valise with her calicos when she floated across the
river. She had changed, and now she fit in nowhere and belonged to no
one. She could never be a Southerner, yet thanks to Alexander's influence, she no longer felt like a Yankee.

Margaret graciously changed the subject. "Would you like to see
the fabrics we brought from France? We can each have a new dress even
if we must sew them ourselves."

"Of course I would." Emily forced self-pity from her mind and
immersed herself in the girls she'd missed so much. At least it allowed
less time to think about Alexander. Nothing in the world could help
that particular situation.

"Tea, ladies?" Lila carried in a tray with a pot and cups, and then she
stayed for the remainder of the afternoon. The four laughed and shared
stories to fill in the gaps in their lives. Emily told about dancing under
the stars at the outdoor harvest festival. When Lila provided an amusing pantomime of Emily's dancing, the Bennington girls laughed until
tears streamed down their cheeks. Emily didn't mind Lila's reminder of

her awkwardness. But in return, she provided a worthy tableau of Lila swooning after the indomitable William.

"Cousin Alexander's valet?" Margaret squealed with delight. "Oh, do tell. I love to hear tales of romance. Such talk was strictly forbidden in the convent school." Margaret leaned toward the group conspiratorially. "One day the headmistress found mention of a single kiss in a poem, and she threw the volume into the fire."

Annie provided a smacking sound with her lips.

Although she relayed no further details of first kisses or poignant glances across the room, Emily knew where Lila's heart lay. In Alexander's absence, William worked as valet to both Mr. Hunt and Dr. Bennington.

No lessons, recitations, or musical skits were held that afternoon in the parlor. Four hearts took simple joy in recalling the past and reconnecting in the present. The future, as uncertain as it was for all of them, could wait.

The young women, still engrossed in their reminiscences, didn't notice Alexander at first when he stepped into the room. Then Lila spotted him and gasped, followed by Annie, who threw down her sewing and ran toward the doorway. "Alexander! Is it really you? I've missed you so!" she cried, wrapping both arms around his waist.

Alexander lifted his younger cousin off her feet, swinging her around in a wide arc. She squealed with delight. "And I've missed you."

Margaret approached when her sister's feet were no longer a danger. "Welcome home, cousin. One year gone and only a few letters to assure Aunt Rebecca you remained among the living? She will take a switch to you, despite your size and reputation." She arched up on tiptoes to peck his cheek demurely.

"I'm afraid it couldn't be helped. My men needed to blend back into their lives quietly. I couldn't come home until all had done so."

Even Lila dropped her needlework to pump his hand enthusiastically. "I'm so glad you're safe, Mr. Hunt."

Emily had paled to the color of milk but remained in her chair. She sat as motionless as a statue. Once greetings were complete, everyone's eyes turned toward her.

"Miss Harrison, aren't you going to welcome Cousin Alexander to Richmond?" asked Margaret.

"Don't you wish to come get a hug?" Annie asked impishly.

"Have you turned to stone?" Lila inquired.

With her eyes focused on the floor, Emily struggled to find something to say.

"Why don't we see about a fresh pot of tea while you two get reacquainted?" Margaret moved smoothly toward the door as Lila followed with the tray. But Annie remained in her chair, determined to see what might happen between her cousin and governess.

"Annie, Lila needs both of us to help." Trilling like a songbird, Margaret dragged her sister from the room by her arm.

"I'm surprised to see you, Miss Harrison." Alexander waited to speak until they were alone.

"Why would you be surprised?" Emily's voice sounded foreign to her ears. "As of yet, I haven't been fired by Mrs. Bennington."

Alexander turned his back to her and stared out the window onto the street below. "Yes, but isn't your work here done? Mr. Lincoln's proclamation took effect last January, freeing all those held in bondage in those states in rebellion. Any who hadn't already run away surely left then. Your railroad no longer has much purpose." He faced her with unreadable eyes.

"Yes, Mr. Hunt. The president's edict gave me great joy."

"Isn't that what all of this was about?" His hand flourished around the once-elegant parlor. "Isn't that what *we* were about? You came into our home under my aunt's employ to free our slaves from bondage."

"Well, yes…in the beginning. I came under false pretenses and deceived the Benningtons and your parents." Her mouth and throat suddenly went dry.

Alexander withdrew a packet of papers from his frock coat and tossed them down on the table between them. "I had these drawn up but waited too long. I'd wished to provide them adequate money for travel, but there had never seemed to be enough."

Unsteadily, she rose and walked to the table, filled with an unexplainable sense of dread. Loosening the ribbon, Emily began to read the first sheet of dozens. "By the powers vested in me by the Commonwealth of Virginia, I hereby grant the complete and irrevocable manumission of the following named slave. From this day forward and for all time, he shall be free, from any and all...." Her voice trailed off as she gaped at him. "Manumission papers. You freed the Hunt Farm slaves?"

"It took a while for my father to agree with me. This should have been done years ago." He walked back to the window, where the rain beat steadily against the pane. "If you only had asked me, I would have given you this. And anything else you wanted in this world."

Emily opened her mouth to speak, but he held up a hand to silence her. "Oh, I nearly forgot. I have something else for you." Alexander withdrew a thin gold chain and burnished locket from his pocket. It swung for a moment before her eyes like a hypnotist's pendulum.

"My locket!" Emily tried to snatch it from his fingers. "Wherever did you find it?"

"On the carpet of my room. You must have dropped it when you came snooping. Was this your talisman, your motivation for your underground work? Allowing you to say words you didn't mean?"

"Of course not! Why would you say such a thing?" With her hands on her hips, she faced him defiantly.

He opened the locket to reveal a faded daguerreotype of Matthew, her former fiancé. She gaped at a young face she could barely remember. Her heart clenched in her chest, not for Matthew but for the implication.

"Then why did you wear it when you came to my room to find me?"

"It was a gift from my parents at my graduation from Miss Turner's School for Ladies. I wore it to remember them, not Matthew. I hadn't opened it since leaving Bennington Island." She sounded like a weak and helpless child.

"Didn't you serve your abolitionist cause in Matthew's memory? Didn't you come south determined to let nothing or no one stand in your path?"

Tears of shame filled her eyes, but she refused to tell more lies. "Yes, that was true when I arrived." She joined him at the window. Below on the street, a farm wagon splashed a hapless pedestrian from head to toe. She felt every bit as wretched. "But after I met you, the locket became nothing more than a gift from my parents." Sounding shaky and uncertain, she forced herself to continue. "I regret deceiving your family in light of their kindness to me. More than that, I regret the lies I told you. But on my heart, I pledge that I care for you. Despite how our situation started, I love you, Alexander." Emily exhaled with relief. She had finally voiced the words she'd withheld too long. The man she wanted stood before her in all his glory. She yearned to caress his stubbly chin, run her fingers through his hair, and kiss away the fatigue around his eyes.

But someone pounding on the front door just then was making enough noise to wake the dead.

"Sakes alive! Who would be calling on Aunt Harriet at the supper hour?" Alexander strode across the room toward the commotion in the hallway.

Emily froze in place, partially obscured by the heavy drape, as an ominous foreboding tightened her gut. She jumped when the parlor door flew open, thudding against the stopper. Three uniformed soldiers marched in boldly, followed by a distraught Mrs. Hunt and a nearly prostrate Mrs. Cabot.

A young officer, dressed in Confederate gray, scanned the room until his gaze found her. "Miss Emily Harrison?" he asked coldly. He didn't immediately notice Alexander partially hidden by the door.

Emily straightened her back with every ounce of dignity she could muster. "Yes, sir. I am she."

"What is this about, Lieutenant?" In three strides, Alexander stepped between Emily and the soldiers.

"Sir!" The lieutenant snapped a quick salute to a superior officer.

The other two followed suit. "I'm Lieutenant Rose of the Richmond Home Guard. I apologize for intruding on your household this afternoon. I have orders signed by the Secretary of War himself, sir." He handed Alexander a rolled parchment with Secretary Seddon's stamp emblazoned in the wax.

Mrs. Hunt and Mrs. Cabot, flanking the other two soldiers, offered indignant protests. Alexander broke the seal and began to read the document. Margaret, Annie, and Lila slipped into the room, huddling against the wall like abandoned kittens.

Without waiting for the colonel to peruse the document, Lieutenant Rose stepped around him. "Miss Emily Harrison, you have been charged with espionage and treason against the Confederate States of America. We are placing you under arrest."

"You most decidedly are not!" Alexander drew his sword in one fluid motion.

But the lieutenant had anticipated such a response. Pulling a long-barreled Colt from his holster, he aimed it slightly to the left. "I deeply regret this, Colonel Hunt, in light of your extraordinary service to the Cause, but I must ask you to step back, sir." He enunciated each word so no one would misunderstand his intentions. "I'm sure you have no wish to further distress your family." With a gloved hand, he gestured at the frightened faces of the five waiting women.

Alexander didn't flinch. "Then I suggest you leave at once. Miss Harrison will remain with me."

Lieutenant Rose pointed the gun barrel at the center of his chest. "You may take the matter up with Secretary Seddon, sir, but I intend to follow my orders."

A horrible silence filled the room as Margaret Bennington circled around to join Emily's side. "There must be some mistake. I can vouch that this woman would never do such things." She bravely slipped her arm around Emily's waist. Against the wall, Annie began to cry.

"There is no mistake, miss." The lieutenant offered a slight bow without lowering his weapon. "Your governess is responsible for exposing the Gray Wraith and curtailing his vital work. Unfortunately,

Colonel Hunt has fallen under a siren's spell. Prison will be too good for this Delilah." The two soldiers trained their guns on Alexander as the lieutenant approached Emily. "Miss Harrison, if you give your word to accompany us without incident, we'll forgo the use of restraints." He glared at her with ill-concealed contempt.

"You have my word." On rubbery legs Emily walked to the door with Lieutenant Rose at her side.

"I demand to know where you are taking her." Sheathing his sword, Alexander advanced to follow.

The stockier of the two guards placed his gun barrel beneath the colonel's jaw. "You and me will wait right here until their carriage leaves, but it's no secret as to where she's going. She's on her way to Castle Thunder—where all Union spies hang."

NINETEEN

I will ask you again, Miss Harrison. How did you come by the information that the Wraith would be at the home of his uncle in Middleburg?"

The thin provost marshal stood so close that Emily could clearly see tobacco stains on his teeth and smell the pomade in his hair. She leaned as far back as the chair would allow. "I told you, sir. I came by the information in an innocent fashion and not from collusion with the Union government." Emily spoke in a dry, raspy voice.

The last few days were starting to take their toll. She had been taken by carriage from Mrs. Cabot's to a tobacco warehouse, presently being utilized as a jail for Confederate soldiers sentenced by a military tribunal. Castle Thunder also held Rebel deserters and the accused enemies of the Confederacy, including spies. Rarely did they incarcerate Union soldiers; they sent those men to the notorious Libby Prison. Guards had locked her in a small, austere room, where the smell of curing tobacco still permeated the air. Her cell contained a cot with a soiled mattress, a washstand with pitcher and basin, and one chair. Emily had thrown the threadbare blanket into a corner for fear of crawly things wishing a change of residence.

The provost marshal splayed his hands across the table. "You would have us believe such sensitive information is discussed at teas and afternoon social calls?" His derision anticipated no response. "Few in our government knew the Wraith's identity for his protection, yet a Yankee governess was privy to it?"

"I learned of his identity accidentally while a houseguest at Hunt Farms, sir. I'm employed as a companion to Mrs. Porter Bennington, Mrs. James Hunt's sister."

"Yes, I see that." He shuffled through papers to locate an earlier report. "You were a governess to the Benningtons of Martinsburg. Is that correct?"

She nodded in reply.

"Please speak up, Miss Harrison." Following her affirmative murmur, he continued. "The Benningtons sent their daughters away to be schooled in Europe after they moved from Parkersburg. Isn't that true?"

"Yes, sir, that is true," she said with growing trepidation.

"Why then would you choose to relocate deep in the Confederacy when your services were no longer necessary? Your pupils weren't even in the country. Why not return to your home in Ohio, where people shared your political sentiments?" With a smug smile, the young man tossed the papers down on the table.

Emily pressed her fingertips to her temples to stem a throbbing headache. How could she explain why she had accompanied the Benningtons without revealing her work on the Underground Railroad? Helping slaves reach freedom was considered theft in Virginia, also a serious crime. She couldn't expose the conductors who provided food and shelter to those making their way north. "I had grown fond of Mrs. Bennington and appreciated her offer to remain part of her household."

"After so brief a period of employment? Didn't you miss your own family?"

"I had no family left in Ohio, sir. My parents were killed in an accident and our farm sold to satisfy a mortgage. Dr. Bennington and his wife provided the only home available to me." Emily hoped her sorrowful plight might arouse sympathy among the officers.

The provost marshal snorted with contempt. "When you were hired, were you not engaged to be married to a Union soldier?"

"Yes, sir, that is correct."

"What happened to that soldier?"

A lump rose in her throat. "Matthew was killed at Bull Run. I believe you refer to the battle as First Manassas."

The man's moustache twitched. "I can imagine only one reason for a Yankee to move to the heart of Dixie while mourning the loss of her betrothed—to avenge his death. You ingratiated yourself into the

Bennington and Hunt households and took advantage of their kindness. Because you weren't teaching anyone, you spent your time keeping tabs on the Army of Northern Virginia and then reported troop movements back to the Union camp at Winchester." He glared at her with cold hatred.

"I did no such thing, sir. I will swear to that fact." Her voice cracked as her nerves frayed.

"Miss Harrison, we have testimony from a reliable source who saw you and your maid in Berryville several times, not five miles from Union headquarters. Do you care to explain your mysterious nighttime outings?"

Emily hung her head. Nathan Smith. He was the only one who could have made such a report. Memories of the captain's flushed face and cold eyes flooded back. He was one enemy she wished she never had made. "No, sir," she said in a barely audible voice.

"I will ask you again. After you learned that Alexander Hunt was the Gray Wraith, how did you find out he and his men would be at his uncle's house that night?"

Fear gnawed at her empty belly. They had given her little to eat and only weak tea to drink since her arrest. Remembering the abrasive Thompsons of Upperville, Emily wished she'd never laid eyes on them, but she wouldn't expose their work. It could unravel the labyrinth of homes, causing untold damage to those involved.

"I cannot say, sir."

Looking thunderous, the young man leaned across the table. "Who did you give this information to at the Union camp? Who was the Yankee you betrayed Colonel Hunt to?"

She stared into his dark eyes with feigned bravado. "I took information to no one. I rode to Middleburg solely to warn Alexander of the trap."

As soon as the words were out she realized her mistake. She'd just admitted knowing about the trap in addition to his identity. Her churning stomach took another nasty tumble.

A smile spread across the marshal's face. "Why would you do that, Miss Harrison? Why would you warn the man responsible for relieving your Federal Treasury of a fortune?"

How could she tell him she'd fallen in love with a Rebel Ranger after her fiancé's death? It sounded scandalous even to her, and this pitiless soldier probably wouldn't believe her anyway. Focusing her gaze on a stain on the wall, Emily sat mute and motionless.

The marshal kicked the leg of his chair, sending it flying.

"Lieutenant Loomis." A man's voice from across the room addressed the marshal. "Would you please bring Miss Harrison another cup of tea? We wouldn't want word of our inhospitality getting back to Washington."

Emily hadn't paid much attention to the officers sitting against the wall during her questioning. Now one of them, apparently the provost marshal's superior officer, approached the table, walking with a decided limp. She realized that part of his lower leg was missing.

"Miss Harrison, I am Captain Reynard, commander of this prison." He righted the chair upset by the lieutenant but did not sit down.

"Captain Reynard." She bobbed her head politely.

"I don't think you understand the serious crimes you have been charged with." Captain Reynard leaned some of his weight on the chair's back. "You have been charged with treason against the Confederate States of America. Your punishment if convicted will be death by hanging. Frankly, based on the evidence, I don't see any other possible outcome. Your sentence will be at the discretion of the judge advocate, advisor to the tribunal. It will be entirely out of our hands. Military tribunals don't look kindly on spies, not even females of tender age." There was no softness in the captain's threats. "If you are protecting others out of some misguided loyalty, I suggest you tell us what you know and not delay. Perhaps the judge advocate will be merciful if you were duped by Yankee officers who took advantage of you."

There was no mistaking the evil glint in his eye. This soft-spoken, wounded soldier frightened Emily more than the blustery lieutenant. "No, sir. I'm not protecting anyone. I have nothing more to say."

Captain Reynard swept his hair back from his forehead, revealing a nasty scar. "Very well, Miss Harrison, you have had your chance. We shall set your case for trial and hope your accommodations here will be satisfactory until then." There was a ripple of laughter from the soldiers along the wall as the captain limped toward the door.

Lieutenant Loomis offered one last glare as he followed his superior from the room. She was probably the first female spy he'd ever met. Emily would have plenty of opportunity to consider his anger and resentment once the matron returned her to her cell. She had little else to occupy her time.

Alexander's shoulder and back muscles ached, yet he wouldn't rest until he had some answers. Since Emily had been taken to Castle Thunder, there was no reason to remain at Aunt Harriet's. No one in his family had any information. Hour after hour he waited for an audience with Secretary Seddon at the War Department in Richmond. Unfortunately the Secretary of War was at the Petersburg camp and no one seemed to know when he would return. After two days Alexander decided to ride to Petersburg and track down the man who had ordered Emily's arrest. Patience never had been his virtue.

With his father's directions, he found the stable where the remaining Hunt horses had been boarded. What he hadn't expected to find was his childhood friend and trusted valet. "Great Scot, William! It's good to see you." Alexander slipped from the saddle and tied Phantom's reins to the post.

William jumped from the sudden interruption of his chores. "Not as glad as I am to see you, sir. I thought for sure you were on your way to a Yankee prison. With winter comin' on, no less."

The two men embraced clumsily in the dusty stable. "Don't you worry—I can outride a Yankee even on a mule." He gazed around the stalls marked with his family's insignia. "You managed to get our best mares across Federal lines? I'm impressed. If I wasn't so broke, I'd recommend you for a raise in pay." He clamped his arm around William's neck. "I feared all our stock had fallen into Union hands."

William tucked the brush into his back pocket. "Let's write down that part about a raise, sir. I'll hold you to that when the war is over."

"Have I ever gone back on my word, William?" Alexander thumped his chest with his fist.

"No, I can't say that you have, and we've known each other a long time." William looked his employer in the eye. "Have you been to your aunt's house yet on Franklin Street? Have you seen your family and Miss Harrison?"

Alexander's joy over finding William safe faded with the mention of Emily's name. He began to pace between stalls like a caged animal. "Yes, I saw her. We barely had time for our first argument when she was arrested by the home guard. Arrested for treason against the Confederate States, of all the ridiculous ideas." He kicked an empty water bucket across the floor. "I rode to the War Department to speak to Secretary Seddon, but I never saw him. Emily needs to explain how she found out about the Middleburg raid and then I can clear up this nonsense."

William averted his eyes toward a floor littered with spilled grain and dirty straw.

"Do you know something about this?" Alexander stopped pacing as the hairs on the back of his neck rose.

"First, let me ask you something, sir. Was Miss Amite at your aunt's when the guards came? Did they arrest her, too?"

"Miss Amite?"

"Miss Lila Amite. She and her parents work for Dr. and Mrs. Bennington. Wherever they go, Lila goes too." The big man scuffed his boot in the dust.

"I know who she is," Alexander snapped, his patience wearing thin. "What I don't understand is why you're asking about her."

"Well, Miss Amite has agreed to be my wife."

Alexander stared at him, trying to tamp down his temper. "You're not making a lick of sense, man. I'm happy Lila agreed to marry you, but what does this have to do with Miss Harrison?"

"I should have told you a long time ago, sir. I'm ashamed I didn't." William yanked his felt hat from his head.

Rapidly losing control, Alexander grabbed his friend by the lapels of his coat. "Out with it, all of it. What do you know about Miss Harrison that I don't?"

"I know what she was doing the day you went to Middleburg. It was the same thing she was doing in Berryville and a good while before that. She was helping slaves find the way to Freedom Road. And you need to know Lila has helped her ever since they came from that island in the Ohio River."

Alexander released his grip on William's coat, as the puzzle pieces clicked together in his mind. "Whose slaves—my father's?"

"A couple were yours, but mainly they were runaways from the Carolinas and Georgia." William looked as if he would rather crawl into a hole than admit his part in the deception. Alexander had trusted him without reservation.

Suddenly, the barn doors swung wide, breaking the uncomfortable standoff between friends. Dr. Bennington rode inside on a lathered mount. "Oh, thank goodness, nephew. You're alive and well. It's been so long. Your parents didn't know where you had gone after leaving Harriett's house."

Alexander grabbed the bridle to steady Porter's horse. "Sorry I didn't wait until you got home, Uncle Porter, but I had to see about the ridiculous charges against Emily."

Dr. Bennington reached for his hand as he dismounted, his troubled expression deepening. "Then it's true. She's been arrested. Tell me what I can do to help."

"The War Department is in chaos with Petersburg under siege. I'm on my way down there now. The best thing you can do is pray."

SPRING 1864

When Emily awoke at dawn in the damp clamminess of her cell, her nose started to run, her scalp itched, and she sorely needed a bath. The previous evening's meal had consisted of cold rancid bacon that turned her stomach and a shriveled apple. When she unwittingly wrinkled her nose at the meat's putrid smell, the matron had chastised her.

"The fare is not to your liking, miss? Perhaps you can tell your friend Ulysses S. Grant to lift the blockade of the port so we can all get something decent to eat." The woman set the plate down with a clatter and scowled as she left the cell.

"Sorry, I've never met the gentleman." Emily replied to the closed door. Today the matron delivered mealy corn bread and weak tea. But at least she returned a short time later with a basin of warm water, a sliver of soap, and a threadbare towel. She also brought something fresh for Emily to wear. Falling in a straight line from her shoulders to ankles, the garment looked as though it was fashioned from feed sacks. Another woman could have fit between the side seams with her, but at least the dress was clean and free of vermin. Months of confinement had whittled her far from ample figure to mere skin and bones.

Her mood initially improved after her sponge bath until she heard the cacophony in the prison yard. Standing on a chair to reach the dirty window, she watched three men sawing and hammering industriously. In the light drizzle, they lifted beam after beam of fresh pine timbers into place. Although their project was far from complete, Emily realized they were constructing a gallows. *Is it for me? Or do they have another incarcerated spy responsible for the exposure of the Confederate's greatest asset besides the loss of many ranger lives?*

The enormity of her actions sank in with each blow of the hammer. Stepping down from the chair, Emily buried her face in her hands and cried for the first time since her arrest. She sobbed not for her dismal future, but for the way she treated people who had trusted and loved her. How Dr. and Mrs. Bennington must despise her. Armed with her Quaker ideals, she had moved to Virginia with the intent to dupe and defraud. Her motivations may have been noble, but these Southerners considered her a garden-variety thief and their enemy.

And what about Alexander? The torrent of lies she told ran through her mind like a fast-moving river. She should never have let herself fall in love. Perhaps it was good she would hang for her crimes because then she would never see the hatred and revulsion in his eyes. She should have told him the truth long ago—about her abolitionist work and the fact that she loved him. Now it was too late. All the love in the world heaped onto a platter wouldn't convince him her heart was true. Alexander would be her only regret on her way to the gallows. And she had no one to blame but herself.

Emily had little time to pine over past mistakes. Minutes after the matron carried away the basin and wet towel soldiers arrived at her cell door. They bound her wrists with a cord and led her through the prison warehouse like a lamb ready for slaughter. A few prisoners jeered, a few whispered words of encouragement, and one elderly man bowed his head and wept. The matron wrapped a thin shawl around her shoulders as they stepped outdoors into a biting wind. A burly soldier pushed her up the steps into a carriage.

"Where am I going?" she asked the matron timidly, peering around the shabby interior. A private joined them inside the dark conveyance. He stared out the window as though even one glance from her treacherous eyes could trap him spellbound.

"To your trial before a military tribunal." The woman dabbed her nose with a sodden handkerchief. "Take a gander at the lovely city of Richmond. It may be the last time you lay eyes on it."

Emily complied dutifully as they rolled past deplorably crowded streets and alleyways. Refugees seemed to have encamped in every doorway or bridge underpass. The sight of so many dirty, sunken faces broke Emily's heart, even though her current situation was no less grim. Icy needles of wind blew through cracks in the carriage, causing her teeth to chatter.

"What's the matter, dearie? You cold?" The woman's question held not a hint of kindness. "Had I known, I could have ordered you something warm from Par-ree, France." She cackled with amusement as the guard shifted uncomfortably on the seat.

Briefly considering the matron's bulbous red nose, the cracked skin of her hands, and a dress colorless from too many launderings, Emily couldn't summon an ounce of animosity. What she thought about instead during the bumpy ride was her home in Marietta. Why had she ever left? She could have slept on the church steps until someone took her in. She could have continued her work in Ohio, never venturing into a strange land of lilting voices and polite behavior that often belied cruel natures. But she had come south and sealed her fate.

They stopped so abruptly in front of an imposing building that Emily slid from the seat onto the floor. In one smooth motion, the guard pulled her upright as though no heavier than a knapsack and then motioned the matron out the door first.

"You need to use the privy 'fore we go inside?" he asked, red-faced, once the matron left the carriage.

Emily blanched at such an impertinent question from a complete stranger. "No, thank you."

Holding on to the rope binding her hands, the guard stepped down to the muddy street below. With stiff legs and flagging courage, Emily followed them up steep stone steps and into a smoky corridor where people gaped at her clothes. *I assure you, ladies and gentlemen, feed-sack dresses are quite the rage this season on the Continent.* From fatigue and anxiety, Emily's mind wandered from ridiculous asides to a summer day on a riverbank at Hunt Farms. It was the first time Alexander had kissed her. Nothing in life had tasted so sweet…and nothing ever would again.

When they reached the end of the hallway, the guard and matron halted before carved double doors and knocked. Emily gaped at her almost unrecognizable reflection in a gilded mirror on the wall. Her cheekbones protruded from nearly transparent skin, her arms hung from the coarse sack like mere sticks, and her hair was in a tangle down her back. The waif in the reflection was a shadow of the woman who had come to Virginia, full of life and full of vinegar, as her grandmother would say. When the courtroom doors swung open, Emily's fear and apprehension vanished. *Let's just get this over.*

She felt the weight of dozens of pairs of eyes on her back as the matron prodded her up to a rail at the front of the room, beyond which five cigar-smoking, bleak-faced men sat at a long table. Each regarded her as though she were a worm that had crawled from a half-eaten apple. "Emily Harrison, I am the judge advocate who will hear your case," said the tallest of the men. "I will then make recommendation to the military tribunal you see on my left and right. You have been charged with treason against the Confederate States of America."

Emily straightened her back, but she couldn't look at the imposing judge.

"How do you plead?"

She opened her mouth to speak but not a sound issued forth.

"How do you plead to this capital offense?" He thundered loud enough to be heard on the street.

"Not guilty," she said, after moistening her lips with her tongue.

"Very well, be seated." The judge pointed at a small table complete with an armed soldier. "We shall begin with signed testimony sent to the tribunal."

On her way to the table, she glanced around at her accusers, but instead found the weary faces of Dr. and Mrs. Bennington. Augusta's eyes were round as saucers, while Porter looked as if he hadn't slept in days. Mr. and Mrs. Hunt sat behind them in the second row. Mrs. Hunt lifted one gloved hand in a wave as though she'd spotted Emily across the room at a ball.

Instead of on my way to the gallows. Emily returned her smile. Then her focus fell on Alexander. He was studying a sheaf of documents in his lap, expressionless. Dressed in an expensive frock coat, starched shirt, and fashionable cravat, he looked every bit the son of a wealthy planter, not the legendary Gray Wraith. The sharp rap of a gavel jarred her attention back to the bench.

"Miss Harrison, serious charges have been brought against you, but apparently you are not without friends in the Confederacy." Dressed in a general's uniform, the judge advocate glared down his nose at her.

Her stomach took another tumble and her knees weakened, but she didn't dare sit down. She supported her weight with one hand on the table.

"Dr. Porter Bennington has submitted a signed deposition, testifying on your behalf. His wife, Mrs. Augusta Bennington, also submitted a second affidavit. You seem to have made quite an impact during your employment. I hope these good people don't regret extending Christian mercy to someone so cunning and devious." There was no mistaking the judge's opinion of her. "Colonel Alexander Hunt has also provided sworn testimony regarding your activities in Virginia, young lady. The colonel testified you were a conductor on the so-called Underground Railroad while in Ohio and continued your work here." His lips pulled into a tight frown. "He swears under oath you limited your crimes to leading slave women and children across the Potomac River, mandated by your religious upbringing and your Quaker heritage."

Emily gasped, not daring to turn around to look at him. How did he know? Had Lila betrayed her, or was she simply not as clever as she thought? And what did it matter now?

"Colonel Hunt has refuted Captain Nathan Smith's allegations, insisting that you committed no treasonous acts of espionage. He added he would stake his life on that fact." Pausing, the judge glanced left and right to the tribunal. They murmured amongst themselves with great agitation.

"I am not a spy, your honor, nor have I ever been one." Emily spoke with every bit of courage she could muster.

"I must stress that we do not treat the matter of aiding and abetting runaway slaves lightly here." Every man on the tribunal looked at her with ill-concealed disdain. "No matter what your personal opinions, religious or otherwise, slaves are considered property in this state and your actions amounted to thievery, plain and simple. It is no different than if someone came to your father's farm and stole his team of horses or a wagon."

Emily felt her spine stiffen. "Sir, one cannot compare a human being to a wagon or—"

The judge interrupted, giving her no opportunity for a platform. "However, Miss Harrison, in light of the fact Colonel Hunt tracked down and paid several owners for their loss and pledges to seek out the rest, we won't recommend prosecution by Virginia courts for abetting fugitive slaves. This is a military tribunal. Our concerns are crimes against the Confederacy."

Emily lifted her chin to meet the judge's gaze. "You are not going to hang me?"

"Not today, Miss Harrison, but I'm also not inclined to release you, either. This will serve as an example for others who might contemplate using our homes for the purpose of thievery."

At that Dr. Bennington rose. "Sir, if I may address the tribunal. It was I who brought Miss Harrison from Marietta, knowing her people were Quaker abolitionists. I am the one who sent her on errands for medical supplies and took no exception as to how long those errands took. It wasn't difficult to deduce what Miss Harrison was up to. As a former Quaker, my wife asked me to turn a blind eye. I take full responsibility for her behavior in Virginia. If you release Miss Harrison to my care, I will see she causes no further harm."

The judge banged his gavel on the desk, trying to restore order to a rambunctious gallery. "I'm sorry, Dr. Bennington, but I intend to keep Miss Harrison at Castle Thunder for an indefinite period until additional evidence can be collected. I am not convinced she had no involvement during the Middleburg ambush. Besides exposing and thwarting the work of the Gray Wraith, many good soldiers lost their lives." He nodded deferentially at the colonel, causing another stir.

When the courtroom grew silent, Alexander rose to his feet. "Sir, if I may address the tribunal."

Every pair of eyes turned in his direction. More than one female gawked at the larger-than-life man whose exploits had been well chronicled in the newspapers. Now they had a handsome face to put with the lore. Several young ladies fluttered their fans, trying to attract his attention.

The judge nodded. "In appreciation for your service, Colonel Hunt, I will allow it. But I won't allow these proceedings to turn into a public circus."

Alexander bowed deeply. "Thank you, sir. Although I appreciate his offer, it's not necessary for Dr. Bennington to vouch for the future behavior of Miss Harrison." He nodded in his uncle's direction.

"I take full responsibility for her actions—past, present, and future. I am bound to duty by Christian sacrament." He aimed a withering glare at Emily for the first time that afternoon. "After all," he continued, "she is my wife."

TWENTY

*S*top wiggling, Lila. I must weave these flowers through your hair before the stems wilt." Emily thumped her friend on the shoulder.

"I can't seem to sit still."

"What are you fretting about? Are you afraid William will discover your uncooperativeness or how disagreeable you are in the morning, and refuse to marry you?"

"No, he already knows and is willing to marry me anyway."

"A brave man, that William, marching off to his fate with a stout heart." Emily inserted one last flower as a knock drew their attention. "Stay where you are." Emily pressed Lila back into the chair before answering the door.

"Matilde sent this up for Lila, miss." The laundress held out a dress as she offered a curtsey.

"Thank you." Accepting the dress, Emily held it up to admire. She turned to her friend. "You will make a lovely bride, Lila."

"As will you, Emily."

"As will I? Pigs will fly before I find a man stupid enough to marry me."

"Stranger things than that have already happened. Now you go take your bath while I put this on. I've already filled the tub." Lila hugged her shyly and disappeared behind the screen with the dress.

Emily felt a blush climb all the way to her hairline as she headed into the bathing chamber. She'd never had a truer friend, nor been filled with as much joy as today. The last six months since her release from Castle Thunder had felt like a fairy tale. After she'd resigned herself to remaining incarcerated until the end of the war, Dr. Bennington arrived one dreary October morning to bring her home. He'd continued to champion her case as though she were a member of his family. Emily would be forever grateful to him and to Mrs. Bennington.

But it was Alexander who produced Charles Mimms, a disgruntled former ranger, along with receipts and signed statements from those who had lost slaves due to her handiwork. She would never know why Mimms testified he had been the one in collusion with the Union Army. The colonel's powers of persuasion must have been as uncanny as his ability to evade the Yankees all those years.

According to Mrs. Bennington, Emily had fainted upon Alexander's announcement that she was his wife. That had been a blessing. Otherwise she might have undermined his plan to save her from the gallows. Once again she had underestimated the persuasive power of the Gray Wraith. The military tribunal had been shocked by his admission, yet no one would question the word of the South's most celebrated hero. Why would anyone claim to be her husband unless it were true? According to Mrs. Bennington, the judge had stared at Emily as she lay prostrate on the floor and replied, "In that case you have my sympathy for your misfortune, sir."

Alexander had bowed deeply and had replied, "We all have our crosses to bear. I pledge she will cause no further trouble."

But the judge had still refused to release Emily into Alexander's custody, despite his testimony and signed affidavits. Emily was carried from the courtroom unconscious as the gallery erupted with shouting. She regained her senses in the carriage next to the unpleasant-faced matron.

She'd still had to wait some months longer in her cell before she was eventually released, but at least her suffering was alleviated. Mrs. Bennington and Mrs. Hunt had been permitted occasional visits, and they brought with them good food, books to read, and warm blankets and clothes.

When Emily was finally set free, the Benningtons had taken her back to Mrs. Cabot's, where Margaret and Anne fussed over her, insisting she eat every few hours as though she were dying of starvation. Considering her deception, her employers could have provided train fare and sent her back to Ohio. Even if they preferred not seeing her hang, they didn't have to allow a liar and thief to remain in their home.

Alexander had been conspicuously absent during these long months, disappearing right after the military tribunal. As kind as the family was, no one would answer any questions about him. Emily couldn't get the truth until she was alone one day with Margaret. The girl relented and said that she knew only that he'd joined the regular Cavalry and was presumed to be somewhere west of Petersburg, providing a screen for infantry during their retreat. Her mother and aunt hadn't wanted Emily to worry while locked away and unable to do anything but fret.

That had been months ago. Everything changed when newspapers announced what everyone had been anticipating—and Southerners dreading: Robert E. Lee's surrender at Appomattox Courthouse to Ulysses S. Grant. At long last, the war was over. That spring, when surrender seemed inevitable, Dr. and Mrs. Benningtons returned to Front Royal to help the Hunts restore what was left of Hunt Farms. With few alternatives, Emily had tagged along like a burr stuck to a dress hem.

Emerging from the dressing room bathed and refreshed, Emily heard a second rapping at the door. "Shall I get it?" she asked.

Lila appeared wearing her beautiful gown. "No, I'll answer the door. You wait behind the screen."

Emily stepped around her. "You are not supposed to be seen on your wedding day."

"Only not by William, and that man knows better than to peek at me ahead of time. You can't very well open the door dressed in your drawers and shimmy." Lila bolted in front of Emily, blocking her path with arms akimbo.

"It's probably another maid with a tray of coffee—"

"Let me work on my last day as a lady's maid." Lila insisted. "Tomorrow I become a horse trainer's wife."

"Heaven help that man if he goes through with this."

"Heaven will."

"As you wish." Emily relented as the pounding grew more insistent.

"Someone open this blasted door." A furious voice permeated solid oak. "I wish to speak to Miss Harrison."

Recognizing the voice, Emily froze where she stood on the thick Oriental carpet.

"I'm afraid that's not possible, sir." Lila sounded sugar sweet.

"I need to see her and I'm not leaving."

"But she is *indisposed,* Mr. Hunt."

"Espionage charges were dropped based on my word that Miss Harrison will cause no more mischief in the South. She may have climbed out a window and be halfway to Ulysses S. Grant once she saw me ride up." Alexander changed his voice to match Lila's tone.

This is too much. Emily flew to the door like a swarming hornet. "Even in Front Royal, we've received word that the war has ended." Emily nudged Lila to the side and threw the door open wide. "General Lee signed Articles of Surrender with General Grant in Appomattox."

Alexander's eyes roved from Emily's bare feet up to her damp curls in disarray around her shoulders. "Goodness, Miss Harrison. Where are your clothes?"

Realizing she wore only a chemise and pantaloons, Emily tried to slam the door, but his boot was too quick. "Please, Mr. Hunt. You have no right in a lady's boudoir." She reached for the long wrapper Lila was holding out and knotted it tightly around her waist.

"Not even when the lady happens to be my wife?" Alexander pushed his way into the room.

Recovering some of her composure, Emily replied in her best finishing school voice. "Yes, I haven't had the opportunity to thank you for your ruse in court. If not for you I would have been hanged or at least still be in that loathsome place. I am truly grateful." She extended her hand politely.

Alexander glanced at her hand but shook his head. "A thank-you will not do, Miss Harrison. The way I see it, you have to marry me or I'll be made a liar. Everyone in that courtroom heard my testimony. And thanks to a reporter in the gallery, everyone who can read a Virginia newspaper believes you're my wife. I don't wish to bear false witness in so public a fashion."

Perplexed, Emily remained mute for several moments. "But the war is over. A Confederate military tribunal has no power to reinstate charges against me. The Union will be restored."

"Do you think it's all right if I appear a liar now that your lovely neck has been saved?" He lifted his chin as he placed a hand over his heart. "What about my honor?"

She scoffed, moving to increase the distance between them. "Yes, there is your famous Southern honor, but I'm sure a slight smudge would be infinitely better than being saddled with a lying, Yankee infiltrator for a wife."

He arched an eyebrow. "Perhaps, but it would be no slight smudge now that I've returned to the Christian flock. I would be breaking a Commandment, and I would rather not. So instead I'll take the lying, Yankee infiltrator, if you don't mind." Alexander winked at her just before a grin overtook his face.

"I made up my mind this morning about my future." She met his eyes squarely. "I cannot impose on the Benningtons' hospitality forever. Because their daughters are too old to need a governess, I've written to several female academies for possible positions. So please, Alexander, do not tease me." Feeling color flood her face, she stared down at her bare feet. "I owe you and your family so much, including my life. Must you demand my humiliation in return? The pain of leaving those I've come to love should be punishment enough."

"I would not tease you about a matter so important." He closed the gap between them and gently drew her against his chest. "Nothing has changed for me since the night I told you I loved you." He lifted her chin to meet her gaze.

Pulling away, Emily walked to the open French doors. Workers, slaves no longer, were erecting a tent in the back garden next to the pasture fence. Although the Hunts had grown fond of Lila, setting up something so fancy for an employee's wedding surprised Emily. "That was long ago. Much has happened since." She didn't turn around even when she sensed him behind her. "I won't have you marrying me from some misguided sense of honor."

"Tarnation, Emily. Do you really think I would marry you to protect what people think of me?"

Not daring to answer, she stared at the floor with eyes awash in tears.

"Let me ask three questions and you must tell the truth. You owe me that much."

"What haven't I already confessed?"

"Did you feign passion for me in the garden during the ball?"

"Certainly not. I couldn't possibly pretend something like that."

"Did you come to Middleburg that night to warn me of something you had no part of?"

"On my honor, I never would hurt you or your family." Emily bit her lower lip to stop it from quivering.

Unfortunately, his third question remained unasked as Margaret and Anne marched into the room with youthful exuberance. Margaret carried a gown draped over one arm, and Anne waved a pair of embroidered slippers.

"What on earth is that?" Emily demanded, pointing at the garment.

"It's your wedding gown, of course." Margaret answered as though her governess had taken leave of her senses.

"*Lila* is getting married, not me. If you will look, she already has her dress." Emily flourished a hand at Lila, who had been standing silently as she watched the proceedings in her fancy dress.

"You look lovely, Lila. Best wishes to you." Margaret smiled at her former maid before turning back to Emily. "No, Miss Harrison. You are *both* getting married today."

"Papa said he wants to 'rid himself of both thorns in his foot in one fell swoop.' Begging your pardon, Miss Harrison." Annie added a demure half curtsey.

"Both thorns in his—"

"Please stop fussing and feast your eyes on the *couture* Mama ordered six months ago." Margaret held up the most magnificent gown Emily had ever seen.

"Ordered six months ago?" The room felt overly warm as Emily stared in amazement. Made of satin with a full lace overlay, it had a tight bodice, a sweetheart neckline, fitted lace sleeves to match the overlay, and a full skirt. An elaborate bustle would catch the sweeping lace and satin train.

"It arrived and not a moment too soon." Margaret ignored Emily's bewilderment. "Look at all the delicate seed pearls the seamstress added."

"It's breathtaking, but it certainly isn't for me. How on earth did you get such an idea, besides what your father said? I can't blame him for being angry with me."

"Oh, he's not angry with you, Miss Harrison. He's pleased as punch. He plans to walk you down the aisle if you'll have him."

Emily wasn't getting through to her. Margaret must have discovered yellow-backed novels while in France that filled her head with romantic nonsense. She turned to Lila. "Does this make sense to you?"

"Of course. I have Papa to walk me. You can't very well skip down the aisle by yourself." Lila smiled sweetly.

"He got the idea from me." Alexander replied in a quiet voice.

Emily turned to face him as something stuck in her throat. "You had better explain yourself, sir."

He had been leaning against the wall during the discussion like a spectator. "I asked my parents and Aunt Augusta to arrange a wedding as soon as I got home. Because William had already told me his plans, I thought why not go to our certain doom together? According to my mother, everyone invited has arrived. Even your former teacher, Miss Turner, and Reverend and Mrs. Ames from Marietta are downstairs. Because the blockade has been lifted, I will arrange a wedding trip to Paris so you can see for yourself if the Eiffel Tower was worth the money. The press says it wasn't. And you certainly can't blame Uncle Porter for wanting to give you away. That's one less person on his pay register. My well-paid cooks have prepared a feast, and my cousins are eager to be bridesmaids for both lovely brides." Anne and Margaret nodded in agreement. Then he inhaled a deep breath and said, "As you can see, no detail has been overlooked."

"Except for the fact I never agreed to marry anyone, mainly because no one has bothered to ask me. Perhaps my accommodations at Castle Thunder are still available."

"Alexander, do you mean to say you never properly proposed?" scolded Margaret. She thrashed his arm with her fan.

"What woman wouldn't want to marry a fine catch like me? Now, if you'll excuse us a few minutes, I'm sure we can straighten this out." Alexander spoke with exaggerated politeness as though it were a simple misunderstanding. The three women filed out, each casting sympathetic glances at Emily.

"No one can possibly be this arrogant." Emily railed the moment they left. "Not even you, a blue-blooded son of Virginia aristocrats with your land grant stemming directly from King Charles himself."

"You would hold my family's heritage against me? You would refuse to marry me because of circumstances regarding my birth?"

"No, of course not." Emily stomped her foot in exasperation.

"Then what is your reason? All our slaves are free. Those who have chosen to remain are paid fairly for their work. I'm no longer in the Confederate Army. And the Commonwealth of Virginia has been restored to the Union." He closed the distance between them and grasped her upper arms. "I love you more than anything in the world. I will honor you and cherish you forever if you agree to become my wife."

She swallowed hard as his face sobered, all her clever or sassy retorts gone. "You never asked your third question."

"What?"

"Before we were interrupted, you said I must answer three questions."

"You're absolutely right." He tangled his fingers in her hair. "Do you love me, Emily? I need to know if you love me."

The question wasn't what she expected. But it was the one she would treasure the rest of her life. "Yes, I love you, Alexander." Emily wrapped her arms around his neck. "And considering that someone went to a lot of trouble making this dress and people have shown up expecting a big party, I suppose I will marry you." Emily heard giggling at the open doorway, where three women stood unashamedly watching them. "Besides, I need to be right there to make sure William doesn't come to his senses and dash off at the last minute."

"Splendid, an excellent choice—one I'll see you never live to regret." When he bent to kiss her, his eyes caught the sparkle of something gold. Curiously, he drew the delicate chain from beneath her dressing gown. "I see you still wear your locket," he murmured. "The gift from your parents upon graduation from Miss Turner's."

"Well, why wouldn't I? It's truly a lovely heirloom, don't you think?" Pulling the locket from his hand, Emily pressed it to her lips. "But I'm no longer a woman of subterfuge." She opened the clasp to display the locket's interior.

Alexander peered down at his own likeness. "That's me."

"I asked your mother for a daguerreotype. I would have preferred one in your uniform with your dashing plumed hat instead of this drab suit of clothes, but alas, it was the only one she had of the correct size." Snapping the locket closed, Emily briefly kissed him and then said, "Now hurry and get changed. I want to make sure you have no time to come to *your* senses."

DISCUSSION QUESTIONS

1. Why did Emily Harrison have difficulty adjusting to life on opulent Bennington Island?

2. Porter Bennington frees his slaves before moving his medical practice to Martinsburg. What factors led to this decision?

3. How could Emily better serve the abolitionist cause if she moved further west in Virginia?

4. Emily forms an almost instantaneous bond with Lila Amite. What life experiences provide common ground for the friendship, and which ones put them at odds with one another?

5. Initially, Emily has little respect for Alexander Hunt because he didn't enlist in the Confederate Army. Why would she want him to join enemy ranks?

6. The Gray Wraith's ethical code adversely affects his effectiveness as a cavalry officer. How does he circumvent his decision not to bear arms?

7. Even in the midst of war, the bloody carnage in Middleburg shocks and shames Alexander. How had he remained insulated up until now?

8. Emily views the privation among the residents of blockaded Richmond with mixed emotions. Why is she troubled by the decline of the Confederacy?

9. Alexander changes dramatically during the course of the story in several ways. How was his faith impacted by the war?

10. Both sides, North and South, believed God was on their side. How did this help the individual soldier but hurt the overall progression of the Civil War?

Discover the exciting, brand-new story of a woman of beauty and courage in Book 2 of The Civil War Heroines Series by bestselling author Mary Ellis

THE LADY AND THE OFFICER

LATE JUNE 1863
Cashtown, Pennsylvania

*G*entlemen, please take heed to what your horses are doing to my flowers!" Madeline Howard spoke with as much authority and indignation as possible after two long years of war.

Four blue-clad officers paused in their conversation to gaze down on her heat-wilted ageratums and hollyhocks. Beneath their horses' hooves the flowers were trampled beyond recognition. The soldiers offered faint smiles and then resumed their postulating and pointing, affording her as much attention as a gnat.

Except for one officer, who straightened in his saddle and removed his broad-brimmed hat. Tugging gently on his reins, the man guided his mount out of the flower bed toward the road. "Good afternoon, miss, General James Downing, at your service. I apologize for the damage." He tipped his hat and then turned his attention back to the others.

"Madeline Howard, General. *Mrs.* Howard." She marched down the porch steps. "Now, if you would kindly move your meeting to someone else's yard, I shall be forever in your debt."

A thin, gangly officer mounted on a sorrel mare was quick to retort, "See here, madam. In case you're unaware, the war has come to the fine

Commonwealth of Pennsylvania with the arrival of Robert E. Lee's infantry. Your posies are of no importance to the Union Army."

"I'm well aware of the war, sir. My husband died on the banks of Bull Run Creek, leaving me alone to run this farm." Madeline settled her hands on her hips with growing indignation. "Those Rebs you're chasing marched through last week, stripping every ear of corn from the fields and every apple from my orchard. They stole my chickens, killed my hogs, and led my milk cow away on a tether. So if I request that you not to trample my flowers for no apparent reason, I would think you could oblige me." Maddy completed her diatribe with a flushed face and sweating palms. After months of privation, she had lost her temper.

For several moments silence reigned as the officers stared at her in disbelief. Then General Downing addressed the wiry, haughty officer. "Major Henry, order the troops to remain within the confines of the road and not damage civilian property." Along the highway, enlisted soldiers trudged in formation toward town, raising a cloud of dust that would linger for days.

Saluting, the major and the other officers spurred their horses and rode off in different directions, leaving her garden ruined.

"Please accept my apologies, madam. And thank you for your husband's sacrifice to our country." General Downing pulled off his leather glove and extended his hand down to her.

"Thank you." Temporarily flummoxed, Maddy reached up and gave his callused fingers a quick shake.

"I will do my best to protect your town from further harm." He held her fingers and gaze far longer than necessary...or proper.

Tugging her hand free, Maddy retreated backward so quickly she trampled the few remaining blooms missed by the horses. She felt a flush climb her neck as she picked up her skirts and ascended the steps. Pausing in the shelter of her porch, she stared at the man who still sat watching. He bowed a second time, replaced his hat, and galloped away, adding another cloud of dust to the heavy air.

Madeline retreated inside and slammed the door, not pleased with her behavior. She wasn't normally a woman who became flustered in the company of men. Remembering the trampled flowers under her feet, she shook her head. At thirty years old and widowed for the last two, she had no time for silly flirtations or coquetry. When her wits returned, Madeline headed to her stable to check the animals. The din of artillery shelling all morning made her mares skittish. If it hadn't been for quick thinking last week, her beloved horse stock—Tobias's pride and joy—would also be in the hands of the enemy. She stroked the horses' flanks and rubbed their noses, trying to calm them with soft words and a gentle touch.

Her own fears were another matter. Widowhood had inspired a determination to keep her husband's farm flourishing. War had created a constant demand for the horses she had bred and raised. Although she would never become wealthy, the bills were paid. Tobias would have been proud of her.

Tobias. It seemed so long ago when he had marched proudly off with the Sixth Pennsylvania Volunteers. He died at a battle the papers were calling First Manassas—first because a second unsuccessful battle was fought at the same loathsome place. He died before she'd grown used to the idea he was a soldier. Madeline had missed him fiercely during the first year, but endless chores filled her hours, allowing no time for grief. She couldn't remember a day she hadn't fallen into bed exhausted. But usually a sense of satisfaction accompanied her fatigue, so she persevered.

The marauding Confederates took everything she had, all but her beloved horses. The moment she had spotted ragged butternut uniforms on the road, she had hidden her horses in a nearby cave—a cave known only to the neighborhood children. Now, while her mares munched hay from their bins, Maddy stood in the barn doorway and watched wave after wave of boys in blue march toward the center of Cashtown. The war had come to Pennsylvanian soil. What would happen to her sleepy little community?

JUNE 30

"Reverend Bennett?" Madeline softly called the man's name through an open window; no one had answered her knock at the door. From every indication her preacher and his wife were both home. Laundry fluttered on the line, the barn door was open, and the back-door was ajar to catch a rare breeze. As she'd ridden her mare through the town square and down the cobblestone streets, she'd seen very few people—nothing like the way things usually were, with friendly neigh-bors hanging over picket fences or milling on the church steps Sunday mornings. "Reverend Bennett?" This time she hollered his name in an unladylike fashion.

The middle-aged preacher's face appeared in the doorway. "Mrs. Howard, come in. Why are you out and about on a day like today?"

"I rode my horse instead of driving the carriage, so I caught a nice breeze. I tied Bo to your water trough in the shade. I hope you don't mind."

The reverend slowly lowered himself into an upholstered chair. "Of course not. Sit and make yourself comfortable. I refer to the commo-tion on the roads, not the heat. With so many soldiers afoot, my wife insists we remain below in the cellar. Haven't you heard the news?"

Madeline sat on the edge of the couch. "I've seen troops moving for several days. First the Rebs stripped my farm, and now our boys in blue are stirring up the dust."

"Everyone appears to be headed to Gettysburg. Entire brigades of cavalry have been spotted, along with long caravans of wagons. And all those poor boys marching in this heat." He fanned himself with a folded newspaper. "Many of my neighbors are scared. They packed up their possessions and left."

"Where were they going?" Maddy asked, sounding childish. The fact she had no nearby relatives to offer shelter undermined her con-fidence.

"North, east—anywhere away from what's about to happen. But the time for leaving is long past. It's no longer safe. Rabble follows every army. You must stay with us until this ordeal is over. There most certainly will be a great battle."

"No, Reverend. I couldn't possibly stay. I need to tend Tobias's horses. If I'm not home, who knows what will happen to them?" Madeline rose, regretting her decision to ride to town for news.

"All right, but at least come below and share a bite with Mrs. Bennett. She worries about you alone on your farm."

Maddy loved the preacher's wife like a dear aunt, so she followed him on the rickety steps to the cellar.

After arriving safely home that evening, she relaxed as she rocked serenely on the porch. Lamplight from the kitchen window illuminated the handiwork of a spider. The thin gossamer strands weren't organized into a web, but were tiny trapezes strung between porch rails. Maddy stared, mesmerized by the artistry. As she waited for the spider to reappear, the glittering yellow eyes of some creature peeked from the shrubbery. She felt no fear, only mild curiosity. The opossum issued a high-pitched squeak and then crept off toward home.

Heat lightning danced and shimmered over the dark hills. The faint report of gunfire miles away was soon drowned out by peepers and cicadas. The frog and insect summer symphony soothed Maddy's nerves with its familiarity. The war, although close at hand, was far from her mind that night. Her thoughts drifted to a tall Union officer with silver glints in his hair and sparkling teeth beneath a black mustache. Strength and power seemed to emanate from him. For the life of her, Maddy couldn't remember why the situation in the garden had so vexed her. They were *silly flowers*. She had lost much more just days ago. She'd lost her entire world a mere two years ago. For the first time, the face of General Downing replaced Tobias's in her imagination as she replayed their conversation over and over.

"Foolish woman," she muttered. Rising, Maddy peered up at a sky studded with bright stars. The moon had already finished its nightly path when she climbed the steps to her room. She undressed without lighting a lamp, donned her long cotton gown, and slipped beneath the cool sheets. Forcing away thoughts of the general, she quickly fell asleep and slumbered fitfully…until the scrape of a rusty latch roused her senses.

With her heart pounding in her chest, Madeline bolted upright. The sound of a whinny lifted tiny hairs on her neck. Someone was in her horse barn! Maddy ran to the window and drew back the gauzy curtains. Peering into darkness, she could see nothing until the moon finally broke free from the clouds. Speechlessly, she watched as her prize-winning mares were led from the barn by several men.

What should I do? Grab Tobias's squirrel rifle from above the fireplace? Race outside and open fire on those who would pillage in the dead of night? Clad in my nightgown?

Instead, Madeline did nothing. This time the thieves weren't the marauding enemy who had stolen her chickens and milk cow. The men riding away with her beloved horse stock tethered to their mounts wore the blue uniforms and gold emblems of the U.S. cavalry.

JULY 1

The next morning dawned hot and hazy, with acrid smoke hanging heavy in the air. Soldiers in every shade of blue, from recently conscripted recruits to sage veterans, marched in both directions on the road. Horses pulled limbers of artillery and caches of ammunition, while farm wagons hauled food to a hungry army. White Conestoga wagons with red painted crosses carried the wounded from an early skirmish or boxes of medical supplies. Young couriers galloped down Taneytown Road at breakneck speed, perhaps with vital dispatches.

In the hectic fervor, few soldiers took notice of a woman who headed to town on the side of the road. Walking in ninety-degree heat through clouds of dust didn't put Madeline in the best of moods. She arrived at the parsonage on Hemlock Street three hours later sweaty and thirsty. No one answered her knock until she pounded relentlessly on the door.

"Mrs. Howard," said an astonished Reverend Bennett. "What brings you back so soon? I told you to stay indoors today—"

"May I come in, sir? And perhaps trouble you for a glass of water?" Madeline leaned against the door frame.

"Forgive me, my dear. Come in. Rest in the parlor while I get you something to drink."

Maddy slumped onto a dainty embroidered chair and closed her eyes. The minister returned within a few minutes with a glass, a pitcher of chilled well water, and plate of gingerbread.

"Thank you." She filled the glass, drank it down, and refilled it. "I'm afraid this isn't a social call. If I may, I would like to borrow one of your horses. I have business in Gettysburg." She pressed the glass to her forehead.

"Of course you may. But why not ride one of your fine Morgans?" Reverend Bennett pushed the plate of cookies closer.

"They were stolen. That is my business down the road."

His face blanched with anxiety. "Goodness! That's awful, but you must not endanger your life because of horses. Soldiers are fighting down the road. There is a battle right here in Adams County." He whispered as though the enemy might lurk nearby.

Madeline straightened in the chair. "Those Morgans are all I have left. Please, Reverend, I've never asked you for anything before. I promise to return your horse safely."

"I cannot refuse you, Mrs. Howard, although I strongly advise against pursuing this. I will saddle my gelding once the sound of artillery ceases." He lifted his hand to forestall argument. "You must wait. I won't permit you to blunder into the fray. Rest for a few hours and refresh yourself. You can leave as soon as it's quiet. It should be cooler by then too." He pointed at the settee and left the room before she could object.

Madeline sat quietly for several minutes. Then she devoured the plate of gingerbread and reclined on the couch. She'd intended to close her eyes for a just short while, but she awoke hours later to someone shaking her arm.

"My horse is saddled. Go with God, Mrs. Howard. I will pray for your safe return."

Mumbling her thanks, Maddy went out the back door and swung up in the saddle. The sun was already low in the western sky. She reached the Chambersburg Pike within minutes at a gallop and then slowed her pace. At the outskirts of Gettysburg, she had no difficulty locating the headquarters of the second corps. Her spirits lifted when she spotted a beehive of activity surrounding the vacated farmhouse. Confusion might allow her to enter unnoticed. Maddy sucked in a breath, set her jaw, and rode into the fenced yard, stopping at the hitching post.

A stout lieutenant shouldered his rifle and grabbed the gelding's bridle. "Hold up, miss. The Martins no longer live here. This here's army property now."

"I'm well aware of that. I have business with General Downing. He's expecting me." She didn't like lying to the man, but she was feeling desperate. Madeline slid from the horse and marched up the front walk, leaving the lieutenant still holding her bridle. Determination got her as far as the open doorway.

Then the same wiry, arrogant major she'd met in her flower garden blocked her path. "I cannot allow you to enter, madam. State your business to me." He spoke with obvious disdain for the intrusion.

"My business is that someone in this corps is a horse thief. My brood mares were stolen last night, and I expect redress from your commander."

"If it's financial restitution you seek, that is a matter for the quartermaster. You'll not be troubling the general with—"

"It's not money I'm interested in, sir," interrupted Maddy. "I want my property returned." She fought to control her voice as her courage flagged. Then the door swung open, startling woman and aide alike.

General Downing appeared as shocked to see her as the minister had been. "Mrs. Howard! Come in. I consider your visit a propitious omen." He turned toward his staff member. "It's all right, Major. I will spare a moment to settle a civilian injustice." He stepped to the side so that she could enter. Then he closed the door in the astonished officer's face.

In an austere room smelling faintly of tobacco, Maddy's waning confidence vanished in a heartbeat. "You may not be pleased to see me once you hear me out." She tucked several loose wisps of hair behind her ear. "All of my horses were stolen from my barn last night while *Union* troops were moving through Cashtown." She paused to moisten her dry lips. "From my window I saw blue uniforms on the thieves. I can only surmise they were your soldiers." Surreptitiously she glanced at the maps and drawings spread across the desk.

The general appeared to choose his words carefully. "'Thief' is a harsh word that some might consider treasonous. Considering your husband died fighting for this great nation, would you deny the army desperately needed replacement mounts? Our officers and cavalry require horses." He dropped his voice to a murmur. "Today, there was a cavalry battle east of Gettysburg. Many good men died on the field. Many horses were lost as well. Everyone must make sacrifices in times of war."

Madeline's stomach churned, but she forced herself to meet his gaze. "I pray that the Union army prevailed on the field." She swallowed hard and continued with far less zeal. "I understand your predicament, General, but those horses are my livelihood. Without them, I will have to throw myself on the mercy of friends and neighbors this winter. But beyond my selfish desire to survive, I respectfully request that *one* of those horses be returned. Bo is a medium-sized, brown Morgan with a distinctive white blaze down her face. She was bred from the best blood-lines in Pennsylvania. I hand-raised and trained her myself. You may keep the others as my contribution to the war, but not…not Bo…" Maddy's voice trailed off as she willed herself not to cry.

The general reflected for a long moment. "If you will make yourself comfortable, I'll only be a minute." He pointed at a chair and closed the office door behind him.

Madeline strained to hear through the solid maple, but the

commotion outdoors masked all but the intensity of his discussion with the major. She inhaled a breath to steady her nerves and perched on the edge of the straight-backed chair.

What an effect this man had on her. She felt as skittish as she had during her brief courtship with Tobias. Never had she been affected by a man's looks, yet her attraction to him was undeniable. Tall and broad shouldered, the general had thick dark hair that curled over his jacket collar. So dark they were almost black, his eyes transfixed a person with their intensity. He wore a meticulously neat uniform that was distinguished but with none of the flashy gold tassels seen in daguerreotypes. Yes, he was handsome, but his appeal stretched beyond physical attributes. He possessed some unseen quality—a magnetism that drew her like bees to nectar.

And she didn't like that one bit.

Maddy's woolgathering was abruptly curtailed. "What have you learned?" she asked as soon as the door swung open.

He crossed the room in a few strides. "I've sent word to the cavalry commander with my chief-of-staff. When the situation and time permits, he is to look into last night's *unauthorized* acquisition of civilian livestock, specifically for the horse you described. I cannot promise, but you have my word I will do my best to find Bo." He bowed from the waist as though they had just been introduced socially.

Madeline leaned back from his close proximity. "Thank you, General. I'm sure your best will be more than adequate. It's truly more than I expected. Good day." In her haste to leave she knocked over the chair she'd been sitting in. She should have paused to pick it up. Then she might have recovered enough composure to make a graceful exit. But when she noticed the deep wrinkles around his eyes and the smile tugging at his lips, she fled the room like a startled rabbit.

He is laughing at my clumsiness!

The lieutenant was still holding Reverend Bennett's horse when she reached the porch. Maddy crossed the dusty yard, mounted, and rode toward home as though the entire Rebel cavalry was breathing down her neck.

James Downing had seen pain and suffering without measure during the past two years. He had witnessed deprivations of every sort in both civilians and soldiers alike. Yet something in Mrs. Howard's tender plea for a beloved horse tore at his soul. From his window he watched her disappear into a cloud of dust on the road with her bonnet ribbons streaming behind her. His intrigue with the perplexing woman went beyond a pretty face and comely figure. Was it small-town living that had preserved her sincerity and innocence? Why else would she worry about ruined flowers when the eastern theater of war had arrived at her doorstep? Yet she possessed enough spunk to ride into chaos to rectify an injustice.

He allowed himself one long moment to stare after her before turning back to his duties. *Great Scot, did I just agree to find a blasted horse in the middle of an engagement?* But before he slept that night he would endeavor to keep his promise. If he had it to do over, he would agree to that and more. The realization that Mrs. Howard had such power over him didn't sit well. Closing his eyes, his brain etched a picture of her face to carry into battle tomorrow. With creamy skin dusted with freckles, wavy hair the color of ripe wheat, and green eyes that flashed in amusement or pique, Madeline Howard would be a hard woman to forget. He'd been smitten the first time he saw her on the road to Cashtown and would remember her long after he moved his corps to the next battlefront.

Her long limbs had moved gracefully beneath the cotton dress in her woebegone garden. Considering the fierce look on her face, his staff thought they had met the enemy sooner than anticipated. Never in his life had an upbraiding been so pleasurable. The moment she marched from her house, he lost his entire train of thought, having no idea what they had been discussing. And when he glanced back over his shoulder, he thought the window curtains had parted an inch. Had Mrs. Howard been peeking from between the lace panels? If he thought so enchanting a woman could be interested in him, he had indeed gone mad.

There was a surreal quality in the air before a battle. The din of the afternoon had mercifully yielded to an unholy quiet that evening. The common sounds of crickets and tree-frogs failed to calm Maddy, but instead added to her trepidation of what the morrow would bring. She barely touched her dinner. She completed her chores in a dream-like state and headed to the porch to read her Bible. Tobias's squirrel rifle, leaning against the post, offered little security. She had just settled into her favorite rocker when the distinctive sound of a sliding latch gripped her heart.

What on earth? There is nothing left in the barn to steal.

"Who's there?" she called into the dark. "Identify yourself or I'll shoot." She lifted the single-shot musket to her shoulder. Moments passed interminably until a familiar face stepped into the circle of light from the kitchen window.

"Please don't shoot. It's me, Mrs. Howard." General Downing pulled off his hat. "I returned your horse to the barn. You'll not be troubled by future procurements." Fumbling with his hat brim, he looked more like a schoolboy instead of the highest commander of an army corps.

"Thank you, General. I'm deeply grateful for the return of Bo, but I was very selfish to make such a demand on a day like this. Forgive me." Setting down the gun, she extended her hand over the porch rail.

He walked up the steps and shook briefly. "You're welcome. It's true that my adjutant thought me mad to trifle with such an errand, but if the horse was to be found, it had to be tonight. Tomorrow will bring a different world than the one we know today." He walked to the end of the porch and peered into her trampled flower garden.

A fission of fear snaked up her spine. "Did the battle go well? Did your soldiers prevail?"

"My troops were only marginally involved today. We are still awaiting final casualty numbers from the cavalry commander, but it would seem they did *not* prevail. We have entrenched and established our lines around Gettysburg, positioning our artillery on high ground. We are prepared to meet the enemy." He turned to face her, leaning back against the rail. "Tomorrow my infantry will yield nothing. They won't be pushed back, but I'm afraid the outcome is far from decided."

"You must think me foolish to ride to Gettysburg about a horse."

"I thought you were very brave to pursue what you wanted." Two or three moments passed before he added, "Your husband must have been proud of your fearlessness."

She struggled to keep her voice steady. "I had little chance to be brave during the brief time we were married. He signed up at Mr. Lincoln's first call for volunteers."

"My sympathies, madam, for your loss."

Madeline shook away her painful memories. "I have coffee left from supper. Would you like a cup before you return to camp? Inside—away from these infernal mosquitos?" She pulled open the screened door.

His laughter was an unanticipated response as he followed her into the overly warm room. "Forgive me, but your question took me by surprise. On my ride here, I wracked my mind for some excuse that would allow me to sit at your table, even for a brief while."

"Why would you be eager to sit in my kitchen? I have nothing to offer you except black coffee." With a flutter of nerves, she reached for the china cups above the stove.

General Downing gripped the back of the chair but didn't sit. "Because I'm far from home, and this war has stretched far beyond anyone's early estimations. Your kitchen is like a desert oasis." He gestured at the low-burning lamp sitting on the delicate lace tablecloth. "But mainly because I yearned to gaze again on the loveliest woman I've ever seen." He spoke the words as though they were painful. A bead of sweat formed below his lip.

Madeline stared, dumbfounded, and then resumed filling two cups with the tepid brew. "Goodness, General. This war has certainly dragged on if that description fits me. My feet are blistered, my hair needs washing, and I can surely use a new dress." She laughed to ease his discomfort.

Blushing, he averted his eyes as he accepted the cup. The confession, hanging in the humid air, had embarrassed him.

"Please sit and enjoy your coffee after an eventful day." She slipped onto the opposite chair.

For a few moments he stared into the dark liquid. "Don't leave your house tomorrow," he said. "There will be heaving fighting. A young woman was killed today by a stray bullet through her kitchen door. I understand she was engaged to be married, and she was only twenty years old. Spend the day in your root cellar, where you will be safe."

"But I can't possibly. I need to return my minister's horse—"

"*Please,* Mrs. Howard. I have a better idea of what's coming than you."

"Very well." She nodded in agreement even as her chest constricted. The air seemed to have left the room. *Who is this man who so affects me?* His brash compliment had pleased her, stirring emotions long dormant. Yet at the same time, she felt disloyal to Tobias's memory.

General Downing drained his cup in one long swallow and then stood. His hypnotic gaze held her transfixed. When he lifted his hand, she feared he might reach for her face. Madeline held her breath, unable to move. He was a stranger—a man she had met only two days ago.

At that moment they both heard horses in the stable yard, followed by the clatter of boot heels on her porch steps. She pushed up from the table as someone rapped insistently on her door.

"General Downing, couriers have brought word that General Buford is on his way to headquarters and wishes to confer." The unmistakable bark of Major Henry broke their unexpected tête-à-tête.

"Thank you, Mrs. Howard, for the coffee. I'm afraid the demands of war have returned. Remember what I said about tomorrow." He donned his hat and swept from the room without a backward glance.

She heard their horses' hooves thundering down the road before she could reach the window. The war had returned indeed.

July 2

Madeline awoke coughing in the hazy dawn. Her sleep had been dream filled and restless. The window she'd left open to catch evening breezes admitted the acrid smell of smoke. Her eyes burned and began to water as she struggled to close the sash. A thick fog hung over the grassy paddocks and stripped cornfields. She bathed and dressed in her coolest frock.

After braiding her long hair in a loose plait, she donned a full-length apron and headed to the barn. Chores would occupy her hands and keep her mind off the general's warning. How could she cower in the cellar when she had two hungry horses to feed? Physical labor would relieve the anxiety building inside her. She sought relief from her restless thoughts of James Downing too. *How on earth did he find Bo among hundreds of cavalry horses?* After filling the grain bins with the last of her oats, she brushed Bo until her coat gleamed and her mane was free of tangles. Later she would return the Bennetts' gelding and buy horse feed with her dwindling cash. At the well she hauled up enough water to overflow the troughs and last throughout the day. The incessant sound of gunfire and cannon fire had begun at first light.

Carrying two more water buckets, Madeline retreated to the barn to crosstie and calm the horses. Both the gelding and her mare had turned skittish with the increasing cacophony. With chores complete she slumped down on a bale of straw in between the stalls. This was as good a place as any to wait out the bombardment. But two hours later, Maddy returned to the shelter of her house. She'd grown jumpier than her equine companions. After sponging off with cool water, she changed her dress and rummaged in the pantry for something to eat. Yet before she finished eating her meal, a deafening roar of artillery began in relentless succession. Blast after blast shook her house to its stone foundation.

Madeline threw herself into a frenzy of activity to keep from going mad. In her room, she filled her largest valise with her favorite garments, personal mementoes, Bible, and framed daguerreotypes. She emptied her small horde of cash into her reticule as if embarking on a pleasant shopping trip instead of retreating from bedlam. She wasn't sure why she packed a bag, but when smoke began filtering under the door she grabbed a jug of water and her valise, and then headed to the root cellar.

The general's plaintive words flowed through her mind as she batted away cobwebs in the cellar's driest corner. Settling onto a rickety bench, she tried to collect her wits as the clamor increased outside her home. For an undeterminable length of time she labored to read in the light from a streaky window while waiting for the battle to cease. Cramped and exhausted, she finally closed her Bible and leaned her head against the cool stones of the cellar wall. Heedless of what spiders might lurk nearby, Madeline fell asleep in the dank confines as darkness fell across the blighted land.

Hours later, stiff and clammy, she awoke to discover that the shelling had stopped. She fumbled around for a match to light the kerosene lamp. As she struggled to ignite the wick, there was a new assault on her senses. Wood smoke—not the sulfurous fumes from cannons but the definitive smell of burning wood. It took several moments for her eyes to adjust in the dark, and then she saw with chilling certainty smoke drifting through the floorboards.

Fire. The kitchen above—her beloved home passed down from Tobias's parents—was on fire. For several seconds she sat paralyzed until panic cut through her stupor. The cellar, her refuge during the battle, was rapidly filling with smoke.

Stuffing her Bible back into her bag, she crawled on hands and knees in the direction of the steps. Not the wooden treads from her kitchen, but the stone steps leading to her backyard. Her parched throat and seared lungs ached, and she kept her watery eyes clenched shut against the smoke. Something repulsive skittered over her fingers, while sparks and embers drifted between the cracks overhead.

Coughing and choking, with lungs desperate for air, Madeline at last bumped into the hard bottom step. She pressed her cheek against the cold stone and prayed not to die in such a loathsome place. With almost no strength left, she pulled herself up toward air and light and life, but before she reached the third step, she sank into black oblivion.

ABOUT THE AUTHOR

Mary Ellis and her husband live near the Cuyahoga Valley National Recreation Area, home to the last remaining GAR Hall in Ohio, and Hale Farm and Village, home to annual encampments and reenactments of Civil War battles. She is an active member of the local historical society and Civil War Roundtable, where she served as secretary for several years. She has enjoyed a lifelong passion for American history.

Mary loves to hear from her readers at
maryeellis@yahoo.com
or
www.maryellis.net

A Tragedy…a Refusal…a Shunning
Will Their Young Love Survive?

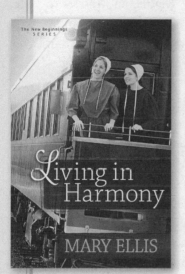

*A*my King—young, engaged, and Amish—faces life-altering challenges when she suddenly loses both of her parents in a house fire. Her fiancé, John Detweiler, persuades her to leave Lancaster County and make a new beginning with him in Harmony, Maine, where he has relatives who can help them.

John's brother Thomas and sister-in-law, Sally, readily open their home to the newcomers. Wise beyond his years, Thomas, a minister in the district, refuses to marry Amy and John upon their arrival, suggesting instead a period of adjustment. While trying to assimilate in the ultraconservative district, Amy discovers an aunt who was shunned. Amy wants to reconnect with her, but John worries that the woman's tarnished reputation will reflect badly on his beloved bride-to-be.

Can John and Amy find a way to overcome problems in their relationship and live happily in Harmony before making a lifetime commitment to each other?

**A New Home… A New Friend… A Catastrophe…
Does She Have a Future to Hope For?**

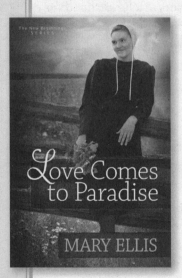

nora King is a woman in love. When Elam Detweiler leaves the ultraconservative Amish district of Harmony, Maine, and moves to Paradise, Missouri, Nora boldly follows soon after. But is she in love with the man or the independence and freethinking he represents? Though she soon finds work she enjoys and a new best friend in Paradise, Nora can't decide whether she wants to capture Elam's *Englisch*-leaning heart or commit finally to her Amish faith.

And then, unexpectedly, Lewis Miller comes from Harmony to offer Nora what every woman hopes for—a lifetime of unconditional love. As Lewis attempts to claim her affections, Elam's interest piques. Suddenly, Nora is irresistible to him. Wooed by two such different men, will Nora come to her senses before Elam's thoughtless choices ruin her reputation beyond repair? Will Lewis's pursuit survive the challenge?

Love Comes to Paradise is about fresh starts…and how faith in God and His perfect plans provide peace and joy in a turbulent and ever-changing world.